LANESBROUGH HALL

Elisabeth Linley

Creative Classics Publications US

Cover design by Chapman & Wilder
Printed in the United States of America

ISBN 979-8-218-05333-8

For Ellie

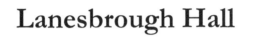

Lanesbrough Hall

Chapter One

January 2019

It was on days like this that Isabelle hated her job. Footsteps sounded on the stairs, and her shoulders tensed. She took another look at her computer screen, wishing that it was telling her something different. After all, who liked to be the bearer of bad news?

The footsteps stopped outside her door. Isabelle took a breath, like a diver ready to slice the water. She raised from her chair before the knock came, feeling like an executioner about to lead a prisoner—an innocent one—to the gallows and opened the door. Her own trepidation was reflected in the face of the woman standing there, who was only a couple of years older than Isabelle.

Isabelle grimaced a smile, hoping to alleviate some of her visitor's anxiety. 'Hello, Melanie. Please come in.'

She stepped aside, wanting to add that it was good to see her, but it wasn't. It was anything but. Isabelle closed the door. The room seemed to have shrunk. The scent of the rose diffuser was sickly-sweet, like mildew. She wanted to open the window, but the sound of London traffic changed her mind. She straightened her shoulders and donned her professional mask as she walked across the room. She gestured for her visitor to take a seat and returned to her chair, facing this woman who looked as fragile as a fledgeling. She was holding an arm around her waist as though protecting a broken wing or perhaps to deflect the words

1

she knew were about to assault her like the pellets of an airgun. Part of Isabelle wanted to freeze time like an image trapped in a photograph for eternity—no past, no future, just this moment in the present. If only.

There was no escaping the inevitable; Isabelle cleared her throat. 'Melanie, I have your results…. I'm afraid I'll have to refer you to oncology. The cancer is back.'

There, it was out. And in that instant, the woman's face broke into fragments of emotions like a pane of glass hit with a sledgehammer. The sound that shattered the room was the universal cry of devastation.

Isabelle fought to keep her composure. She knew she had to say something, to give this mother of two children under the age of five some hope. But deep down she knew all she could offer were platitudes. Instead, she rolled her chair to the other side of the desk, leaving the safety of the professional barrier.

Isabelle took Melanie's hands, hoping to give her some warmth, to thaw the iciness that gripped her. The room was silent except for Melanie's cries in tandem with the tick-tock of the clock, marking the time. The ten-minute consultation had long overrun. Isabelle had other patients waiting downstairs. Some would be staring at the information posters telling them about the annual flu-jab, heart disease, and diabetes. Others would be engrossed in their phones, answering work emails, or playing games to pass the time. More would be swearing under their breath and tapping their feet in frustration like dancers waiting to take the stage.

'Thank you, Dr Rousseau,' said Melanie as though reading Isabelle's thoughts, and she stood.

Isabelle steadied her as she swayed. 'I will ring and make sure the referral is fasttracked.' Except she had already done it that morning. With her arm around her charge, she accompanied her to the door. 'Would you like me to call anyone for you?'

'No thank you, doctor. My mum is meeting me in the coffee shop around the corner. I'll be fine.'

Isabelle doubted Melanie Stewart would be 'fine' anytime soon but also knew she had to be, for the sake of her children.

This just sucks.

She made a mental note to call her in a few days, just to make sure. She shut the door and leaned against it for a moment and let the strength of the wood seep into her body before she returned to her desk. Isabelle felt an almost physical jolt as the door flew open and banged against the wall. The sound was followed by a barrage of words.

'How dare you call yourself a doctor?'

Isabelle stared at the man who had barged into the room.

'You had no right to put my daughter on the pill without my permission,' he growled at her.

The image of a nervous sixteen-year-old flashed in front of her. Isabelle had been forced to reassure her repeatedly that, from a legal point of view, she was no longer deemed a minor and the consultation would remain confidential. This man had no right to invade her office and give her abuse.

'You can't just walk in here. I could have been in consultation—'

'I knew you weren't. I've waited long enough for that lady to come out. And you're gonna listen to me.'

Isabelle held up her hand. 'You'll need to make an appointment. And now if you'll excuse me, I have to get on with my patients.'

'We're not finished yet.'

The sound of footsteps reached them. Relief washed over Isabelle at the sight of Mrs Hargrave, the practice manager.

'I'm sorry for the disruption, Dr Rousseau,' Mrs Hargrave said as she laid a hand on the man's arm. 'Now, come along please, Mr Patrick, and we'll sort this out.' She sounded like a bouncer trying to shimmy along a drunk.

The man yanked his arm away. 'I'll sort this out when I speak to the General Medical Council and have your licence taken away. We'll see how you like it then.' His voice boomed one last time as he lumbered out of the room.

Isabelle shook her head. The GMC was her professional regulatory body, and whilst they had the obligation to take every complaint seriously, Mr Patrick would soon realise his mistake, should he ring them.

'I'm sorry, Dr Rousseau. This won't happen again,' said Mrs Hargrave.

'It isn't your fault, Mrs Hargrave. Don't worry about it.'

Isabelle let herself fall back on to her chair. The clock on the wall told her it was only 11:30 a.m.

How can I survive another six hours?

The desk phone rang as if to confirm she needed to get on.

'Yes?' she answered, feeling haunted.

'Dr Rousseau, there's an urgent call for you,' said the receptionist.

'I really need to get on. Can you take a message or perhaps someone else can deal with it.'

'It's your mother.'

Isabelle put a hand on her forehead. Today couldn't possibly get any worse. Right now, she just didn't have it in her to talk to her mum.

'Please, Mrs Dobson. Tell her I'll call her this evening.'

'I'm sorry, I've already tried; she is rather insistent.'

Isabelle didn't miss the woman's emphasis on the last word. She closed her eyes. Yes, her mum, Bonelle, was insistent all right. It had always been her way or the highway.

'Fine,' she breathed out the word—that word again. 'I'll take it.'

There was a click, then a pause before her mum's voice penetrated her ear. 'Isabelle, why haven't you been answering any of my calls and messages?' said Bonelle, her tone as sharp as a scalpel.

Isabelle's fingers dug into her temples. 'I'm at work, Mum.'

'And this is an emergency. I need you to go to Scotland. Mimi's been admitted to the hospital. She's in a coma.'

Time stood still. A sudden image of Mimi abandoned in a hospital bed flashed in Isabelle's mind. Nausea rose from the pit of her stomach, choking her. The words *Mimi, coma,* and *hospital* kept repeating themselves like a mantra foretelling doom.

'Isabelle? Are you still there?'

'Yes,' she said, unable to hide the tremor in her voice as she brushed away tears.

'Isabelle, I know what you're doing. Stop it now. You always have to see the worst in everything, don't you?'

And why are you always as cold as a reptile? Isabelle wanted to say. Instead, she asked, 'Will you be coming over?'

'I would, but I have a few things in the diary I'd rather not cancel. For all we know, it's much ado about nothing. Call me when you know more. And Isabelle, try not to worry too much.'

Isabelle clenched her jaw to stop herself from saying something she might regret. But she needn't worry. True to form, Bonelle had already hung up.

Anger propelled her into action. Isabelle found Jeremy's number and prayed her semi-retired colleague would answer.

'Isabelle?'

'Listen, Jeremy, can you fill in for me for a few days, ideally starting today?'

'That urgently?'

'Yes.'

There was a pause, but Isabelle didn't intend to fill the gap.

'Okay, I'll be there in the next hour, but you owe me.'

She breathed a sigh of relief. Next Isabelle opened WhatsApp before she forgot. *Charlie, won't make it tomorrow. Family emergency. Sorry lovely. Speak soon xx.* She'd been looking forward to catching up with her best friend from uni, but she knew Charlie'd understand.

She dashed downstairs. The reception was heaving. She ignored the stares that bored into her and made her way to the side door.

'Is James free, Mrs Hargrave?'

'He's between patients, just go ahead.'

Isabelle knocked on the door, and without waiting for an answer, strode in. James looked up from his screen. He creased his brow, and she knew she wasn't welcome.

'I'm sorry, James, but I have to leave. I should be back in a few days.'

'This is highly irregular, Isabelle. What about your patients? You can't just up and go.'

Colour crept up his neck, but she ignored it. 'I've arranged for Jeremy to cover my clinics. He'll be here in an hour.'

'That's as maybe. But this is not helping your chances of making partner in this practice.'

Isabelle nodded, turned on her heel, and left, resisting the temptation to slam the door behind her.

Chapter Two

Isabelle had never been to the Royal Infirmary before, but it reminded her of Guy's Hospital in Battersea where she had trained. The lights almost blinded her as she rushed past others hurrying like her, their faces etched with worry and tiredness.

She rubbed her nose as the smell of disinfectant hit and followed the signs to the ICU on the fifth floor. A nurse directed her to room 11. She hastened her steps towards the end of the corridor, the soles of her shoes sticking to the linoleum. Then she was at the room. The blinds were half open, and she could see her grandmother, Mimi, wearing an oxygen mask that made her look as if she'd shrunk.

The sight was enough to drain the last vestiges of her composure. Isabelle gripped the door handle for a moment to stop the tremor in her fingers before opening the door. She almost screamed when a man stood up from the seat in the corner.

'Angus!'

He frowned. His eyes were still liquid silver, his hair auburn as autumn leaves, but now it cascaded in waves past his jawline. Of course, it had been six years since she'd seen him. Why wouldn't he have changed his hairstyle?

'Sorry,' Isabelle said. 'I wasn't expecting you. Or anyone.'

'I'm sorry; I didn't mean to frighten you. How are you, Belle?'

'Quite frankly, a bit confused. What are you doing here?'

Isabelle's words came out sharper than she'd intended, but she didn't care. The last thing she wanted right now was company—or to dredge up old hurts. She just wanted to be alone with Mimi.

'I'd think that's obvious,' Angus snapped back. 'I'm staying with Mimi, seeing as her *family* wasn't at hand. Poor Mrs Murray was beside herself when she rang.'

Isabelle was relieved to hear that Mimi's housekeeper had been with her when it happened, but the heat rose in her cheeks at Angus glowering at her, as though challenging her to defy him. She raised her chin and fixed her eyes on him.

'In case you haven't noticed, some of us don't live just around the corner. It's kind of you to have come, but I'm here now. There's no need for you to stay. So if you'll excuse me, I'd like to sit with my grandmother.'

She knew she'd crossed the line as the words came out and for a moment regretted her outburst.

'Look, I didn't mean to snap,' said Angus, running his fingers through his hair. 'I'm sorry. I've missed you.'

Isabelle blinked, surprised. 'Well, my number hasn't changed, you've had six years to get in touch. To fix things.'

'I know …' He swallowed. 'You have every right to be upset—'

'Yes, I do,' she said, her jaw clenched. 'But I don't want to go over this now. You chose your girlfriend over your friend. A lot of people do. Or maybe you just didn't need me around anymore when you found someone better.'

Angus groaned. 'It wasn't like that, honestly. You were the most important—'

Isabelle held up her hand. '*Please,* Angus, not now. I just want to be alone with Mimi, okay?'

His face fell. 'Sure. I'll go and get a coffee. Do you want anything?'

Isabelle gazed towards Mimi and shook her head. Mimi would be so disappointed if she could hear them right now. She'd refereed enough of their childhood; she didn't need them arguing over her bed now that they were adults. She looked at Angus; pain distorted his face. She hardened her heart.

'Nothing, thanks,' she whispered and turned her attention back to Mimi.

After Angus left, she exhaled to release the pressure weighing on her chest and took Mimi's hand, without disturbing any of the machinery. With her other hand she stroked Mimi's hair.

'Oh Mimi, what happened? I can't bear to see you like this. But I'm sure you'll be out in a few days. Then I'll come and stay at the Hall and look after you.'

Her words belied the dread that had taken up residence in her stomach. Try as she might, she couldn't shake off the feeling of doom that had penetrated every inch of her body.

She sat there, as still as Mimi, listening to the pressure-relieving mattress breathe and hiss. The heart monitor flashed and bleeped like a warning signal. Isabelle's mind wandered back to the phone call, less than a month ago, when she'd told Mimi she wouldn't be coming to the Hall for Christmas. Tears of regret stung her eyes. How she wished she could turn back the time. She should've gone, should've made the effort to spend the holiday there.

Isabelle heard the door open, and her body tensed, but she didn't turn around. Why did Angus have to be back so soon?

'Hello, there.'

Isabelle turned to see a woman in a suit, wearing glasses that overwhelmed her face. The stethoscope around her neck was the colour of cherry blossoms, which seemed at odds with the rest of her appearance.

'I'm Dr McCormick.' She offered her hand.

'I'm Isabelle, Mimi's granddaughter. What happened?'

'Ah, your mother mentioned you'd be coming. If you'd like to step outside for a moment, I can explain everything.'

Isabelle was taken aback. Why hadn't her mum told her she'd spoken to the doctor? She must have been more worried than she'd let on.

In the corridor the doctor paused as though to weigh her words, just as Isabelle had done with Melanie Stewart the day before. 'I'm afraid your grandmother has suffered a ruptured intracranial aneurysm. That's when a weak blood vessel in the brain balloons, and as the pressure increases it bursts, causing internal bleeding.'

'Thank you, I understand.' Noting the doctor's look, Isabelle added, 'I'm a doctor myself.'

'I see. That makes it easier in some ways.'

'Do you plan to operate?' asked Isabelle though she already knew the answer.

'Can I talk to you, one colleague to another?'

Isabelle's shoulders slumped. She nodded, not trusting herself to speak.

'I'm afraid the severity of the bleed, combined with her age, preclude surgery. Unfortunately, the prognosis is not good. I'm so very sorry that I don't have better news for you. I'll check on her again later.' The doctor brushed Isabelle's arm and walked off.

Isabelle stood as though she'd forgotten how to walk. She couldn't quite process what she'd just been told, as though her brain no longer knew how to deal with medical information. There must be *something* they could do. Yet, at the same time, as a doctor she was aware of the futility of her thoughts.

'Hey, what's happened? Is Mimi okay?'

Isabelle dragged her head up and saw Angus standing there with two cups of takeaway coffee. He was looking at her with eyes full of fear.

'She's not going to wake up.' Isabelle's voice sounded to her own ears like she was speaking under water. 'I'm going to get some fresh air.' She walked away without waiting for a response.

Outside, she took out her phone, she had to call her parents although talking to her mum was not what she wanted right now. Still, she steeled herself and rang Bonelle's mobile. When it went to voicemail, Isabelle hung up. She felt a surge of anger at her mum's attitude, both towards Mimi and herself.

'She can bloody well ring me if she wants to know what's going on,' she muttered. Next, she tried her father and jolted when she heard a female voice.

'Aurelie? Is that you?'

Aurelie was her stepmother, for want of a better word. Every time Isabelle heard her voice, she remembered her horror when her father had told her, 'I met the love of my life,' then introduced her to a beautiful girl closer to her age than his.

'Of course, it's me, Isabelle. Who else could it be? Hang on, Jean-Francois is coming.'

And then her father's voice. 'Isabelle?'

'Oh, Papa,' she managed to say before the dam of tears burst.

'Isabelle, chérie, what's the situation?' Isabelle could hear his concern and tried to still the sobs.

'Mimi's dying, Papa…' Isabelle said as a spasm of pain gripped her body.

'I'm so sorry, ma petite. Papa's here, just take your time.'

Her father's voice wrapped around her like an embrace, and she calmed enough to give him the details.

'Is your maman there with you?'

'Of course not!' she said, 'Sorry, Papa, I didn't mean to snap, it's just—'

'I know, I know. Not to worry. I'll drive straight to Lyon airport. I should be with you before midnight.'

'Thank you, Papa. I love you.'

'And I love you, ma petite. Hang in there.'

Isabelle made her way back up to the ICU. The ground felt more solid beneath her feet. Isabelle had learned early on to only rely on herself, but every so often she wished her family wasn't so scattered. Still, at least Lyon wasn't as far away as LA.

She took her place at Mimi's side, relieved that Angus seemed to have gone. She stroked Mimi's hand, wondering if she was soothing herself or the unconscious Mimi. She shook her head at the irony of the situation, how their roles had reversed. Then she bent down and kissed the woman who had so often comforted her.

Chapter Three

The limousine glided over the carpet of snow covering the road. Isabelle watched as the flakes danced, obscuring her view of the hearse in front that was carrying Mimi's body.

'As if today isn't bad enough, we have to stand in the snow as well,' moaned Bonelle.

Isabelle clenched her jaw and suppressed the urge to rise to her mum's remark. Her father took her hand, and she looked at him. He shook his head and gave her hand a squeeze. He was right; it was neither the time nor the place for an argument, though she'd have loved to hurl some of her grief and anger at her mother.

The car came to a halt. Isabelle's heart pounded in her chest, sending a rush of blood through her veins. She wished she could stay in the car; she didn't think she had the courage to face the mourners outside the church in the small village of St Abbs. They stood in groups, huddled under umbrellas as black as the mood of the day. They all turned around at once to stare at their convoy. Isabelle realised she'd been digging her fingernails into her father's flesh and loosened her grip on his hand.

She was that little girl again, watching her father carry her twin sister's coffin over his shoulder. The idea that Chloe was locked in that crate, no bigger than her toy box at home had made Isabelle hyperventilate. Knowing even then that she would get no comfort from her mum, she had turned to Mimi, hidden her face in her skirts, and sobbed. This time there was no Mimi to turn to, no Mimi to hold and comfort her.

The usher opened the car door for them, and as her father stepped out, the snow blended with his hair. He fixed his eyes on hers as he helped her stand. Then she linked her arm in the crook of his and was glad of its strength. Isabelle kept her eyes on the ground as she passed the mourners, just like she had at Chloe's funeral. Even so she felt Angus standing to one side, his eyes on her, sympathetic and filled with his own grief.

She exhaled as they arrived in the sanctuary of the Norman church. The scent of Frankincense brought back the memories of the many services she and Mimi had attended. Memories that once used to fill her heart with joy were now tearing at it. In her mind's eye she saw Mimi standing at the altar with the village choir singing 'Amazing Grace' at the Harvest Festival service. Mimi's voice rang through the space with a strength and clarity that belied her age.

Now it was the sound of the organ playing Beethoven's 'Moonlight Sonata' that filled the air. It was Mimi's favourite. Isabelle gazed at the lilies and roses adorning the front of the altar, but soon the tears blurred the veil between the past and present again, transporting her back to many afternoons at the Hall spent listening to the classical masters. Her heart contracted with a pain as if she were drowning, making her gulp for air. She tried to suppress the wail that was determined to push its way out of her.

The music stopped and the vicar, who'd known Mimi for years, talked about her. Isabelle was trying to listen, but her mind wasn't willing to absorb the words that like everything else seemed to have lost all meaning.

Her father whispered her name. 'It's your turn, ma petite. Do you want me to come and stand with you?'

'Yes, please, Papa.'

Isabelle left the safety of the pew, hoping her legs would bear the weight of her grief. She caught her mother's look. Disapproval was painted on her face like makup. Looking away she focused on the weight of her father's hand on her back and let herself be guided towards the altar. Then she climbed the three steps up to the pulpit. The piece of paper in her hand was trembling. It contained the words that were meant to honour Mimi. But how could any words be enough?

Wiping away tears with the heel of her hand, Isabelle looked at the crowd. Angus was sitting near the back of the church with his parents, Margot and Jonathan. His head was bowed, as if he didn't want to burden her with the heaviness of his own sadness.

Then her eyes fell on her poised and elegant mother, sitting at the front. Despite her age, her mother turned heads, but instead of her almost ethereal beauty, what struck Isabelle was Bonelle's expression. She knew that Mimi and her mum had a strained relationship, but why the absence of any emotion?

She tried to clear the grit in her throat and opened her mouth to speak, but nothing came out. Her head was spinning; she swayed. Isabelle dropped the paper and held onto the pulpit, praying she wouldn't faint. Angus lurched to his feet, as if he might be able to catch her from the back of the church, but it was her father who put his arm around her shoulder, pressing her into his side.

'Do you want me to read it?' he murmured.

Isabelle nodded.

He picked up the paper. 'I am speaking for my daughter, Isabelle,' he said, more loudly, then cleared his throat. 'There are no words that could describe what Mimi meant to me, and no words to capture the enormity of my loss. Mimi was a compass whenever I was lost. She was the smell of cookies, the sound of laughter, and the voice of reason. She was the warm blanket of comfort, the safe, guiding hand …'

Every memory the words conjured up was a small wound. She yielded into her father's embrace, pressed her head into his chest, and succumbed to the force of her grief, losing all awareness of her surroundings.

After the service Isabelle stood by the graveside with her parents on either side of her. The snow had calmed, but the wind was still blowing with a vengeance. She glanced at the line of the bereaved, waiting to pay their respects, and once more her eyes settled on Angus, who was helping his mother to stand against the gale. They were no longer friends, but her stupid heart drew strength from his presence. Perhaps because so many of her memories of Mimi were also memories of him.

Mimi and her family had been embedded in this small

community for generations, being the laird of the land, and there were so many other mourners who wanted to express their condolences that she had to focus on each, shake each hand, nod.

Finally, she was approached by Mimi's housekeeper, who like a loyal guard had remained by her side until the end. She was dwarfed by a coat as brown and heavy as the soil beneath her feet.

'Mrs Murray, thank you for coming.' Isabelle's voice was hoarse. 'I know how much you meant to Mimi.'

The old woman folded Isabelle in her arms. 'Oh, Miss Isabelle, I'm so very sorry for your loss. Those words of yours went right through my heart. Your grandmother would have been very proud of you. There was not a day gone by that she wasn't talking about you. We'll all miss her terribly.'

Mrs Murray dabbed away at her tears, and Isabelle had to look down to hide her own.

'Isabelle, please, no more hysterics. I think we had enough of those,' Bonelle said after Mrs Murray left.

Isabelle looked at her mother and contempt washed over her. But Bonelle was staring ahead, avoiding eye contact. She was about to say something when she heard her father.

'Bonelle, leave her alone.'

'What a surprise, Papa to the rescue. You always took her side. Surely, even you must agree that her performance earlier was an embarrassment.'

With that, her mother turned and walked away.

'Don't mind your maman, chérie. She has her own way to deal with her grief.'

'I know, Papa, but we're all in the same boat, aren't we?'

She didn't understand why Papa and Mimi had always made allowances for her mum's attitude. It sucked. Isabelle took a deep breath, kissed the lilac rose she held in one hand, then dropped it onto the coffin.

The limousine drove through the gates, the driveway wound around the side of the hill. Linden trees lined the avenue in a parade of welcome. The car turned the bend, and there was

Lanesbrough Hall, seat of the Lanesbrough family since 1614. The family crest hung on the apex of the door, depicting an osprey with the motto: *Truth and Wisdom*. With its triple-gabled roof covered in snow and the light glowing through the windows, the Hall resembled a picture-perfect Christmas card.

The wake was already in full swing, with laughter and banter filling the house. Waitresses with trays of refreshments weaved in and out of the crowd milling in the hallway. The chandelier illuminated the scene like a stage in a theatre. Isabelle overheard a circle of women she thought were from the Women's Institute, commonly known as the WI.

'This is wonderful; even in death good old Mimi is outdoing us. Come on ladies, let's have a toast to our lovely Mimi.'

Isabelle made her way through the guests, smiling and nodding like an automaton, knowing she was seeking Angus but refusing to acknowledge it. She saw her mother listening to a lady, her expression one of boredom.

'My dear, we'll sorely miss your mother. She was very generous to us all. The Lanesbroughs have always looked after St Abbs. They rebuilt all the fishermen's cottages in the harbour after that dreadful storm in 1868. My grandmother used to tell me the stories when I was a wee bairn. They made sure we were looked after during the war and …'

Isabelle found her father in conversation with a kind-looking older man.

'Hamish, this is Isabelle, my daughter,' Jean-Francois introduced them.

Isabelle shook his hand and nodded.

Hamish smiled. 'This place brings back so many memories for me. My father was estate manager here. We used to live in Burns Cottage on edge of the estate.'

A range of emotions was displayed on his face, but Isabelle couldn't read them all.

'This place is steeped in history,' her father said.

Bonelle parked herself at Isabelle's elbow. 'I wonder how long we need to put up with this before we can have the house back to ourselves. I hate funerals.'

Hamish stiffened and took his leave; Isabelle shot her mother a look. 'Don't be rude, Mum. It just shows how much everyone cares about Mimi.'

'As you say. Personally, I find the whole thing distasteful.'

'Isabelle's right, Bonelle,' said Jean-Francois. 'You should know better than anyone how much your family means to this village.'

'Oh, for goodness' sake, JF, don't you start. This is my family's home, and I can behave any which way I please.'

Isabelle wasn't used to being in the same room with both of her parents since their divorce and once again listening to their squabbling. At least her father hadn't brought Aurelie.

'Please don't bicker. Remember, today is about *Mimi.*'

She turned and saw Angus approaching, but now he had Alex at his side. Alex hadn't been at the funeral, had she? No, Isabelle would have noticed her. Alex did not exactly blend into the background. She was an exotic bird with her raven hair and emerald eyes.

At the sight of Angus, Jean-Francois brightened. 'How are you, young man? It's been a long time. Too long! Are you going to introduce us to this lovely lady?'

Alex put her hand on Angus's arm as though to claim him. Angus's eyes crinkled with his smile. As he turned to look at Isabelle, she dropped her eyes and focused on her fingernails.

He paused, then spoke. 'It's good to see you again Jean-Francois. This is Alex, my fiancée. Alex, meet Jean-Francois, Bonelle, and this is Belle. These are the old family friends I told you about.'

'It's a pleasure to meet you all,' Alex painting on a smile that did not reach her eyes.

Isabelle couldn't help thinking that meeting her was not the pleasure Alex claimed. Instead of staying to see if her theory was correct, she used the interruption as an excuse to escape upstairs. She needed a moment alone to grieve in peace before she returned to the fray.

Chapter Four

The few days after the funeral had been a nightmare, with just Isabelle and her mother rattling around the Hall. The memories of Mimi were enough to deal with, but on top of that her mum had been snapping at her at every opportunity.

'Why are you walking around with a long face all the time?'

'Why aren't you eating more?'

'Why are you sleeping so much?'

It reminded her of growing up when she'd been the subject of her mum's constant criticism. Now she and Bonelle were approaching the building that housed Morgan McDougal Solicitors.

'I still think it's ridiculous that we have to go for a will reading.' Bonelle tossed her hair. 'Nobody does this anymore.'

Isabelle frowned. 'Mimi wanted a will reading, so she's getting one.' *And I can go back to London right afterwards*, she thought.

Before they had the chance to reach the receptionist, a young man appeared out of nowhere.

'Hello there,' he said, shaking their hands. 'I'm James Morgan. But please, call me James.'

His demeanour and looks were not what Isabelle had expected. The same was true for his stylish office. He pointed towards the chairs facing his desk.

'Please take a seat.'

Isabelle sat on the edge of the chair, crossing and uncrossing her legs, and playing with the elastic hair band on her wrist. She caught her mum looking at her watch. James must have noticed too.

'This won't take long,' he said. 'Mrs Lanesbrough wished for this meeting to be private. I've written to the few people she bequeathed token gifts to. Then there is, of course, Mrs Murray,' he consulted his papers, 'who has been given leave to stay in Burns Cottage, for the rest of her life for free and will receive a monthly pension.'

Bonelle leaned forward. 'For free? What was my mother thinking?'

Isabelle winced at her mum's outrage. But before she could say anything the solicitor continued.

'I shan't bore you with reading the whole will. I've made a copy for each of you to take with you.'

Isabelle was pleased he'd ignored Bonelle's question.

'In brief, Mrs Lanesbrough's property portfolio—the house in London, the two cottages in Yorkshire Dales, and a sum of £150,000 pounds—goes to you Ms Smeatson.' He looked at Bonelle, who pursed her lips and nodded. 'The Lanesbrough Estate—the Hall, including over two thousand acres of land, the old staff cottages, of which there are six, and the stables— will go to you, Miss—I mean, *Doctor* Rousseau.'

He turned his gaze onto Isabelle, who could think of nothing to say and only stared at him.

He added, as if he'd been saving it for dramatic effect, 'But *only* if you live at the Hall for twelve months.'

The words hit Isabelle like a slap in the face.

Mr Morgan carried on, oblivious to the effect his words were having. 'You could, according to the terms of this agreement, choose to sell the estate after the year is up, should you so wish. However, if you decide not to live at the Hall for the first year, it will be bequeathed to the National Trust for Scotland. But you would keep the cottages,' he said almost as an afterthought.

'Apart from Burns Cottage, three of the others are currently rented out, and two would need some work before they could be used. The proceeds go towards the daily upkeep of the Hall. In addition, should you remain at the Hall, you would also be entitled to a sum of £250,000.'

Isabelle shook her head, she couldn't take it all in. 'I'm sorry, I don't—'

'Do you care to explain, Mr Morgan?' Bonelle's voice cut the air.

Isabelle noticed that he fixed his eyes on her. She too avoided her mum's gaze. He explained the same stipulations. Isabelle stared at him as if he were talking in code.

'Can I ask when my mother changed her will? As far as I knew, as the next in line, the entire Lanesbrough Estate would be passed on to me.'

Isabelle noted the twitch in the corner of her mum's eye and her set jaw. She too felt nauseated by the turn of the events. Why would Mimi bypass her mum?

Probably because Mimi knew Bonelle would sell *that horrid place* as she always referred to the Hall. But Mimi also knew that Isabelle had her life in London. Why would she want to move to Scotland?

'As you may be aware, my father always dealt with Mrs Lanesbrough, but he has retired. Let me check. The date of the will states, *the seventh day of September 1993*, so almost twenty-six years ago.'

The year Chloe died, thought Isabelle.

'Thank you, I can count.' Bonelle clasped her hands in her lap. 'Is there any reason given?'

Despite her words, Isabelle had not missed the shadow that darkened her mother's face.

'I'm sorry; I'm not aware of any.'

Part of Isabelle couldn't help feeling a certain schadenfreude. For once someone else seemed to have the upper hand over her mum. But she also knew that Bonelle wasn't going to just sit there and take it, which meant trouble for Isabelle.

'We'll be in touch.' Bonelle's voice was followed by the clapping of her heels as she strode away. Isabelle stood. Her insides were churning as if someone had taken a mixer to them. She'd not expected the meeting to take such a turn.

'One moment, Dr Rousseau, this is for you. I'm sorry, I don't know the content,' added Mr Morgan.

Isabelle frowned as she took the A4 envelope. When she saw *For Isabelle* in Mimi's familiar handwriting, tears clouded her sight.

'Isabelle, are you coming?'

She blinked to stop the flow and put the envelope in her handbag then walked out of the solicitor's office. Bonelle took charge

'Come on, your train isn't going for a couple of hours. I think we could both do with a drink, and you should eat something.' She pointed to an eatery across the road. ''There. That'll do.'

For once, Isabelle was relieved her mother had reverted to her pragmatism. The bistro was crowded with office workers on their lunch break.

'What can I get you?'

Isabelle looked at the waitress. Questions were assaulting her brain. What the hell was she going to do with an estate? She dreaded to think what this would do to her relationship with her mum, which was already stretched to its maximum. If she were honest, she was annoyed at Mimi for putting her in this situation and not even thinking to warn her.

'I can come back if you need more time,' offered the waitress.

'No, thank you; we'd be here all day,' Bonelle said. 'We'll have two glasses of your best red and the soup of the day.'

After the waitress brought their wine, Bonelle took a sip and wondered, 'What on earth was my mother thinking?'

Isabelle sighed. 'Mum, please. The whole thing is just too upsetting. I'm sure Mimi had her reasons.'

What reasons though? She just couldn't get her head around the whole thing. None of it made any sense.

Bonelle gritted her teeth. 'Why do you always have to defend her? Can't you see what an imposition this is?'

Yes, of course Isabelle could see, but right now, she didn't have the capacity to carry on this conversation. Besides, despite her anger she couldn't bring herself to say anything against Mimi. After all, Mimi had been more of a mother to her than her own.

'Mum, please just leave it. It's done now.'

But was it done? She wished her mum hadn't rushed her; she could have asked Mr Morgan.

'No, it's *not* done. How can you be seriously thinking of uprooting your life?' She rolled her eyes. 'Honestly, Isabelle, I sometimes wonder whether you've inherited any part of me.'

There it was again, that disapproval. The heat burned Isabelle's cheeks as images of her childhood flashed through her mind. A few weeks before Chloe died, they had each drawn a picture for Bonelle.

'This is wonderful, my darling, you're a clever girl,' Bonelle said to Chloe. 'Give Maman a hug.'

Isabelle had waited her turn to show Maman her picture.

'That's pretty, Isabelle, but you need to go over the colours again. It'll look much better, darling.' Bonelle patted her back.

The waitress placed Isabelle's soup in front of her, bringing her back to the here and now and the conundrum of Mimi's will. She busied herself with eating, though her appetite had vanished.

'Talk to me, Isabelle,' Bonelle said loudly enough to draw looks from the neighbouring diners.

Isabelle wished she could teleport herself back to London and away from all the miasmas.

'What do you want me to say, Mum? Didn't you hear? I can't sell the Hall until I've lived there for twelve months.'

'Nonsense.' Bonelle flicked her wrist at her. 'I'll tell you what. We'll swap. You give me the Hall and the estate, and you can have the properties and the cash. I'll deal with that solicitor.'

It was some offer. She could retire just by renting out the properties. But the Hall had been in Mimi's family for generations. She had loved the house and trusted Isabelle with it. How could she betray Mimi and let go of it, just like that?

'Mum, please stop. I need time to digest all this, so don't go on about it. Why do you want the Hall anyway when you hate the place?'

'There are some things you don't understand, Isabelle.'

'Then tell me.'

'You've always put Mimi above everyone, even yourself. You think Mimi was a saint, but let me tell you something, young lady, your grandmother was a selfish and secretive woman who doesn't deserve your loyalty.'

Isabelle took a breath. 'Really, Mum? That's enough. Why would you even say something so horrid about your own mother?'
'Never mind. One day maybe you'll find out for yourself.'

Chapter Five

Isabelle took a taxi to the bar and spotted Charlie at one of the tables. She stood and hugged her.

'Hey, gorgeous. You look done. I'm sorry I couldn't be there for you. I tried to get out of the work trip but…'

'Hey, I understand.' Isabelle took off her coat and sat down.

Charlie gave her a glass of wine. 'I thought you could do with this. How did it all go?'

'An absolute nightmare,' said Isabelle. 'Mimi's left the Hall to me instead of Bonelle, so of course Bonelle is raging. She wants to swap inheritances. I'd get the houses in London and Yorkshire, and she'd have the Hall. She'd probably knock it down first chance she got.'

'Well, you can't let her do that!' Charlie squeezed her hand. 'Hey, so, you're rich now?' She grinned. 'Does that mean you're getting the next round in!'

'Not exactly. I have to live there for a year first.'

'What?' Charlie gaped. 'In Scotland? It's like the plot of a haunted house novel! Is the Hall haunted?'

'Don't be daft, Charlie. I can only assume that Mimi thought if I lived there for a year I would fall in love with the place and be unable to sell it.'

Charlie looked at her wide-eyed. 'Have you decided what to do?'

Isabelle sighed. 'I don't know what's best. I don't want to go. I like my life in London. I know the job's been stressful recently, but I was thinking I could go private and work fewer hours.'

Charlie nodded.

'Oh Charlie,' Isabelle groaned, 'I'd miss my home, the hustle and bustle of London and, of course, *you*.'

'I know, lovely.'

'What am I supposed to do in Scotland in the middle of nowhere, in a mansion all on my own?' She bit her lip.

'Then, I suppose you should swap with your mum, like she suggested.'

Isabelle sat back and slumped in her seat. 'I was kidding about her knocking the place down, but she *would* sell it. I can't bear the thought of the Hall going to strangers.'

'I'm sorry, I don't know what to say. You're truly between a rock and a hard place.'

'And there's something else.' She leaned forward. 'I saw Angus.'

'No way! The ghost himself? And he actually spoke to you?'

'He said he missed me.'

'What a jerk! I hope you told him that you stopped missing him years ago, after he crapped on your years of friendship for some random chick.'

Isabelle shook her head. 'It wasn't the time. If I see him again. Maybe.'

'So, he's living in Scotland again? Back from Dubai? Or did he just come home for Mimi?'

'I'm not sure. I got the impression he was back, but I didn't ask.'

'Wow, well, that's another thing to factor into your decision. All I'll say is take your time and don't rush into anything.'

'I don't have the luxury of time.'

'What are you on about? Of course, you do.'

Isabelle looked her in the eyes. 'I don't, Charlie. I have exactly one more week to make my mind up.'

'Seriously? That's insane. Poor you. That's no time to make a life-changing decision.' Charlie blew out her breath in bursts as if she was whistling.

'I know…'

'Okay, I'll tell you what; forget about it for one evening and enjoy yourself. The answer will come to you. And remember, regardless of what you decide, I've got your back.' She put an arm around her.

'Thank you, Charlie. It means a lot. I think I will get us another drink after all.'

Isabelle reached into her bag for her wallet, and her fingertips brushed Mimi's letter, still waiting for her, unopened.

It wasn't until the following day that Isabelle gathered the courage to open the envelope. She swallowed and tipped the contents onto her lap. There was a notebook and a letter. She reached for the letter first, carefully unpeeled the top not to rip it, and withdrew the paper. She noticed it was dated the same day Mimi had written her will. With her stomach roiling, Isabelle read her grandmother's words.

My sweetest Isabelle,

You're the daughter I wished for—what a terrible things to say, you must think to yourself. But we both know that your mother and I were never close. For this I accept full responsibility. I know I failed her terribly as a mother, and sadly nothing I tried could remedy our relationship. Perhaps I should have tried harder. I just hope that one day she finds it in her heart to forgive me, for her own sake. I cannot ask for redemption, but her hatred of me is eating away at her, I know.

My dearest child, if you are reading this letter then it means that, despite my hope, I never mustered the courage to tell you my story in person, the story that would have helped you to understand both the past but more importantly, the future and the reason I have left the Hall in your hands.

I know that my desire to preserve the Lanesbrough Estate and our ancestry has placed a huge burden on your shoulders, and I pray you will forgive me, my darling Isabelle. But I also know that you are strong and courageous and will do it justice more than your mother ever could. There is only one last thing I ask of you: should you discover the past, I beg that you do not judge me too harshly. You see, whilst I know you will be brave, I was not.

I was too much of a coward, and I silenced that guiding voice, the one that told me the right path to take. Instead, I chose to bow to fear and others' expectations and caused great unhappiness. Not just for me but for others too who became casualties of my cravenness. And for that, I feel truly regretful. But it is too late to change what has happened, and all I can hope for is that you will make better decisions in your life than I did in mine.

Know that I'll always carry you in my heart and watch over you.

With all my love, my sweet, sweet angel.

Your loving Mimi

PS: I left you something which will give you a starting point, and help you decide if you wish to unravel the past and accept your legacy.

The letter was drooping in Isabelle's hand. Her eyes were puffy and hurt from crying. Her heart ached at the thought of never being able to hear Mimi's voice again or hug her. Worst of all, she realised she knew nothing of young Mimi or her life, bar a few stories. Now the opportunity to talk to her was gone. She read and reread the letter, and each time she found more questions than answers. What was Mimi talking about? What did she mean she was a coward and not to judge her too harshly? She couldn't imagine what decisions Mimi had made, or why she would ever need forgiveness.

Bonelle's words echoed in her mind. *You think Mimi was a saint … Your grandmother was a selfish and secretive woman.* Could what her mum said be true? Should she talk to her?

Isabelle looked at the notebook. Did she want to know the truth? If Mimi *had* done something to cause hurt and unhappiness to others, could she bear to know about it? What if that were to change her memory of Mimi? Isabelle shouted her frustration into the room. She may as well find out what the hell she was dealing with. She snapped up the notebook, flicked the cover open, and began to read.

Chapter Six

Mimi, August 1953

Dear diary,

> *I'm on the threshold of adulthood. In exactly six hours and twenty-three minutes I'll be eighteen. Alasdair has organised a party for me. I was allowed to choose some guests for myself and, of course, the usual crowd of the vicar and his wife, the good doctor, and our family friends, the Fairbairns, will be attending. I've invited Abigail and Rosie from my boarding school. I don't know what I would have done without them for the last four years.*

At the sound of a car, I put my diary away, jumped off the bed, and ran to the window, shrieking at the sight of the Aston Martin, Alasdair's pride and joy. I flew down the stairs, ripped open the front door just as he got out of the car, and ran straight into his arms. Alasdair lifted me up and twirled me around, making me shriek with delight. He put me down and planted a kiss on my forehead.

'Hello, my favourite sis.'

I wagged my finger at him. 'I'm your only sister.'

He winked, his eyes dancing, and ran a hand through hair that was wind-swept like the crop of barley in the fields. We linked arms and walked back towards the Hall.

'How's your big day been so far, little sis?'

'Lovely, thank you. I'm glad the sun is shining. The men are setting everything up on the terrace by the rose garden, so we can enjoy the sunset over the sea.'

'That's a grand idea.'

'Maybe after lunch we can go to the beach?'

'You're the birthday girl; your wish is my command.'

Alasdair bowed, which made us both laugh. He ruffled my hair and strode inside the Hall.

I walked around the bend of the drive, but there was still no sign of Abigail and Rosie, so I made my way to the rose garden to talk to Mama about my day. I sat on the bench that Papa had made with the inscription, *In loving memory of Catherine*. I thought of my tenth birthday, Mama and I sitting under the lilac rose, her favourite spot, making lanterns. It had been the last birthday before Mama got ill, and I felt as though someone had draped me in darkness.

'Happy birthday, Miss Mimi.'

Will's voice intruded my thoughts and brought me back to the present. 'Thank you, Will.'

He stood there looking at me, his eyes the colour of the sky above, making my stomach flutter.

'This is for you.' He handed me a package. 'I didn't want to give it to you in front of everyone else.' He blushed and looked away.

My fingers trembled as I untied the twine and unwrapped the paper to reveal a box decorated with inlays of birds and flowers. When I lifted the lid, the scent and the sight of the lilac rose petals that filled the box brought tears to my eyes. I closed the lid, wanting to preserve the perfume for as long as I could.

'Thank you, Will,' I whispered. 'This is …'

I looked up at him, and the tenderness in his eyes gave me courage. Before I could change my mind, I stood up and hugged him. The warmth of his body heated mine. He smelt of hay and musk. Then he stroked my hair, and waves of pleasure rippled through me.

'What the hell?'

I was about to step out of Will's embrace and turn around, but Alasdair tore us apart.

'What do you think you're doing?' Alasdair pushed me to one side and then shoved Will backwards. 'Are you trying to ruin my sister's future?'

He turned away as if he couldn't bear to look at Will and swiped his hands through his hair. His face was flushed. Drops of sweat glistened on his forehead and above his lips.

I couldn't stop shaking. I'd never seen Alasdair this angry.

He faced Will again, jabbing the air with his finger. 'If I ever see you touching my sister, you can kiss your position here goodbye.'

I looked at the ground, wishing it would open and swallow me. The sound of Will's footsteps moving into the distance was replaced with Alasdair's voice.

'Mimi.'

I didn't look up. I didn't want him to see the tears of shame.

Alasdair came closer. 'Hey, look at me.'

The anger had left his voice. He tipped up my chin with his fingers and bent his head. His breath tickled my skin. I swallowed and forced myself to speak.

'It was all my fault. I hugged Will, not the other way around. I'm so sorry, Alasdair.' I burst into tears.

'Shh, come here.' He put one arm around my shoulder and with the other, he cradled my head and let me sob into his chest.

I tasted the saltiness of tears and snot. I don't know how long we were standing there. But at last I stopped crying. Alasdair loosened his grip, took my hand, and tugged me down to sit with him on the bench.

'Look. Mimi, I'm sorry I lost it. This was the last thing I wanted on your birthday.'

I still couldn't bear to look at him and stared at my lap.

'I know you're a young woman now, and sooner or later you'll fall in love. But not all men have the best of intentions, and you have to be really careful who you trust. Especially as I won't always be around to watch out for you.'

I nodded.

'Of course, I want you to have fun and enjoy yourself, but remember, this is St Abbs. People are still behind the times when it comes to women having more freedom.'

I knew that things had changed for women after the war, and Alasdair was right: it would take another fifty years for it to reach us here.

'And on top of that we're Lanesbroughs. People look up to us, they expect us to uphold certain values. Do you understand what I'm saying?'

'Yes, I think so. I'm sorry, Alasdair. I promise, I'll be careful.'

He kissed the top of my head. 'Now, enough of that. Let's go and see if those friends of yours have arrived.'

'Thank you for the lovely feast,' I said that evening as Mrs Quinn brought in the birthday cake.

'Here's to Mimi,' everyone chorused, raising their champagne glasses to me as I blew out the candles.

I looked around. All the staff was standing to one side with parcels in their hands, but I couldn't see Will anywhere.

'Now, sis, I have two presents for you. Open this one first.' Alasdair handed me the first gift.

I unwrapped the present and inside there was a photo album embossed with dragonflies. They looked so vivid as if they were still alive.

'I thought you could choose some pictures and take them with you when you go to university in a few weeks, so you don't miss the Hall too much.'

I gave him a hug, overjoyed with my present.

'Now, this is from Mama…' His voice caught as he handed me a box. 'She asked me to give you this on your eighteenth birthday, just as her mother had given it to her and her mother before that.' His eyes glistened with tears.

Inside the box, nestled on a cushion was a locket. The tears stung my eyes. I tried to speak, but my throat was closed.

Alasdair reached out, freed the necklace, and fastened it around my neck. We held each other for a long moment, both knowing how the other was feeling, the way we always seemed to.

The next morning, I was on my way to the orchard to help Mr Murray, the head gardener, collect fruit when I sensed a presence. I looked over my shoulder and found Will standing in the shadow of the cedar. Our eyes met and I flushed. Alasdair's words rang in my ears, but I couldn't stop holding Will's gaze and savouring the feeling that spread through my body like sunshine. Then the memory of my upcoming departure came like a grey cloud. I'm not sure if I imagined it, but I read similar thoughts in Will's countenance. I was about to close the gap between us, to tell him how sorry I was about what happened, when I heard Mr Murray.

'Miss Mimi, are you coming? These apples won't pick themselves.'

I turned towards the orchard and then looked back to Will, but he wasn't there anymore.

Chapter Seven

Isabelle was moved by Mimi's account. It was like she'd been watching a movie, and yet she'd felt as though she could have reached out and touched her.

'I love you Mimi,' she whispered and with her fingertip wrote the words in Mimi's diary. And in that moment she knew there was only one choice she could make. She had to move to Scotland.

The sun was reflecting on the sea like a million diamonds glittering on a bed of cobalt carpet. The coastline seemed to rise and fall like a breathing giant, slithering along the shore. Isabelle looked out the window and some of the tension released from her body as she marvelled at the beauty of nature.

Then the taxi stopped at the Hall.

Isabelle couldn't help but be mesmerised by her ancestral home. It'd been standing on the same spot for the last four-hundred years and although it had started to show signs of wear, it would very likely stand for four-hundred years more. She remembered Mimi telling her that the Hall had been built on the ruins of a twelfth century fort. How many lives had it been privy to, and would it give up any secrets to her? She closed her eyes and listened, but it felt as though the Hall was in a slumber, frozen in time.

She closed the door behind her and raised a hand to her face as the smell of decaying flowers greeted her. The scent reminded her of working in the morgue all those years ago as a resident. There was a heaviness that made her feel claustrophobic as if the Hall were grieving. It was like she'd entered a tomb.

She took the stairs to her room. The wallpaper and curtains looked as though someone had drained the colour from them with a syringe.

Still, she remembered the day this room had become hers. Mimi had met her at the Edinburgh airport, and she was going to spend her summer holidays at the Hall.

'Mimi, Mimi!' Isabelle threw herself into her grandmother's arms.

'Hello, angel.' Mimi pulled her into an embrace. 'I missed you.'

'I missed you too, Mimi. I can't wait to get home. Do you know if Angus is back from his school? Will I see him today? I want us to go to the beach.'

'Slow down, darling,' Mimi laughed, 'I don't know about Angus, but there's a surprise waiting for you at the Hall.'

Isabelle had pestered Mimi to tell her about the surprise, but Mimi hadn't budged. Back at the Hall, Mimi had taken her upstairs and opened the door to this room.

'Seeing as you're twelve now, I thought you needed a room suitable for a young lady. This used to be my room when I was your age. Do you like it?'

'Oh Mimi, you're the best!' She gave Mimi a hug and lunged onto the four-poster, giggling with delight at her newfound kingdom.

The sound of the front door closing made Isabelle jump. She was sure she'd locked it behind her, and it could only be opened from outside by a key. She rushed downstairs in time to see a figure disappearing into the cloakroom.

Her heart pounded, and her palms were slick with sweat. She looked around for something she could use as a weapon, but there was nothing. She was about to go back upstairs for a fire iron from the master bedroom when the figure reappeared. Both let out shrieks at the sight of the other before recognition dawned.

'Christ, Mrs Murray, you scared me.' Isabelle softened her tone when she saw Mrs Murray's face. 'I'm sorry, I didn't mean to shout. I just hadn't expected anyone.'

'No, no, it's my fault. I'm sorry to give you a fright,' said Mrs Murray, her hand still resting on her chest.

Isabelle sighed. 'I think we could both do with a cup of tea, don't you?'

'Don't look so worried, Miss,' said Mrs Murray when Isabelle put the tea on the table. 'I thought I'd come over to see if I could help with anything. The place is in a terrible state.'

'That's very kind of you, but I'll manage.'

Mrs Murray's brow creased into deeper lines. Her fingers started to twist the fringes of the scarf in her lap. She raised her eyes and looked at Isabelle.

'The thing is, after the funeral I went to stay for a wee while with my daughter in Dumfries. I came back a couple of hours ago and thought I'd give the place a good going over. But now you're here … maybe I could still look after the Hall for you?'

Isabelle reached out and placed a hand on Mrs Murray's arm. 'Thank you. But the truth is… I…' The heat rose up her neck, burning her cheeks. 'I can't afford your services.'

Mrs Murray chuckled then fixed her eyes on Isabelle. 'Oh, don't you go worrying about that, Miss. Your grandmother's been more than generous to me. I'm sure you know about the arrangements she made for me. It's more than I need. And I just can't see myself getting up every morning with nothing much to do after spending a lifetime getting up at dawn and going to bed past midnight. You'll be doing me a favour.'

Isabelle smiled, reached over, and gave her a hug. 'Well, that's an offer I can't refuse.'

'That's settled then. I'll see you tomorrow, Miss.' Mrs Murray heaved herself off the chair with one hand and left.

Isabelle's mood brightened knowing that at least the Hall would be taken care of. She was back in her room when her phone rang. Isabelle checked the caller ID, sighed, and accepted the call.

'Hi, Mum.'

'Isabelle, are you at work?'

'No, I'm at the Hall.'

Isabelle braced herself for a barrage that didn't come. She dreaded her mum's silence even more than her anger.

'I see. Here I was thinking I wouldn't rush you into a decision, and you didn't even have the courtesy to let me know.'

'I'm sorry, Mum. I had a lot to deal with. I know I should have told you.' Why did she always let her mother guilt trip her?

'It's me who is sorry. I hoped you had more sense. I'm going to a retreat, but I'll be coming to Scotland next week. This is not over.'

Her shoulders slumped. Why couldn't her mum just let her get on with her life?

After the call, Isabelle pulled a pen and notebook out of her handbag to write a shopping list, only to realise she'd picked up Mimi's diary instead. It was as if she was holding a part of her grandmother close. Isabelle closed her eyes, heard young Mimi's voice, and wondered where her story would take her next.

Oh Mimi, I miss you so much.

Although she had things to do, she could not resist opening the diary. Isabelle was about to read on, when she realised she'd written the words with the pen in her hand.

Oh well, she thought, settling in to read, *it didn't matter. Mimi wasn't going to write in her diary again.*

Chapter Eight

Mimi, September 1953

I was in my room in St Andrews, unpacking my things, lingering on the box Will had given me and trying to decide where best to display it, when there was a knock on the door.

'Come in,' I called and looked over my shoulder.

The woman standing in my doorway was as glamorous as any movie star. Her hair was styled in curls around her face, and her dress hugged her figure to perfection.

'Hey, I'm Eilean. My room is next door to yours.' She pointed her thumb to her left. 'I arrived a few days ago.'

'I'm Mimi.'

I wondered what she must think of me. I felt every inch as frumpy as a country bumkin.

'I was about to go for a walk, but if you'd like I can give you a hand, then we can go together?'

I looked around the room, there wasn't much left to do. 'Let's go, I can finish later.'

I put Will's box on the table beside my bed. I could fall asleep with the scent of rose petals.

'Great!' Eilean beamed. 'Let's go.'

'Would you mind if we have a look at the university?' I asked as we walked down the cobbled streets.

'Not at all. It's just around the corner.'

'Oh wow,' I said at the grandeur of the sight that greeted me.

The Gothic buildings of the six-hundred-year-old university sprawled on two sides of a quad. The lawn in the middle was bordered by walkways. Gravel crunched underneath our feet as we made our way around.

'That's St Salvator's Chapel and the college tower,' Eilean pointed out.

The sunlight reflected off the stained-glass, bringing the images alive. My heart soared like the spires and the tower of the building in front of me as the realisation hit me that for the next three years, this would be my home.

'Come on, enough of the boring stuff.' Eilean tugged at my arm. 'There's this pub, where all the students go.'

Five minutes later, she dragged me through a crowd of men and women, sitting on benches outside the pub. Glasses of wine and beer chinked, and their laughter filled the air. I'd never seen so many people my age in one place. A flutter danced in my tummy like the wings of a bird, but I couldn't tell if it was excitement or my nerves. I was relieved when Eilean grabbed my hand and dragged me inside.

'Fancy a beer?' she asked.

'I've never had beer, only wine or champagne,' I said.

'Don't worry, you'll like it.'

I watched as Eilean ordered our drinks, and the man behind the bar whispered something in her ear. She threw back her head and laughed. I looked away to stop myself from staring at them.

'There. Let's go outside.'

I took the glass of beer and followed her.

'Hey guys, would you mind if we shared your bench?' Eilean asked.

'Of course not, anytime,' said one of the men as he took in every inch of her.

'So, Mimi, what do you think?'

I looked around. The women wore makeup and hairstyles like Eilean's. Some were even smoking. I wondered, *Was that what Alasdair meant about women having fun?*

'What's the matter Mimi? Don't you like it here?'

'Nothing. It's just, I think I need a new wardrobe.'

'Oh, Mimi. Don't look so worried. We still have a couple of days before it all kicks off. Leave it to me.'

'Are you ready?' Eilean asked the next day as we came to a stop outside the beauty salon. 'I think I'm more excited than you are.'

Her enthusiasm was infectious. I clapped my hands, breathed in, and followed Eilean inside. I sat there mesmerised by the snip-snip of the scissors as the stylist cut through my hair and wondered whether I'd have any left by the time she finished with me. Next, she put rollers in, wrapped a net around my head, and I joined the line of women under the driers. My head was buzzing with the heat and the sound, and I doubted if I could bear to do this once a week.

I looked over at Eilean, who was flicking through a magazine and sipping tea.

'I think you're done,' the stylist said and led me back to my chair.

She rushed through my hair with her fingers as she undid the net and the curlers, pulled and smoothed strands of hair with her comb, and doused me with a cloud of hairspray. At last she stood aside, and I looked in the mirror.

I couldn't take my eyes off the image that was looking back at me. It was like it belonged to someone else. My hair, which now reached to just under my chin, was arranged in layers of curls that looked and felt as smooth as silk. The top was swept up to one side like a wave.

Eilean squeezed my shoulder. 'You are absolutely transformed.'

Once outside we headed for the shops. I couldn't help bouncing my new hair with the flat of my hand in front of every shop window, which earned me a sharp look from Eilean.

'You're going to ruin your hair. Come on, Mimi, time for clothes and shoes.'

We walked into a store. Although it was not as sophisticated as Jenners in Edinburgh, where Alasdair had taken me a few times, Eilean knew exactly what she was doing and several hours later, we carried the myriad hat boxes and bags of dresses, shoes, twinsets, trousers, and blouses back to my room.

'My feet are hurting, and I need a nap.' I took off my shoes and rubbed my toes.

'Not yet. Come on, sit. I'm going to show you how to put on your makeup, so you don't end up looking like a clown.'

I dragged myself to the chair and sat in front of my mirror.

Eilean opened a compact, swept the pad over the powder and blew on it. 'Now dab this in. Pad it over your face.' She took the pad off me and replaced it with a brush. 'Now stroke this over your eye-lashes. Like so.'

She swiped the brush up and down in the air.

'Ouch,' I shouted, as mascara stung my eye. I wiped at the tears.

'Look at you!'

'What?'

I looked up at the mirror and to my horror my face was smeared with streaks of black. I looked back at Eilean, and we broke into peals of laughter.

After Eilean fixed my face and left, I grabbed my diary and stretched out on my bed. I wanted to make sure I recorded every detail of my adventure. I opened to a new page and caught my breath at the sight of the words **Oh Mimi, I miss you so much**, written in an unfamiliar hand.

Was it possible that Will had followed me to St Andrews? Was he staying out of the way, as Alasdair had demanded, but had left me this message? I missed him too. I thought of how thrilled I had been by his touch. Perhaps if I replied, he'd see my own message and write back.

With a secret smile I wrote: *Who is this?*

Chapter Nine

The February mist had gathered over the sea, and only the sound of waves crashing against the rocks revealed its existence. The fog was closing in, forcing Isabelle to concentrate on where she was going. The screech of a seagull made her jump. She took a breath, filled up her lungs, and broke into a run.

By the time she reached the end of the beach, her clothes were stuck to her from the mist and sweat, and she'd started to feel the chill. She should go back, but the idea of being in the house on her own put her off. She walked on towards the village instead. There was no sign of any activity, no sign of the buzz she was so used to in London. The streets, blurred by the haze, were deserted. Even the fishing boats bobbing up and down on the waves looked abandoned. Isabelle's heart sank; the whole place seemed like a ghost town.

Determined to find some sign of life, she hurried towards the coffee shop. The lights shining through the window lifted her spirit and the smell of coffee and cinnamon greeted her as she pushed open the door.

It seemed the entire village was gathered inside. She returned the few nods of greeting. All the tables were taken except for one seat at a table for two that was occupied by Hamish, one of the very few villagers she hadn't met before Mimi's wake. She approached the table, and before she had a chance to ask, he gestured towards the seat.

Isabelle looked at him. Like a sailor's, his face was weathered, carved by the years, and framed with a beard that covered the line of his jaw.

He must have been a looker as a young man, thought Isabelle.

'There you go, love.' The waitress put the coffee and pastry she'd ordered in front of her.

'So,' Hamish said, 'I hear you've been living at the Hall?'

Of course, he'd heard. That was village life for you.

'Yes,' she said. But if she were honest, the reality of her decision hadn't sunk in one bit. 'Do you live here yourself?' she asked, hoping to deflect the conversation from herself.

'Yes, on the outskirts of the village. You've heard of Silcraig Farm? Mind you, all that's left of it is the house.' Isabelle didn't think she'd heard of it. It must have shown because Hamish added, 'It used to be a dairy farm. It's on the right-hand side if you're going towards Edinburgh.'

'Yes, I think I've passed it in the car a few times.'

Remembering their conversation from the funeral, she thought perhaps she could learn something about the history of the Hall from Hamish. Since she'd had more time to digest everything, she was drawn to discover Mimi's story. She couldn't shake the feeling that whatever happened all those years ago was, as Mimi had said in her letter, the key to the past and future. She needed to know the reason she had left behind her life in London.

Isabelle leaned forward. 'So, how long was your father estate manager?'

'All his life, and his father before that. My family were estate managers at the Hall for generations. I broke a century long tradition.'

The sadness in his eyes didn't escape Isabelle. She empathised with him. Although she hoped she'd be able to fulfil Mimi's wish, she was terrified of failing and being the one to give away the Hall.

'I left fifty-seven years ago and moved to the Highlands,' Hamish continued. 'I came back only a week before Mimi's funeral.' He looked out of the window.

'But why?' Isabelle couldn't help asking.

'My lovely Elspeth, my wife, passed away a year ago. It was time to come home,' Hamish said, still not looking at her.

'Sorry, I meant why did you leave?' asked Isabelle, her curiosity getting the better of her.

'That's a story for another time, lassie.' He chuckled, but she could see the weariness in his eyes. 'Aye, I'd best be on my way. Come and visit me at the farm,' he said, and got to his feet with a groan.

Isabelle's shoulders slumped. There was clearly something that Hamish didn't want to talk about. But did it have anything to do with Mimi?

It was well past midday when Isabelle got back to the Hall, and it was only when she spotted the removal van in the drive, that she realised she'd forgotten they were coming. *Thank goodness for Mrs Murray*, she thought, who was directing men loaded with her belongings to a corner in the hallway.

'Now you're here, I'll be off, Miss Isabelle. I'll see you tomorrow. Aye, before I forget, I left you some soup in the fridge,' added Mrs Murray.

Once the removal men finished and left, Isabelle had the Hall back to herself. But instead of unpacking her cases and the few boxes, she headed for Mimi's room. She had to find the rest of Mimi's diaries if she wanted to find out what Mimi had done that had caused everyone involved such pain. The diary she was reading contained the story of the girl. She needed the diary of the woman.

She turned the handle and took a step inside. The sight of Mimi's belongings, and even more so the scent of Chanel No 5, made her heart contract. Tears filled her eyes as she was bombarded with memories. She closed the door behind her. She couldn't go in there, not yet. Instead, she dragged herself up the stairs to her room for a shower and rest.

When Isabelle woke, she willed life into her limbs and walked over to the window, drew back the curtains, and was greeted by a blizzard. Rapt, she watched as the wind picked up snow and hurled it around with a fury. The North Atlantic seemed to mimic the motion by crashing the waves back into its depth. The sky and the sea had merged in a wrestling match. How lucky that the removal men had been and gone already.

Stuck indoors during the storm, she may as well unpack her bags. Isabelle was emptying one of the boxes when her eyes fell on the framed photo of her and Chloe that she always kept on her bedside table. She reached for it, running her thumb over the glass. They both had their hair in pigtails tied with butterfly scrunchies and displayed identical toothy grins. Isabelle's arm was around Chloe's shoulder, pulling her closer.

She stroked Chloe's cheek with the tip of her finger. It seemed like yesterday. They'd been on holiday to the South of France and were staying at a villa by the sea. Every evening they all sat on the terrace, knees drawn up to their chests, arms around their legs, watching as the big sun sank into the sea.

But Maman, why is this sun bigger than the sun back home? Chloe had asked on the first night. Isabelle could still hear her parents' laughter.

At the sound of the phone, Isabelle reached for her mobile before realising it was the house phone ringing. She put the frame back in the box and dashed down the stairs to the hallway. She loved Mimi's rotary dial phone, the type that was in fashion again. She'd seen imitations in London shops, but Mimi's was the real deal. She halted for a moment before picking up the receiver, wondering who was calling her—or rather, calling Mimi. Her stomach churned at the thought of having to explain to a stranger that Mimi had passed.

'Lanesbrough Hall.'

She answered just as Mimi used to in her Queen's English voice, the one that had always baffled Isabelle, considering the Lanesbroughs were of Scottish blood through and through.

'Isabelle? It's Margot.'

Isabelle frowned. Why was Angus's mum calling her?

'I thought I'd check to see how you are, darling girl. I saw the van passing through the village this morning.'

Isabelle rolled her eyes. 'News travels fast in this part of the world,' she said, followed by a forced laugh. Not wishing to upset Margot, she added, 'I'm fine, thank you. It's very kind of you to call.'

'Is there anything we can help you with? It won't be any bother at all, just say the word.'

Isabelle was glad Margot's tone remained the same as before. She softened her own in response. 'Thank you, but I already unpacked everything. There wasn't much to begin with.'

'Well, it would be lovely to see you again. Why don't you come over for Sunday lunch? Angus and Alex will be here too. It'll be nice for you youngsters to spend some time together. What'd you say?'

Isabelle paused. Though she was amused by being called a youngster, she wasn't overjoyed at the prospect of seeing Angus and Alex.

'It'll be no trouble if that's what you're thinking,' Margot said. 'In fact, I'll be offended if you don't come. It's been so long since you visited us!'

Isabelle wanted to tell her exactly who was to blame for that, but she bit her lip. The last thing she wanted was hostility. This was a village after all, and it'd be hard to avoid people.

'That'll be lovely. I look forward to seeing you on Sunday. Shall I bring anything?'

'Just yourself. Come over at midday. And Isabelle, just call if you need anything—anything at all.'

Isabelle placed the receiver back in its cradle and let out a sigh. She wished she were in London where she needn't please anyone unless she wanted to.

As she walked back to her room the emptiness weighed on her. She checked her Facebook and Instagram, looking at images of friends. Out of habit she checked her emails, but there was nothing from work, only spam from Dune offering her a discount on shoes that were certainly not designed to weather a blizzard.

Her mood plummeted, and she asked herself if she'd made the right decision. She called Charlie but it went to voicemail. She left a message.

'Hey, just wanted to say hello. Hope all is good with you, chat soon.'

She was here for a reason; she may as well get on with it. She opened the diary and gasped. Right next to her own words: **Oh Mimi, I miss you so much**, someone had written *Who is this?* in what very much looked like Mimi's own writing.

'Very funny,' she said, then frowned. Who, other than Mrs Murray, could have accessed the diary? She didn't think that Mrs Murray was the type to play tricks.

She touched the writing. It looked old, the same pen faded in the same way as the diary entry.

'How?' she whispered.

It was as if Mimi herself had replied to her comment.

She half-laughed, but the situation wasn't funny. Isabelle sat there chewing her lip. She touched the pen next to the book. Should she reply?

The scientist in her told her Mimi wouldn't answer. Couldn't answer. It had to be a trick someone was playing. But then again, there was much that science couldn't explain, Isabelle thought as she looked out of the window.

The snow-covered landscape glittered under the full moon, and for a second Isabelle wanted to believe in magic. What did she have to lose? But should she tell Mimi she was her granddaughter? Of course not; she didn't even exist in Mimi's world yet. She wrote:

I'm Isabelle. A friend.

And she began to read.

Chapter Ten

Mimi, October 1953

'Oooh, you look glamorous,' said Eilean as I caught up with her outside the pub. I blushed. 'It's a bit early. Let's have a drink first before we go to the party.' Eilean pointed to a table in the corner as we walked in. 'You grab this table, and I'll get the drinks.'

'I wanted to ask you something,' I said as Eilean handed me a glass of wine.

'Of course, what is it, Mimi?'

I took a sip of wine and braced myself. 'Someone else has written in my diary.'

'What do you mean, *someone else*. Someone not you?'

'Yes.'

'What does it say?'

'Mimi, I miss you so much.'

Eilean was silent for a few moments and then burst into laughter. 'Do you know what I think?' Her eyes danced. 'You have a secret admirer.'

'A secret admirer who broke into my room and wrote in my diary?' I rolled my eyes at her. 'How do I find out who it is?'

'Simple: you ask around.'

'But if they wanted me to know who they were, why would they write a secret note?'

'Can you think of any other ideas?'

I shrugged. I didn't want to tell Eilean I'd already written back. I'd thought about it since and had to admit it'd been a stupid idea.

'Come on, let's go to the party,' Eilean said. 'Your admirer might even be there.'

'I'm not sure I want them to be,' I said with a small shiver and Eilean laughed.

Ten minutes later we arrived at a Victorian house ablaze in lights like a forest fire. The door was open, and people were smoking and talking outside. It was my first house party, and I had no idea what to expect.

'Stop dithering.' Eilean pulled me inside. We pushed our way through the crowd and into the kitchen.

'Eilean, darling, over here,' a man beckoned.

He towered over everyone else and was even more good-looking than Will.

'Mimi, this is Julian,' said Eilean as she looped her arm in his. 'Julian meet Mimi.'

'Pleasure to meet you, Mimi.' He shook my hand and gave us a glass of wine. 'Come on, you must meet Roger.'

'Eilean!' said Roger when we found him. He tapped the side of his head with two fingers. 'And who is this loveliness?'

'This is Mimi.'

'Enchanted.'

Roger took my hand, bent, and kissed it, then he looked up into my eyes. I couldn't help giggling.

'Come on,' he said and pulled me towards the dance floor.

I looked over my shoulder at Eilean who nodded her encouragement, so I let myself be swept away. Roger held my right hand in his, placed his other palm on the base of my back and pulled me close. Our bodies touched, and a tingle ran through me. He swayed me from side to side to the rhythm of the music. I looked around us and saw other couples dancing and to my horror a few that were kissing. Part of me wanted to look away, but I couldn't.

'Are you having fun, Mimi?'

'I… yes, thank you.' Trying to find a safer ground, I asked, 'What do you read?'

'Literature, and you?'

'Biology.'

Roger nodded. 'Where do you—' He paused, looking past me. 'Would you excuse me? I just saw someone I've been looking for; I'll be back in a moment.'

Without waiting for a reply, he left me standing in the middle of the crowd. The heat rose to my cheeks. I looked around and was relieved that no one seemed to be taking any notice of me. As I made my way back to the kitchen for a glass of water, I looked for Eilean, but she was nowhere to be seen. I roamed around some more, recognising a few faces, but everyone was busy chatting amongst themselves, and I didn't know how to break the ice.

I leaned against the wall, listening, and swaying to the music for a while, but I couldn't help feeling the odd one out. It was much later when I spotted Eilean at the bottom of the stairs.

'Eilean!'

I shouted at the top of my voice but doubted if she could hear me with all the noise. I quickened my step, pushing through the crowds, but by the time I reached the spot, she had vanished again.

'Darlin' Mimi.'

I turned to find Roger with his hands in his pockets, rocking back and forth on his heels. His eyes were shining, and he closed his lids over them at intervals.

'Are you all right?' I asked.

He grabbed my hand and pulled me into him. His breath was hot on my neck, and I felt the wetness of his lips. I turned my head away from him.

'Playing hard to get?' He slurred the words and pulled me closer.

His arm closed around me with such force that I thought my lungs might collapse. To my horror, I felt his hardness against the softness of my stomach, and nausea rose up to my throat. I tried to free myself, but his grip tightened.

'Let me go,' I shouted, but before I knew it, his lips were pressed against mine.

I thought I was going to throw up. Then someone pulled Roger off me.

'The lady asked you to let her go.'

For a moment I flashed back to Alasdair pulling me from Will's embrace, but this wasn't my brother. It couldn't be. The man stood between me and Roger, with his back to me. I didn't wait to hear more. I pushed my way through the crowds and didn't stop running until I got home.

I headed for the bathroom, looked in the mirror, and traced the mascara lines where I had cried. I washed, changed into my nightgown, and went to bed. I lay there staring at Will's box, the events of the night going around in my head like a carousel. In my panic to get away, I realised I had never stopped to thank the stranger.

The next morning, I woke with a headache. Perhaps a walk would help clear it. The clouds were the colour of pewter, and the wind was slicing the air like a scythe, but the weather was no worse than I was used to at home. I pulled my shawl up to protect my face, headed for the seafront, and sat on my favourite bench close to the castle. There I watched the seagulls diving into the waters of St Andrews Bay, thinking about last night and my own naivety.

'They're quite skilled divers.'

I turned in the direction of the voice and frowned.

'How are you this morning?' the stranger asked.

'I'm sorry, do I know you?'

'I was going to introduce myself last night, but you were gone. I was the one who intervened when, well … you know.'

'Oh, I'm so sorry. I should have thanked you, but I just had to get away.' I blushed.

'I understand. I'm Glen Smeatson, by the way, originally from Edinburgh.' He offered me his hand.

I shook it. 'I'm Mhairi Lanesbrough, but everyone calls me Mimi, and I'm from St Abbs.'

'Ah, the beautiful Scottish borders. I visited the Ettrick Valley a few times with my family, but that was a long time ago.'

'I must admit, I've rather been enjoying the novelty and hubbub here until…' I averted my gaze.

He cleared his throat. 'It's getting rather chilly standing still. May I be so bold as to ask you on a walk?'

Another image of Roger from last night flashed in front of me, but I pushed it aside and looked at Glen. His clothing and demeanour also reminded me somewhat of Alasdair. He seemed a gentleman, so I ought to be safe, particularly in broad daylight.

'That would be lovely,' I said, though nerves in my stomach jittered.

'Is this your first term, Mhairi?' he asked a while later.

It was strange to hear him call me by that name, but I didn't mind. 'Yes. I'm reading biology.' I gave him a sideway glance. 'What about you?'

'I'm a historian. It's the last year of my PhD. I also assist with lectures for first-year students. May I invite you for a warm drink?'

'I think I'd like that very much,' I said, my own face by now numb with the cold.

We walked in silence, but unlike last night I actually did feel safe.

'Here we are,' said Glen and we walked into a tearoom I had seen before but hadn't had a chance to visit.

We ordered hot cocoa for me and a coffee for him.

'What is it your family do?' I asked.

'My father's a surgeon and university professor, and my mother was a concert pianist when they met. But she gave it up after she had me and has since been giving piano lessons. What about your family?'

I swallowed. 'We're landowners. My parents passed away, and I live with my brother at the Hall on Lanesbrough Estate,' I said, missing each of them more with every word.

'I'm very sorry about your parents, though I must admit living on an estate must be charming. Perhaps one day I will have the pleasure of seeing it for myself.'

There was a look in his eyes that I couldn't decipher, but which made me blush.

We carried on talking, and by the time he escorted me to my accommodation, I had a feeling I knew him well.

'It was a pleasure to meet you, Mhairi.' He smiled, making dimples appear on his cheeks, which I thought took away some of his seriousness. 'Would you like to go to the pictures? I'm home this weekend, what about the Friday after?'

'Yes.'

My entire body whirred with excitement at my own boldness. But perhaps this was the new me, the more elegant, confident, and grown-up Mhairi, rather than little Mimi from the Hall.

As soon as I got into my room, I reached for my diary. My heart froze in my chest as I read the words:

I'm Isabelle, a friend.

I ran through the names of all the girls I knew and couldn't think of any Isabelle. Besides, this time I knew for a fact that I'd left my diary locked in my room. How was this possible? Could it be a ghost?

I laughed at my own silliness, but then a memory flashed before my eyes. I was walking with my mother hand-in-hand through the woods at the Hall. It was summer, and we were heading for the burn. I must have been about six or seven.

'Do you see that spring, Mimi?' my mother asked.

'What about it, Mama?'

'Well, the local stories say that's where Shellycoat live.'

I frowned. 'Shelly what?'

Mama laughed. 'Shellycoat, they're fairy folk.'

'Do they really live there?'

'I'm not too sure, but what I can tell you is that your grandmother could see things others didn't.'

'You mean like ghosts?'

'Something like that.' She squeezed my hand.

I don't know how long I sat there, but it was dark now. Could it be I was fey like my grandma? Before I could reconsider I wrote:.

Are you a ghost?

Chapter Eleven

Isabelle rubbed her eyes. Her head was buzzing and her stomach growling. She had to get out, but the only place where she could go was the village pub. She couldn't walk there in the snow, so she would have to drive Mimi's Volvo. The car was sitting in the open garage like a relic, as though lost in time. She turned the key in the ignition, but nothing happened. She tried a few more times before it sputtered into life.

The drive took less than ten minutes of creeping, with the occasional swerve that made her heart fall into her knickers. There were no streetlamps in the village, but the Fox & Hare was illuminated like a beacon with fairy light garlands hanging underneath the eaves and a spotlight over the pub sign that aptly depicted a sitting fox and a hare.

The sounds of chatter and laughter enfolded her before she even opened the door. Inside, the warmth of the fire and the smell of food formed a warmer embrace. As she made her way towards the bar, a few people nodded a greeting in her direction, which made her feel welcomed. Perhaps it wasn't that bad after all to be in a place where everyone knew each other.

She waited in the queue at the bar and glanced around. Every table seemed to be taken. She wondered if it were always this busy. She looked back towards the bar, spotting the blackboard there announcing, *Pizza Tuesday*. Great news, at least that was a takeaway food she still could enjoy in the sticks, and it explained the crowd.

'What can I get you?' asked the barmaid. She had a shock of curls so red they glowed.

'I'll have a G&T please.'

As she was waiting, Isabelle admired the beams aged by the years and the pictures of foxes and hares in Victorian costumes on the walls. They reminded her of the Peter Rabbit stories Mimi used to read to her. It felt like yesterday that she'd been in her PJs on her bed with Mimi next to her.

'That'll be £4, love,' said the barmaid as she placed the drink on the counter.

Isabelle tapped her card on the machine. She turned around before the waitress noticed her shiny eyes and felt as though she'd walked into a wall.

She heard a voice she recognised. 'Belle? Hey, are you all right?'

'Angus.'

'Well, I'm glad we remember each other's names.' He winked, and despite herself she laughed. 'It looks like you'll be needing another drink, let me buy you one.'

Isabelle noticed the wet patch on Angus's jumper from her G&T. 'Gosh, sorry, Angus,' she said, and began to wipe at the stain.

'Oh, that's nice. Don't stop.'

Isabelle slapped his chest. 'Behave yourself. I'm still angry with you.'

Angus chuckled. 'Siobhan, another G&T and a pint of Elvis Juice please,' he shouted over the noise.

'Aye, I'll bring them over.'

'Come on.' He grabbed Isabelle's hand and led her to a table in the corner.

She was relieved to see that Alex wasn't there. On the other hand, maybe she was in the loo.

'Is Alex here?'

'No, she was having a Zoom party with her friends in Dubai, so I left her to it.'

Isabelle breathed a sigh of relief.

'There you go.' Siobhan placed the drinks on the table. 'Any food for you?'

'Probably later,' said Angus. He took a sip of his beer then asked, 'How're you settling in?'

'All right.' Isabelle tucked her hair behind her ear.

Angus cleared his throat. 'Listen Belle, I just wanted to say how sorry I am for not having been in touch since I left.'

Isabelle nodded. Then she set her jaw. 'Why though? I mean, you just ghosted me. If it hadn't been for your posts on Facebook and Instagram, I would have thought something had happened to you.'

He looked down.

'You really hurt me, Angus. I thought we were friends. But I guess not. You of all people should know how hard I find it to trust people—'

'I know.' He took her hand. 'It's hard to explain. Complicated. The thing is, when I first got to Dubai, I was just swept up with the novelty of it all. I was insanely busy. Then I met Alex, basically on my first day at work—'

Isabelle pulled her hand away. 'And you promptly forgot about me. Is that it then?'

'No, no.' Angus swiped his hair out of his face and looked at her. 'It wasn't like that. It's … Alex saw a message from you and asked me who you were. And let's just say, she didn't understand why I needed a friend like you, when I had her.' Angus swiped his hair back again. 'She made such a song and dance about you every time you got in touch that in the end, it was simply easier to let you go, especially with you in London and me in Dubai.'

Isabelle knew Alex had been behind it. *That cow.* But she was not going to relent that easily. She crossed her arms and sat back.

'So it's Alex's fault.'

'No, it was mine. I shouldn't have given in to her. I should have explained *us* better. But every time I tried, she said I was just in love with you, and it all went wrong. Can you forgive me?'

Isabelle looked at him. He wore the same expression he used to have as a kid when he was pleading with her.

'Fine. But you're still with Alex. How's she going to feel

about our friendship now?'

Angus sighed. 'To be honest, I don't care. When I saw you, I realised what I'd thrown away so carelessly. If she asks, I'll tell her that our friendship doesn't change my relationship with her.'

Isabelle nodded. 'It's a shame you didn't think of that six years ago. But luckily, I'm feeling magnanimous. And I missed you. So, I'll give you one more chance. Now, enough of that. I'm starving.'

'*That* I can remedy in no time. Pizza's coming up,' he said and headed for the bar.

Isabelle watched him go and thanked her stars that at last she had her friend back.

Back at the Hall, Isabelle got ready for bed, but her mind wouldn't shut down. She thought about texting Charlie that Angus would be back in their lives again, but Charlie would only be angry that she hadn't read him the riot act—or at least a lot more of it.

Instead, she turned the light on and reached for Mimi's diary, hoping there would be a new message. Isabelle opened the diary and burst out laughing at the sight of Mimi's words asking oif she were a ghost.

Was she a ghost? Isabelle wondered before the madness of it hit her. This was beyond reason, but it had worked. Then another thought struck her. If this were true, if she could communicate with the young Mimi, did it mean that she could change the past? Could she find out what Mimi had done to alienate Bonelle and perhaps fix it, fix her family? Isabelle shook her head at the outrageousness of her idea and turned her attention back to the diary and wrote:

> **I suppose, I am. But not really. It's hard to explain. I'm sorry about what happened at the party. You really need to be careful, Mimi. I hope it won't happen again, but if it does, next time knee the guy between the legs; that should teach him a lesson! I'm glad Glen stepped in. He seems like a nice guy.**

Then she began to read.

Chapter Twelve

*M*y dearest Alasdair,
    Please forgive me for not writing sooner, but as you can imagine, it's been a busy couple of months since I arrived. I now know my way around the city and enjoy taking walks along the ruined remains of the once magnificent cathedral that was built in 1158. I get on well with the girls in my Hall and have become quite close with Eilean, who like me also reads biology like me. We often study together or go for walks; I'm so glad I met her. In fact, I have a confession to make. I'm afraid Eilean persuaded me to buy an entire new wardrobe, which made rather a large dent in the generous allowance you gave me. But you'll see for yourself that it was worth it. As you know, Christmas is coming up, and I'd like to get everyone some nice presents.

    I hope all is well at the Hall, and do give my warm regards to everyone. Please send me news from home, and I look forward to seeing everyone at Christmas.

    Your loving sister,

Mimi

I thought it was prudent not to mention the party, and as for Glen, I didn't want to worry Alasdair. I'd tell him when I saw him at Christmas. At the thought of going back to the Hall, I realised with a jolt that I hadn't thought of Will for several days. My birthday seemed like another lifetime.

The church bells pulled me out of my reverie. I grabbed my coat and scarf and ran out. Glen was waiting for me. He must have heard my steps; he turned around and his face broke into a smile that warmed my heart.

'You look lovely.' He kissed me on the cheek, then he offered me his arm.

'Thank you.' *And you look rather dapper*, I wished to say but thought better of it.

'Have your exams started yet?' he asked after a few minutes.

'No, but I have a few assignments to do. What movie are we going to see?'

'I thought you might enjoy the new one with Glynis Johns?'

I beamed at him. 'How exciting; she's one of my favourite actresses.'

When we arrived at the pictures, Glen bought the tickets and a couple of drinks before we went in and took our seats. Soon after, a hushed silence descended over the theatre as the lights went out and the screen flashed. The excitement in the room ran through me like an electric current. The touch of Glen's hand on mine brought a smile to my face before I became engrossed in the movie and enchanted by Glynis.

At some point Glen draped his arm around my shoulder. My chest warmed, and I leaned into him. I noticed a few couples kissing and was relieved that Glen was a gentleman. Still, I hoped that he would kiss me soon.

'Oh Glen, that was wonderful. Thank you,' I said after the movie finished and we emerged into the foyer.

'My pleasure, Mhairi. Shall we have dinner together, or do you wish to go back?' he asked and helped me into my coat.

'I'd love—'

'Hello, old chap.' Roger grinned at Glen. 'I see it worked.'

He looked at me and tapped his nose. I looked from him to Glen and shook my head in disbelief, my heart thumping in my chest.

'You two know each other? What is he talking about, Glen?'

But Glen wouldn't look at me.

'I'll leave you to it, folks,' Roger said as though nothing had happened and walked away.

'Glen?' I asked again and couldn't hide the tremor of disbelief and anger in my voice.

His shoulders slumped. He rubbed his palms up and down his face and when he took his hands away, I could read only misery in his eyes. When he finally spoke, I had to strain to hear him.

'I'm sorry, Mhairi. It wasn't meant to happen that way.' He looked away. 'Roger was just meant to come on to you, but he took it too far.'

'So you two planned the whole thing?' I raised my voice.

His face contorted, and he jolted at the force of my words. 'Mhairi, please, I know it looks bad, and it was stupid. I just wanted to impress you. I thought if I asked you straight out, you would turn me down. I know I was wrong. I've regretted it ever since. I...'

Words failed him and remorse wrapped around him like his coat, softening my anger enough for my hurt and confusion to find a way in. I didn't want him to see the tears that stung my eyes.

He brushed my arm. 'Mhairi, I'm so, so—'

I slapped his arm away and walked off.

'Mhairi, wait.'

I ignored his call and dragged myself home with the weight of my pain. By the time I was back in my room, my eyes hurt from crying, and I was shivering with cold, shock, or exhaustion, I didn't know which. I lay on my bed and closed my eyes, replaying the scene in my mind like a film on an endless loop.

I was startled awake by a knock on my door and opened my eyes. The room was doused in sunshine. I threw the blanket off me and noticed that I was still in last night's clothes. I didn't dare to think what I must look like after all that crying. I went to the door but didn't open it.

'Who is it?'

I heard an unfamiliar voice say, 'I've got a delivery for you.'

Alasdair must have sent me a parcel. 'Just leave it at the door, please.'

'Sure, Miss.'

I heard a rustling followed by the sound of footsteps moving away. I opened the door and saw a bouquet of roses so large that it looked like one of Mama's rose bushes. I smiled despite myself. I picked up the bouquet and closed the door before anyone could see me. As I bent down to inhale the scent I noticed a card, but even before I opened it, I knew—or did I hope?—that it must be from Glen.

Can you forgive me, Mhairi?

I don't know if I projected my own sadness onto the words or was somehow able to sense his. I shook my head to dislodge my confusion and put the flowers in a vase. I needed to clear my mind, but I wasn't ready to talk about it yet.

Two days later, I'd just left the St Salvadore's Chapel after the Sunday service and was headed towards town to treat myself to tea and perhaps a sandwich when I heard, 'Mhairi, wait.'

I turned around to see Glen running towards me. A stab of anger flashed in my chest at his sight, and I carried on walking.

'Please, Mhairi,' he said when he reached me and caught his breath. He put up his palms towards me like I was a flighty horse about to bolt. 'Please, just hear me out.'

He looked like he hadn't slept since I'd seen him last. His complexion was even paler than usual and stubbles the colour of rust covered the lower part of his face. I crossed my arms over my chest and waited.

'Thank you. Listen, I'm truly sorry for what I did. It was unforgiveable. I'm deeply ashamed of myself. But what upsets me most is the hurt I caused you. I... is there any way you could find it in your heart to give me another chance?'

The sincerity of his words was reflected in his eyes, and I knew he meant every word. I could stay angry at him, but unless I was ready to let go of him, there was no point. He must care for me if he was prepared to make such an effort. Besides, I had no difficulty believing that Roger would have taken things into his own hands. Glen had no doubt made an error of judgment, but in every other respect he'd been nothing but a gentleman.

'Fine,' I said at last and watched as relief washed away the tension in his features.

'Thank you, Mhairi. I promise I won't disappoint you.' He cleared his throat. 'Will you let me take you out for lunch?'

I didn't answer. Was I sure I wanted to get involved with him? What if he let me down again?

'Please, give me a chance to make it up to you,' he said as though he'd read my mind.

'All right.'

It was only lunch, and my stomach was rumbling. Besides, I couldn't ignore the flutter in my chest at the thought that it wasn't yet over between us.

'Thank you,' he said and offered me his arm. 'My car is just around the corner.'

As I took his arm, the familiar warm feeling rushed through me. Though still cautious, a part of me was pleased that we'd made up. A few minutes later Glen stopped in front of a cerise Chevrolet and opened the passenger door for me. The leather interior was as soft as my kid gloves. I settled in and watched as Glen sat behind the wheel and turned the ignition.

'It'll warm up soon,' he said as he fiddled with the buttons.

He pulled onto the road. His driving was measured, unlike Alasdair's—my brother was fond of speeding as though he were a racing driver—and soon I became engrossed in the scenery.

Half an hour later, over a lunch of game pie in a country pub, I asked, 'Do you plan to leave Edinburgh once your PhD is finished?'

'No, I've been already asked to set up a research project and will have my own lectures.' He took another fork full of pie and seemed to study me as he did so. 'What made you study biology?'

'I guess living at the Hall, I've always been surrounded by nature and was interested to know more.'

'And do you plan to work once you graduate?'

It was such a simple question, yet I felt at a loss for an answer. I'd never really thought about any plans for my future and in that moment I realised that somehow I must have thought I'd always be living at the Hall, and the absurdity of it hit me.

'I'm not sure,' I finally answered. My shoulders tensed at my own naivety, and Glen must have noticed my discomfort because he moved the conversation on to friendships, and I was grateful that he had read me so well.

By the time we reached my residence, it was dusk. We stood in front of each other, neither of us speaking. It was as though we both wished to delay the moment of parting.

'Thank you for your wonderful company, Mhairi.'

I nodded and wondered when I'd see him next.

'Would you like to go to the theatre on Saturday?'

I beamed at him. 'Oh, that would be marvellous.'

'I'll collect you here at six.'

He leaned forward and kissed me on the cheek. When he pulled back, my hand had wandered to my face and was covering the spot, as though trying to keep his kiss in place. I blushed and dropped my hand, but from the smile on his face, I knew he'd already noticed.

He tucked a strand of hair behind my ear, making my skin tingle. 'I'll see you soon, Mhairi.'

I ran up to my room, pulled off my gloves and coat, and grabbed my diary. I wanted to write it all down before I forgot any details. I opened my diary and saw Isabelle's message.

I suppose, I am, but not really....

It's nice to have a friend no matter what strange thing you are.

Her advice put a smile on my face.

The party seems ages ago, but I sure learned my lesson! I should have listened to my brother's warnings. But if I'm honest, I just wasn't expecting it. You're obviously a feisty girl. I'll need to toughen up more. The only good thing that came out of it is that I met Glen. We're stepping out. But you'll read about that anyway.

Though I wondered what she'd think about what Glen had done. I hoped she wouldn't think badly of him. I didn't really know her. She wasn't like anyone I'd met, and I was curious about her.

Tell me about yourself.

As I thought about what to write next, I looked at Will's box on my bedside table. With trembling fingers, I picked it up and slid it into a drawer.

Chapter Thirteen

Isabelle arrived at the Old Steading, relieved that she and Angus were friends again and that the awkwardness of their broken bond was not going to raise its head during lunch.

The farmhouse had been built in local stone. It sat on its own grounds separated from the road by a wall, overflowing with ivy. The glow of the pyracantha berries livened up the flowerbeds.

Margot greeted her with a hug. Stepping across the threshold, Isabelle felt as though she was stepping back in time; even the smell of the farmhouse seemed the same, that of milk and biscuits.

'Sit down, lovely.' Margot pointed to the kitchen table made of railway sleepers worn by time. 'I'll put the kettle on.'

Isabelle looked around, taking in the beams and the hearth. A sense of familiarity washed over her, and she began to relax.

'That's a nice smile,' said Margot.

Isabelle laughed to cover her embarrassment at being caught out. 'I was just thinking of the times Angus and I used to sit here with glasses of milk. How we scoffed our faces with the chocolate biscuits you used to bake.'

'I remember that too. You two were like feral cats, dirty and hungry all the time,' said Margot with a shake of her head. She placed a hand on Isabelle's arm. 'How're you keeping up, darling?'

Her throat tightened and Isabelle looked away to gather herself. 'I miss her very much.'

Margot bent and took Isabelle in her arms, just as someone called out from behind her. Isabelle recognised the voice and freed herself from Margot's arms. She swiped away the tears with her sleeves, just as Alex and Angus strode into the kitchen.

'Hi, Belle,' said Angus. He kissed her on the cheek.

Isabelle tilted her head away from him, no need to actively wind up the jealous girlfriend. She looked at Alex.

'Hi, Alex,'

'How was your walk?' Margot asked.

Alex wrinkled her nose. 'Very wet and muddy.'

Her hair was falling around her face in waves. She had no makeup on and still looked like a model.

'That was nothing. You'll get used to it eventually,' Angus said with a wave of his hand.

'I don't think so, and I'm not sure I want to either. You keep forgetting, I'm a city girl.'

Isabelle felt some sympathy for that and nodded in Alex's direction but was ignored.

'How can I when you keep reminding me of it?' Angus said, not smiling.

Isabelle looked at Margot, who rolled her eyes.

She must be used to the bickering, thought Isabelle.

The room felt like a punctured lung that was slowly losing air, taking Isabelle's nostalgic feelings with it. This was not the same picture that Angus and Alex had presented at the wake. *Relationships*, she thought.

'That smells grand,' Jonathan said as he joined them in the kitchen. 'Come on you lot, sit down. I'm famished.'

His cheerfulness dispelled some of the tension, but not all of it. Isabelle noticed Alex glowering at her and wondered how long Angus would stick with his determination to reignite their friendship in the face of his fiancée's antagonism. She decided to make her excuses and leave as soon as she could without offending Margot.

'Any news, Belle?' Angus asked as they sat down around the table.

Before she had a chance to answer, Alex said, 'I thought your name was *Isa*belle?' her cut-glass accent emphasising the first three letters of her name.

Isabelle wondered whether the hint of irritation in Alex's tone was directed at her or Angus.

'It is,' Margot said, piercing a roast potato with her fork. 'But our Angus always called her Belle. He was too young to say the name properly and it stuck.'

Isabelle nodded and looked at Angus. 'And no, there's no news here, I'm afraid. My next step is looking for a job.'

Jonathan looked up. 'I might be able to help you. A golf buddy of mine, Calan, has been running the surgery in Haddington for yonks, and I'm sure he said he was looking for a locum. I'll give you his number. Give him a call and say hello from me.'

'Thank you. I'll do that.' Isabelle looked at Alex, who had yet to eat a single thing. 'By the way, congratulations on your engagement. The pictures popped up on my Facebook. I was going to send a message, but then everything with Mimi happened and I forgot to mention it to Angus the other night…' She trailed off for a moment, then forced herself to continue. 'How are the wedding plans coming on?'

Alex just looked at her. 'They're not, and what do you mean by *the other night*?' She looked from her to Angus.

Isabelle too looked at Angus, who closed his eyes and looked down. So he hadn't mentioned to Alex they'd met at the pub.

'Angus?' Alex's eyes bored into him.

'I met Belle at the pub the other night.'

'And you just forgot to mention it?'

'Are there any problems with the wedding plans?' asked Margot.

'What?' Her question seemed to throw Alex off balance. 'No, I meant we haven't had much time recently.'

Isabelle shifted on her chair, trying to think of something to say and regretted bringing up the subject in the first place. There was no doubt she'd put her foot in it. But then, how did Angus expect Alex to support their friendship, if he lied to her about it, even by omission?

'You guys go; Alex and I will take care of this,' said Angus after they finished their meal. His hand swept around the kitchen, and it was unclear what he and Alex would be taking care of, the dishes or their differences.

'Thanks, love. Come on, Isabelle.'

Margot ushered her into the living room, and Jonathan went to stoke the fire. Isabelle wished she were miles away in London, pursuing her Sunday ritual of a walk around Primrose Hill followed by a lunch at the café in the park where she'd spend her afternoon reading and watching life go by.

'You all right, darling?' Margot asked, looking at her with concern.

'I'm fine. I'll just be a second.'

Isabelle excused herself and headed for the loo to have a moment alone. As she walked past the kitchen, she overheard Angus and Alex arguing.

'You can't help yourself, can you, Alex? You had to advertise our business. You know Mum and Dad aren't stupid. And in front of Belle as well. Honest to God, what the hell were you thinking?'

'Why didn't you tell me you met her? And besides, what do you care what she thinks?'

There was a frustrated sigh. 'Never mind, let's just get in there. We'll make up an excuse and leave after we've had a coffee.'

Isabelle hovered beside the open doorway. She knew she should go, but it was as if she were spellbound. God, that woman hated her. Before she could walk away, Alex turned to leave the kitchen. When she saw Isabelle a shadow crossed her face.

'Can I help you?'

The edge in her voice made Isabelle's back stiffen. 'No, I was just on my way to the loo,' she said and made her escape.

Isabelle closed the bathroom door behind her, leaned against it, and focused on her breathing. She walked over to the sink and splashed her face with water. *Not long to go*, she thought.

Back in the living room, all eyes fell on her, except Jonathan's; he was snoring by the fire.

'Ah, there you are. Come on, sit down.' Margot patted the seat on the sofa next to her.

'Did you find the loo, Isabelle?' Alex looked at her, eyes narrowed and chin raised.

She thought Alex's attitude sucked, and she wasn't going to sit there and take it. She put on her biggest smile.

'Yes, after a detour to the kitchen.'

Isabelle watched with satisfaction as the colour rose in Alex's cheeks as though she'd slapped her. And when Angus roared with laughter, Isabelle could have kissed him. Though Isabelle felt some guilt for having intruded on the couple, it wasn't all her fault; they shouldn't have aired their differences in someone else's kitchen.

Shortly after, she said her goodbyes and headed back to the Hall, the walk helping relax her. She poured herself a glass of wine, took it to the living room, and opened Mimi's diary to distract herself from her visit. She wondered what Mimi had got up to and if she'd replied to her message.

It was beyond reason, but it had worked.

It's nice to have a friend ... you're obviously a feisty girl...
Tell me about yourself?

Isabelle smiled. It was clear that Mimi had fallen for Glen. But as she read of Glen's perfidy, Isabelle clenched her jaw. She would have given him a piece of her mind. And what of Mimi? She was sexually assaulted by Roger. How could she have got over it so quickly? And as if that wasn't bad enough, she had taken Glen back!

Isabelle shook her head. *I wouldn't trust that man.* She had to try and warn Mimi without putting her off. She picked up her pen.

I'm sorry to hear so much has happened, Mimi. Are you really all right after what happened with Roger? I can see you like Glen. But it'll take time to get to know someone properly. And I'm sure you know that. I'm a doctor. I used to live in London but moved to Scotland. It's been a big change, but I'm slowly finding my feet.

Isabelle felt like she was writing to a pen pal. She kicked off her shoes, tucked her feet under her, and began to read.

Chapter Fourteen

Mimi, Christmas 1953

Since we made up that day outside the chapel, Glen and I had been for many more walks, teas, and lunches. Although we had come across some of his friends around the town, this evening was the first time I was to meet them all, and it was a debate night. As Glen and I approached the building, my grip tightened on his arm, and my stomach churned. I knew for fact that they all were rather serious intellectuals, while I, well…

'What if they don't like me?'

Glen patted my hand. 'Of course, they will.'

And I realised I'd spoken the words.

Glen pressed the bell, and the door opened at once.

'Come on in,' George said and shook our hands. I had met him once before.

The flat was much larger than I'd expected and decorated in furniture that like the house itself was Georgian. A group of young men and women were sitting around a fire.

'Hello, everyone; this is Mhairi,' Glen introduced me.

Everyone nodded in greeting. George gave us our drinks and a buffet was laid out on the dining table. After a few sips of wine, the tension eased. I watched the room descend into a debate about politics and history.

'Glen, what do you think of Churchill's *A History of the English-Speaking People*?' asked one of the men I hadn't met before.

'I think he deserved the Nobel Prize. Of course, it's not written the way a professional historian would have. It's his view. However, considering the man's aptitude and experiences...'

I looked around the room and could see everyone was listening as though it was the gospel, though personally, I found myself losing interest. As the evening progressed my mood dampened further by Glen's complete lack of interest in me.

'Glen,' I whispered and touched his arm to get his attention. But it was as though he'd forgotten I was there. I took myself to the window and watched as snow covered the city.

'Ah, here you are.' Glen appeared at my elbow sometime later. 'Are you enjoying yourself?'

I wanted to say *No because you've been ignoring me all evening* but instead, I replied, 'Yes. And you? You seemed so engrossed.'

'Yes, you're right, and now I realise I must have neglected you. I'm sorry.'

He reached and took me in his arms, and I nestled against him, my disappointment draining from me.

Soon after we said our goodbyes. Glen and I were walking arm in arm through the snow, his umbrella containing us in our own bubble when he stopped in his tracks and turned to face me.

'Mhairi...' He cleared his throat and continued. 'You must know I'm very fond of you.'

It sounded to me more of a statement rather than a question, so I continued looking at him, trying to focus on my breathing whilst wondering what was coming next. But nothing did.

'And I like you,' I eventually said, speculating on where all this was going.

The words were barely out of my mouth when the gap between our faces closed, as did my eyes, and a whisper of a kiss touched my lips. It stopped, gained momentum, and returned passionately. After Glen had ignored me all evening, it had been the last thing I'd expected. But I couldn't deny feeling a sense of pride that a man of such standing was interested in me.

The next morning I packed my bags and took out my diary. I had a couple of hours before Alasdair would be here to take me back to the Hall for Christmas. I hoped Isabelle had written to me.

Are you really all right after what happened with Roger?

I frowned. I hadn't really thought about it since Glen and I got back together. And though the memory of it sent a shiver through me, I pushed the image aside. There was nothing I could do about it and focused on the rest of Isabelle's message.

I'm a doctor.

I was impressed as I read her note and how wonderful that she lived in Scotland. *Perhaps we could meet?* I thought. But then I realised that was impossible. I shook my head. I still couldn't figure out how all this was working, but I shrugged and wrote a response.

You must be very clever. I read biology but you already know that. Why did you move to Scotland? It must be very different from London. Alasdair's been to London, but I've never been there. Do you have any siblings? What about your parents?

At the sound of a car horn, I looked at the clock. Could it be Alasdair already?

The way he drives, I wouldn't be surprised, I thought and left for downstairs.

'Mimi!' Alasdair shouted, hastened his steps, and lifted me.

I dropped my bag and wrapped my arms around his neck. 'Oh, Alasdair, I missed you so much.'

'And I you, little sis.' He kissed the top of my head, put me down, and opened the car door. 'Now get in there. Everyone's waiting for your arrival.'

We were half an hour into our drive when a blizzard began, and Alasdair had to slow down.

'Are we going to make it?' I asked. The last thing I wanted was getting stuck on the road in this cold.

'Let's hope so,' said Alasdair.

It was the last light of day by the time Alasdair and I arrived home. As soon as the car came to a halt, I jumped out and ran into the Hall.

'Miss Mimi, I'm so glad you're home,' said Mrs Kerr.

'Miss Mimi!' Mrs Quinn rushed into the room, held me by the arms and looked me over, her eyes twinkling with joy. 'Oh my, you look a proper lady now, doesn't she, Mrs Kerr? I've made your favourite meal: roast chicken and for pudding there's apple crumble and custard.'

'Thank you, Mrs Quinn.'

I gave her a hug before I ran up the stairs to my room. I stood in the doorway and looked around me. It was my room, and yet it felt as though it belonged to another me from another time, and for one moment I longed for Glen and my life in St Andrews.

Early the next morning I was in the stables greeting my horse, Rionnag, when I sensed a presence. I turned around to see Will standing a short distance away from me. My pulse galloped in response, and a rush of warmth coursed through my body. I frowned to cover it up. Surely, I shouldn't still feel like this? Not when I had Glen; not when I had moved on?

'Hello Miss Mimi, it's good to see you back.' Will said, his voice quivering.

'Thank you, Will. I'm glad to be back,' I managed to say.

A silence that seemed to last an eternity descended on us. I don't think I was ever so pleased to hear Alasdair's voice.

'Good morning,' he said and stopped in his tracks, looking at Will. 'Would you mind saddling Target? I'll help Mimi.'

I hadn't missed the tension in my brother's voice. I stepped aside so Will could pass and tried to compose myself. It occurred to me this was the first time after the incident at my birthday that the three of us were together, and judging by his demeanour Alasdair was still on alert.

On the twenty-first of December, the winter solstice, the doors of the Hall opened for the traditional Christmas party. It'd been snowing for the last three days, and the flakes were still coming down.

'You look very festive,' Alasdair said and pecked me on the cheek.

I too was pleased with my choice of dress, which matched the colour of the holly berries. I'd spent more time than I dared to admit, styling my hair the way Eilean had showed me, and applying my makeup, without once having to correct a stroke.

Tables were arranged along one side of the hallway, decked with platters of food and glasses of port and whiskey that would be filled and refilled over the course of the next hours.

Alasdair and I took our place by the Christmas tree and greeted our guests as they arrived.

'Everything looks so wonderful,' said Mrs McCallum, the doctor's wife.

I was about to reply when I was distracted by Alasdair greeting Will. Mrs McCallum, who was known to love her food, was already heading towards one of the maids.

I forced myself to look at Will, and heat enveloped my body. This was the first time since the morning in the stables that we were standing face to face. I'd seen him around the grounds, but apart from a nod of the head, neither of us had attempted a conversation. I knew that we'd been avoiding each other. Or at least I had.

'Merry Christmas, Miss Mimi,' Will said. He looked at me for a moment before averting his gaze.

'And a Merry Christmas to you, Will.'

I was more in control but still confused as to how it was possible to have feelings for two men. I decided that my feelings for Will must be reminiscent of my adolescent crush, and I understood for the first time how improper a continuation of it would be. But something inside me knew that Will still felt the same.

Chapter Fifteen

Over breakfast, Isabelle was pondering how to find out more about the past. Maybe she could have a nose around her study, where Mimi had kept all her paperwork.

Half an hour later, she opened the door to Mimi's study and found it plunged into darkness when it'd usually been full of light. Even so, time had stood still. The desk looked as tidy as always. A lamp was perched on one corner, and an ink set that had belonged to Mimi's father sat in the centre. On the other corner was a frame that Isabelle knew held a photo of Mimi's parents, taken on the lawn in front the Hall. And there in the middle were Mimi's reading glasses, as though she'd put them there only moments ago.

In her mind's eye she saw Mimi sitting there, her glasses perched on the tip of her nose, and her head bent over some papers. It brought back the memory of a day when Angus had been playing with his other friends, and Isabelle had run out of ideas to entertain herself, so she knocked on the study door.

'Hello, sweet girl.' Mimi looked at her over her glasses.

'Why don't your glasses fall off your nose Mimi?' Isabelle asked. She'd often thought about that but kept forgetting to ask. She was surprised when Mimi laughed out loud. She didn't think she'd said anything funny.

'Oh, come here you and give Mimi a hug, and tell me what you've been up to.'

The memory made her swallow hard. She crossed the room and opened the curtains. The rain was stroking the windowpanes. The garden looked asleep.

Isabelle turned her attention back to her task. Where would Mimi have hidden her diaries? She sat behind the desk and opened the first drawer. She picked up some receipts and pushed aside a cheque book and a few pens. She closed the drawer and moved on to the next one, which didn't yield anything of interest either except the usual array of stationary. She opened the third drawer and took out a couple of new-looking note pads. She noticed a key ring with three keys that looked as if they would fit a lock. She tried them in the desk drawers, but they didn't fit.

Isabelle looked around the room and hit her forehead with the palm of her hand as she spotted the filing cabinet. It reminded her of the Victorian apothecary cabinets, only this one took up an entire wall. She went to work, opening drawer after drawer, only to find years of what looked like estate accounts, household ledgers, and more paperwork, but no diaries. She opened the penultimate drawer and found a box. It looked similar to a shoebox. She removed the lid and inspected the inside. Smiling, she left the room with her find.

'You look like the cat that got the cream, Miss Isabelle,' Mrs Murray said, making Isabelle jump. 'What've you got there?'

'It's a box full of photos.'

'Aye, your great-uncle was always at it, snapping away with them cameras of his,' said Mrs Murray as she put on her coat and wrapped her shawl around her neck. 'I'll be off then; see you tomorrow.'

Isabelle carried her treasure to the kitchen, emptied the contents on the table, and started going through the pictures. Most of them depicted the Hall and the grounds, some in black and white and some in colour but all yellowed with age.

It struck her that nothing much had changed except for some of the trees and shrubs, which had matured over the years. There was nothing that gave her a clue to any secrets. In one of the photos a group of people, including several children, were lined up in the hallway in front of a Christmas tree that reached the first-floor landing. Isabelle bent her head and studied the photo. She thought one of the teenage boys in the picture looked familiar, but she couldn't place him. She turned over the photo, and on the back was written *Christmas, 1945*.

The first Christmas after the war, Isabelle thought.

She picked up the next photo as though in slow-motion and pressed it against her chest as if to hide the jab of pain that struck her. She closed her eyes and let her mind take her back to the last time Chloe had been at the Hall.

'Elle, Gus, where are you? This isn't funny,' shouted Chloe.

Isabelle and Angus giggled behind cupped hands. Peeking out of the reeds by the pond, Isabelle watched her twin sister. Chloe's face was all scrunched up, and her cheeks were red from running around. She was out of breath. She had her arms crossed over her chest as she stomped around, pounding the grass with her bare heels.

'This is boring. I'm going to tell Maman you're mean.' Chloe thrusted her bottom lip forward; she always did that when she was in a strop.

Isabelle knew the routine. In a minute Chloe'd be all upset and run to Maman crying, then Maman would shout for Isabelle to Come here this instant! *She hadn't known what instant meant and had asked Papa who told her it meant* this minute.

Then she would huff and go to Maman who'd say, 'Isabelle, how many times should I tell you not to upset your sister?'

'But Maman—'

'No, Isabelle, you know Chloe is not well; her heart can't cope with too much upset.'

Maman never let her say what happened. It was always her fault, which she thought was very unfair.

'Come on, let's go,' she said, nudging Angus with her elbow.

'No, Belle, don't.' Angus urged, holding her back by the arm. 'You know it's a trick.'

'Angus, let go.' Isabelle pulled her arm away and ran out onto the lawn.

'Nyah-nyah, nyah-nyah, nyah, nyah. I found you,' Chloe taunted in a singsong voice. She stuck out her tongue at Isabelle and ran inside.

Isabelle realised that she didn't have many memories of Chloe and her together at the Hall. For that matter, she probably only had about two years' worth of memories of her sister altogether. She could barely remember anything before the age of four and of course by the time they were six, Chloe was dead. And it hadn't been the heart disease that killed her.

The sound of the front door closing disrupted her reverie. She put down the photo and went to investigate.

'Isabelle?'

'I thought you were going to one of your fancy retreats?' She kissed her mother on the cheek.

'You mean Aja Malibu, and yes I was. And as you know it's business, not pleasure. Anyway, I'm here now.'

'I'll go and put the kettle on.'

Isabelle made coffee and put it on the table.

'So, what exactly are you doing here?' Bonelle asked as she sat down.

Isabelle took in her mother's set jaw and her trademark raised left eyebrow. She wanted to say it was her house now, and she didn't need a reason to be here, but she knew better than to ruffle Bonelle's feathers.

'Mum, please, we've already talked about this.'

'And I told *you* it wasn't over.' Bonelle tossed back her hair.

Isabelle averted her gaze but tried to stay her ground. 'Remember the will, Mum? I'm meant to live here for twelve months.'

'Don't you have any sense? You've uprooted your life for this pile of bricks?'

The expression of disdain on her mother's face reminded her of the bitchy girls at her boarding school.

'I told you, we'll contest that ridiculous will. In fact—'

'It's not your decision. It was Mimi's final wish, and I'm honouring it.'

Isabelle knew her statement wasn't the entire truth. Following Mimi's wish had been part of the reason she moved her life to the Hall. The other reason had been to find out about her family's past and uncover Mimi's secret. But she was not about to tell Bonelle any of that. Instead, she crossed her arms over her chest and raised her chin. She knew she was being childish but couldn't help it. Her mum always brought out the worst in her.

'*It was Mimi's final wish,*' Bonelle mocked her. 'Mimi. It's always been Mimi with you, hasn't it?'

Isabelle looked away from the scorn in her mother's eyes.

'Well, whether you like it or not, I've spoken to my lawyer in LA, and we're exploring the option of contesting the will. I was hoping you'd see sense, but I should have known better than curtail my plans and come here.'

Isabelle looked wide-eyed at Bonelle. 'But why?'

'It's the principle. Apart from a gift token to you, the rest should have gone to me. The Hall is my rightful inheritance to do with as I wish.' Bonelle's eyes were dripping with contempt.

'I'd bet any money you wouldn't be like this if Mimi had left the Hall to Chloe.' Isabelle dared to say, and with a sense of satisfaction saw Bonelle shift on her seat.

'This has nothing to do with Chloe.' Bonelle glowered at her. 'So, stop it.'

A surge of adrenaline shot through her. Her mum never wanted to talk about Chloe. It was as if she'd never existed.

'I won't stop. She was my sister, and if I want to talk about her, I will. You always shut me down when I so much as mentioned Chloe's name.' Isabelle burned with the heat of all her pent-up emotions. 'Have you ever thought what it must have been like for me? Of course not! Mimi was the only one who cared—'

'Enough of this!' Bonelle said and looked away.

What a mess, what a bloody mess. It had always been about what her mum wanted. For once, Isabelle was going to do what she wanted and if it upset Bonelle, so what?

'Fine. There's no point in discussing this. You're going to do what you want anyway, no matter what I say. But just know: if you contest the will, I'll fight you.'

Isabelle stood and left. She was at the top of the stairs when she noticed she'd left her phone behind. She retraced her steps, but the sound of crying halted her at the kitchen door. Bonelle was rocking back and forth in her chair with something in her hand.

'Mum?'

Isabelle closed the gap between them and saw that Bonelle was looking at the same picture of Chloe that she had. After a moment's hesitation she put her arms around her mother's shoulders, and as if she'd absorbed her mum's sadness and grief, Isabelle too began to weep and for the umpteenth time wished they could always be this close. After a while Bonelle stirred, and Isabelle let go of her.

'I'm going to bed. The jetlag is catching up with me.' She stood.

'Are you—'

'I'm fine.' Bonelle patted her arm. 'I'll see you tomorrow morning.'

Isabelle put the photos back in the box and went to her room. She wished Mimi was here so she could talk to her. But the diary was the closest she could get to her.

When she opened it, she saw Mimi's message:

You must be very clever... Why did you move to Scotland?

Good question, Isabelle thought. Had she really done the right thing?

My grandmother died and left me a house and a secret past she wants me to uncover. But now my mum wants the house. She never liked me as much as my twin who died when we were really young. But Papa and I are close, and I have a little sister.

As she read, Isabelle wondered if Mimi had really gotten over her feelings for Will. Should she ask her? No, she would wait and see what happened. But she wasn't pleased about the way Glen had treated her on debate night or that afterward Mimi had given him a second chance. What a jerk. Why couldn't Mimi see it?

Isabelle sighed and remembered she had to be careful.

It looks like everything is working out between you and Glen. I hope you don't mind me saying, but I wasn't pleased he ignored you at his friend's house. You've got to tell him he can't treat you like that.

Chapter Sixteen

Mimi, Easter 1954

I needed Alasdair to collect me as I had too much luggage. But Glen also wanted me to meet his parents. Not to matter, however, because it all tied in at the end. Darling Alasdair had been a good sport about it and agreed to accommodate the visit on our way back to the Hall and play taxi for the day.

'Alasdair,' I shouted and ran into his arms. He closed his arms around me and kissed me.

'I missed you, little sis.'

'And I missed you.' I turned around to Glen who'd been standing at a distance. 'Alasdair, this is Glen.'

The two men greeted each other, but I could sense Glen's tension from the way he clenched and unclenched his jaw, making his dimples appear and disappear.

Alasdair held out his hand. 'I've heard much about you.'

'It's a pleasure to meet you.' Glen shook Alasdair's hand.

Alasdair nodded. 'We'd best set off.'

'It's very kind of you to accommodate the visit.' Glen said after a while. 'Mhairi has told me about the Hall. You must be a very busy man indeed.'

'Not at all. We'd have had to pass by Edinburgh anyhow. A few hours here and there won't matter.'

'How big is the estate?'

'A few thousand acres, almost as many farmers and staff.'

'What a responsibility,' Glen replied.

He was right, and for the first time I realized how I'd taken it for granted that everything had always been *there*. Whilst Alasdair was shouldering all the work, I was living my life.

After a while I heard Glen snoring in the back, and Alasdair and I grinned. It wasn't long before I spotted the Holyrood Palace and soon after we turned into Regent Terrace and stopped at No 17.

'Right, I'll collect you in couple of hours,' Alasdair said once we were out of the car.

Glen gestured towards the house. 'Why don't you come in?'

'Thank you, but perhaps later. Have fun, sis!' Alasdair said then drove off.

Though I'd been looking forward to meeting Glen's parents, now that the moment was here, there was a flutter in my chest. I breathed in to calm my nerves.

'Let's go.'

Glen took my arm as we climbed the steps. A curtain twitched and the door opened as we reached the last step.

'Glen!' The woman looked even more stylish than Eilean. 'And you must be Mhairi. I'm Jane.' She grasped my hand. 'Glen has told us so much about you. Do come in. You must be tired from the journey.'

A maid in a uniform appeared from nowhere and took our coats.

'Come this way into the living room; I'll go and get my husband.'

The room was just as elegant as the owner. Two windows took up almost an entire wall and overlooked the garden that was filled with spring flowers and hedges.

'It's very lovely here,' I said.

Glen nodded. 'Yes, Ma likes everything just so.'

Did I detect an undertone?

'Hello, hello.'

I turned. The man entering the room looked like an older version of Glen, except unlike him, he looked like he'd dressed in a hurry.

'Henry Smeatson. Pleasure to meet you, Mhairi.'

'And you.' I shook his hand. He exuded warmth and that put me at ease.

The maid entered the room with plates of pastries, tartlets, cakes, and tea, followed by Jane, who poured the tea.

'Glen told me your family are landowners,' she said, handing me a cup. 'The Hall sounds rather impressive, I must admit. But tell me, how do you entertain yourself? I mean there are no theatres, restaurants, or shops.'

'I suppose—'

'I'm sure there's plenty to do, Ma,' Glen replied for me.

He must have thought that Jane was trying to put me down.

'It's different,' I said.

Sometime later the uniformed maid walked in. 'Ma'am, there's a gentleman at the door, asking for Miss Mimi.'

Jane raised an eyebrow. 'Mimi?'

'Yes, that's what I'm usually called. And that must be Alasdair, my brother.'

I stood, wondering what on earth he was doing back so soon. Then I looked at the clock on the mantlepiece and realised it was much later than I'd thought.

'I must agree with my son. Mhairi is much better suited to a young woman,' Jane said. 'However, your brother must come in for a refreshment; I'd like to meet him.'

I could see why Glen came to my defence earlier. Jane was a stuck-up cow, and I tried not to let her words get to me.

'I'll go and ask him.'

I left the room, glad to escape. When I reached the door I told Alasdair, 'Glen's parents want to meet you.'

'I haven't got long. I'll just lock the car and join you in a moment.'

I went back in and was about to enter the living room when I heard voices.

'What do you think, Ma?' asked Glen.

'She's a nice enough girl, but I still think you could do better.'

My heart dropped and tears smarted my eyes. It was one thing if she didn't like me much but trying to put Glen off me was another. My instinct was to turn around and leave.

Then I heard Henry say, 'I think she is a lovely young lady, son.'

At least I had him on my side.

'You didn't need to wait for me,' said Alasdair. 'Come on, let's go in.' He put his hand on my back.

I don't think I'd ever been so pleased to have my brother on my side. I heard the greetings in a haze and couldn't bring myself to look at Jane.

'You have a delightful home, Mrs Smeatson,' Alasdair complimented.

'You're very kind, though I'm sure it's not as grand as the Hall.'

'Well, you must come and see it for yourself soon.'

I drank my tea and admired my brother's ease and charm around others. He'd always been that way even when we were children.

Shortly after, we'd said our goodbyes to Glen's parents, and after a chaste kiss on the cheek from Glen, Alasdair and I set out on our way back home.

'They seemed nice people,' Alasdair said.

'Yes.'

He glanced at me. 'You don't sound very convinced.'

'No, I think they are. It's just… I had the impression that Jane thought maybe I wasn't sophisticated enough.'

'Nonsense. I thought she was impressed with the Hall.'

'Maybe.'

We drove the rest of the way in silence, and I was relieved when we finally reached the estate.

'Where's everyone?' I asked as we went in.

'Mrs Kerr's visiting her sister, and Mrs Quinn must be somewhere in the kitchen. I'll see you in a couple of hours. I must catch up on some paperwork.'

I headed to my room and took out my diary. I needed to get rid of the turmoil inside me. I wished I could speak to Eilean but alas. My mood lifted when I saw Isabelle had written to me. But poor thing, her grandma had passed away and her sister before that. I wondered what secrets she was going to uncover, and if she would tell me about them.

I'm sorry you lost your sister. It must have been awful for you. I should know because I lost Mama and Papa when I was young too. But unlike you, Mama and I were close. I think I can understand why your mother wants your house, but it was your grandmother's decision. So if I were you, I would fight for it. It's all very intriguing. I'm sure you'll unravel the secrets, and I hope you'll tell me more about them. I'm afraid I haven't had a good time of it, but that's got nothing to do with Glen. He's been as good as gold. It's his mother that worries me.

And I told her of my visit.

Chapter Seventeen

'Yes, I should be back by the evening, New York time. I'll call you then.'

Bonelle put the phone down as Isabelle walked into the kitchen the next morning.

'I thought you were staying for a few days.'

'So did I, but something urgent has come up. Before you ask, it has nothing to do with yesterday.'

I bet it does, thought Isabelle. 'Are you sure?'

'Look, Isabelle, I know we're very different, but I hope you know that I love you and that's why I can't just stand by and watch you ruin your life.'

'But Mum—'

'No, Isabelle. You do what you have to and so will I. We just have to agree to disagree.' The front doorbell rang. 'That must be the taxi.'

Isabelle followed her mum into the hallway, wondering why they could never leave on good terms.

'It'll work out, you'll see,' said Bonelle.

She kissed her on the cheek and got into the taxi. Isabelle stood there, watching the car disappear around the bend of the drive, then went back inside. She wasn't sure if she should be relieved or worried about her mum's departure. She couldn't shake the feeling that there was more to come.

She walked around the house. Today the Hall seemed determined to show her all its faults as though to confirm that Bonelle was right. The paintwork around the windows was peeling, wallpaper had curled around the edges in some places, and there were watermarks on the ceilings. Portraits and photographs of her ancestors were hung alongside paintings of hunting and country life, and they all looked crooked and abandoned.

How come she'd never noticed any of this before now?

And what had it been like for Mimi, dealing with all this alone for years? She shook her head but couldn't dislodge the idea that decay was creeping through the fabric of the Hall like a disease. She felt sick at the thought that all this would soon be her responsibility.

Was her mother right? Was she ruining her life? It was as though the Hall was an orphaned child at her mercy, and she didn't know whether she was going to look after it or abandon it in the end. She pushed aside the guilt and was about to head for Mimi's room in search of the diaries when she heard the door. It must be Mrs Murray, who wouldn't approve of Isabelle snooping around Mimi's room, so instead she went to her own. She may as well make that call.

'Could I speak to Dr McKenzie, please?

'Who is calling?'

'Dr Rousseau,' said Isabelle knowing there wouldn't be any more questions.

'I'll see if he's free, one moment please.'

'Dr Rousseau, Dr McKenzie here. How can I help you?'

'Well, I got your number from Jonathan, at the Old Steading?'

'Oh aye, Jonathan, the old rascal. What's he doing giving out my number to young women, heh?'

'He's an old family friend. I've recently moved into the area, and he thought you might have some work for me.'

'I see. Well, we may have an opening in a few months, and we have locum work on and off. Why don't you leave your number with me, and I'll be in touch.'

Isabelle gave her number and ended the call. Though part of her hadn't been looking forward to going back to work again, she'd soon be needing a job. She grabbed her laptop, looked for other surgeries around the area and shot off a few emails. She sat there tapping her foot and wondering what she could do until Mrs Murray left and she could search Mimi's room.

Then she had a thought. It was time she took Hamish up on his invitation.

The gate to Silcraig Farm stood open. Hamish had his back to her, kneeling on a cushion similar to one Mimi had. He was planting marigolds.

'They look lovely,' she said.

'Hello, Isabelle.' Hamish looked at her over his shoulder. 'I see you've found your way here. Come on in. I won't be long; it takes these knees a few minutes to stretch.' He heaved himself upright.

'I hope I'm not disturbing you.'

'Disturbing me? Nonsense, lass. Now let's get in. I'll make us a nice cup of tea, and we can enjoy the sunshine in the back garden. What'd you say?'

'That'd be lovely, thank you.'

She followed Hamish in, noting the beams and seascape paintings on the walls. She didn't know what she'd expected. The cupboards and dressers in the kitchen were painted in a shade of teal, and a table sat in the centre of the room.

'This is very pretty,' she said, watching Hamish prepare the tea and wondering how she should broach the subject of Mimi and the Hall.

'How's everything at the Hall?' he asked, solving her problem as he carried the tea tray outside.

'It's all good. It can get lonely sometimes, so it's nice to have Mrs Murray around.'

He chuckled. 'Who would have thought the old bird would still be there.'

'You both were working at the Hall at the same time?'

'Of course. Back then she was the housekeeper's daughter and a few years younger than Mimi. She took over from her mother not long after Mimi and her husband moved to the Hall. That's when everything took a bad turn. Aye, that man.' Hamish sighed.

Isabelle's ears pricked. Could *that man* be Glen? She realised that she'd never seen any pictures of Mimi's husband. Once or twice she'd asked Mimi, who'd only say that he'd died a long time ago but had been a lovely dad, which had made it harder for her to understand why her mother had never wanted to talk about him. But then again, her mother never wanted to talk about Chloe either.

'You see, he was from a wealthy Edinburgh family,' Hamish explained. 'A born and bred city boy and some professor or something. He didn't understand our ways. Always looking down on us as if we were goons—do this, do that. And my, that man had a temper on him. Sometimes, we'd overhear them shouting. Huge arguments. We were all worried for Mimi. You see, she didn't have a family no more. Da told me we all had to watch out for her.'

Hamish's features tensed and Isabelle wondered what images were crossing his mind.

'It wasn't a happy place after Glen arrived. I'm telling you, if it hadn't been for our loyalty to the Lanesbrough family and Miss Mimi stepping in, folks would have left.'

Although she hadn't particularly taken to him when reading Mimi's diaries, Hamish made Glen sound positively vile. If true, why would Mimi have married him? Isabelle couldn't even begin to imagine what it must have been like for her.

'Is that why you left?' Isabelle asked.

'That and other things, lass,' he said, averting his eyes.

Isabelle watched Hamish stare into the distance and knew the old man had reached the end of his story—at least for now. She'd have to ask about what happened to Alasdair next time. She stood and put a hand on Hamish's shoulder.

'Thank you, and I'm sorry if I've upset you.'

Hamish patted her hand. 'It's not your fault, lass. Maybe it's time for me to face the past instead of trying to forget it. Come on and see me again soon, will you?'

He looked at her with a sadness etched on his face that broke Isabelle's heart.

As soon as Isabelle got back to the Hall, she headed for Mimi's room. She needed to get to the bottom of this.

She opened the door and was hit again with the scent of Chanel No 5, but to her surprise, this time it comforted rather than pained her. She opened Mimi's bedside table and her heart jumped at the sight of the notebook. She flicked through it. It was Mimi's diary all right, but only a few pages were written in, and nothing jumped out at her.

She walked towards the wardrobe that covered the length of the wall. Mimi's clothes were hung in rows, with shoe and hat boxes stacked on the floor beneath them. She sat down and began to open boxes. Several stacks later, Isabelle struck gold when she opened a hat box, and Mimi's diaries stared back at her. She carried the box back to her own room and put it into her own wardrobe. Then Isabelle picked up the diary she was currently reading and saw Mimi's note. Isabelle frowned. Poor Mimi. Jane sounded like a right dragon.

If anything, she'd have thought it would be the other way round. And Glen sounded like a bore. Should she warn Mimi off Glen to save her from an unhappy marriage? She picked up the pen, then paused. She only had Hamish's word that Mimi had been so miserable. And he hadn't lived at the Hall for years. What if he were wrong and Isabelle destroyed a happy relationship?

And of course, if Mimi didn't marry Glen, then she wouldn't have Bonelle. And if Mimi didn't have Bonelle, well then, what would happen to her?

Isabelle rubbed her temples. She was developing a headache. Because if she was never born, then she wouldn't be able to write in the diary and there would be no one to warn Mimi not to marry Glen. Which would mean that Mimi married Glen, had Bonelle and then her—

'This is impossible,' she whispered.

She rolled the pen between her fingers. No, she couldn't warn Mimi not to marry Glen. But perhaps she still had a role to play. Perhaps she could make sure their marriage was happier. Play counsellor. Taking a breath, she wrote:

> **My mum never got on with her mother, and she hates the house. She just wants to get rid of it, I think because she believes it will ruin my life.**
>
> **I don't know why she and my grandma never got on, but I hope I'll find out.**

Glen and his dad are on your side. Jane's probably just jealous or perhaps overprotective. But you need to try and get on her good side, Mimi. She sounds the type that could cause you a lot of grief if she chose.

Chapter Eighteen

Mimi, July 1954

I looked out of the window; it was a glorious day for a party. I flicked through my dresses in the wardrobe and settled on a dress with the colours of a marbled peony. It was fitted on the top, and the skirt puffed around my legs and ended just below the knees, showing off my figure. I wrapped a cardigan around my shoulders and headed downstairs. Glen was waiting for me. He was wearing a shirt and trousers the colour of sandstone and holding a matching blazer over his shoulder with one hand.

'You look lovely.' He kissed me on the lips.

'Thank you. You look rather dapper yourself,' I said and took his arm.

We walked our customary route. Everywhere students were celebrating the end of another university year. As we reached the bench where it all started on that October day, Glen came to a halt.

'Sit down, Mhairi,' he said and wiped his brow.

Before I had a chance to voice my confusion, he went down on one knee and opened a box, displaying a sapphire and diamond ring that shimmered in the sunshine. I stared at the ring, looked down at Glen and back at the ring. For a moment my heart seemed to stop but then just as suddenly started pounding against my chest.

'Glen—'

'My darling Mhairi, I cannot tell you how impatiently I've been waiting for this day. Will you do me the honour of becoming my wife?' His voice shook, and his eyes misted.

It all seemed like a dream. I don't know for how many seconds or minutes I stared at him, as though I was sealed in time, before I said, 'Of course! I mean yes, I will.'

'I love you,' Glen whispered and kissed me.

It was like a spell was broken and a rush of pleasure washed over me. Tears stung my eyes as I watched Glen lift the ring from its bed and place it on my finger.

'Do you like it?' he asked.

'I…it's beautiful.'

I watched the stones reflect the light as I twisted my hand this way and that.

Glen swept me up into his arms and kissed me so hard that it took my breath away. We pulled apart at the sound of cheers and clapping and saw a group of passers-by dotted around us. Glen handed me an envelope which I opened and read.

My favourite sis,

If you're reading this, then Glen must have popped the question. I want you to know I'm very happy for you and wish you both a bright future.

Your loving brother,

Alasdair

I swallowed the dam of emotion that was constricting my throat and dabbed under each eye with the tip of my index to stop the tears from ruining my makeup.

We arrived in Edinburgh early afternoon the next day.

'I guess congratulations are in order,' Jane said as she greeted me and kissed me on the cheeks without her lips touching my skin.

'Thank you,' I said and swept a strand of hair that wasn't there out of my face to avoid looking at her.

'You must want to freshen up. I'll meet you on the terrace,' she said and strode away.

I was relieved for the break. In the bathroom I dabbed my face with my handkerchief and put on some more lipstick.

That'll do.

I straightened my shoulders and left. In the hallway, I met Henry, who gave me a hug.

'Mhairi, congratulations, my dear.'

He offered me his arm and we walked into the garden, which was a riot of colours and scent. I glimpsed champagne glasses and a selection of petits fours laid out on the table.

'Here you are.' Glen patted the chair next to him.

'I say we toast the happy couple,' said Henry, and we all picked up our glasses. 'Welcome to our family, Mhairi.'

'Have you set a date yet?' asked Jane.

I almost choked on my champagne.

'Ma,' said Glen, elongating the two letters.

'What, dear? It's a feat to plan a wedding. Then there is the question of the venue that must be booked.' Jane's gaze settled back on me.

I still had no idea how to respond. Glen and I hadn't had time to discuss the subject, but the one thing I was sure about was the venue.

'I was hoping we could hold the wedding at the Hall,' I said with some trepidation, wondering how Glen but more importantly, Jane would take it.

'Of course, that's one option,' she said and took a sip of her champagne.

My heart sank and I looked at Glen.

'Let's not rush into anything,' he said without looking at me.

'But—'

He turned and fixed me with his eyes. 'There's plenty of time.'

My face was burning. Not wanting to cause a scene, I swallowed my anger and hurt at not only Jane belittling me but Glen shutting me down in front of his parents, which made it worse. I stared at my lap.

Glen must have noticed my discomfort for he laid a hand on my arm. But he said nothing to reassure me.

I jumped out the car the moment Glen and I pulled up at the Hall.

'Alasdair,' I shouted and ran into his arms, doing my best not to burst into tears.

'Congratulations, little sis,' he said, holding me to his chest. 'And to you, Glen, welcome to the family,' he added, shaking Glen's hand.

I hurried inside and saw Mrs Kerr and Mrs Quinn smiling as they came rushing towards me with congratulations and embraced me. I was just peeling myself away from Mrs Quinn's grasp when I heard footsteps behind me. I turned around and saw Glen frowning at me.

'Glen, come and meet Mrs Kerr and Mrs Quinn,' I said, and this time I didn't miss the disapproval on his face.

He nodded once and carried on walking. I blushed and turned to Mrs Kerr and Mrs Quinn and saw my own discomfort mirrored in their features. I looked away and carried on after Glen.

'I didn't realise you are on such friendly terms with your servants. It seems rather irregular,' Glen chided.

I was about to say something but let it go. I didn't wish to create unpleasantness on his first stay at the Hall.

Later that afternoon, Glen and I were sitting on the terrace reading, when I saw Will running up to the Hall. I couldn't help the warm feeling that arose in my chest.

'Ah, you! Bring that parasol over here,' Glen shouted.

'I'm sorry, sir, but I need to speak to the master urgently. I'll send someone over,' Will said, his tone even.

'Come on man, it won't take a minute,' Glen insisted.

Will's face turned red, and his fists clenched by his side. I was about to step in when I saw Alasdair approaching.

'What's going on here?' he asked.

'This young man's not been very forthcoming.'

Alasdair ignored Glen and turned to Will.

'It's Target, master. There's something wrong with him.'

'Fetch the vet at once,' said Alasdair, already running for the stables.

'I'll take a rest in my room,' said Glen. The shadow on his face didn't bode well.

I sighed as I watched him stride indoors with his ego bruised. But there was nothing I could do, so I went to the stables to see what was happening with Target. I could hear him whinnying as I approached. I came to a halt at the door to the stables. Will was kneeling beside Target, stroking his coat, and whispering to him. The sunshine was slanting through the box, illuminating the scene. As though sensing my gaze upon him, Will turned and looked at me. The expression on his face took my breath away. I remained rooted to the spot long after he was gone, but I told myself to push the feeling aside. I was marrying Glen; there was no room for feelings like this.

Over the next few days Glen and I found our equilibrium again. It helped that Will was nowhere to be seen.

On the morning of Glen's departure, we took a walk. I'd been thinking about broaching the subject of our wedding venue with him, and with the grounds dazzling in myriad colours in the sunshine, it seemed a good opportunity.

We stopped by the pond and watched the Koi fish dance amongst the lilies. 'I hope you enjoyed your stay,' I said.

'Yes, it's been good.'

I ignored the lack of enthusiasm in his voice and pressed on.

'I really would like to have our wedding here.'

Glen's shoulders tensed, and he fixed me with a glare. 'I told you we'd discuss it. But now is not the time.'

I crossed my arms. I was not going to be put down a second time in so many days. I imagined what Isabelle would say and knew she'd tell me to stand my ground.

'Glen, listen to me—'

'Look, I still need to pack.' He raised his voice. 'I haven't got time for this.'

'Is everything all right, Miss Mimi?'

I turned around at the sound of Will's voice and saw him marching towards us. I was about to say something when Glen stiffened next to me.

'Mind your own business,' he shouted across the lawn.

But Will continued to stride towards us. I looked at Glen and the expression in his eyes sent a shiver up my spine.

'Everything's fine, thank you, Will,' I assured him.

After a moment of hesitation, Will nodded, turned around, and walked away.

Feeling fortified by Will's loyalty, I pushed on. 'Glen, I don't care about anything else, but this is the one thing I will not compromise on. Unlike you, my parents are no longer with us and at least if the wedding was here, I'd have a sense that they're with me.'

Glen looked at me for a long time. The tension came off him like mist. I held my breath in anticipation.

'Fine, have it your way,' he said and strode away.

I didn't set eyes on Will again until I was due to go back to St Andrews. On the day of my departure, I saw him in the stables with Rionnag.

'Will you be riding, Miss Mimi?' he asked without looking at me.

His coldness startled me. 'No, I'll be leaving shortly,' I said, trying to hide my hurt.

'Very well. Goodbye, Miss.' Without making eye contact, he stuck a piece of paper in my hand and left.

My instinct was to call him back, but I realised the futility of it all. Nothing changed the fact that I was engaged to another man, that Will was a member of my staff, and there could never be anything between us. I sighed and read the note.

Dear Miss Mimi,

I wondered for a long time if I should write this. Though I know it's not my place, I couldn't keep my silence. I beg you not to marry that man for he won't make you happy. Please forgive me for speaking out of turn.

Yours, Will

The words chilled me to the bone, but after each time I reread the note, anger replaced shock.

How dare Will overstep the mark like this?

Glen was not perfect, but he loved me, and Will didn't understand our relationship. How could he? My shoulders slumped as I realised that perhaps that was my own fault. I must have encouraged Will.

It was time for me to let go of my girlish crush. I headed for the house and back in my room picked up my diary. Isabelle's message about Jane made my heart sink. How was I supposed to get on her good side? She didn't seem like someone who'd change their mind easily. I sighed. I wrote:

I'll try.

What else could I do? As I read on I felt sorry for Isabelle. It must have been hard for her growing up if her mother and grandmother didn't get on. Alas relationships.

I too am beginning to discover that relationships are not always straight forward. If I'm honest, I think I'm in a spot of bother and rather confused about my own feelings. I think I could do with your advice.

I told her everything.

Chapter Nineteen

Isabelle had just put the flowers on the table in the hallway when she heard the sound of tyres on the gravel. She couldn't wait to see her father and her sister, Emilie, but her heart sank at the thought of seeing Aurelie again. She opened the front door, shifting her weight from one leg to the other as she waited for the passengers to get out of the taxi.

'Papa.' She rushed straight into her father's arms.

'Isabelle, ma petite.'

He kissed her on the cheek and held her tightly. Isabelle was overwhelmed with love, and her heart expanded in her chest.

Another door opened and Isabelle saw Emilie, standing on chubby legs, clad in socks and pumps. She wore a dress, dotted with daisies and a cardigan. Her curls were stuck to her head. She was rubbing her eyes with her fists as though she'd just woken up. Her father bent and picked her up.

Isabelle greeted her sister in French, but Emilie hid her face in Papa's chest. It tugged at Isabelle's heart that she was a stranger to her own sister, despite her efforts to FaceTime her most weeks. She knew that the fear of losing another sister had prevented her from getting too close to Emilie, and now she was at a loss for how to bridge that gap.

She heard the door slam and turned around. Aurelie nodded in her direction.

'Isabelle.'

She looked at Aurelie with dismay, noting that her outfit and jewellery had no doubt cost her father a fortune. She forced herself to give Aurelie a hug. Her stepmother's body tensed up, mirroring her own discomfort.

'*C'est manifique.* You must be very pleased, Isabelle,' said Aurelie, gazing at the Hall.

Isabelle looked at Aurelie in disbelief. Could this woman be more insensitive?

'I'd rather still have my grandmother.'

'Isabelle, I'm sure that's not what Aurelie meant,' her father said.

'No, it was not,' Aurelie agreed.

But it was always money with Aurelie, wasn't it? Isabelle picked up a couple of bags and guided them to their room to refresh.

'Would you like a coffee? Or do you want to head out straight away?' she asked her father.

'No, let's go now,' Jean-Francois said. 'Emilie has already had a long day, and she'll need her bed soon.' He stroked Emilie's cheek.

'Sure, I'll just grab my bag and meet you at the front.'

They walked down the side of the house to the crowded beach where children were playing football after school, mums were standing in groups chatting, dogs were chasing sticks, and people were relaxing and enjoying the sun. They found a spot by the sand dunes and settled down.

Jean-Francois and Aurelie took Emilie's hands and headed for the shore. Isabelle laughed when she heard Emilie's screech as she dipped her toes in the cold water. She watched this little family that was hers and yet wasn't. She didn't feel she belonged to them. A pang of sadness hit her. As she watched Aurelie playing with Emilie, she had to admit that despite her dislike of the woman, she wished her own mother could have been more like her.

Images of childhood flashed through Isabelle's mind. She remembered sitting in the garden, breaking the thorn on the tip of the agave plant, and pulling it down the length of the leaf. She'd watched with satisfaction as the fibres came off unbroken. She'd made a knot at the bottom of the strings; now she had her thread and needle, so she could stitch the hole in the rabbit's foot. She laid the toy rabbit with its matted and worn fleece on a bed of grass.

'*Don't you worry, Peter Rabbit, it won't hurt, I promise. Why don't you just close your eyes and sleep.*'

Isabelle sang a nursery rhyme, the one her father used to sing to her and Chloe. '*Dodo, l'enfant do, dodo, l'enfant do, l'enfant dormira bien vite, lullaby child, lullaby child, the child will soon be asleep.*'

'*What are you doing here, all on your own, ma petite?*' *asked Jean-Francois.*

'*Papa!*' *Isabelle jumped up, forgetting she was mid-operation and threw herself into her dad's open arms. Jean-Francois picked her up, held her to his chest, and stroked her hair.*

'*Where's your maman?*'

Isabelle peeled herself away so she could see him. '*I don't know; I haven't seen her since lunch. She said she'll sleep for a little.*' *Isabelle watched her father's brow wrinkle.*

'*But that would have been hours ago, ma petite.*'

'*Sorry Papa, I didn't check on her, it's just,*' *she swallowed hard.* '*I don't think Maman likes it when I wake her up and last time…*'

Isabelle stopped herself just in time but not before her body gave a little shudder like it did when she was cold.

Isabelle could vividly still remember it now. Her mother's wide eyes had stared at her.

'*Maman, are you all right? Will you come and play with me?*'

Then there'd been lots of caterpillars in her tummy that had made her feel sick. But Maman had just kept staring at her.

'*Maman say something, please.*' *She bit her lip and tried to be brave and not cry.*

'*Just go, and leave me alone, Isabelle.*'

Isabelle ran out of the room, tears running down her face. '*Oh, Chloe,*' *she whispered.* '*Why did you have to go and leave me all alone?*'

The Fox & Hound was packed with Saturday night punters. Her father had wanted to catch up with everyone, so Isabelle had booked a table for them and the Fairbairns, including Angus and Alex to her annoyance.

Alex and Aurelie looked as elegant as one another. Isabelle had made an effort to jazz-up but couldn't help feeling like the ugly sister next to the other two women. Introductions were out of the way, and everyone seemed upbeat.

'Aren't you a wee cute bundle.' Margot stroked Emilie's hair.

'So how long are you staying?' Jonathan asked Jean-Francois.

'We're setting off for the Highlands in a couple of days and fly back to France from Glasgow.'

Isabelle had been disappointed to learn she'd only have her Papa and Emilie for a couple of days. She knew Aurelie must be behind the plan.

'Is there a problem?' Aurelie asked Isabelle, rolling her Rs at the back of her throat.

Isabelle realised she'd been staring at her. 'No, not at all.'

She admired and envied Aurelie's ability to always say what was on her mind.

'Oh, how delightful. I wish I could go back with you,' Alex said.

'Are you French?' asked Aurelie.

'No, my father's Spanish and my mother's Lebanese. My father is a diplomat, so we moved around a lot, but we settled down in Dubai when I started high school.'

'Magnifique, what an interesting life. You must find it monotonous here, no?'

Isabelle noticed Angus tense his jaw and tried to think of something to divert his attention.

With a glance at Angus, Alex said. 'Yes, it is … different here—'

'Yes, in Dubai, it's the typical expat life,' Angus said, cutting Alex off. 'Fancy houses, apartments, partying, drinking and everyone busy outdoing everyone else.'

Aurelie raised an eyebrow at the unmistakable contempt in his voice.

Alex flashed her eyes at him. 'If I remember correctly, you were a big fan.'

'That sounds like great fun to me,' Aurelie said.

'Excuse me,' Isabelle stood and could feel all eyes on her as she made her way to the bar.

She was about to order when she felt a hand on her shoulder. She turned and saw Angus.

'Can you get me a shot?'

'That bad?'

'I don't know how much longer I can take it.'

Isabelle got their drinks, and they stood aside to make room for others.

'You want to talk?'

'Thanks, but not now. That'll just make it worse. Let's get back.'

Isabelle nodded. But she couldn't understand why Angus was putting up with Alex.

Back at the table, Angus sat next to her. Aurelie was still discussing the merits of Dubai versus Scotland with Alex. Meanwhile, her dad, Margot, and Jonathan were engrossed in their own conversation. It irked her that Aurelie ignored that group, feeling she belonged with the younger crowd. She seemed to want the best of both worlds.

Isabelle caught the tail end of Alex's answer.

'We'll probably go back in a couple of years. I can't imagine it'd be very entertaining bringing up children here.'

'We will? Because that's the first I've heard of it.' Angus chuckled and took a swig of his beer.

Isabelle saw his face twitch, a tell-tale sign of irritation that hadn't changed since childhood. She so wanted to reach out and put a hand on his arm, but Alex was staring in their direction.

'Ah, I wouldn't be so definite, madam,' Jean-Francois said, turning to join their conversation. 'I can assure you that Angus and Isabelle had very entertaining childhoods. As I remember, you two got up to all sorts of mischief.'

Margot nodded. 'Yes, go on, tell her.'

'Yes, go on, Angus, do tell,' Alex seconded Margot, her body language stiff.

Isabelle looked around the table wondering if everyone else was aware of the power play that was going on. Angus caught her eye, his grin signalling he had mischief up his sleeve.

'Belle, do you remember the time we went on our holiday?'

Isabelle burst into laughter at the memory. 'Yes, we packed our rucksacks and asked Mimi for some sandwiches for the trip.'

'Yes, we even told her what we were planning, but she clearly thought we were only messing about.'

'Gosh, we walked for what seemed like miles before we ended up in that field and were chased by those bloody massive cows.'

'Man, we were running for our lives. I don't think I ever realised how fast cows can run,' said Angus, chuckling.

'I've no idea how we managed to clamber over that fence and when we thought we were safe we heard the farmer shouting and legged it. That's when you had your tremendous idea.'

Isabelle pulled a face and they both burst into giggles.

'Yeah, but it was only meant to be until the coast was clear. It was you who said: *We should have a rest and eat our lunch*,' Angus mimicked in a child's voice.

Isabelle snorted with laughter. 'Yes, but you were the brainchild behind us doing it in the trailer where, I quote, *nobody would see us*.'

'And it would have been an excellent idea, had we not fallen asleep.'

They burst into another fit of laughter.

'You two were quite the adventurers,' said Aurelie. 'That was some story.'

'Wasn't it just,' Alex said, her voice full of sarcasm and an expression like thunder on her face.

Isabelle's laughter died, and she wondered again what Angus had seen in someone like her. It made no sense to her; some people just seemed to end up with the wrong people.

The same thought echoed in her mind later that night when she read Mimi's account.

She had already decided not to warn Mimi but to act as counsellor. Perhaps if she put the wedding off a bit, until she was more certain of everything. She grabbed the pen.

Congratulations, Mimi. And well done for standing up to Glen. Now you can take your time and get to know him better. After all it's a huge decision you're making. Especially if, as you said yourself, you have feelings for

Will. I mean sometimes we can love someone but still feel attracted to others. All I can say is there's no rush. As for me, you're right, it wasn't easy growing up, but I had my papa and grandma to love me.

Chapter Twenty

I was sitting on the bench in Mama's rose garden and telling her about tomorrow, wishing she and Papa could be with us, when I opened my diary and found Isabelle's message. My heart missed a beat.

Take your time and get to know Glen better.

Isabelle was no better than Will with his *He won't make you happy*. Her disapproval filtered from between her words. How dare she.

I knew Glen could be opinionated and devoted to his work, but there was no doubt in my mind that he loved me. Why else would he want to marry me? And as for Will, I just had to keep reminding myself I didn't love him.

The sound of an engine announced the arrival of the first guests and roused me from my musing. I ran to the Hall just as the Jaguar with its open top roof came to a halt.

'Hello, Mhairi.' Jane pecked me on the cheek. 'So this is the Hall. I can see why you wanted it as a venue.'

'It's a slice of paradise,' Henry said, then hugged me.

Alasdair stepped out and accompanied the couple inside, giving Glen and me some privacy.

'How is my beautiful bride?' he asked, and as his lips touched mine, a tremble ran all the way down to my legs. 'I can see all is under control here,' he said, nodding towards the men who were setting up the marquees on the lawn.

'Yes, the whole week has resembled a military operation. Mrs Quinn has enlisted half the women in the village to help her with the cooking and baking, and Mrs Kerr has deployed the other half to spruce up the Hall.'

'But you are happy, my darling Mhairi?'

'Yes, I am.'

And in that moment, I meant it.

The next morning, the Hall seemed to awake even before the birds' first choir. Annie, Mrs Kerr's daughter, was helping me with my dress when there was a knock on my door.

Jane peeked her head in. 'Mhairi, can we come in?'

'Of course.'

'This is Maggi, and she's here to attend to our hair and makeup.'

'That's so very kind of you, Jane,' I said and welcomed Maggi.

I wasn't sure whether it was out of kindness or whether Jane wanted to ensure I looked the part for groom's guests. I brushed aside the thought and reminded myself of Isabelle's words to stay on Jane's good side.

Two hours later, I looked in the mirror and could barely recognise myself. The dress gathered in folds at my feet. The sleeves were sprinkled with pearls and stones shimmered like stars. Mama's veil was held atop of my head with a comb. And I admired Jane's foresight regardless of her motivation.

There was another knock on my door and Alasdair stood there, looking the part in his wedding suit tails.

'You look spectacular, sis,' he said, and kissed my cheek.

I beamed at him. 'Thank you.'

He held a box in front me and opened the top, revealing a Celtic knot heart in white gold, studded with diamonds.

I gasped. 'Alasdair, is that the one Mama wore on her wedding?'

'Yes, Papa gave it to her. Apparently, every bride wore it and he asked me to give it to you. This comes from Papa's side of the family,' he explained. 'Apparently, every bride wore it. Papa asked me to give it to you on your wedding day.' His face contorted as though he couldn't decide whether to smile or cry.

I, on the other hand, didn't even attempt to hold back the tears as Alasdair fastened the necklace. It sat just below my collar bone. I picked up the posy Mr Murray had put together of Mama's roses. Even if my parents couldn't be here, at least they were close.

I walked down the stairs on Alasdair's arm. My insides were doing somersaults with excitement and apprehension. It was normal, wasn't it, to feel nerves on one's wedding day?'

'Congratulations Miss Mimi,' I heard someone say amongst the staff who had gathered in the hallway in their Sunday best. Everyone cheered. I was touched by their warmth. Tears smarted my eyes as I looked at them one by one and realised that after today, the Hall would no longer be my home. My home would be with Glen from now on. My heart sank at the thought. My gaze met Will's, but I couldn't bear the sadness and the intensity in his stare and looked away.

Alasdair and I embarked in the Rolls-Royce and despite the open top, I felt as though there was not enough oxygen.

Alasdair looked at me sideways. 'Are you okay?'

'Do you think I'm doing the right thing? Should I have waited longer?' I blurted out. Isabelle's words rang in my ears.

'Of course, you are. Don't second-guess yourself. It's normal to get cold feet.'

'How come you're not married yet?'

Alasdair laughed. 'I'd love to, but I haven't found anyone yet who'd be prepared to shoulder the responsibility of running the estate with me. But I'm sure I will.'

Poor Alasdair. I felt a pang of sadness for my brother. His life was so much determined by his inheritance. I was lucky indeed.

'Yes, you're right,' I said.

The church came into view, and the crowd of villagers cheered. I heard their comments as we alighted from the car.

The bride's here.

Doesn't she look beautiful?

With every step my pulse accelerated. I reached the altar, and when I saw Glen's eyes brimming with love and happiness, I felt as though I could finally breathe.

'You look amazing,' he said and took my hand.

The church fell silent as the reverend began to speak. 'Today we're here to celebrate the holy matrimony...'

But relief was short-lived as Isabelle and Will whispered doubts in my mind and hushed the reverend's voice. Mentally I screamed at them to go away, and Glen must have noticed something was amiss for he tightened his grip around my hand as he said his vows.

Then it was my turn. I focused my gaze on Glen as I repeated each word.

'And now I pronounce you husband and wife. You may kiss the bride,' said the reverend.

Glen bent and whispered in my ear, 'I love you.'

And as his lips touched mine, I knew I'd made the right decision.

Back at the Hall we were swept up in the celebration, and I felt as though part of me was there while the other part lingered in a haze.

It was just before midnight when Glen took my hand, and we stood at the bottom of the stairs.

'Ladies and gentlemen, thank you for sharing this special day with us.'

The guests cheered us one last time as we ascended the stairs.

'To the happy couple!'

Glen carried me over the threshold and sat me on the bed.

'I promise I'll be gentle,' he said, and his kisses became more urgent.

He took off my wedding dress. 'You look beautiful, my darling,' he said and ran his hands up and down my body.

I responded to his touch, and yet my mind was whirling. It was the first time ever I'd been naked in front of a man, and part of me just wanted to cover myself up. I wondered if that was normal.

Glen's weight crushed me, and as he pushed himself inside me, I gasped. It hurt, as Eilean had warned it would. I was just getting used to the feeling when Glen made a few jerky movements and collapsed on top of me.

'That was amazing, Mhairi,' he whispered and lay next to me. I couldn't help feeling let down by the act itself, which could not have lasted longer than ten minutes. Was this what all the fuss was about? As soon as Glen rolled off me, I went to the bathroom, and cleaned up. By the time I was back, Glen was snoring.

'You're sure you won't stay longer?' Alasdair asked Glen over breakfast two days later.

'Unfortunately, I can't old chap. Duty calls, as I'm sure you understand.' Glen drank the last of his coffee and stood.

I dropped my serviette on the table and followed him out to the car. He bent down and kissed me.

'I'll miss you, my darling.'

'I'll see you next week,' I said and waved as he drove down the drive.

I sighed. If I were honest, I was looking forward to some time on my own to get my head together. I walked to the stables and took Rionnag for a ride around the estate. We stopped by the burn to have a rest. I took off my boots, pulled up my jodhpurs, and waded into the water. Every so often a stone captured my imagination, and I'd pick it up with my toes as I used to do when I was young. I was doing just that, my leg up across my thigh, when I was disturbed.

'Hello, Miss Mimi,' said Will.

Despite being now married, everyone on the estate had continued to call me Miss Mimi, which pleased me. To me, Jane was Mrs Smeatson.

I almost lost my balance, waving my arms in the air to find my footing, when Will reached out and steadied me. We stood there with his hands still around my waist. I was already agitated through the exertion, but the heat magnified with the closeness between us.

'I'm sorry, I didn't mean to scare you.'

The intensity of his gaze almost took my breath away. This was the first time we'd been alone since that summer day he gave me the note in the stables. Bewildered and overwhelmed by the resurgence of the old feelings, I nodded, unable to speak, look away, or for that matter, release myself from his grip. At last he took my hand and led me back onto dry land.

'Congratulations on your nuptials,' he said without any emotion.

I took a breath before I trusted myself to speak. 'Thank you. How have you been, Will? How's your mother?'

'We're both well. Mother is still away at my aunt's,' he said, but his eyes were full of fervour.

Silence reigned again between us. Part of me was wondering how to end the encounter, the other part deciding whether I wanted it to be over. I finally took Rionnag's rein and walked along the burn, leaving Will behind.

Back at the Hall, I couldn't settle, and I knew I had to talk to Isabelle.

I think you were right to tell me to wait. I wish I hadn't ignored your advice. But at the time, I guess it seemed like you were critical of Glen, and I became defensive. I was so determined to forget about Will. But why am I still feeling this way about him?

Chapter Twenty-One

Isabelle had been waiting for the right time to catch her father alone, but Aurelie was determined not to give them any opportunity. She was running out of time; tomorrow would be the last day of their visit.

'Papa, could we go for a walk please?' asked Isabelle.

'That would be lovely,' Aurelie jumped in before Jean-Francois had a chance to answer. 'We could go back to the beach. The sun is shining, Emilie would love it.'

'Actually, Aurelie, I'd like to discuss some family matters with Papa alone. I'm sure you don't mind.'

That put Aurelie in her place, Isabelle thought with satisfaction, which dissipated when she saw a flicker of sadness in her father's eyes. And that didn't sit right with her.

'Of course, chérie, let's go. Then we can go to the beach afterwards,' Jean-Francois suggested.

And with that Isabelle knew he'd put her in *her* place. And she deserved it. She had to stop acting like a child.

'I keep forgetting how enormous the estate is.' Jean-Francois said. 'The upkeep must cost an absolute fortune. Though judging by the state of the grounds not much has been done.'

Isabelle looked around through her father's eyes. It was true; there were signs of neglect everywhere: the trees and shrubs were overgrown, weeds covered the beds, and leaves and debris littered the lawn.

'That's one of the things I wanted to talk to you about. Bonelle says she is checking the feasibility of contesting the will. So I wanted your advice.'

Jean-Francois whistled. 'That's quite some news, eh? I'm almost certain it's not the money she's after. Maybe it's got something to do with her relationship with Mimi and the Hall?'

Isabelle nodded. 'Yes, I think so too. She told me that Mimi was this terrible person, and I didn't know the real her. Which I would have ignored, but then Mimi left me this letter.'

'A letter?'

'Yes, it said that she had made mistakes, ruined her relationship with Mum, made bad decisions.'

'Surely not! What bad decisions?'

'She didn't say. She just … she left me her diaries. She wanted me to live at the Hall and find out for myself I suppose. I think Mrs Murray knew her secrets, but I don't want to ask her, I feel like … like it's betraying Mimi. But I'm determined to find out what's going on.'

Isabelle hesitated. Should she tell her father about the strangeness of the diary? The fact that she seemed able to communicate with the young Mimi? No. He would think she'd gone mad and drag her from the Hall himself.

Jean-Francois looked at her with concern. 'I know how much you love Mimi. But make sure you look after yourself. And let's hope whatever reason your maman has, she changes her mind. Come here.'

He folded his arms around her. Isabelle yielded into her father's embrace and let his strength envelop her.

'You know I'm always here for you.' He paused. 'I know it hasn't been always the case.'

Isabelle pulled herself away from her father's embrace and looked at him. 'What do you mean? You and Mimi have—'

'No.' Jean-Francois shook his head. 'I've never should have let your maman sent you to boarding school. You were only ten, so young. I failed you, ma petite.'

He rubbed her cheek with the back of his hand, and Isabelle's heart contracted with love for this man who was big enough to admit he'd made a mistake.

'Thanks, Papa. It means the world to me to hear you say that. If I'm honest, it's the one thing that made me angry at you. I guess because I never understood why you didn't stand up for me.'

Jean-Francois cupped her face. 'Our life changed beyond recognition after Chloe's death, and in my efforts to keep your mother from falling apart—'

'It's okay Papa. I think I'm beginning to see that side of Mum now.'

Back at the house she put a picnic together and resolved to be on her best behaviour as they headed for the beach. The moment Emilie's feet touched the sand, she grabbed her dad's hand and dragged him to the water.

'I'll miss Emilie; she's growing up so fast,' said Isabelle.

'Will you? Why don't you visit us more often then?' asked Aurelie.

Isabelle was about to say something contradictory but reminded herself of her resolve. Besides, Aurelie's question was valid. But she still didn't feel like getting into the complexities of her relationship with her living and dead sisters.

'It's a bit complicated,' she said.

'Look, Isabelle, of course I know about Chloe. And I'm not blind; I've seen the way you sometimes look at Emilie.'

'What do you mean?'

'Pfft, come on.' Aurelie waved a hand in the air. 'There's much love when you look at Emilie, *but* there's also a lot of sadness and something else, like you're… *prudente*,' Aurelie said, using the French word for cautious.

Isabelle was taken aback that Aurelie had paid her that much attention. She looked up at her and saw nothing but empathy in her eyes.

'Just remember, you can't bring Chloe back, but Emilie is here. Voilà, I'm finished.'

Aurelie made to move away, but Isabelle touched her arm.

'You're right.'

She stood up and together they joined her father and Emilie.

'Elle, Elle,' Emilie shouted, unable to say her name in full.

It was yet another reminder of Chloe, thought Isabelle. She watched her sister bounce up and down in the water, then took off her sandals and joined her. As her feet touched the water, she screeched to make Emilie giggle. This was the first time she and Aurelie had agreed on something. She needed to let go of the past so she could move forward.

That night, as Isabelle finished reading about Mimi's wedding, she knew Mimi had not listened to her and had married in haste. What was the old saying? Marry in haste, repent in leisure?

She couldn't understand how Mimi could have married Glen when she was still drooling over Will? And Hamish had been right about Glen; Isabelle didn't like her grandfather one bit. But that wouldn't help Mimi. She put her counsellor hat back on.

> **I'm glad you had a lovely wedding day. And I'm sorry you thought I was criticising Glen. That was definitely not my intention. As for Will, remember we talked about having feelings for two different people. But you don't have to act on them. Try not to worry, and things with Glen will improve. I'm sure you're just experiencing teething problems.**

Chapter Twenty-Two

Mimi, May 1955

'I'll make some sandwiches for the hike,' I said.

'Actually, Mhairi, would you mind staying put? With all the wedding stuff going on, I'm a bit behind with work and would like to catch up,' said Glen.

'But it's our honeymoon, and you've taken leave,' I said, unable to hide my disappointment.

'Yes, but the work won't do itself. Come here.' Glen closed me in his arms. 'I'm sorry, but I promise I'll be all yours after today.' He kissed me.

I nodded and left the cabin. Then I wound my way up through the valley. It seemed that everywhere I looked there were couples walking hand-in-hand and a twinge of envy—and I guess, self-pity—pierced my heart. I gazed at the hills covered in heather and the loch stretching in front of me like an ocean, but try as I might, I couldn't feel any joy at the beauty that surrounded me. The clouds started drawing in, so I made my way back.

I opened the door and saw Glen bent over his paperwork.

'How was your walk?' he asked without looking up.

'I missed having you with me.'

I don't know if it was the words or something about my tone, but this time he glanced at me.

'I'll tell you what, why don't we go somewhere for an early dinner, and I'll do some more work afterwards?'

'Oh Glen, that'd be lovely.'

I closed my arms around his neck and kissed him.

But my joy was short-lived. For the rest of the week, despite his promise, Glen continued working for at least a few hours every day.

'Mimi!' shrieked Eilean as she rushed to hug me. 'How are you? How was the honeymoon? Oh, there's so much to catch up on!'

'Come on in, and we can chat as I'm unpacking,' I said, but the truth was there wasn't much to say.

'Go on, spill the beans.'

'It was nice.'

'Is that all? Honeymoons are meant to be the best time.'

I averted my gaze, and stared down at my hands, trying to supress the heaviness that had descended on me.

'Mimi? What's wrong?' Eilean sat next to me and put an arm around my shoulder.

I sighed. 'Nothing really, except that Glen carried on working throughout the entire week.'

'I'm sorry, Mimi.'

'It is what it is. Maybe I just need to be patient.'

Eilean was silent for a moment, then asked, 'Do you love him?'

I looked up at her. 'Of course, I do.'

Eilean nodded. 'Look I can see you're disappointed, and I don't blame you. But I've known more guys than you, and I can tell you Glen is one of the good ones. It's just he's a bit obsessed with work. Better than chasing after other women or being a drunk, wouldn't you say?'

'Yes, you're right. I'm sure I'll be fine.'

'Besides, it's not a good thing to be in each other's pockets. You're going to be busy with studying, and of course you have me.'

She patted my hand. I hugged her.

'In that case, you'd better help me find a house because I don't think Glen's going to have any time.'

I was right. Glen spent all the hours God sent either holding lectures or working on his book, so Eilean and I looked at houses.

Most I didn't like, and the ones I did were always gone by the time I got Glen to see them. It was a month later when at last it all came together.

'What do you think?' I asked Glen as I led him through the two-bedroom terraced house just behind the university, pointing out the stripped floors, the fireplaces in each room, and the views over St Andrews Bay. I hoped he'd like it because I was getting fed up with house searches and viewings.

'It seems adequate for our needs, and the rent is feasible. I think we should take it,' he said and looked at his watch.

I was aware of Glen's tendency towards pragmatism but still, I couldn't help feeling disappointed at his lack of enthusiasm for the house that would be our first home.

We moved in two weeks later, at the beginning of July. I was giving everything a thorough clean when the bell rang.

'Eilean, come in.'

I wiped my brow with the back of my hand and kissed her.

'It's looking lovely. But I think it could do with some colour,' she said, looking around.

'Yes, I have a list as long as my arm. The floors could do with some rugs. I'd like some cushions, throws, and curtains.'

'Don't forget pictures. And some lamps,' added Eilean.

'I know you just got here, but do you fancy going shopping?'

'Now you're talking.'

By the end of the same week, I was satisfied that I'd put my stamp on the house.

I made a beef stew with dumplings and put a bottle of champagne in the refrigerator to toast our new home. Close to seven, I checked myself in the mirror and sat on the sofa reading a book, expecting Glen to walk through the door any minute. But with each tick of the clock my irritation became an itch I couldn't get rid of. Eventually I went to my room and took out my diary, glad that I had Isabelle to talk to. I was pleased when I saw Isabelle's note. She was right. I should focus on my marriage and stop finding faults with Glen.

You're very wise, and I've been trying. It's just sometimes I feel like no matter what I do it's not enough. Glen is as busy as ever, and I can't help feeling second best to his work. But I guess as Eilean pointed out, it could be worse. Do you have someone special?

'Mhairi. Mhairi.'

I heard Glen's voice. I looked at my watch, it was almost ten. 'I'm coming.'

I closed my diary and made my way downstairs.

'I'm so sorry, Mhairi, but I lost track of time. Have you had any dinner yet?' Glen asked and kissed my mouth.

'Why don't you sit down, and I'll bring you something,' I said.

The stew was dried and congealed, and the dumplings were like shrivelled prunes. As I laid the table, I realised I no longer cared about the champagne or celebrating anymore.

'Look Mhairi, I'm sorry. I know I haven't been as attentive as I should recently. It's just, there are a lot of eyes on me right now and much pressure to prove myself at work. Do you understand?'

I didn't miss the serious look in his eyes. 'Of course,' I said, and refrained from asking: *But what about me?*

Chapter Twenty-Three

At the village shop, Isabelle picked up some cheese, and as she put a few bottles of French chardonnay in her basket, she thought of her father's visit a week ago. They'd be heading back to France today.

'Blimey woman, are you going to drink all that on your own?'

Isabelle turned to see Angus and laughed. 'Just stocking up, but then again who knows?' She winked at him.

'Well, I could always come over and help you? I was meaning to pop around anyway. Unless of course you're busy?'

'That'd be great. We could have some lunch and maybe go for a walk?'

'Grand. I'll meet you in a couple of hours?'

'Sure, see you then.'

It was only as she was preparing lunch that Isabelle remembered she hadn't asked about Alex. Would she be coming too? She hoped not.

She set the table, realised she hadn't bought any dessert, and went about making chocolate brownies—Angus had a sweet tooth. She was putting the first batch in the oven when the doorbell chimed.

She waved at Angus. 'Come on in.'

'I got these.'

He gave her a box of Dairy Milk as they walked to the kitchen.

'Thank you. Great minds think alike,' she said, gesturing to the oven. As she picked up the mixing bowl to put it away an image crossed her mind.

'Do you remember that time, or should I say the last time, we helped Mimi bake a cake?'

His eyes lit up after a few seconds and he grinned. 'You mean the time you managed to drop the bowl full of chocolate batter?'

'Oh, the forever gallant Mr Fairbairn. You'll find it was you who pulled it out of my hand, and it slipped out of your greasy fingers.'

'Nonsense, and you know it. Mimi was absolutely livid, wasn't she? I was proper scared of her.' Angus shook his head. 'It all seems like another lifetime.'

'It was over twenty years ago. A lot has changed since.'

'Yes. I miss those days. We had so much fun.'

Isabelle didn't think Angus knew just how much those summers had meant to her. It was the only time her life had felt normal, free of guilt.

'I always used to be jealous of you for having Mimi to yourself all the time,' admitted Isabelle. 'You had her after school most days, didn't you?'

'Yeah, I was lucky. But I used to miss you a lot during term time.'

The expression on his face sent a wave of heat through Isabelle's body and she had to look away.

'At least you had your other friends to keep you entertained.'

'Yes … but they weren't like you. At least being at the Hall made me the cool kid.'

He burst into laughter. Isabelle slapped his arm but was glad they were on safe ground again—or were they?

'Where's Alex today?' she asked as she busied herself with washing the bowl.

'Off to Edinburgh shopping.'

'Won't she mind you being here? I mean—'

'You know what? She seems upset with me all the time anyway, so…' he shrugged and sipped his wine.

Isabelle didn't say anything, but she couldn't understand. Why didn't they just break up? Neither of them was happy.

'I know what you must be thinking,' he said as though reading her mind. But then again, they'd always been like that. 'Truth is I'm hoping it's just a phase.'

Isabelle nodded. There was nothing she could say to that. He must love Alex. The moment of silence was disrupted by a ping, causing them both to check their phones.

'It's Alex. She's on her way. I'd best go. I promised I'd do a spot of tidying up.' Angus grimaced.

'It was good to catch up.'

'Thanks for the lunch. Give me a buzz if you need anything.'

He pecked her on the cheek. Looking at him, Isabelle knew she could have fallen for him head over heels, but of course, that was nonsense. He was her oldest friend, and besides, he was with Alex.

Isabelle walked back to the kitchen when her phoned pinged with an email notification. It was from Mrs Hargrave at her old surgery. She frowned. Why would she write to her? She opened the email.

I'm sorry to contact you, Dr Rousseau, but I thought you may want to know that Melanie Stewart passed away yesterday.

Poor, poor Melanie. Isabelle's heart went out to her small children and her husband who were now left behind. But her feeling of sorrow was replaced with guilt. Had there been anything she could have done? Perhaps if she had stayed, she could have kept a close eye on her?

Isabelle jolted at the sound of the phone buzzing in her hand. She pressed the green button and saw Charlie beaming at her. Her smile quickly faded.

'Hey, Isabelle, what's wrong? You look dreadful?'

'One of my patients died. Cancer. I thought maybe I could have...' Isabelle shrugged

'Saved her? Bloody hell, not every death is your fault. People die. In fact it's the one sure thing about life.'

Isabelle hung her head.

'Look sweetheart, I know you still torment yourself because of Chloe, but really, you've got to let it go.'

Isabelle tucked her hair behind her ear. She knew Charlie was right and yet she couldn't help the feeling.

'I know, I know.'

'How's your sleuthing coming on?'

Isabelle knew Charlie was trying to change the subject. There was no point moaning, so she went along with it.

'I found the diaries, at last. But I'm still reading the first one. Nothing strikes me as the terrible behaviour Mimi mentioned yet.'

'Maybe it all happens later. The whole thing is pretty strange.'

If you just knew, thought Isabelle.

'I can't wait to see you; nothing's the same here without you. How's it going with Angus and the prickly Alex?'

'Actually, Angus was just here for lunch.'

'Was he now. And her ladyship didn't mind?'

'She was out shopping in Edinburgh. Anyway, it doesn't matter. There's nothing between Angus and me. She's just the jealous type.'

'Hmmm, but I bet you wouldn't mind if there was—'

'Stop that, Charlie Higgins.' Isabelle knew Charlie was trying to cheer her up, but she wasn't in the mood.

'Just saying.' Charlie shrugged. 'Anyway, I've got to go, gorgeous. Keep me posted.'

Isabelle pocketed her phone and sighed. She wondered how much longer she could carry on rattling around the Hall on her own. Her only hope was that she'd soon have a job. She switched on the TV and flicked through the channels. But her mind kept going back to Melanie Stewart. There was nothing she wanted to watch. She went up to her room. The best thing she could do was carry on with Mimi's story.

She opened the diary and saw Mimi's message.

I've been trying… it's not enough.

That didn't sound good at all to Isabelle. But what was she supposed to do? Glen was selfish, and she didn't care that Eilean thought he could be worse. As far as she was concerned, Glen was bad enough. She wished she could tell Mimi to leave him, but then there would be no Bonelle. She bit her lip and started writing.

It must be very disappointing for you, Mimi. I know you're trying to be patient, and I understand Glen has to impress the people at work, but I also think that you need to be honest with him and tell him how you feel. It

can't be about him all the time; there has to be some sort of compromise.

The answer to the second part of Mimi's message wasn't straight forward. *Did* she have someone special in her life? There was Angus of course. She couldn't admit it to Charlie, but she found herself wanting to tell Mimi. She would have loved the idea of the two of them if she'd been alive.

There is someone I like. We kind of grew up together, but he's engaged to another woman.

There, it's out, she thought and carried on reading.

Chapter Twenty-Four

Mimi, December 1955

Alasdair and I were sipping wine in the hotel restaurant near the golf course. It was already almost eight, and there was still no sign of Glen.

'Shall we order?' Alasdair asked.

Knowing my brother only too well, I could sense his dismay. We were having our starters of scallops some twenty minutes later, when Glen put in an appearance.

'I am so sorry to keep you waiting; I completely lost track of time,' he said, running his hand over his head. 'Mhairi, my love, you look beautiful.'

Almost as an afterthought, he bent down and kissed me on my burning cheek. I was struggling to suppress my anger at his usual excuse.

'Do you always work this late?' Alasdair asked after the waiter had taken Glen's order.

'What, old chap? Oh work. Well, the term has just ended, and there's a lot to wrap up, and I'm working on my book.'

'I see,' was all Alasdair said.

'I'm sure Mhairi will enjoy having some time on her own at the Hall. I should be with you for Christmas Eve.'

He touched my hand, but I didn't respond.

'Is Glen joining us today?' asked Alasdair over Christmas Eve breakfast.

'Your guess is as good as mine,' I said, unable to hide my irritation.

'I know it's none of my business, sis. But are you happy?'

I looked at my plate. 'Yes, it's all good.'

'Are you sure? It's just, you know, things between you and Glen seem a bit tense.'

I slumped into the seat, averted my gaze, and stared down at my hands, trying to quell the feeling that pressed on me these days like a weight whenever the subject of my marriage came up.

Alasdair reached across and touched my arm. 'Mimi? What's wrong?'

I exhaled as though to breathe out the heaviness. 'It's been dreadful, Alasdair. Our honeymoon was a disaster because he worked every day. If it wasn't for me, we still wouldn't have a home. Maybe I just need to be patient.' I repeated my mantra, which was wearing rather thin.

'I'm not an expert on marriage. Glen is a decent enough chap, but it seems a bit excessive.'

Yes, he may as well never have married I thought, but I didn't want to worry Alasdair more than I already had.

'Can I ask you something?'

'Of course,' he said and took a sip of his coffee.

'Do you remember Mama and Papa arguing?'

'No, they always seemed so in love, didn't they?'

'Yes, they did.'

Which meant that Glen and I weren't.

'Do you want me to have a word with him?' Alasdair asked.

'No, I'm not sure it would change anything. But thank you.' I reached across the table and touched his hand.

'I know; let's go for a ride. What do you say?' suggested Alasdair in the tone he always used when he wanted to cheer me up.

'You're on.'

I was fed up with waiting for—and being irritated by—Glen.

Alasdair and I had just returned from our ride when the telephone rang.

'For you, Miss.' Annie gave me the receiver.

'Mhairi, darling,' said Glen.

'Where are you?' I asked, not in the mood for pleasantries.

'I'm afraid, darling, that I won't be able to make it tomorrow. I had a set-back. I promise I'll come for Hogmanay.'

I could hear the regret in his voice, but it left me cold. I'd been married for barely eight months, and it already felt as if I had no husband. I thought of Mama and Papa's marriage again, and it pained me to think just how much my own was lacking. How was this the same man I'd been so giddy over in the beginning?

On New Year's Eve Mrs Kerr's daughter, Annie, was getting married to Mr Murray's son, Ewan, and of course Alasdair and I were invited as guests of honour.

We were sitting in the front pew of the church, and as I turned around to see Annie walk in, I glimpsed Will. I don't know whether it was the way he looked in his suit or the glow in his eyes, but I felt a flutter in my stomach and was gratified when later at the Fox & Hare for the wedding breakfast, I found myself facing him, albeit sitting at separate tables, of course.

It was a celebration full of laughter and banter. Annie and Ewan looked so in love, and I hoped that their union would be happier than my own.

'Alasdair, it's time to leave,' I said and had to repeat myself twice before I got his attention.

'Just one more whiskey, sis, and we'll be off.' Alasdair slurred the words.

I knew ten wild horses couldn't now drag him away from this party. Though I'd rarely seen him drunk, when he was, it was with style.

'It's all right. I'll see you back at the Hall.'

'Just wait a few minutes; I don't want you to go on your own.'

I was about to reassure him when Will spoke up.

'It's okay, Master Alasdair. I'll walk Miss Mimi home.'

'Cheers, Will, you're a good man.'

Alasdair then downed his whisky as though he'd forgotten about that incident on my birthday. But then again it had been a few years, and I was a married woman.

My heartbeat picked up at this turn of events, and I allowed myself to bask in Will's attention. I didn't feel even a morsel of guilt, being still rather angry at Glen for not turning up for Christmas or Hogmanay. Just as we were to approach the bend of the drive and were still hidden from the Hall, I slipped. Automatically I clung onto Will.

'Are you all right?' he asked, as he held on to me.

I managed to steady myself and looked up. His face was so close to mine that his breath warmed my skin.

'What the hell?'

On hearing Glen's voice, we jumped apart.

To my horror, he was half-walking, half-sliding down the path, his face red as flames, and he was shooting daggers at Will with his eyes.

'It's you again!' he boomed and pushed Will back.

'Glen, please! I slipped, and I was the one who held onto Will. Would you rather I'd had a fall and broken a leg?'

I stood between the two men even though my insides felt as if they had turned into mush. I hoped my legs wouldn't buckle under me. To his credit Will stood there so silent I wondered if he was even breathing. But I suspected he knew anything he did or said would only worsen the situation. I clenched my hands and tensed to stop the tremors that had grasped hold of me. Thankfully, my words somehow got through to Glen, for he threw a quick look at my face and didn't make any further move towards Will.

'I don't ever want to see you near my wife. Do you hear me?' Glen growled.

I didn't dare so much as look in Will's direction. My head was spinning, and nausea was heaving my stomach as Glen took my arm and led me towards the Hall.

As soon as we were inside, he left me standing in the hallway and headed for the living room.

'I shouldn't have bothered.' He threw back at me over his shoulder.

With everyone at the wedding, I headed up to my room, sat on my bed and wept. Later, I asked Isabelle:

What am I to do? It's a terrible situation. I see you too have fallen for the wrong man. It's not easy, is it? But maybe you're the lucky one. I'm finding marriage isn't that great after all. I tried to be patient, but it's getting worse. Has Glen stopped loving me? And of course there's Will. He seems to care so much more about me. And when I'm with him, I feel like I'm alive. I wish Glen would make me feel that way.

Chapter Twenty-Five

In the April sun the harbour had come alive. The reds, blues and yellows of the fishing boats looked as though they'd just been painted. Fishermen were sitting in groups on upturned baskets mending their nets. Tourists in their walking gear and rucksacks were trailing the coastal path like ants, and soon the place would be crawling with them.

Isabelle spotted the tables outside the café, where villagers were enjoying a drink and basking in the sun. It reminded her of London and the Sunday afternoons she used to spend in the coffee shop reading. It seemed like another lifetime.

Before long she was seated at one of the outside tables with a cup of coffee and Mimi's diary. But she couldn't concentrate on reading; her mind wandered to her lunch with Angus. In the week since, they had swapped a few messages, but she hadn't seen him.

Finally, Isabelle began to read Mimi's diary.

What am I to do?... It's a terrible situation. I wished Glen would make me feel that way.

Well, Mimi was right; they both had fallen for the wrong man. But if she thought she had trouble in her love life, Mimi's was on another level. Isabelle was furious at Glen for the way he was treating Mimi. She too wondered if he loved Mimi; it was obvious that he was driving her towards Will.

She knew it was a different time back then; divorce wasn't something to be entered into lightly. She wasn't even sure on what grounds a woman could get a divorce. Isabelle took her phone and wrote *Scottish divorce law* in the search engine. The first entry told her that divorce could be achieved only on the grounds of desertion, insanity, and cruelty.'

'Christ. Poor Mimi.'

But Mimi had to make a decision. Was Will going to be cause of the arguments that Hamish said had driven him from the Hall?

> **It sounds absolutely dreadful, Mimi. I don't know what to say. I can see why you're questioning your marriage, and I must say I agree with you. But Will and your feelings for him aren't helping the situation either. Perhaps when you're back in St Andrews, you could take some time to think about what it is you really want. I also think it'd be a good idea to do something for yourself. You've been studying hard. Maybe you could look for a job after you graduate. You could build your own career. At least that way you'll have another focus rather than your whole life being about Glen or Will.**

She put the diary away and was about to take out her book when, as if thinking of him had called him forth, Hamish was at her table.

'How are you, lass? Do you mind if I join you for a quick cuppa?'

Isabelle could hardly say no.

'How's life at the Hall treating you?' Hamish asked as he sat down.

'It's been okay. There's still a lot to learn. Would you mind telling me more about its past?'

'Aye. There's so much to tell.' He paused. 'What is it you'd like to know?' Hamish raised his eyebrows and looked at her with an expression Isabelle couldn't read.

She would have loved to ask him if he knew any secrets, the type of secrets Mimi would be worried about sharing.

'What was it like to live there?' she asked instead.

Hamish looked thoughtful. 'You must remember times were different. We're talking over half a century ago. The Hall was the heart and soul of the community around here.'

Isabelle nodded. 'Mimi told me.'

'I don't mean just St Abbs, but Coldingham and a couple of the other hamlets. The estate spread over a few thousand acres. Nigh everyone around these parts worked for the Hall. At its height, there were a thousand folks.'

'Wow,' Isabelle tried to imagine what that would have been like. 'Was that when Mimi was young?'

He nodded. 'Everyone worked hard, but the old master and his son—that'd be your great-granddad and your great-uncle, Alasdair—were good to us. Always treating everyone with the respect due to them, you know?'

No wonder. Isabelle thought of what Alasdair had told Mimi about the responsibility.

'But as I told you last time, things changed when Master Alasdair died. He was so young.' Hamish's face sagged with sadness. 'He was only a couple of years older than me; he didn't make it to thirty.'

Isabelle gasped. 'Oh, no! How did he die?'

Mimi had mentioned Isabelle's uncle Alasdair a few times when Isabelle was little, but she'd had no idea Alasdair had died so early.

'A car accident.'

The young Mimi Isabelle was communicating with would be devastated. Alasdair was her last living family, and they were so close.

Isabelle did a quick calculation. 'Mimi must have been in her early twenties. How did she manage?'

Hamish abruptly stood. 'Sorry, lassie, I must get back for the electrician. Make sure you come and visit me soon.' He patted her shoulder and was gone.

Isabelle ordered another coffee, mulling over Alasdair's death. Could she warn Mimi? She would have been horrified if Chloe's death had been somehow foretold. But on the other hand, what if instead of *foretelling* Alasdair's death, she could prevent it. Maybe she could come up with a plan.

Mimi needed Alasdair. Perhaps she'd have a happier marriage if her brother was around to intervene, to make Glen step-up and be a good husband, to give Mimi sensible advice and a shoulder to cry on—one that wasn't Will's.

The waitress had started stacking up chairs. It was time to go. Isabelle knew she should go and look through the Statutory Register of Deaths for Alasdair's death certificate. She had to find out the exact date. She wished Hamish hadn't rushed off. But she had time. And the thought of spending the evening on her own didn't seem very appealing. She needed company to take away this feeling of being surrounded by the dead.

She'd been sitting in the Fox & Hound for almost an hour. Two gin and tonics later, she was still trying to piece together what she knew. It seemed to her as though the more she found out about her family's history, the less she understood. She looked around and saw the pub had filled. She needed the loo but didn't fancy losing her seat. She spread her jacket on the chair like she used to do in London when she was alone in a coffee shop and left her book on the table.

On her way back she noticed that the other chair at her table had been taken. Her dismay deepened when she recognised the offender.

'Alex, what are you doing here?'

'Hello, Isabelle. I suspect the same as you,' she said with a raised brow. 'Having a drink.'

'I didn't mean it that way. I just wasn't expecting to see you.'

'Don't worry, neither was I. And I'm afraid I'll be staying. There aren't any other seats, and I'd really rather not stand at the bar.'

Isabelle didn't like Alex's tone at all. Charlie was right to call her *prickly Alex*.

'You know what, don't worry, I was finished here anyway.'

As she went to pick up her jacket, Alex snapped, 'For God's sake, Isabelle. We're not in a playground. Just sit down and finish your bloody drink.'

The cheek of her!

Isabelle ignored her and picked up her handbag.

'Please, Isabelle. I didn't mean to snap.'

Isabelle looked at Alex. Her eyes were glassy with a faraway look. With a groan, Isabelle sat back down, but she couldn't dislodge the discomfort in the silence that stretched between them. She took a sip of her drink and stole another glimpse at Alex. Her jaw was set and there was a tremor to her chin.

'Are you okay?' Isabelle asked. Whatever their differences, the woman was upset.

'Yes, thank you. Do you come here often?'

She knew Alex was trying to change the subject and went along with it. 'Not really, I've been in a few times. I was out and didn't fancy going back to the Hall yet. What about you?'

'Same reason really. Angus is working late, and I just needed to get out of the house and be around people. Have you moved to the Hall permanently then?'

'Yes.'

'But don't you miss your life in London?'

Isabelle didn't want to discuss her situation with Alex. 'Of course, it's normal. But it's getting easier.'

'Well, it isn't getting easier for me. In fact, the opposite. It becomes more unbearable by the day.'

Isabelle couldn't help feeling irritated with Alex's whinging. 'Why don't you go back?'

'It's not that simple.'

It didn't look like Alex was going to explain, and Isabelle didn't want to ask. But she felt a pang of guilt as she wondered whether her friendship with Angus was one of the reasons.

'I'm sure you'll work it out,' she said.

'You know, I really admire you living at that place all on your own. I think I'd go out of my mind.'

'I get by.' Isabelle realised she meant it. She had Mrs Murray and Angus. And there was Hamish. And Mimi.

Alex glanced at Isabelle. 'Life's strange, isn't it?'

Isabelle didn't know what to make of that comment, but based on her recent experiences she admitted, 'Yes, it is.'

Alex slumped into the chair as though withdrawing into herself.

'Are you gonna be all right, Alex? It's just, you seem so … sad.'

Alex didn't respond. But then again, it wasn't like they were friends. She saw a tear falling from the corner of her eye, which Alex wiped away with her fingertips.

'Are you sure you want to hear this?' Alex said at last, looking at her.

Isabelle shrugged. 'Only if you're happy to talk about it.'

'I don't really know where to begin.' Alex reached out a fingertip and traced a circle in the moisture that had gathered on the outside of her glass. 'I guess you know Angus and I've been going out for the last six years. The first five were amazing. But then Angus started getting restless, wanting to get married, have children. And come home.'

Isabelle hid her disappointment. Angus must really love Alex to want children with her.

'You're probably wondering what's wrong with that?' Alex looked up, catching Isabelle's eye. 'Honestly, I'd love to have a family with Angus. But not *here*. We had a lot of arguments about it, but eventually I agreed to at least give it a go and here we are. I'd hoped Angus would realise the move was a mistake and we'd go back. But he wants to stay.'

Isabelle thought of what Mimi had said about her being better off without a relationship.

'So, I'm afraid you didn't meet me at my best. If it's any consolation, it hasn't been anything personal.'

Isabelle wasn't so certain after what Angus had told her about Alex being jealous of her. Or maybe now that Alex had met her, she didn't think of her as competition.

'I'm sorry, Alex.' Isabelle touched Alex's hand. 'It doesn't sound like an easy situation for either of you. But I hope you and Angus work it all out.' And she meant it.

Finally, Isabelle had a glimpse of the real Alex and understood why—apart from her looks—Angus was attracted to her.

If she didn't want to come between them, she had to keep her distance. Angus was a friend and that was that.

Chapter Twenty-Six

Mimi, July 1956

'Congratulations, darling sis, I'm very proud of you,' said Alasdair.

The graduation ceremony had just finished, and we were standing with a circle of friends on the lawn in front of the university, sipping champagne.

'Yes, Mhairi, it's certainly a big day,' added Glen.

He put his arm around my waist and kissed me on my brow. There was a warmth in his eyes I hadn't seen since New Year's Eve when he found—for want of a better word—me in Will's arms. I hoped that the shadow of that day had at last left us.

Alasdair turned to me. 'So what are your plans now?'

'Actually, I've got a post,' I beamed at him.

Thanks to Isabelle for putting the idea in my mind, I thought, but of course I couldn't tell my brother that.

Alasdair hugged me. 'That's wonderful. Well done, Mimi. What will you be doing?'

'I helped out on a project for one of my genetics assignments, animal breeding. I must have done a good job because my professor offered me a post as an assistant researcher. Isn't it great?'

I was still floating on the cloud of validation and accomplishment.

'I'm very proud of you, Mimi.'

'Thank you. If it wasn't for you, I wouldn't be here.'

I looped my arm through his. Only too aware that, despite Alasdair being tied down by the Hall, he never begrudged me my freedom and had always been there to encourage and support me.

'You're the best brother in the world and I love you very much.' I kissed him on the cheek.

He grinned. 'Of course, I am. And I love you too, little sis.' He ruffled my hair like he used to when I was little. But for all his cheeriness, I didn't miss the glossy sheen in his eyes. 'But I'm afraid the best brother in the world has to take his leave.'

'What? You aren't staying?'

'Sorry, sis, it's the big market day tomorrow, and you know I can't miss it. Besides, I'll be back in two weeks to collect you anyway,' he said and squeezed my arm. 'And we'll have a proper party at the Hall.'

'Of course,' I said, unable to hide my disappointment.

The truth was, Glen was as busy as always, and if it hadn't been for my studies, I wouldn't have known what to do with myself. I had been looking forward to spending a couple of days with my brother.

'Chin up.' Alasdair lifted my chin with the tip of his finger. 'Now give your best brother a hug,' he said as he enveloped me in his arms.

The next morning, I was jerked awake by a sound. Disorientated, I checked the alarm, it was just before eight. Glen was nowhere to be seen; he must have left for work already. The ringing resounded around the house until I realised it was the telephone. I rushed into the living room, still wrapped in the haze of sleep, and picked up the receiver.

'Hello?'

'Miss Mimi, is that you?'

'Yes.' I knew the voice but couldn't place it. 'Who's this?'

'It's Williams, the estate manager of the Hall. Miss Mimi, I'm afraid I have bad news.'

His voice seemed to have lost its substance, and a shiver ran through my body, freezing my bones.

'It's Master Alasdair, Miss. He… he had an accident on his way back. We only heard early this morning.'

I gripped the phone. 'An accident? What do you mean an accident?'

'A car accident, Miss.'

'A car accident?' Why could I only repeat what was being told to me?

'Yes, Miss. I'm afraid…' His breath hitched, and my own mimicked the sound. 'I'm afraid it was quite bad.'

'Which hospital?' I whispered, as fear tightened my chest.

'He… Miss, he didn't make it. I'm so very sorry—'

His voice broke off and was replaced by what sounded like a growl. That was the last sound I heard before darkness claimed me. I have no clear memory of returning to the Hall or the three weeks leading up to the funeral, for I seem to have spent it in the oblivion of sedation. Glen joined me the day before the funeral, and on an August morning that was as grim as the depth of winter, a sea of mourners flocked to the village church. I felt like a ragdoll, propped up by Glen.

'We are all gathered here to pay our respect to the most important pillar of our community, Master Alasdair…'

I heard the reverend's words as though from a distance before everything was lost to silence.

I stood on top of the staircase. The Hall was immersed in darkness except for the light coming through the window. Where was everyone? We needed to get to the funeral.

A wave of dizziness and nausea washed over me at the image of my beloved Alasdair beneath the ground. I grabbed the banister and waited until it passed.

'Glen! Mrs Kerr!' I shouted, but there was no reply.

I hurried down the stairs and tightened my grip on the banister to break my fall as my knees buckled under me without warning. I straightened up and carried on.

'Glen? Mrs Kerr? Where are you?' I shouted again into the void that had seeped through me.

Mrs Kerr grabbed me by the shoulders. 'Annie, find Mr Smeatson,' she said without taking her eyes off me.

'Why aren't you ready, Mrs Kerr?' I asked as I took in her dressing gown. 'Where is everyone? We need to go to the funeral.'

'Miss Mimi, the funeral was yesterday. You fainted, and we brought you back.'

'No, you're wrong,' I wailed.

Glen came rushing down the stairs and wrapped his arms around me. 'Mhairi, Mhairi, everything's fine, come with me.' He looked at Mrs Kerr. 'Call the doctor, will you?'

'I don't need a doctor,' I shouted. 'Let me go; I need to go to the funeral. Alasdair needs me.'

I tried to pull myself away from Glen. But his grip tightened.

'It's okay; it'll all be fine,' he whispered the words into my ear over and over until the fight went out of me.

I collapsed like a heap in his arms and dissolved into tears. Glen picked me up like a small child and carried me into bed. I must have fallen asleep at some point. The next time I awoke, the sun was shining, and I saw Glen sitting on the edge of my bed.

'How are you feeling?' he asked.

'Okay,' I said with effort. My throat was parched, and I had trouble keeping my eyes focused on Glen. 'What happened?'

Glen cleared his throat. 'The doctor had to sedate you, Mhairi. You just weren't coping. You came to the funeral but … we had to bring you back to the house when—'

'No, please, dear God!'

The wail of despair shook my core and burst out of me at the thought that I had missed Alasdair's funeral. I clawed at my face as it hit me that I'd lost my last chance to say goodbye to my beloved brother, to tell him how much I'd miss him.

I would never forgive myself.

Chapter Twenty-Seven

'*No!*' Despair and shock clutched at Isabelle's heart. Alasdair had died. She had failed to stop it. Charlie's words pushed themselves to the forefront of her mind.

Not every death is your fault.

But Charlie was wrong. She could have tried harder. If she'd just followed through with her plan and found the death certificate instead of sitting in the pub listening to Alex's problems, Alasdair would have been alive. She could have told Mimi not to let him go back to the Hall that afternoon without giving anything away. But it was too late. She was too late.

Again.

She rubbed her hands over her face and forced herself to read on. Every word of Mimi's agony and devastation broke another piece of her heart. As she sat there with the diary in front of her, Isabelle could no longer hold back the tears. She cried for Mimi and for Alasdair who, like Chloe, never had a chance of a future.

As Isabelle read the last sentence, she realised that despite what she'd thought, she couldn't begin to imagine what Mimi was going through. She had lost everyone—her entire family—by the age of twenty-one.

Isabelle had to forget her own guilt and self-pity. She couldn't undo Alasdair's death, but she'd make sure she was there for Mimi. Should she tell Mimi that she was her granddaughter? Would it help her to know that life moves on?

No. Isabelle shook her head. She'd already told Mimi that her grandma and sister had died. If she told Mimi who she was, she'd be giving her notice of her own death and the loss of her granddaughter. No. She had to let Mimi grieve Alasdair's death.

With new resolve, she picked up her pen.

> **Mimi, I'm so sorry. I know there's nothing I can say to take away your anguish. I wish I could reach across time and space, hold you in my arms and be there for you. But I still want you know that I'm right here, Mimi. You're not alone, I'm here for you.**

Isabelle paused, she wanted to say: *Like you were there for me,* but she couldn't. She blinked back the tears and focused on her message.

> **And I deeply care about you. Sending you all my love.**

'I'm so glad you're here!' Isabelle said as she parked the car in front of the Hall.

The entire week she had been either beating herself up for failing to save Alasdair or telling herself to stop being so self-centred and focus instead on Mimi. She was fed up and couldn't wait to spend the next couple of days with her friend.

'It's been far too long,' Charlie agreed as she got out of the car.

'I missed you so much. I missed just picking up the phone and meeting up,' Isabelle said as she led them inside.

'I know, my lovely; I missed you too. There's so much to catch up on.'

'Let's get you settled first.'

Isabelle took Charlie's arm and led her down the hallway to the guest room.

Charlie stood in the room, open-mouthed. 'Wow, this is unbelievable! I know you said it was big, but this is *enormous*.'

Isabelle grinned. 'I'm glad you approve. Have a shower if you want, and I'll show you the rest of the house. Then we'll head for the pub.'

Charlie flopped herself onto the four-poster bed and grinned. 'Gosh, this is ridiculous, I feel like I'm in a fancy hotel.'

Charlie's enthusiasm for the Hall gave Isabelle a glow of pride. Somehow she'd forgotten how special the Hall was.

As though Charlie had read her mind, she said, 'I don't get why you were in a quandary. I'd drop anything for this,' sweeping her hand across the room.

Isabelle smiled. 'Yes, it's amazing. But it's also the antithesis of my life in London. And there's a hell of a lot of responsibility.'

'Responsible is your middle name!'

Isabelle picked up a cushion and threw it at her.

'And what's going on with Angus?' Charlie asked, rolling over.

'He's just a friend.'

'Come on, out with it. Something's happened, hasn't it? I can see it written all over your face.'

Isabelle couldn't help laughing. 'Do you know, you missed a career in interrogation. It's nothing really. I've met up with him a couple of times, without Alex. I thought maybe ...' Isabelle shrugged.

Charlie cocked her head. 'What?'

'Oh, I don't know. Then I saw Alex in the pub. She told me Angus wanted to get married and have kids. He's not free, and he isn't into me.'

Charlie took her hand. 'He'd be crazy if he wasn't.'

Isabelle laughed. 'You haven't seen Alex. Anyway, the only thing standing between them is this question of where they have this family. Alex wants to go back to Dubai. Angus doesn't.'

'That's a pretty big thing. What if they can't work it out?'

'I don't know. But whatever happens I don't want to be a factor in their decision. Angus might end up resenting me for destroying his chance at a family with the woman he loves. He has to sort it out alone.'

'I didn't realise so many people even lived here,' Charlie said a couple of hours later, looking over the crowd gathered in the Fox & Hare's garden.

'Some will be weekend tourists; the season starts now in May and usually ends around October.'

'Belle!'

Isabelle turned to see Angus standing by one of the picnic tables. There was no Alex in sight.

'Ooh, who is that handsome devil?' Charlie asked, nudging her with her elbow.

'Angus, dummy.'

'No, I mean the other one.' Charlie pointed. 'The older one: Colin Firth meets Henry Cavill.'

Isabelle frowned. 'I've never seen him before.'

They made their way over to Angus. Feeling a little awkward, Isabelle kissed him on the cheek.

'You remember Charlie?' she said.

Angus nodded. Isabelle didn't miss his clenched jaw and sighed. Despite her efforts there'd always been a dislike between Angus and Charlie.

Angus cleared his throat and pointed to the stranger. 'This is Scott. He's back visiting his dad. Thinking about making a permanent move.'

'Hi Scott,' Charlie sidled nearer to him and grinned.

'Hi.'

Scott's voice was deeper than Angus's—sexy deep, like whiskey and honey. Charlie's eyes widened. If Scott was single, he'd just signed his death warrant, thought Isabelle.

'And where's Alex tonight?' Isabelle asked.

'She went to Dubai for a long weekend,' Angus said and emptied the rest of his glass.

Noting his discomfort, Isabelle was sorry she'd brought up the subject.

'I'll get the drinks,' Scott offered.

'I'll come with you,' Charlie said, taking his arm. 'I want to see what local delights they've got.'

'Cheers mate. Could you get me the same please?' Angus raised his glass.

'The usual for you?' Charlie said to Isabelle.

Isabelle nodded and watched the pair head towards the bar. 'Scott's in trouble,' she murmured.

'Scott loves trouble,' Angus said.

'Is everything all right?'

'Why shouldn't it be?' Angus shot back and looked away from her.

Isabelle couldn't remember when she'd last seen Angus this wound up. She laid a hand on his shoulder.

'Hey, it's me, remember?'

Angus turned around. 'I'm sorry, Belle. I didn't mean to take it out on you.' He swiped his hand through his hair. 'It's been God-awful.'

'Come on, let's go and sit down.'

She led Angus to a bench. They sat and gazed over the harbour and the sea beyond. The clouds were scattered like pink candyfloss across the sky. Isabelle turned and looked at Angus.

'Now, what's wrong?'

'Nothing really—at least nothing new. We had an argument a few days back. They're getting worse. Nothing is being resolved. Then she said she'd booked a flight home. She *needs a break.*'

'Maybe a break isn't such a bad idea. You know, give you both some time to cool down?'

'It's not that.' Angus looked away and steepled his hands over his face. 'I... I don't know whether I should just give in and agree to move back.'

Isabelle's heart sank. She'd just found him again. She knew if he went back to Dubai, he'd cut her out once more. Alex would make sure of it.

'I mean, yes, I missed Scotland, and I was bored with the Dubai lifestyle, but we were happy. It only started going pear-shaped when I insisted that we move here.'

Isabelle wanted to tell him that if he were that happy, he wouldn't have wanted to move, but she remembered her words to Charlie; she couldn't influence Angus's decision.

'Ah, that's where you two are hiding,' said Charlie.

Isabelle took her G&T out of Charlie's hand and raised a brow in Scott's direction. But Charlie only beamed at her and returned her attention back to him.

'So, Scott, you're moving here to be closer to your dad?' she asked a little while later. She didn't miss Scott's arm around Charlie's shoulders as they stood there.

'Basically, yes. Mum died not that long ago. Dad was originally from here, so he wanted to move back. I know the place, and there's nothing keeping me in the Highlands.'

Charlie's eyes brightened.

'In fact, I've heard your name, Isabelle. Dad mentioned you the other day.'

'Me?'

'Scott's Hamish's son,' Angus jumped in.

'Oh, I didn't know.'

Scott was older than Charlie and her but not old enough to be Hamish's son. It didn't add up. Perhaps Hamish's wife had been much younger than he was.

'Scott's a wildlife photographer,' Charlie told Isabelle, breaking into her thoughts. 'He's been travelling the world. Isn't that cool?'

'Do you exhibit your pictures, Scott?' Isabelle asked.

'Sometimes, but I mainly sell them to magazines or put them up on my website as stock images.'

'Sorry to interrupt, guys.' Angus said. 'But I should be off. I'm expecting Alex to Facetime me.' He looked at Charlie. 'It was nice to see you again.'

Charlie made a face at Isabelle and jerked her chin towards the exit. Isabelle rolled her eyes.

'Hang on,' she said to Angus. 'I'll walk with you.'

'Are you sure? What about Charlie?'

She leaned in and whispered, 'Charlie wants to be alone with Scott.'

Angus snorted. 'Oh, I see. Come on then, walk me home.'

'Are you okay? Is there anything I can do?' she asked him once they were out of the ear shot.

'I'll be fine.' He gave her shoulder a squeeze. 'Thanks, Belle. You're a good mate.'

Chapter Twenty-Eight

Mimi, September 1956

*D*ear diary,
    I'm sitting in the sunshine on the terrace, looking at the waves lapping at the shore as they've done for millennia, a usually comforting sight but not today. I feel like I'm drowning underneath a sheath of ice, suffocating in my grief. The thought that the last member of my family, my dearest Alasdair, has died is beyond unbearable.

    It's shameful to admit, but since Alasdair's death just over a month ago, I've been asking myself if life is worth living. Everything seems an effort and every morning I awake to the same nightmare. My marriage is nothing but a hollow shell, and my husband nothing but a self-absorbed academic. I was moved by Isabelle's message and could tell she was genuinely touched by Alasdair's death.

    'Thank you so much, Isabelle. I too wish you were here. I haven't heard from Eilean since she embarked on her new life with Jonathan in America. So you're truly the only friend I have left. Please keep writing to me. I don't think I could bear it if one more person disappeared from my life.

I put the diary away and let despair and loneliness engulf me.

'Miss Mimi, you haven't touched any of your lunch,' said Mrs Kerr, bringing me back to present.

'I'm sorry, Mrs Kerr, but I wasn't hungry.'

'You can't carry on like this. There's nothing left of you. Mrs Quinn won't be pleased to have another tray returned untouched.'

But I didn't care. A short while later, on my way up to my room, I overheard the two women talking.

'I'm worried about that lass. She's fading away by the day,' said Mrs Kerr.

'What a tragedy,' Mrs Quinn said in reply. 'So young and all alone with her grief. I may be speaking out of turn here, but for the love of God, where's that husband of hers, I ask you? What can be more important than his wife at a time like this? And what's going to become of the Hall?'

I felt as though someone had poured ice over me. My feet were stuck to the ground. Though touched by the compassion and concern of these two women who were like family to me, I was ashamed that I had neglected my responsibilities as mistress of the Hall. With Alasdair gone, the entire estate relied on my strength and guidance, and it was a task I didn't feel equipped to shoulder. I turned on my heels and headed for the beach. I walked in a daze until I came to a halt by the Moonlight Cove. Then I sat and stared out into the sea until it blurred into nothingness like everything else.

'Hello, Miss Mimi.'

Will's voice was as solid as the rocks around me. I looked over my shoulder and watched him settle next to me, his eyes glazed over with his own grief at losing his friend. Though I had caused somewhat of a rift between my brother and Will over the last few years, they'd been friends all their lives.

We sat there in silence; it was the first time we'd been alone since the incident with Glen on New Year's Eve. Tears assaulted my eyes as I remembered Alasdair's jolly drunkenness at Annie's wedding.

'Da wants to talk to you tomorrow morning.' Will's words chased away the image.

'Is something wrong?' I asked, unsettled by the request.

'No, he just thinks it's time he started stepping back a bit.'

'But Will, I can't manage!' I jumped up, unable to contain the panic that gripped my body.

'It's all right.' Will reached for my hand, and I lowered myself back down. 'He wants me to start taking the reins a bit more.'

Will's words eased some of my discomfort.

'I've been preparing for the job for the last five years and besides, he'll still be around. All you need to do is make the decisions; I can oversee everything else, and Da will help if needed. We can do this together.'

He laid his arm around my shoulders, and we sat there until my heartbeat had calmed down.

'Thank you for doing this for me,' I said though I wasn't sure whether *this* was the comfort or his support and guidance with running the Hall or both.

'I'd do anything for you,' he whispered.

He leaned towards me, and before I had a chance to respond, his lips sealed mine. Without thinking, I responded as he breathed life into me. He undid the zip of my dress and pulled it down to my waist, as his mouth continued to caress my lips, my neck. An image of Glen fleeted across my mind, but I pushed it aside. Will's lips reached my bare chest, and a groan of pleasure escaped me.

As if on cue, we tore at the rest of each other's clothes. I'll never forget the moment Will and I became one, a feeling I'd never experienced with Glen. As he made love to me, my body and soul began to thaw with the heat of our passion.

Chapter Twenty-Nine

With Charlie returned to London, Isabelle turned her attention back to Mimi. She wondered how she was coping after Alasdair's death.

The guilt at having missed the opportunity to do something raised its head again. Alasdair had died in an accident she could have prevented if she'd let Mimi know it was coming. After everything Mimi had done for her, Isabelle had let her down in the worst possible way.

She had reached the end of Mimi's first diary. The last pages had been filled with pain caused, at least in part, by Isabelle herself. Although Mimi seemed to have found some hope at the end, Isabelle worried. What would happen when Glen found out about Will?

She had promised Mimi that she'd be there for her, and she would. She took her pen.

> **Mimi, of course I'll keep writing. I'd never leave you.**

Isabelle paused and looked out of the window. She had to say something about Will without alienating Mimi. Should she tell Mimi that perhaps now was the time to leave Glen and take the risk that Bonelle wouldn't be born? But where would that leave Isabelle herself? And if Isabelle wasn't here, how could she help Mimi?

> **I'm pleased you have Will and believe me I understand why you no longer care about Glen or what he may think. But Mimi, as long as you're married to him, he can make**

life difficult for you. I want you to be happy, but please be careful.

She needed the next diary. But she was nervous. What if the next diary lacked the magic of the first? What if the very last thing she was able to say to Mimi was *Please be careful*, not *I love you* or *Thank you for looking after me*. What if she never got to tell Mimi who she really was?

Bracing herself, she retrieved the hat box with Mimi's diaries from the bottom of her wardrobe. As she searched for the next diary in the series, a bundle fell on the floor.

Letters. All addressed to Mimi. She sat there for a moment looking at them before picking them up. Could these letters contain the answer to the mystery of what Mimi had done?

She ignored the knot in her stomach and undid the ribbon. Then she touched the paper that had yellowed with age as she fanned them out in front of her like a hand of cards. She wondered if there were put together in an order. She unfolded each letter and laid them side by side on the floor. A couple bore no date, the rest ranged from 1957 to 1964. She picked up one of the letters at random. It took a minute to get used to the writing; it was not Mimi's. Then she started to read.

21 January 1957

My dearest Mimi,

 Last night I couldn't find sleep, and when I was finally spirited away, I had the most dreadful nightmare. In the dream you told me you never wanted to see me again and that your love for me had died. You turned around and started to walk away. I kept calling your name, but I had no voice. I was woken up by my own strange sounding scream. My whole body was shaking, and it took a while before my heart calmed.

 I don't know if I could ever bear to be separated from you, my love. I miss you with all my heart. I must see you urgently. at the Moonlight Cove.
Yours always,
W

It was a love letter, Isabelle realised. She read and reread the letter. It was written after Alasdair had died, and she suspected that the W stood for Will. Obviously, the affair had continued. Was this the great mistake Mimi had spoken of, a sordid affair with her estate manager? What had Mimi been thinking?

Then Isabelle shook her head. This affair couldn't have caused Bonelle to hate Mimi. Bonelle hadn't even been born yet. Perhaps she should ask Mrs Murray about Will. There was no Will in the village, and Mimi had never mentioned him. Perhaps he died too, like Alasdair.

Isabelle was unable to stop herself feeling disappointed in Mimi. She knew Mimi had been harbouring a crush on Will and had found a moment of comfort with him, but the idea of her having an affair was absurd. Mimi had always seemed, to Isabelle's mind, so straightlaced. But that had been the old Mimi and not the young girl devastated by her brother's death and abandoned by an uncaring husband. Who was she to judge? What would she have done under the circumstances?

There was only one way to find out what had really happened. She had to read Mimi's next diary.

'Isabelle, where are you?'

Surely not. Isabelle's heart gave a thump at the sound of her mother's voice.

She had no time to wonder if the new diary would let Mimi see her message. She piled the letters back in the box and shoved it to the back of the wardrobe. She put the new diary in her bedside table on top of the old one and left the room.

'I'm coming,' she shouted once she reached the top of the staircase, not wanting her mum to know what she'd been up to.

'Where have you been? My throat's sore with all the shouting,' Bonelle complained.

'Come on, Mum. I didn't know you were coming, did I?' Isabelle looked at Bonelle, unable to hide the irritation in her voice. 'Anyway, what brings you back?'

'Why? Am I disturbing your super-busy schedule? And in case you've forgotten, this is my family home, and I can come and go as I please.'

Actually, this is my *home*, Isabelle wanted to remind her, but that would guaranteed lead to an argument, and after the truce they'd reached last time, Isabelle was disinclined to rock the boat.

'Of course, you know I didn't mean it like that. As I said, I wasn't expecting you, that's all.'

'Well, if you must know, I have meetings in London in a couple of days. And you and I need to talk.'

Isabelle knew what Bonelle wanted to talk about, but she needed to buy herself some time. She was still distracted by the thought of Mimi's letters.

'Sure. 'Why don't you have a little rest, I'll go for a run, and we'll talk over dinner?'

'Fine.'

Isabelle headed for the beach in search of the Moonlight Cove. Where was it? A memory started to take shape. She closed her eyes.

'Where're we going, Mimi?' Isabelle asked, hopping up and down, waiting for Mimi to pack the little picnic basket.

'It's a surprise.'

'What kinda surprise?'

'Speak your words properly darling, as I have told you. We say what kind of surprise.'

'Sorry, Mimi, I forgot,' said Isabelle and repeated her question.

'A very special one.' Mimi winked at her.

'Is Angus coming with us? I'll bet he'd like a special surprise too.'

'Not today, sweetie. Perhaps next time.'

They'd headed for the beach, and Isabelle remembered the heat of the sun burning on her skin.

'Mimi, are we there yet?' She was getting hot and wished she could just go for a swim.

'Just a little longer,' Mimi assured her.

'But my legs are getting tired,' Isabelle moaned.

Mimi laughed out loud.

'It's not funny, Mimi,' Isabelle pouted, thinking Mimi was not being very nice today.

'Oh lovey, I'm not laughing at you. It's just you and Angus can spend all day running about, and I don't hear you complaining your legs are tired.'

Isabelle didn't have anything to say to that. She just hoped they'd be there soon.

'Do you see that big rock there?'

Isabelle put the flat of her hand to her forehead and looked at a rock that came out of the sea like a mountain, with lots of others that looked like hills around it.

'That doesn't look very special, Mimi,' she said, and her shoulders slumped in disappointment at her surprise.

'Come, let's run this last bit and you can see for yourself.'

Mimi grabbed her hand, and they ran for the rocks.

They'd climbed over the boulders, waddled briefly in the shallow water and once they'd got around *the* rock, there was an opening. Mimi had stepped into the gap and helped Isabelle in.

'Oh wow, Mimi, this is like in a story book. Is it real?'

With her mouth open in awe Isabelle stared at the white teeth hanging from the ceiling of the cave. Water dripped from the tips of them like raindrops falling into a little blue pool.

'Yes, sweetheart, it is, but it looks magic, doesn't it?'

'Has it got a name, Mimi?'

'It's called the Moonlight Cove.'

Chapter Thirty

Mimi, October 1956

I'd never leave you...I just want you to be happy...but please be careful.

Isabelle hadn't judged me. Not that I had been anxious about it, for nothing much seemed to matter these days, but I'd have been sad if she hadn't understood. I was glad I could still call her my friend. And she was right to warn me.

Thank you for being a real friend and for being concerned about me. Believe me, I know what you're saying. But over the last months, it has been Will who has brought me back to life with his love and devotion. He's been beside me every step of the way as I've grown in confidence and taken ownership of Lanesbrough Estate.

What I didn't write but was sure she'd read about anyway was that almost every night Will and I had met at the Moonlight Cove, our makeshift love nest.

Tonight was different. As I reached the Moonlight Cove my mind was still on the phone call I'd had with Glen earlier. Will stepped out of the shadows and took me in his arms. I closed my eyes, savouring the moment, but Glen's words kept pushing to the forefront of my mind. I sighed and looked up at Will.

His eyes searched mine. 'What's wrong?'

There was no point delaying the inevitable. 'Glen's coming tomorrow,' I whispered.

'Is he back for good?'

A shudder ran through my body at the thought of having to live under the same roof and share the same bed with Glen again.

'Come here.'

Will wrapped his arms around me, and we laid on the blanket. I closed my eyes as we made love and wished the moment would last forever. But alas. Under the cover of night, we walked towards the Hall. We stopped at the top of the stairs that led to the terrace and hung onto each other like the only two survivors of a shipwreck amidst the ocean.

'I love you, Mimi. I wish we didn't have to part—ever.'

'I know. But at least we have our love,' I said and kissed him goodnight.

I stood there watching him disappear and wished, as I did every night, that we could walk into the Hall as husband and wife for all to see rather than the guilty lovers that we were, hiding in the shadows like fugitives.

As I approached the terrace doors, I saw a glow in the living room. Mrs Kerr must have forgotten to turn the light off, I thought. I went in and closed it behind me.

'And where have you been?' Glen asked, his voice a mixture of calm and menace.

I almost jumped out of my skin and let out a shriek as he revealed himself from behind an armchair. He had a tumbler of whiskey in his hand and fixed me as best as he could with eyes that were marbled with red.

'What are you doing here?' I snapped, unable to help myself. 'You were supposed to arrive tomorrow.'

'Well, I thought I'd surprise my wife, but as I can see it's turned into a rather unpleasant one. I've been waiting here for hours, and that useless old woman wouldn't say anything.'

'Don't—'

'Now I'm asking you again, Mhairi, where have you been?' he said with such force that his spit landed across the floor.

'How dare you question me and insult my staff?' I shouted.

The dam had broken and all the resentment, hurt, and upset of the last months were finding their way out. He closed the gap between us and grabbed me by my wrists.

'In case you've forgotten, I am your husband.'

I turned my head at the smell of whiskey on his breath and gagged as the bile rose in my throat. I yanked my arms free and walked away, widening the gap between us. My whole body was shaking with indignation and fear.

'My husband? You have no right to call yourself *my* husband. You lost that privilege when you abandoned me after I lost my brother.'

I hurled the words at him. Tears were running down my face, but I didn't care. I stood there, my head held high and stared at him, until he had the grace to look away. Only then did I turn and walk from the room.

My entire being was trembling as I headed for my bedroom. Once inside I locked the door behind me and curled up on my bed, wailing and screaming heartache and rage into the covers.

The next morning I raised myself and walked down the stairs. Glen was sitting at the breakfast table being served by Mrs Kerr. He was still in his last night's clothes. His hair was pressed against his scalp, and he looked like he'd just woken up.

'Good morning, Mrs Kerr, Annie,' I said.

It was not the form to show discord in front of staff, so I earned myself a sideways look from Mrs Kerr for having ignored my husband. But I was past caring. As far as I was concerned, she and Annie were more of a family to me than he was. I didn't bother to sit down. I just picked up the coffee Mrs Kerr had poured me and walked away.

'We need to talk, Mhairi,' said Glen.

I knew we did, but I was not ready yet. I wished I didn't have to talk to him, ever again. So I made my way to the stables. Will was waiting for me there, and we snuck away together, under the guise of exercising the horses around the estate.

As we rode Will asked, 'Is everything all right?'

'Oh, it was awful. Glen was waiting for me last night. He and I had a terrible row.' I tensed at the memory.

Will stiffened. 'Did he hurt you?'

I shook my head.

Will dropped his eyes. 'I'm sorry I couldn't be there for you, my love.'

'It devastates me to say it, but we can't risk seeing each other in the next while.'

I wished Glen would just disappear back to his university, his tomb of books and his students that were no doubt in awe of him, as I no longer was.

'I know, my love. But I've waited for you for years, and I'll wait as long as it takes.' He leaned over and kissed me.

After my return to the Hall, I couldn't settle down. I took out my diary, read Isabelle's warning again and wrote:

> *Yes, I know. But if I'm honest, I don't know how to get myself out of this mess. I can't bear the sight of Glen. And I don't know how I can survive it without Will.*

That evening after dinner, I could no longer avoid the conversation. Glen and I settled in the living room by the fire. I waited until Mrs Kerr had brought our coffee and left.

I walked to the drinking cabinet and poured myself a snifter of brandy. 'Would you like a drink?'

'Whiskey, please.'

I handed Glen his drink, took my seat opposite him, and waited for him to speak. He moved to the edge of the chair, rested his arms on his thighs, and stared down into his whiskey as though the amber liquid held a script.

'I know I've let you down, and I'm sorry. I have thought long and hard as to how we could move forward.'

'Have you?'

Glen looked up at me. I was expecting a retort, but he continued.

'I admit I'd intentionally delayed things, hoping you'd change your mind about running the estate and that we could carry on with our lives in St Andrews.'

Though I had suspected some such scheme, hearing Glen admit it made me want to lean across and strike his face. How dare he assume I would abandon something that meant so much to me, so that we could have a life where he chose? A life that involved me sitting around and waiting for him to throw me crumbs of attention. I stood to leave for I couldn't trust myself, but he held up a hand.

'Please, Mhairi. Let me finish.' He sipped his drink and continued. 'I can see I was wrong, both in making that assumption and the way I went about it.'

I lowered myself onto the chair.

'I've contacted my colleagues at Edinburgh University. They have a project I could work on until the end of this academic year, and after that they'll have a full-time post for me. That means that I'll be able to share my time between the Hall and Edinburgh.'

He was being the voice of reason, and his plan was a compromise I could not disregard. But inside I was despairing. I didn't want him. The hairline fracture that had set in following our honeymoon four years ago had turned into a chasm that could not be bridged. But as I didn't have the courage to tell him the truth, I nodded in agreement, knowing that I'd be bound to hold my side of the bargain.

Glen reached for my hand and led me up the stairs into the bedroom. How could I protest? He was my husband, after all.

I lay there, staring up at the ceiling, my skin crawling with disgust at his touch and all the while hating myself for being such a coward.

Chapter Thirty-One

The next morning, Isabelle awoke with a headache. She'd spent hours tossing and turning, going over the letters she'd found and wondering whether they might be related to the secret Mimi hadn't managed to tell her.

Groaning, she took a paracetamol from her bedside table. Should she get up? She looked at the clock; it was only seven. She picked up Mimi's diary. She may as well see how everything panned out.

Thank you Isabelle for being a real friend…

Isabelle smiled, glad that the new diary had the magic of the first, and that she'd been able to do something for Mimi. As she read on, her heartbeat grew faster. She turned the page and a sense of dread washed over her as she took in Mimi's words.

I don't know how to get myself out of this mess.

She grabbed her pen and began to write.

You're right, this is a mess! But it's not too late to sort it out. I understand Will's been the only one by your side in that horrific time. But Mimi, what is it you want? I can't help feeling that Glen must suspect SOMETHING, don't you think? If I'm honest, I think sooner or later the truth is bound to come out and then what? I can't tell you what to do, but please be brave and think things through.

'Isabelle are you up?'

'Be down in a minute, Mum,' she shouted and put the diary away.

Isabelle found her mother in her usual place at the kitchen table sipping a coffee.

'You look terrible,' said Bonelle.

Charming, Isabelle thought and ignored her. She poured herself a cup of coffee and sat opposite her mum.

Bonelle handed her a Chanel carrier bag. 'Here, I thought you may like this.'

Isabelle opened it and held up the twinset in navy and white. 'That's gorgeous. Thanks, Mum. It'll be perfect for work.' She bent across the table and kissed Bonelle on the cheek.

'Talking of work, have you got a job yet?'

That didn't last long. 'I've got a few things in the pipeline.' The truth was there was only Jonathan's friend Calan left to call.

'I see. Well, you may need to change your plans. I've decided I will go ahead with contesting the will. As a matter of fact, my lawyer is going to write to that Morgan chap sometime today,' said Bonelle, as though she was telling her they'd run out of milk.

Isabelle clutched her cup of coffee in her hand and willed the anger to stay put in the pit of her stomach.

'Isabelle, say something.'

But Isabelle didn't pay her any attention. She knew the moment she opened her mouth she'd no longer be able to control herself. She couldn't even bear to look at her mother right now.

Bonelle raised her voice. 'Isabelle! I'm talking to you?'

'What, Mum?' she snapped. 'What is it you want me to say? Congratulations? Did it even for one moment occur to you how I might feel, knowing that my own mother, who by the way isn't short of money, is trying to snatch away my inheritance?'

Isabelle had the satisfaction of seeing Bonelle look away. Tears of frustration pricked her eyes like needles. She was not going to cry in front of her mum.

'Isabelle—'

'No, Mum.' Isabelle held up her hand. Bonelle clenched her jaw. 'It's enough. *I've* had enough. I've tried to be understanding, tried not to let this come between us. But you know what? I don't care anymore. This is my life, my house, and if you don't like it, tough, *Mum.'* Bonelle flinched. 'Now if you'll excuse me, I have better things to do with my time.'

Isabelle stood and made her way out of the kitchen without a glance at her mother. She ran up the stairs into her room, closed the door and leaned on it. She was buzzing with nerves and excitement. She'd never stood up to Bonelle like this, and she realised that it felt as though she'd finally let go of a dead weight. She sat on the bed and picked up Mimi's diary, then she heard a knock on her door.

'Isabelle, look. I understand you must be upset now but believe me it's for your own good,' he mum said through the door. 'Why is it so hard for you to believe that I'm doing this because I care about what happens to you?' Bonelle's fist banged on the door. 'One day perhaps you'll understand.'

Isabelle didn't answer. She listened to the sound of Bonelle's footsteps fading away down the corridor, then lay on the bed and closed her eyes. She had to calm her nerves.

She woke up with a jolt at the sound of knocking on her door. She rubbed her eyes and looked at the clock. It was eleven.

'Miss Isabelle, are you in there?

Thank God; it's Mrs Murray, she thought. She raised herself and opened the door.

'Sorry, I must have fallen asleep. Is Mum still here?'

'No, Miss. She left an hour ago. Said she'd take the earlier train to London.'

At Isabelle's exhale of relief, Mrs Murray said, 'Why don't you come down and I'll make you a coffee?'

As Isabelle picked up her phone from the bedside table, she saw Mimi's diary and remembered the affair. If it had gone on for a long time, perhaps even years, then maybe her mum had known about it. Was that the problem? She needed to get to the bottom of this.

When she got to the kitchen Mrs Murray put a cup of coffee in front of her and sat down. 'Miss Isabelle, is everything all right?'

'Not really. Mum's being … Mum. Can I ask you something? I found Mimi's diaries.'

Isabelle watched the colour drain from Mrs Murray's face and knew she had the answers, just as Isabelle had thought she would. She ploughed on.

'Do you know who Will is?'

But as the old woman looked up at her, Isabelle's heart sank. The expression in Mrs Murray's eyes told her she'd reached a dead end.

'I can't say. It's not my place, Miss. All I can tell you is that man brought nothing but trouble to this place. I'm sure the Hall will give up its secrets when the time's right. Now, if you'll excuse me.' She pushed away from the table and left the room.

Isabelle rubbed her face. She wasn't sure how much more she could take. The room was closing in on her. She needed to get out. She walked into the grounds and followed the path to the burn.

She sat down on a rock and listened to the sound of blackbirds chirping and the flap of their wings as they dashed in and out of the undergrowth. She watched the rivulets of water wash over the bed of the burn. She and Angus hadn't come here often, only when it was too hot to go to the beach. She almost felt the sensation of the stones under her feet and the water on her legs as they built bridges across the stream.

Her thoughts went back to the argument with Bonelle. Now that her initial elation had gone, a cloak of sadness wrapped itself around her. *What now? Was there a way to come back from here?*

Isabelle knew that Bonelle would never concede. But what about her? Was she ready to let go of her relationship with her mum, however dysfunctional it was? Had it all been worth it? Perhaps she shouldn't have come here. She'd tried her best to honour Mimi's wish and learn more about her family, but it was as if everyone was against her. Her phone buzzed in her pocket, disrupting her reverie.

What now?

'Dr Rosseau? It's Calan McKenzie.'

'Oh, yes, hello,' Isabelle said and crossed her fingers.

'Look, I'm sorry, but there won't be any position available with us.'

'Oh, right. Thanks for letting me know.'

Isabelle stared at the phone. With no job, how was she going to survive? She logged into her bank account and stared. That couldn't be right. She forced herself to focus and examined every transaction. She realised she'd forgotten to take into account the service charge of the flat payable every quarter. She had just enough to scrape by—barely—but if she didn't return to work in London she'd be broke.

Isabelle shouted with frustration, jumped from her perch, and ran towards the Hall. She raced up to her bedroom, threw the suitcase on the bed, opened the wardrobe, and started ripping the clothes off their hangers. She'd had enough of everything. Her life was a mess. She couldn't remember the last time she'd felt so out of control. She slid onto the floor with her back resting against the wardrobe, put her head in her hands and let the tears of frustration run freely.

She had no idea how long it had been. She looked out of the window and saw dusk was falling. She dragged herself up, took out her phone, and checked the time. She put her hand on the wall to let the dizziness pass and remembered she hadn't eaten anything. She looked around her at the disorder that looked like someone else had created it. Then she headed for the kitchen and made herself some toast and a coffee. She needed to function if she were to sort out this chaos.

At least there was one person she knew would be there for her. She took out her phone and FaceTimed Charlie.

'Hey, sweetie, what's wrong?'

Her voice quivered. 'Oh Charlie, it's been so dreadful since you left...' She clenched her jaw and swallowed the lump in her throat.

'Hey, hey, just take your time and tell me what's happened.'

Isabelle cleared her throat. 'Where do you want me to begin? I found out Mimi had a full-blown affair, but it's not just that. I think reading about her life has been affecting me more than I realised. I've been trying to find out who the guy is, and Mrs Murray admitted she knows but wasn't going to tell me.'

'Bloody hell, Isabelle.'

Isabelle put up her hand. 'Wait, it gets better. Bonelle's going ahead with contesting the will. I told her finally what I thought of her and basically threw her out—'

'Woohoo, I love it!' Charlie grinned. 'Well done you.'

'I know, but...' Isabelle chewed the inside of her mouth.

'What? You're not regretting it already are you? Listen, this has been a long time coming. Ever since I've known you, you've been complaining about the way your mum treats you.'

'I know, I know. But what now? Believe me, I know my mum, and there'll be a comeback.'

'Well, then you cross that bridge when you'll come to it.'

'Isabelle shrugged and looked down.

'Isabelle, it'll be fine, honestly.'

'It's not that. I'm ... I think maybe it was a mistake coming here.'

'Don't you go doubting yourself because you had a fall out with your mum.'

'It's not just that, Charlie. I'm broke. I've been waiting to hear from this job, but the guy called earlier and said they don't need anyone. So you see...'

'Crikey. It's been hell of a day. Poor you. So what are you going to do?'

'There's only one thing I *can* do. Come back to London.'

'Oh sweetheart, I'm sorry. I mean I'll love to have you back, but I wish things had worked out.'

Isabelle nodded and looked away.

'Isabelle, look at me. I'm here. Needless to say, you can stay with me for as long as you want. If you needed, I could lend you some money to tie you over.'

'I know, but—'

'No buts. Just get yourself here. I should be out of work by the time your train gets in tomorrow. I'll come and meet you at Kings Cross. What d'you say?'

'Thank you, Charlie, you're amazing. I don't know what I'd do without you.'

'That's what I'm here for. If the shoe were on the other foot, you'd do the same for me. Now go and get some sleep. And Isabelle, I promise you'll be fine, sweetie.'

Isabelle set to work. She emailed a few recruitment agencies in London, then as she closed the laptop, her eyes fell on Mimi's diary. No, she couldn't face Mimi. She knew enough of her secret to put the rest together herself. And though one part of her felt she was letting Mimi down, the other part of her couldn't help blaming Mimi for the mess in her life and all over an affair that might have been a big deal back then but wasn't now. No, she just needed to focus on sorting out her life rather than be distracted by Mimi's love triangle.

Chapter Thirty-Two

Mimi, Christmas 1956

It was the day of the annual Christmas party and the preparations for the celebrations were well underway.

'Hey, you! Stop that racket now!' I heard Glen bellowing and rushed into the hallway.

'What's going on?'

Mr Murray, the gardener, and his helpers all seemed rooted to the spot, as they loaded the tables with bottles of whiskey and wine.

'How am I supposed to concentrate with all this noise going on?' shouted Glen.

'Please continue, Mr Murray,' I said. I gestured to Glen and headed into the living room.

'This has to stop; there's never any peace in this place,' he yelled, waving his hand in the air.

'In case you've forgotten, *this*' I copied his gesture indicating the space, 'is a working estate. It was *you* who insisted on having your study on the ground floor. The Hall is big enough for you to choose another room. And I don't like the way you speak to my staff and treat them.'

'Don't you—'

'No! This is not the first time you've disrespected them, and I'm tired of making excuses for your quite frankly unacceptable behaviour. These people have been taking care of the estate and my family for years, and my loyalty lies with them.'

'How dare you tell me how to speak to my servants,' he shouted.

'Please remember,' I said, keeping my anger under wraps. '*I'm* the mistress of Lanesbrough Estate, and *I'm* the one running it. These people are *my* staff.'

'Don't be ridiculous.'

'No, Glen. You chose to pursue your career, and therefore just as I don't tell you what to do in Edinburgh, you're in no position to dictate what happens on the estate.'

I had turned to leave when Glen's laughter halted me in my tracks.

'I didn't think you'd be quite this naive, Mhairi. Don't forget I'm your *husband,* and as such half of the estate *and* your precious Hall belongs to me. *I* just let you run it.'

My heart froze, and for a moment I thought my lungs had collapsed because I couldn't breathe. It was as though I had lost command over my body. I was still standing there when Glen passed me on his way out of the room. Was it true? Did half of the estate really belong to him? But as the enormity of his revelation hit me, anger replaced numbness. How could I have been so stupid? If only Alasdair was still alive.

The sound of the guests arriving tore me out of my ruminations. I looked in the mirror above the mantlepiece, straightened my shoulders and went to face the guests. As I stood there studying the sea of faces looking up at me, Glen joined me. I stiffened in response. Tears stung my eyes at the thought that Alasdair should have been here with me. But these people were my responsibility now, and I knew I couldn't jeopardise losing the Hall.

I cleared my throat. 'As you all know, the last six months since the tragic death of my beloved brother have not been easy, and I know how much we all miss him.' I paused to clear the tightness in my chest. 'I want to thank you all for your patience and your tireless support of me and Lanesbrough Estate. I couldn't have made it without you. To Lanesbrough Estate and to you.'

I raised my glass to the chorus that followed my cheers.

'To Miss Mimi,' said a voice in the crowd and another cheer went up.

My eyes locked on Will's, and I raised my glass to him, not daring to think where I'd be without him.

'A very touching speech,' said Glen, his sarcasm turning each word to poison.

He walked away, leaving me to entertain our guests alone.

It was a week after New Year that I made my way to the stables, unable to contain my joy at spending some time alone with Will. The landscape was covered in frost, which glistened in the sunlight like crystal.

'How are you holding up?' he asked as we led the horses onto the bridleway.

I sighed. 'I don't know. I sometimes wonder what happened to my life. Where did I go so wrong?'

Though I had asked myself this question so many times, I had yet to find an answer. But the one thing I knew was that if I'd taken my time to get to know Glen as Isabelle had suggested, instead of being swept off my feet, my life would be different indeed.

'Don't be too hard on yourself, Mimi. None of us knows how things end up working out sometimes.'

'Yes, you're right. Not that it matters anyway; at least we have each other.'

We hacked back in silence, each engrossed in our own world. As we arrived at the stables, Will got off his horse and helped me down from Rionnag. His hands remained on my waist, and he pulled me to him. I closed my eyes at the touch of his lips as sweet as honey on mine when he was yanked away from me. I opened my eyes just as Glen's fist landed on Will's jaw.

'You bastard!' shouted Glen.

He shoved Will in the chest with such force that he stumbled over a bale of hay and fell onto the ground. My heart was racing so hard I feared I'd have an attack. Yet I was incapable of any movement. I watched as though trapped in a nightmare as Glen bent over Will, grasped his collar with one hand, and was about to land another punch when something in me snapped into life.

I ran towards Glen and pulled on his arm with all my might, trying to get him off Will.

'Glen, please, please stop.' I begged.

Tears of helplessness were running down my face. The time seemed to stand still for an eternity.

'You're not worth it,' Glen literally spat at Will. 'I want you off this estate, and don't you ever dare come back.'

He grabbed my arm and dragged me out of the door, his fingers digging into my flesh.

'You're hurting me; let me go,' I shouted, and tried to pull my arm away. To my embarrassment, I saw Mr Williams running towards us.

'Miss Mimi, are you all right?'

'It's none of your business, man. Now, leave us alone,' said Glen.

However, that didn't deter Mr Williams who stood his ground. I was touched to the core by his loyalty and was reminded of my position. Yes, on the surface of it, I was wrong, but I was not going to let any man treat me this way and certainly not in public.

'Enough,' I shouted.

I don't know whether Glen realised the humiliation he was subjecting us to or whether he felt outnumbered, but he released my arm.

'We're not finished,' he sneered at me and walked away.

'Thank you, Mr Williams.' I was relieved the ghastly scene was over.

'Is he in the stables?' he asked.

I nodded and watched him go. My nerves were in shreds. I hugged myself to stop the shaking and dragged myself back to the Hall. I went into the living room and poured a measure of brandy. It didn't matter that it was mid-morning. I had just taken a sip when Glen marched in, banging the door behind him.

'How long has this been going on?' he barked.

My heart sank, and I knew I must gather myself. Not trusting my legs to hold me, I lowered myself on to the edge of the sofa and willed myself to speak but was unable to form the words.

'I asked you a question?' he shouted in my face, making me jump.

'There's nothing going on, it was just a kiss.' Even I wouldn't have believed it myself.

'Don't patronise me, Mhairi. I'm not as ignorant as you'd like to think.'

He began pacing up and down in front of me. My head was spinning, and I felt sick. I don't know which one of us I resented more in that moment. He came to a halt in front of me. His fingers bore into my cheeks, forcing me to lift my head and look at him.

'I said how long?' He emphasised each word as though spelling out a word to a child.

'I don't know.'

I looked away. His laugh made me flinch.

'I see. Well, let me jog your memory. You think you're very clever, don't you? Or perhaps you think I'm blind or stupid? Well, you're wrong.' He screamed the words at me. 'You think I didn't see you that night back in August?'

The words made my blood freeze, and I stared at him in disbelief. Satisfied at my reaction, Glen pushed on.

'I didn't say anything, because I held myself partly responsible for not having supported you right after your brother died. Why do you think I came up with this arrangement?'

I lowered my head.

'I thought once I was around more often, you'd tire of your sordid little game. But I should have known better than to trust you.'

The last sentence was almost a whisper. As though he was at last defeated, Glen left the room.

I couldn't bear it. How would I cope without Will? I ran up the stairs to my room, grabbed my diary, and reached out to my friend.

> **You're right; this is all a mess! But it's not too late to sort it out. I can't help feeling that Glen must suspect something. Don't you think?**

I shook my head at my own stupidity.

> **Mimi, what is it you want?**

Her words reverberated in my head. But fear and frustration clouded my mind.

*Oh God, Isabelle, it is too late. I've been naïve and blind.
I wish I had your foresight. Life's been so unbearable since
Alasdair's death and without realising it, I created my own
fantasy world with Will. Now, I have no choice but to face the
reality of my situation. I have to make a decision, but I don't
know if I have the courage and strength to do what would make
me truly happy. Choosing Will means I could lose the Hall.
That's a price I don't know if I could bear to pay. Please help me
get out of this nightmare.*

It was after lunch the next day. I was sitting at my desk staring
out of the window. My eyes hurt from all the crying as my gaze
swept over the grounds buried under the cloak of snow. I didn't
know if Will had already taken his leave, and my heart broke at
the thought that I may not be able to say goodbye. A knock on
the door jolted me out of my rumination. Fear gripped me at the
thought it was Glen. I held my breath with a mixture of weariness
and trepidation.

'Miss Mimi?'

I don't think I'd ever felt so relieved at the sound of Annie's
voice. 'Come in, Annie.'

She entered and held out a letter. 'This is for you.'

'Who gave this to you?' I asked. But Annie turned around
and left the room.

I turned the envelop in my hand but there was no writing
on it. I wondered if it was from Glen, and anxiety churned my
insides again as I opened the missive.

21 January 1957

My dearest Mimi,

    *Last night I couldn't find sleep and when I was finally spirited away,
I had the most dreadful nightmare…*

As soon as I finished reading, I grabbed my cape, ran out of
the door, and headed into the snow. I ran as fast as I could and
arrived at the cave panting for breath. In an instant Will was by

my side. We hung on to each other. I breathed in his scent and tried to memorise the imprint of his body on mine as the sound of the waves crashing against the rocks surrounded us.

'Are you all right? I was worried about you,' Will said at last.

I broke into a sob.

'I know, my love.' He kissed my head and stroked my hair. 'Yesterday, not long after you'd gone, Da came into the stables and told me in no uncertain terms that unless I was prepared to ruin your reputation, I should leave.'

I looked at him in disbelief.

Will's eyes teared up. 'My bags are packed; my train goes in a couple of hours.'

'You can't do this,' I cried and clung onto him.

His arms closed around me. I could hear his heartbeat pounding his chest. He peeled me off him and held me by the shoulders.

'I love you, Mimi. Please come with me.'

I shook my head. This was all happening too fast. How could I leave the Hall in Glen's clutches?

'I can't,' I whispered and closed my arms around him as though trying to absorb the essence of him.

'Then I must go. Just remember I'll always love you.'

He kissed me one last time, and with that he disappeared from my life.

Chapter Thirty-Three

'Good afternoon, Dr Rousseau. Mr Morgan is expecting you.' The receptionist nodded towards Mr Morgan's office.

'Dr Rousseau, it's a pleasure to see you again,' the lawyer greeted her and gestured towards the chairs.

Isabelle took the same seat as last time. It felt like déjà vu, except to her relief, Bonelle was absent this time. At the thought of her mum, anger flared up in her chest.

'Mr Morgan, I'm leaving the Hall,' Isabelle said before she lost her courage.

'I must admit I wasn't expecting that. May I ask what brought about your decision?' He cocked his head.

Isabelle clasped her hands in her lap. 'It's not a specific reason. More like a combination of things. My mum has decided to contest the will. And I don't know what my position would be anyway.'

Mr Morgan nodded. 'I'm afraid Mrs Smeaton's lawyers have written to me by way of introduction and setting out her intentions.'

Isabelle frowned. 'So nothing's happened yet? I mean court dates and so on?'

'I haven't received any formal applications yet. But I'll be happy to act on your behalf if you wish.'

'Thank you.' Isabelle stood.

'Forgive me, but I don't see why you should wish to leave the Hall though?'

She sat back down again. 'Well, as I said that's one of the reasons. The other is my finances. I haven't been able to find work.'

And then there was of course Mimi's diaries and secret, she thought and looked down onto her lap.

'I understand. I just wished you'd come to me sooner. Because I think I have a solution to at least one of your problems.'

Isabelle raised her head. 'You do?'

'Can I make a suggestion? Why don't you just take a week or two off, go somewhere to get some space.'

'But—'

'Then come back, and I'll tell you my plan. If you still feel the same then I'll promise I'll accept your decision.'

He held her gaze. Isabelle shrugged. She could go to France for a few days. In fact it wouldn't be a bad idea to get her father's take on everything.

'Perhaps you're right.'

'Excellent. In the meantime, please don't hesitate to get in touch if you need anything.'

Isabelle left with Mr Morgan's advice on her mind, so she took out her phone and called her father.

'Isabelle,' Jean-Francois answered after a few moments. 'Is everything all right, ma petite?'

Isabelle grimaced and ignored the question. 'Papa, is it okay if I came for a visit?'

'Of course, chérie. We'd love to see you.'

'Thanks Papa. I'll message you with the flight—'

'No, I'll send you an e-ticket. Just keep an eye on your emails.'

'No, Papa, I can—'

'It's fine. I know you're a grown-up woman, but you're also my daughter, and I'd like to treat you.'

'Thanks Papa.' Isabelle hung up, grateful that her father hadn't given in, seeing she was broke.

Next Isabelle called Charlie, but it went to voicemail. 'Hey lovely, I'm going to France tomorrow morning. I'll explain everything when we speak. Thanks again for being so amazing.'

There was one more phone call to make. Isabelle brought up the contact and clicked on the number.

'Hello, Belle. That's a nice surprise.'

Her heart skipped at the sound of Angus's voice. 'I'm going to France for a few days. I thought I let you know in case…'

'I thought you bolted on me?' Angus laughed.

Heat burned Isabelle's cheek. 'Don't be silly.'

'Just pulling your leg. I wish I could come with you.'

'Why don't you?' Isabelle blurted before she could stop herself.

'You know, this and that.'

Yes, Alex. 'I'll call you when I'm back.'

Back at the Hall, there was no sign of Mrs Murray. When Isabelle walked into her room, her eyes fell on Mimi's diary. Poor Mimi, she didn't have anyone to help her.

'Except me.'

Isabelle just couldn't disappear on her. She picked up the diary.

Her heart sank as she read about Glen uncovering the affair and that he'd known all long. Though Mimi hadn't made the best choices, Isabelle couldn't help feeling angry at Glen. How dare he threaten to take away the Hall from Mimi? She'd love to give him a piece of her mind. She picked up her pen to write when she saw a shadow cross the page.

'Jesus Christ! What the…?'

Isabelle dropped the diary as if it had burned her. Her heart raced as she watched the words appear on the page.

> *I had just changed into my nightgown and was brushing my hair when Glen came in. I watched in the mirror as he approached. Then he grabbed me by the hair, so that I had no choice but to bend my head back.*
>
> *'You're hurting me,' I shouted, as my heart began to hammer in my chest.'*

That was Mimi's writing. How was this possible? Was she dreaming? Isabelle rubbed her hands over her face and opened her eyes again, but the words continued appearing right in front of her as though by an invisible hand. She focused on the content.

I opened my mouth to scream at him, but he silenced me with a kiss. My teeth cut into my lips. Pain and a metallic taste filled my senses. My stomach heaved from the smell of whiskey and repulsion. He led me to bed by my hair and threw me onto it.
'You're hurting me, Glen. Stop!'

'You bastard, let her go!' Isabelle screamed and pounded her fist on the bed.

But he ignored my remonstrations. He held me down with one hand and with the other pulled down his trousers, forcing himself on me. Pain shot through me, but the more I struggled the harder he pressed down on me.

'No! Please, dear God, stop.'

In the end I just lay there, closed my eyes, and let the tears wet my face. By the time he finished, I'd died on the inside.

Isabelle broke into a sob. She had to do something. She wiped her face with the back of her hand and put her pen to paper.

Mimi, my lovely Mimi, it's Isabelle. I'm here.

Isabelle? Is that really you? How is this possible?

Yes, it's me. I don't know and I don't care. All that matters is you.

It's too late, Isabelle. I can't carry on.

Mimi, you must listen to me. You're in shock and traumatised.

Isabelle blinked away the tears. She had to push her own feelings away if she were to help Mimi. She had to think of her as a victim of domestic abuse like the patients she used to see and not her grandmother.

I just feel numb. I can't even cry.

We need to make sure you're safe. Where are you right now?

I'm in my room. The door is locked.

Is there a phone?

There's one in the hallway and one in my study.

I want you to call for Annie. Tell her to ring the doctor and the police. You have to tell them what happened and have him removed from the Hall.

I'm not sure I can do that. He threatened to take the Hall away from me.

For crying out loud, Mimi, the man is a violent rapist! An abuser! You can't just let him get away with it. The Hall's been in your family for four-hundred years. Have you even spoken to your solicitor to see if he has a claim over it?

Her answer came after a lengthy pause.

No, I haven't.

Okay, you can do that later. But for now just do what I asked.

Isabelle didn't want to let Mimi go. She wished she could reach through the pages, hold her in her arms, and tell her everything would be all right.

I love you, Mimi. Now call for Annie.

She put her hands over her face and let the tears of sadness and helplessness wrack her body.

Chapter Thirty-Four

Mimi, March 1957

'Miss Mimi, have you seen the doctor?' asked Mrs Kerr one day after I'd rushed to the bathroom again after eating a bite of toast.

Since Will had walked out of my life, I'd been feeling plagued by nausea, unable to keep anything down. At night I'd cry myself to sleep. Missing Will was like a tumour consuming every ounce of my strength.

'I'm fine, Mrs Kerr. I don't need to bother the doctor.' After all, there was nothing any doctor could do for heartbreak.

'Miss, if I can speak freely?'

'Yes.'

'I think you're with child, Miss.'

At Mrs Kerr's words the room began to spin around me. I lifted myself off the chair, ignored Mrs Kerr's side glance and dragged myself to the study and sat there staring into the space. Was I really pregnant? There was no point thinking about it until I found out for sure.

'Miss Mimi, Mr Morgan is here for you.' Mrs Kerr's words brought me back to the present and another problem.

I hadn't called the police or the doctor as Isabelle had suggested. I couldn't have faced the shame it would have brought on the Lanesbroughs. I just hoped Mr Morgan had good news for me.

'Please take a seat, Mr Morgan. Mrs Kerr, could you please bring us some refreshments.'

'No, thank you. I had a coffee before I sat off,' he said and opened his briefcase.

I sat at the edge of my seat, wringing my hands in my lap, and trying to calm my racing heart.

'I have looked into the matter and can confirm that your husband would have no claim over the Lanesbrough Estate.'

I nodded. How relieved I was to hear that my beloved Hall was safe.

'However, it's taken this long to work out whether the estate would survive after he'd claim half of your assets, which I can assure you he would.'

Nausea stirred in my stomach, and I leaned back in my chair.

'These are the properties that we finalised in your name after Master Alasdair's death, which was after your marriage. It is the proceeds of these that has been supporting the estate.'

Bile rose up in my throat, and it took me all my will not to retch in front of Mr Morgan.

'In short, it's not impossible, but I'm not positive that the estate would survive intact. I'm sorry.'

'Excuse me,' I said and dashed to the bathroom.

My last hope was gone.

'There's no doubt you're with child. The baby's likely due sometime in September,' said the doctor as he finished examining me the next day.

'But how can that be? I had my monthly just a few weeks ago.'

'Some women continue their menstruation throughout the pregnancy. I can assure you, you're pregnant. My congratulations.'

He turned his back on me and left the room.

I lay on the bed, staring up at the examination light. I'd heard that women who were expecting should feel delighted, but I felt only relief that I'd continued fulfilling my duties as a wife, even though every moment of it had felt like violation.

But that left one question: was this baby Glen's or Will's?

A shudder ran the length of my spine at the ramifications, and heat rose into my chest and throat, making me want to throw up.

I put my hand over my mouth and forced myself to regulate my breathing. It seemed an eternity before the tremor and nausea let go of my body and I could formulate thoughts with some lucidity.

Both men had similar colouring, but their features were miles apart. What if the baby looked like Will? The coward in me was petrified at the idea of the scandal, but my courageous side rejoiced at the idea that this charade would be over once and for all if it did. I couldn't see Glen raising another man's child.

Maybe Glen would want a divorce? It was frowned upon but perhaps this was a blessing in disguise after all. If that happened, I'd be free to be with Will and our baby.

But then I remembered Mr Morgan's words. *I'm not positive that the estate would survive it intact.* I needed to talk to Isabelle. She always knew what to do.

Back at the Hall I almost walked into Glen as I opened the front door. He blocked my path.

'Where have you been?'

'I'll tell you over dinner.' I said and looked down trying to hide my irritation at his early arrival.

'You've got yourself another lover?' he taunted.

'Don't be so uncouth.'

'Then tell me, woman,' he raised his voice.

'I'm with child.'

I saw something cross his features. Shame? Guilt? I pushed my way past him and went straight to my room. I locked the door as I've been doing whenever Glen was in the house ever since that night.

I took out my diary and flicked through it, my eyes tearing up as I read our conversation all those weeks ago. And I realised just how much I'd come to rely on this stranger who like an angel appeared in my life out of nowhere to support and guide me.

> *Darling Isabelle, you're the most wonderful friend anyone could wish for. I followed your advice and spoke to my lawyer but I'm afraid there's not much hope. And now that I'm pregnant the situation is even more complicated. Please keep writing to me. You're the only one I've got. And Isabelle, thank you for everything.*

Chapter Thirty-Five

'You're quiet,' said Jean-Francois.

Isabelle turned her attention from the French countryside and looked at her father. 'Sorry, Papa. There's so much going around in my head. I don't know if I can stick it out at the Hall. Even if I wanted, I'm completely broke.'

'I know it's been tough on you, ma petite. But don't let money stand in your way. What I've got is yours and Emilie's.'

'Thank you, Papa. It means the world.' She squeezed his shoulder. 'I may well have to ask you for a loan if it comes to it.'

'I'm glad to hear. Just don't be too hard on yourself. I know you're trying to do right by Mimi, but in the end you have to think of yourself.'

Jean-Francois patted her arm as they reached the village of Saint-Haon-le-Châtel and drove the alleys that wound up the hill. The sixteenth century manor that her father had restored to its former glory came into the view, making Isabelle smile.

As soon as they entered the house, Emilie ran towards them squealing with joy. Her curls bounced around her face with every step. Dressed only in her nappy and her top, she looked adorable.

Emilie opened her arms and on cue, Jean-Francois bent down and picked her up. Isabelle greeted her in French, but unlike last time, Emilie gave her a smile that melted Isabelle's heart. All she wanted to do was to reach for her sister and gave her a hug, but she didn't want to push her luck. So she just kissed her on the cheek, which Emilie wiped away with the back of her arm, making Isabelle and Jean-Francois laugh.

'Patience, ma chérie. She'll come around,' said Jean-Francois.

'I know, Papa. I've promised myself we'd never again be strangers to each other. I've lost one sister; I'm going to hold on to the one I've got.'

Isabelle stiffened at the sight of Aurelie as though by reflex but remembering their last encounter and Aurelie's remarks, she relaxed.

After lunch, they settled by the pool.

'Could you watch Emilie please?' Aurelie asked. 'I just need to make a call.'

Isabelle saw that Emilie was sitting on the grass not too far away, playing with her doll. Her phone pinged and there was a message from Charlie.

Sorry missed your call, sweetie. Just get in touch if you need anything. Catch up soon x

She was about to put the phone away when a message from Angus came through.

Hope you arrived all right x

Her mind went back to the Hall, and whether she should leave. But that would mean leaving Angus behind too when she'd only just found him. She wondered how he and Alex were getting on. And what of poor Mimi? A pang of guilt hit her. How could she have contemplated giving up the Hall when Mimi's been through hell and back to keep it. She had to read the diary as soon as she could.

The sound of a splash brought her out of her reverie. She looked around and couldn't see Emilie anywhere. She jumped off the sunbed, knocking it over and ran towards the pool. Her heart pounded as she tried not to let thoughts of her twin penetrate her mind. But she couldn't stop the image of Chloe, in the water—

Emilie jumped out of the pool, running towards Isabelle, and pressed her cold, wet body against her. Isabelle did her best not to recoil from Emilie's embrace as she was engulfed with the feel of Chloe's wet body, which had remained cold, no matter how hard Isabelle had tried to breathe life into her.

And even though she hated to think of it, that day forced itself into her mind. Every afternoon she and Chloe watched a Disney movie whilst Bonelle had a rest. To avoid arguing, the rule was for each to take turns at choosing a film. That afternoon, Isabelle had chosen *The Jungle Book*.

'I don't want to watch this,' said Chloe. *'It's boring; there's no princess.'*

'Chloe, stay here. You know Maman doesn't want us to go outside when she sleeps. You'll get us into trouble.'

But Chloe had only shrugged and left the room. Secretly, Isabelle had been pleased that she could watch her cartoon in peace without Chloe whining every five minutes. At some point Isabelle thought she'd heard Chloe calling her, but she didn't care. Chloe was probably just bored again and wanted her to come out so they could play.

Sometime later when the cartoon had finished, Isabelle switched off the TV and went out to search for her sister.

Chloe! Chloe!'

She called as loudly as she dared, not wanting to wake up her maman, but she got no reply. She walked across the lawn and towards the swimming pool.

'There you are,' she said, watching Chloe lying on her back in the middle of the pool, looking up into the sky. 'Chloe! Stop being silly. Maman will wake up any minute.'

But Chloe ignored her and carried on staring into the sky.

Isabelle stepped out of her of dress, walked into the pool, and swam towards Chloe. Her heart was beating her chest. She reached for Chloe's leg, but Chloe was still. She swam closer and saw Chloe's lips were the colour of the plums on the trees and her face looked like a doll's. Isabelle's chest tightened, and her eyes filled with tears.

'Chloe, Chloe, please say something.'

Isabelle shook her by the shoulders and started to sob. From somewhere in the depths of her mind, she remembered what her father had shown them to do over and over again, if one of them got into trouble in water. She put one arm around Chloe's waist and pulled her to the edge of the pool. She sat on the steps and one by one she climbed out, on her bum, with Chloe on top of her.

She wriggled out from under her sister, put her hands on her knees, and took deep breaths. It was like someone was pounding a hammer on her chest, but it was coming from inside. She pressed her lips over Chloe's. The waxiness of them almost made her sick. She ignored the feeling and started breathing life into her as her tears merged with the drops of water on Chloe's face.

'Ow, ow, Elle.'

Isabelle jolted at the sound of Emilie's voice and loosened her grip.

'Sorry, ma choupette.'

She stroked her sister's arm. She saw Aurelie approach and wiped the tears away just in time, or so she thought.

'Here you go.' Aurelie gave her a glass of wine before sitting down next to her, then said to her daughter, 'Go and find Papa and get changed.'

Isabelle watched her sister skip indoors and took a sip of her wine to steady her nerves.

'*Alors*, what's happening? You're white as these tiles.' Aurelie tapped her foot on the ground. She reached and held Isabelle's hand. 'You're shaking.'

'I'm fine. Thanks.' Isabelle looked down.

'Of course, you're not. I can see that.'

Isabelle remembered her resolve again. She steadied her breathing and looked at Aurelie. 'I... I thought Emile was drowning just now, and I had a flashback of Chloe.'

'I know. Your father told me just what a brave little girl you were. It must have been so traumatising for you.' Aurelie squeezed her hand. 'I'm sure you've been told this before, but you mustn't punish yourself. It was an accident.'

Isabelle realised she'd never empathised with little Isabelle. Instead, she'd punished her—meaning herself—at every opportunity.

Aurelie cocked her head. 'But that's not all is it?'

Isabelle sighed. 'No, my life's turned upside down since Mimi died. I've been reading her diaries, and it's horrible what she'd been through.'

An image of Mimi being raped flashed in her mind and shiver ran through her. Aurelie put her arm around Isabelle's shoulder.

'I'm sorry; I can see how much you care about her.'

Isabelle tucked her hair behind her ear. 'And then there's my mum. She wants to take my inheritance.'

Isabelle saw Aurelie's mouth hang open and laughed.

'*Ça, alors!* That's quite a story. But that's family for you. Sometimes, it's very hard to understand why people do what they do.'

'What about your own family?'

Isabelle realised she knew next to nothing about Aurelie. She noticed Aurelie's faraway look as she sipped her wine like she was engrossed in a movie. After a while Aurelie cleared her throat and looked up at her.

'I was lucky. Papa and Maman were good people. But they never should have had me.'

Whatever Isabelle had been expecting, it wasn't this.

'My parents were a very wealthy young couple and what you English call socialites. The château was always full of guests, or empty because Papa and Maman were holidaying with friends. I don't think I have any memories with just the three of us as a family.'

Isabelle could almost feel the sadness in Aurelie's voice. Her childhood seemed even lonelier than her own.

'Of course, I had the best of everything growing up. Even as an adult, Papa gave me a big flat in Paris. I have a trust fund I could live off for two lifetimes.'

Aurelie shrugged her shoulders in resignation, looked at Isabelle and burst into laughter. 'Oh Isabelle, your face is a picture.'

Isabelle's face was burning. She realised her jaw had literally dropped and clamped it shot.

'I'm sorry. I—'

'Didn't know?'

Isabelle nodded.

'Don't worry, you were not the only one thinking I married Jean-Francois for his money. It's the obvious cliché, and no one ever says anything; it's all just, how do you say—implied?'

Isabelle wished she hadn't been one of those people. 'Yes. That must have been hurtful for you.'

'Of course, but the truth is I always dreamed of my own little family with someone who wasn't just after *my* money or because my parents were glamorous.'

Isabelle shook her head at the irony of it all.

'When I met Jean-Francois, he was just so full of life but so, tranquil, calm with it. There was no bitterness or anger, even when life hadn't been kind to him.'

'Yes, you're right. Papa is very special.'

'You should have heard the way he talked about you. Mon Dieu, there was so much love and pride.'

Isabelle blinked to shy away the tears.

'And that's when I knew he was the one. Perhaps now you understand why I don't mind he is much older than me.' Aurelie smiled and stood. 'I'll go and see what that little madame is up to.'

Isabelle watched her go and a flicker of hope flared in her chest. If she'd managed to put aside her differences with Aurelie, perhaps one day she could do the same with her mother.

Isabelle reached into her handbag for Mimi's diary. She hoped Mimi had left Glen by now. But as she read on, her body tensed up. That bastard had gotten away with it. She balled her fist. She could punch his lights out. She turned the page and groaned as she went over the solicitor's advice. What a bummer.

'Good God, no.'

She cupped her hand over her mouth as she read Mimi was pregnant and didn't know who the father was. DNA testing wouldn't be available, but what about blood types? They would have to wait until the baby was born and then it would only be conclusive if they all happened to have different blood types.

As a doctor she had a fairly good idea. She rooted in her handbag for a pen and began to scribble.

Mimi, it's unlikely that the baby is Glen's! You've been married for almost two years, and nothing. You've been with Will for only a few months, and now you're pregnant. It must be Will's baby.

Isabelle had another thought. Did Bonelle know? Was that the reason for the acrimony between mother and daughter. She shook her head. She had to focus on Mimi.

More importantly, you have got to keep working on leaving Glen. I know you don't want risk losing the estate, but you have to try.

Chapter Thirty-Six

Mimi, September 1957

'Mrs Kerr! Annie!' I screamed in pain.

Annie rushed in. 'Miss Mimi, are you all right?'

'I need to get to the hospital. I think the baby is coming. Has Mr Smeatson arrived yet?'

'No Miss, I'll go and fetch Mr Williams.'

Annie rushed out of the door as Mrs Kerr came in.

'Now, Miss, there's no reason to panic. Just breathe in and out, nice and steady.'

She put an arm around my waist as we made our way outside, where Annie helped lower me into the car. I gasped as I twisted to get my legs in. To my relief though I saw Mr Williams get in the driver's seat.

'You'll be fine Miss. We'll be there in no time.'

'Mrs Kerr, call Mr Smeatson please,' I said as we set off.

'I'll stay here until your husband comes, Miss,' said Mr Williams half an hour later, as he handed me over to the nurse.

The irony that this man could be the grandfather of my child did not escape me.

'Just a few more steps, Mrs Smeatson,' said the nurse as she led me onto the ward with one arm around my shoulder.

'Please, call me Mimi.'

I gasped as another stab of pain sliced through me, making me double over with pain. I had almost reached the bed when my water broke, and the heat of embarrassment burnt my cheeks.

'It's all right, just sit here.' The nurse helped me onto the bed. 'We'll sort you out in no time.'

I lay there sucking for air like a bee that couldn't get enough nectar and wishing it was all over. A new voice intruded into my thoughts.

'I'm Janet, and I'll be your midwife.'

I raised my head and said through gritted teeth, 'I'm Mimi.'

'Now, I need you to slow down your breathing, Mimi. Nice deep breaths in and out.' She demonstrated to leave no doubts in my mind. 'Now, open your legs for me, please. This might feel a bit uncomfortable.'

I felt the cold of her hand between my legs and flinched. What if there was something wrong with the baby? A sob choked my throat, as fear and loneliness overwhelmed me.

'You're almost there. Just a few more hours and we can start.'

I wasn't sure I could get through a few more hours.

'Catherine can walk you around, that usually helps to speed things up.'

Hearing the name of my mother brought the tears to my eyes. I wished Mama was here, holding my hand and telling me it all would be fine.

On cue, Catherine laid an arm behind my back. She helped me up, and we began pacing around the room.

I felt like one of the heifers on the estate as I lumbered around and around in circles to the sound of my own groans. The only consolation was that Glen wasn't here. Why couldn't it be Will I was expecting. And then I remembered that Mr Williams must still be waiting outside.

'I think it may be time,' said Janet as she marched into the room.

I lay back on the bed. All I wanted to do was curl up like a foetus. Instead Janet ordered me to hold my legs apart and push. I don't think I'd ever felt pain like this. It was as though someone was playing tug-of-war with my legs, and I feared I'd be torn apart.

'Hold, now push. Good girl.'

I heard Janet's voice through a haze of agony. I was biting so hard on the sheet I'd stuck in my mouth that my jaw hurt. It felt like hours that I'd been lying there, pushing and screaming. My pillow was soaked with tears and sweat. And my whole body was shaking with effort and exhaustion.

'I can't do it anymore,' I cried.

'Come on, Mimi. I can see the head, just a few more pushes.'

I took a deep breath and as I pushed my screams filled the room.

'The baby's here. It's a little girl. Catherine, run for the doctor,' Janet said.

Panic invoked by her words mobilised me, and I raised my head off the pillow.

'Why? What's wrong with my baby? Why isn't she crying?'

'She'll be all right, Mimi. She just got the cord wrapped around her neck. The doctor needs to check her.'

I wailed my fear and despair into the room and bent forward as much as I could. My daughter was looking blue and just lay there as Janet unwrapped the cord from her neck. I couldn't look. I fell back on to the bed. The thought of losing my baby was too much to bear.

Please dear God, save my little girl.

I heard the sound of the door followed by rushing feet, but it was like I had departed this plane. I don't know how long it was but at last my soul returned to my body at the sound of my daughter's cry.

'Here, you can hold her now. She's fine.'

'How?' I asked as if I still couldn't believe my luck.

'All that matters is she's all right.'

Janet placed my daughter wrapped in a blanket in my arms. I stroked her face, still red from her exertions and followed the contours of her features for clues. There was no obvious resemblance yet to either my husband or my lover. I looked into her dark blue eyes, the same as all new-born babies, and sighed. Only time would release me from the torment of not knowing. As if in agreement, my daughter began to wail. I felt a whoosh of something sticky and wet between my legs and gasped.

'What's happening?' I said and tried to look down.

'That must be your placenta,' Jane said, pressing a buzzer.

Catherine was by my side in no time and began to clean me up and change the sheets.

'You need to feed her, love. Here,' said Janet after Catherine left and helped my daughter latch on to my breast.

It was a feeling I had no words to describe as I watched my daughter, though it was an effort to keep my eyes open. I'd just finished feeding when the door opened, and Glen walked in.

'I came as soon as I could,' he said.

He didn't kiss me. Instead, he took the baby and sat on the chair beside the bed.

'Welcome, little Bonelle.' He kissed the baby's forehead.

I sat upright. 'What did you call her?'

'Bonelle, that was my grandmother's name.'

'But I wanted to call her Catherine, after my mother.'

'I don't want to argue with you. Don't you think that after everything I had to put up with, the least you can do is to let me name my daughter?'

I wished I could scream at him *She's not your daughter*, but even if that was true, I knew I wouldn't have the courage to tell him.

The next day, Glen took us home. We had just pulled in front of the Hall, when the door flew open and Mrs Kerr, Annie, and Mrs Quinn rushed out.

'My goodness, isn't she pretty?' said Annie.

'You're a bonny lass.' Mrs Quinn stroked the baby's head.

'Come in, Miss. We don't want the wee lassie catching a cold.' Mrs Kerr took charge and led us in. 'Have you named her, Miss?' she asked as she settled us in front of the fire.

'Yes. She's called Bonelle Catherine.'

Mrs Kerr raised her eyebrow. 'I see.' Was all she said but her back stiffened.

I stroked my daughter's face.

'Mrs Kerr, bring us some tea, will you,' said Glen as he walked in, took Bonelle, and sat opposite me. He kissed her head.

'So, little Bonelle, tomorrow you'll meet your grandparents.'

My heart sank. 'What time will they be arriving?'

'They're not. I told them we'd go to Edinburgh.'

'But Glen, the baby is too young, and in case you've forgotten, I've just given birth. Why can't they come and visit?'

He looked up at me and fixed me with his gaze. 'Listen to me, Mhairi. I think I've been patient enough with you. My dad's not feeling well, and I promised Ma she'd see her granddaughter tomorrow. I'm not going to disappoint her.'

'Well you can't take her without me. She'll need her feed. And I'm not coming. I'm afraid Jane will just have to wait.'

I looked away to hide my smile. Glen's laughter echoed in the emptiness.

'You've got to stop underestimating me.'

My heart missed a beat, as I tried to figure out what he meant.

'Ma's already arranged for a wet nurse to come.'

I stared at him wide-eyed. 'You can't be serious?'

'You see Mhairi, you can easily be replaced.'

It felt like my heart was pumping rage rather than blood through my veins. I stood up from my chair when, as if in protest on my behalf, Bonelle began to wail and jolted me back to my senses.

'She's hungry,' I managed to say and without looking at Glen, I took my daughter and left the room.

The next morning, with Annie's help, I dressed. I'd had no more than a few hours' sleep the night before and dread filled me at the thought of having to see Jane. The sound of the car horn put a halt to my rumination.

'We should be there in time for lunch,' said Glen as he drove away.

I nodded and closed my eyes. The next thing I knew, Glen was prising Bonelle out of my arm.

'We're here. You can't fall asleep with the baby in your arms. I had to keep an eye on her all the way.'

He had a point, but I couldn't help feeling as though I was under one of his magnifying glasses.

Jane stood by the open door, her hands clasped in front of her. 'Oh my goodness.'

As soon as Glen reached the top of the stairs, Jane took Bonelle from him. My daughter stirred and started to cry.

'Nah, nah, that's not the way to greet your grandma.'

She put the baby over her shoulder and patted her back. I balled my fists on my side to stop myself from snatching my daughter off her as I followed them into the living room.

'Congratulations, darling Mhairi. I'm glad you and the baby are well,' said Henry and he kissed me on the cheek.

His kindness brought tears to my eyes, and I was glad he was there.

A lunch of sandwiches and cold meat was served on a tray in the living room. I wasn't hungry but I nibbled on a sandwich as I watched Jane cooing over my daughter. She looked up and our eyes met.

'You look dreadful, dear. If you don't mind me saying.'

Henry leaned forward in his seat. 'Jane—'

'You can't be getting much sleep,' she continued as though he hadn't spoken. 'I think you should stay here for the next few months. I could look after Bonelle during the day to give you some respite.'

'Thank you, Jane, but I have Annie at the Hall. And of course, you're welcome to come and stay any time.'

'Ma is right, Mhairi,' said Glen.

'Really, Mhairi. There's no need for a servant to look after my granddaughter. Besides, our friends and relatives here wish to see her. After all, apart from you, she has no other family at the Hall.'

I swallowed and burst into a coughing fit as I choked on my sandwich. Tears ran down my face as I struggled for air. Glen was on my side beating my back with the flat of his hand until the coughing stopped.

'Excuse me,' I said as soon as I caught my breath and rushed out of the door.

In the bathroom, I held the sink with both hands and wailed in despair. I wished someone from my family was alive. But now Bonelle was all I had.

That night back in the safety of my room, I watched her sleep, and my breath caught at the thought that if I was not careful, I could lose her. I took out my diary from the locked drawer in my desk and was disappointed there were no messages from Isabelle. Perhaps she hadn't had a chance. But what if something had happened to her? I couldn't bear the thought. Then I would truly be alone.

Isabelle darling, are you all right? I hope so. I have a beautiful daughter, Bonelle. But already Glen's threatened to take her away from me if I don't do his bidding. Then there's Jane. You should have seen the way she looked at Bonelle, like a hungry wolf that has spotted a lamb. She hates me; she just tolerated me all this time so I can give her a grandchild. I feel powerless against them on my own with no family or friend by my side. I so wish you could be here with me. I'd bet they couldn't intimidate you. But at least you're there for me. Please don't stop writing. I don't think I could get through all this without you.

Chapter Thirty-Seven

As the taxi drove through the gates, a smile spread across Isabelle's face at the sight of the Hall. The grounds were overflowing with blooms in the sunshine. As soon as the taxi drove off, the front door opened, and Mrs Murray rushed out.

'Miss, thank goodness you're back,' she said, twisting a cloth in her hand.

Isabelle frowned. 'Is everything okay, Mrs Murray?'

The housekeeper shook her head. 'No Miss.'

She looked to her right. Isabelle followed Mrs Murray's line of vision and noticed a Land Rover and another car that were almost tucked at the side of the Hall.

'Whose are those?' she asked.

'You'd best come in, Miss.'

Isabelle followed Mrs Murray into the kitchen.

'The kettle is boiled; let me just make you a cuppa.'

Isabelle understood Mrs Murray needed to gear herself up for whatever it was that she was going to reveal. She sat at the table and watched her make the tea.

After she put a cup in front of Isabelle, Mrs Murray said, 'It's your mother, Miss.'

'Mum?' Isabelle leaned forward as though to make sure she'd heard her right.

'Yes, Miss. She rang a few days ago and asked if you were here. I told her you were away, and I didn't know when you'd be coming back.'

Isabelle felt a tinge of guilt at not having told Mrs Murray of her exact plans. She hadn't wanted to worry her until she'd made her decision.

'But she could have called me.' Isabelle took out her phone to check but there was no sign of a missed call or message from Bonelle.

'I can't answer that Miss. I would have let you know, but I didn't have any numbers for you.'

'I'm so sorry. If I'm honest, it hadn't even crossed my mind.'

Mrs Murray nodded. 'I'll understand, Miss. Anyhow, a few hours ago, I hear the door opening and think it must be you. But there was Miss Bonelle with two gentlemen all suited and booted.'

Isabelle's heart sank. 'Who are these people?'

'I couldn't tell you, Miss. Your mother dismissed me.'

The colour rose in Mrs Murray's cheek. Isabelle felt anger rising in her own chest.

'But I stuck around out of sight.' Mrs Murray grinned, and Isabelle couldn't help smiling at the woman's cunningness. 'I overheard them talk about making the Hall into flats or a hotel of some sort.'

Isabelle stood. 'You're not serious.'

'I'm afraid so, Miss. I couldn't bear to hear more so I left them to it.'

'Where are they?'

'In the grounds somewhere.'

Isabelle fizzed with rage as she ran out of the door in search for her mum. She was by the pond when she saw a man with his back to her holding up an iPad, looking like he was taking pictures. Isabelle ran up to him.

'Hey, you! What do you think you're doing?'

The man turned around and looked at Isabelle like she was a rare species he hadn't seen before. Isabelle came to a halt right in front of him.

'I asked what you're doing on my property?'

The man took a step back and cleared his throat. 'I'm here with Mrs Smeatson.' He looked around. 'She can't be far away.'

'*This* is *my* home, and Mrs Smeatson had no right to invite you. Now, I want you to leave.'

'Isabelle! What's the matter with you?' Bonelle shouted.

Isabelle turned and saw her mum with another man in tow march towards her.

'What's the matter with *me*? How dare you bring these people here? This is my home, and I want the lot of you gone.'

'Mrs Smeatson, what's going on here?' asked the man next to her mum.

'Nothing, please wait in the car for me. It's all a misunderstanding.'

'Seriously, Mum? Let me tell you what's going on here.'

'Isabelle—'

'No!' Isabelle held up her hand and held Bonelle's gaze. Then she turned and looked at the man again.

'Mrs Smeatson has brought you here under false pretences.'

The man shot Bonelle a look of distaste, 'I don't appreciate this, Mrs Smeatson. It's highly irregular.'

Her mother didn't even flinch.

'Please accept our apologies.' He nodded in Isabelle's direction. 'Come on, James,' he said to the man with the iPad.

'Don't you ever, *ever*, talk to me like this and especially not in front of other people,' Bonelle hissed as soon as the men had gone.

Isabelle took a step back for fear of slapping her mum in the face. She was shaking with rage.

'I talk to you like this because of the way you treat me, *Mum*. I'm not that little girl, so desperate for your love and approval, that I'd pander to your every wish.'

Isabelle watched her words puncture some of Bonelle's confidence and the tightness in her chest loosened some of its grip.

'I want you to leave.'

'Don't you tell me what to do, Isabelle. I will get my hands on this place, even if it's the last thing I do.'

Isabelle turned and began to walk away. 'You are welcome to try. Until then remember the Hall is *mine*.' She threw the words over her shoulder.

'Isabelle!'

But Isabelle walked on. She took deep breaths with each step to calm her nerves. When she reached the Hall the Land Rover was gone. Mrs Murray rushed into the hallway.

'Are you all right, Miss?'

'Not really, but it's okay. I'll be up in my room.'

She brushed Mrs Murray's arm and walked up the stairs to her room. She closed the door behind her and sat on the bed. She held her head in her hands as though it was too heavy for her neck to support it. Her rage was replaced with numbness, and her mind was dulled except for one thought: she would stay and fight for the Hall.

Was that how Mimi had always felt? Was that why, despite all her unhappiness, she had chosen the Hall? She'd best find out. She reached for Mimi's diary and began to read.

Her eyes teared up as she read about Mimi giving birth all on her own and then thinking her baby was dead. She must have been terrified. As a doctor she knew how traumatising childbirth was, both physically and emotionally, particularly when there were complications, a fact that even now many still wouldn't acknowledge. She couldn't help worrying about Mimi. Just how much more could she take? She still couldn't believe Mimi was only twenty-two. It was madness.

As she read on, her empathy was replaced with fury at Glen and Jane for being so twisted and downright vicious. Maybe that's where Bonelle got it from.

She focused on the diary and frowned. Why was Mimi so sure Bonelle was Glen's? She began to write:

> **Mimi, I wish I was there with you. You're much braver than you think. I think Bonelle is Will's, not Glen's, daughter. Didn't you get my last message?**

She hated Glen for threatening Mimi. She wished she could just tell Mimi to ignore him, but she wasn't sure what the custody laws were at the time. She doubted women had fair treatment in the courts.

> **I can only imagine how hard it must be for you all on your own, but you mustn't let them alienate Bonelle from you. See if you can find out for sure if Will's the**

father. If he is, then you have to leave Glen even if it means downsizing the estate. He and Jane are toxic; the sooner they're out of your life the better. I've had a major fallout with my mum today, but nothing anywhere near as bad as what you've been through. By the way, if I were you, I'd find out Will's whereabouts. This is your chance, Mimi. And remember, I'm here.

On that note, Isabelle's mind went back to her own problems. She picked up her phone and wrote an email to Mr Morgan, asking for an appointment ASAP.

Then she needed to get out. With shaking fingers, she Whatsapped Angus.

Fancy a drink?

Chapter Thirty-Eight

Mimi, November 1960

'Bonelle, darling, come on, we need to go,' I said.
'We goin' to Grandma Jane?'

'No sweetheart, to the doctors. Now come here, put your coat on.'

The last three years of our lives had been hell. Going back and forth to Edinburgh for a few days every week was the only way I could persuade Glen and Jane to let us stay at the Hall.

'But I don't want to go!'

My daughter stomped her feet, and I could see from her pout that she was working herself up to a tantrum.

'We can't see Grandma Jane until you've been to the doctors. And if you're a good girl, we'll go to the sweet shop afterwards.'

Bonelle narrowed her eyes at me, huffed, but let me put her coat on. We walked to the surgery, and ten minutes later were called in to Dr Donaldson's office.

'Ahh, little Bonelle, my favourite patient,' the doctor said and pinched her cheek, which earned him a frown from his favourite patient.

'Come on sit here.' He patted the bed and lifted her up. Then he gave her a doll. 'Now, I want you to look after her for me.'

I was sitting in the chair by his desk, waiting to hear Bonelle's scream as the needle pricked her, when my eyes fell on her open file. Automatically I read the details: name, address, date of birth, blood type. It was as though I was choking. Bonelle was type A.

My blood type was O and Glen's B. I remembered one of my lectures and the professor talking about blood types. There was no chance, that Bonelle's could be A, unless one of her parents had the blood types of AB or A.

Bonelle was Will's daughter.

'My God.'

'Is everything okay Mrs Smeatson?' the doctor asked.

My face was burning. 'Yes, yes.'

He nodded, but I didn't think he was convinced. The last thing I needed was for the doctor to think something was wrong with me. But my mind returned to Will and how happy he'd surely be if he knew he had a daughter—that *we* had a daughter.

I looked at Bonelle and tears stung my lids. *How different our lives could have been, had I been braver*, I thought.

'Look, Mummy.' Bonelle showed me the sweet in her hand.

'Good girl,' I stroked her hair. 'Now let's go.'

I couldn't bear going back to the Hall yet. I needed time to think. We walked around the village for a while and onto the harbour, but I couldn't seem able to calm the jingles of nerves.

Bonelle pulled on my sleeve, bringing me out of my ponderings. 'I'm cold. Can we go home?'

'Yes, come on.'

As we arrived at the Hall, Annie opened the door.

'Darling, why don't go with Annie for some hot chocolate and biscuits? I'll be upstairs.'

Back in my room, I walked across to the window overlooking the garden. The frost covered the ground and the trees. At last I knew. Bonelle was Will's daughter, but if anything, it felt as though my torment had just begun. Should I write to Will and tell him? I didn't even know where he was. And what about Glen and Bonelle? What if he found out? Would he abandon her? She loved him so much.

I wanted to scream.

'Mhairi, are you in here?' Glen opened the door. 'Where have you been?'

'At the doctors.'

He closed the door. 'We need to talk.'

My heart sank. Glen was the last person I wanted to talk to right now.

'What's going on?' I asked, unable to hide the edge in my voice.

'My father died.'

Weak-kneed, I leaned against the window ledge. Poor Henry. 'What? When? How?'

'A heart attack. Ma found him this morning in bed.'

'I'm so sorry, Glen. How terrible. Are you okay?'

'Really, Mhairi, what kind of a stupid question is that? Of course, I'm not okay.'

'You know I didn't mean it like that …'

I looked down on my lap. Why did everything have to be a fight with him?

'Just pack your bags, we need to get going. Annie's getting Bonelle ready.'

'Don't you think it'd be better if you went on your own and Bonelle and I join you for the weekend?' I asked, not daring to say we'd only came back two days ago.

'Ma specifically asked that I bring Bonelle.'

'But—'

'Look, Mhairi, I haven't time for this. You can stay here if you like, but I'm taking Bonelle to see Ma.'

I hated it when Glen took that tone with me. 'Yes, perhaps that's for the best. There's much to do at the Hall. I can join you at the weekend.'

'Suit yourself,' he said and left the room.

You weren't there when my brother died, so why should I be there for you?

I wished I'd come out and said it. But really I was sad for Henry. He was older than Jane, but he hadn't been that old. Now I'd lost my only ally.

My thoughts returned to Will and Bonelle. What was I to do?

'Bye, Annie,' I heard Bonelle say and rushed downstairs.

'Bonelle, come and say goodbye to Mummy.' I hugged her, not wanting to let her go. 'Be a good girl.' I stroked her hair one last time, then I watched her run after her father.

'I'll be in my room, Mrs Kerr,' I said and turned to go upstairs.

'Miss, I'd like a word, if you don't mind.'

'Why, what's the matter?' I asked, but she wouldn't look at me. 'Let's go in here.' I walked into the living room.

'Miss, I know it's not a good time, but it's time I stopped. Mr Kerr and I have decided to make the move to Dumfries. My sister lives there and you know.'

I stared at her. I'd known Mrs Kerr all my life, and now her face was lined with the marks of age. *How many years had she served the Lanesbroughs?* I wondered.

'Of course, I should have thought it was time for you to retire. I'll miss you.'

I hugged her and as I held her, I no longer could hold back the tears. There was a knock on the door. I pulled away and wiped at my face.

'Come in.'

'Miss, Mr Williams is here to talk to you,' said Annie, looking from me to her mother.

'I'll leave you to it.' Mrs Kerr nodded and left the room.

'It's all right, Annie, tell him to come in.'

I wasn't sure how much more I could take today.

'Sit down, Mr Williams. What can I do for you?'

'It's okay Miss. It won't take long,' he said and remained standing, turning his hat in his hands like rosary beads. 'As you know Miss, I was going to step back all those years ago but with everything that happened, you know …' He looked down.

My cheeks burned at the memory of Will leaving.

'Anyhow, there's a young chap I know. He ran an estate in Northumberland, but it was sold, and he ain't like the new owners. Sorry if I'm rumbling. I think he'd be the right man to take over.'

I rubbed my hands over my face. 'Is everyone leaving?'

'I'm very sorry, Miss.'

'No, Mr Williams, I understand. I'm grateful you stayed on this long. When can I see this man?'

'His name's Fraser. He's a Scotsman, Miss. He could come at the weekend.'

'That's fine. Thank you, Mr Williams.'

He nodded and turned on his heels. He was halfway across the room when I found the courage to ask.

'Do you have an address for Will?'

He halted and stood with his back to me. I held my breath as I waited for an answer. At last he turned. The look in his eyes scalded my face.

'I'm sorry, Miss. He writes but he seems to be moving around.'

I nodded and watched him go. Bonelle's grandfather. There had been so many times I wanted to ask him about Will and never dared. I wondered what he'd say if I'd told him about Bonelle. I shook my head and sought refuge back in my room. The only silver lining was that I had an excuse not to go to Edinburgh this weekend. I sat on the bed and opened my diary. At least Isabelle had written again.

I think Bonelle is Will's, not Glen's, daughter. Didn't you get my last message?

How did she know? And why hadn't I seen her message? I had assumed she too had left me and had stopped writing in my diary, what had been the point? My eyes swept over the rest of her message.

I'm so glad you understand. I know now for certain that Bonelle is Will's daughter. But I don't know where to find him. You're right; I need to get Bonelle away from Jane and Glen, but it's not that easy. She loves them.

Finally, the last of the mourners left the house on Regent Street, and I put Bonelle to bed, counting the days when we'd be back at the Hall so I could set out to find Will and sort out my life. When I could stall no longer, I crept back downstairs.

'Good night, son. I'll leave you to it,' Jane was saying. She nodded at me as she passed me in the doorway.

'Sit down, Mhairi. Ma and I've been discussing the future. I'm worried about her.'

'Of course.' A sense of dread crept up my spine.

Glen cleared his throat. 'I suggested that Bonelle and I stay here with her for a while. You know, for some company. I also need to sort out my father's estate and talk to the lawyers. I can't expect Ma to deal with all of that.'

'Why can't she come and stay at the Hall? You'll be here for work anyway and the rest you can handle from there.'

Was I paranoid or did he seem always a step ahead of me? I pushed on before Glen could interrupt me.

'I don't think it'll be healthy for Bonelle to be here on her own with a grieving grandma. Besides, her life is at the Hall...'

Glen was already shaking his head.

'Surely, you can't expect Ma to leave her comfort and her friends at a time like this? What the hell is she supposed to do at the Hall? Really, Mhairi, I wish for once you could think of someone else.'

I felt as if Glen had slapped me. Did he really think I wanted his mother anywhere near me or the Hall? This vile woman who since day one had disapproved of me and who, since Bonelle was born, had tried to claim her.

'Fine, but I want my daughter back at the Hall where she belongs.'

'*Our* daughter, Mhairi. Don't ever forget that.'

Oh, how I wished I could shout the truth in his face.

Chapter Thirty-Nine

Isabelle surveyed the crowds for Angus and found him standing on the edge of the garden, gazing over the sea. A rush of pleasure washed over her, and she hastened her step. He turned around and their eyes met, making her heart quicken.

'You look great,' Angus said and kissed her on the cheek.

He held her in his arms a little longer than usual, and when he at last released her, he had a look in his eyes that made her legs go weak.

'And you look great. But also dreadful,' she said to get back on the safe ground of friendship.

But her discomfort was replaced with concern as she took in the circles under his eyes. His cheeks looked hollow, and his chin hadn't seen a razor in days.

'You'll find this is my new look. Clearly it doesn't meet the lady's approval.'

Isabelle ignored his comment. 'I mean it; what's happened?'

'I think I'll need another one of these.' He raised his pint. 'Or actually, something a bit stronger if I'm going to tell you the whole sorry tale, and I'm sure you'll need a drink too. The usual?'

Isabelle gave him the thumbs up. While he was gone, she looked out over the harbour, wondering what kind of sad tale he had to tell her.

'Here.' Angus handed Isabelle her G&T.

'Are your parents all right?' she asked, taking it.

He looked surprised. 'Yes, don't worry. This isn't about them.'

'Okay then, spit it out, Mr Fairbairn,' she said and took a sip.

Angus exhaled through his lips, as though blowing a raspberry, which would have made Isabelle laugh, had it not been for the expression on his face. It reminded her of when they were children and Angus was told to do something he didn't want to.

'It's Alex.'

'What about her?' she asked, hoping nothing awful had happened.

'You remember she went to Dubai for a break?'

'She went for a few days to get her head straight, right?'

'Right. She stayed away longer than we'd planned. But she came back a couple of weeks ago.' Angus swiped his hair back. 'She told me she'd made a decision. She was going to move back there.'

Angus pinched the top of his nose with his thumb and index finger. He turned his face away from her but not before Isabelle saw a tear escaping the corner of his eye. Her heart went out to him; misery and pain were written all over him.

'I'm so sorry, Angus.'

She put her arm around his shoulder, just as she used to do when they were children.

Angus sniffed. 'I tried to reason with her, but she was adamant that the only way we could be together was if I moved to Dubai permanently. She knew it was out of the question for me.'

'Gosh, how horrible, for both of you.'

Angus grunted. 'Wait till you hear the rest. I was going through Facebook and saw pictures of Alex looking all cosy with this guy. You know how you just *know*?'

Isabelle nodded. Her heart sank as she guessed what was coming next.

'I checked some of her older posts more carefully, and I'm telling you, it was like someone poured ice-water over me. He's there in every damn picture: behind her, next to her, his arm around her shoulder or waist…'

'That's awful. But couldn't it be innocent? They could be friends … like we are.'

'Yes, and that's why I gave her the benefit of the doubt. I called her and asked her about him. At first, she denied everything, but eventually, she confessed.'

'No way.'

Angus nodded. 'Apparently, she'd dated him for a while before we met. Somehow, they got chatting again soon after we moved here, and gradually they got closer and closer.' He stood there with his head hanging down as though all life had drained from him. 'I feel like a complete idiot.'

'I'm so sorry, Angus.' She squeezed him tightly.

'Don't worry,' he said, patting her back. 'I'll survive. If I'm honest, it's lovely to have you back. I sort of can't talk about this stuff with the lads and my parents, especially poor Mum. She's been so worried about me. Anyway, what's going on with you?'

'Are you sure you want to know?'

'Will we need reinforcement?' Angus shook his glass.

Isabelle laughed. 'Oh, I'd think so.'

As they walked to the bar, Isabelle looked around the familiar faces. Would she really have left all this behind?

'There, don't drink it all in one go,' Angus winked as he handed her the glass.

'After everything that's happened today, it's tempting.'

Angus nudged her. 'Go on, tell.'

Isabelle took a steadying breath. 'A week ago, I was so close,' she indicated a space with her index and thumb, 'to chucking it all in.'

Angus frowned. 'But why?'

'Ach, just everything: trying to get to the bottom of Mimi's secret, not being able to get a job, and being broke.'

'Belle, why didn't you come to me? I'd never have forgiven you if you'd upped and left just like that.'

Isabelle's heart melted. Why hadn't she? 'Good job I didn't, seeing as you had already plenty on your plate.'

Angus held her arm. 'It doesn't work that way, and you know it.'

'I know … Anyway, to top it all, I came back today to find Mum at the Hall with some property developer guys. You can imagine how that went down.'

'Jeez, Belle. I know your mum, but even for her, that's taking it a step too far.'

'She's not gonna rest until she's got her hands on the Hall or so she said.'

'And knowing you, even if you hadn't wanted the Hall before, you'd fight her tooth and nail now. Am I right?'

'You got it, Mr Fairbairn.' Isabelle punched his arm.

'Come here.' He put his arms around her and whispered in her ear, 'I know how much it upsets you. And I know I've been a lousy friend for the last six years, but I've got your back.'

Isabelle nuzzled into his chest, breathing in the warmth of his body and his words. She wished they could stay like that forever. Maybe now that Alex was out of the way? No, she'd seen how upset Angus been; he clearly still loved Alex.

Angus let go of her. 'We're a right pair, aren't we?' He laughed but that sadness didn't leave his eyes. 'Come on, let me walk you home.'

'You know you don't need to.'

'I want to. We don't want you to go AWOL, do we?' He winked.

On the way to the Hall, Isabelle wondered if she should tell him that she could talk with Mimi and about Bonelle's parentage. No. She'd sound insane. And she needed to find the whole truth before she divulged Mimi's secrets.

'Fancy another drink?' Isabelle asked as they arrived.

'No, thanks,' Angus said, but he had that look in his eyes again.

Or was she just imagining it?

Once inside Isabelle made herself a sandwich and sat at the table with Mimi's diary, wondering if she was going to leave Glen or not. She frowned at the date. Why hadn't Mimi written for the last three years? But she had to smile as she read about her mum as a three-year-old and wondered just how much life changed us. She sat upright as she read of Mimi's discovery. Isabelle realized she'd made a mistake.

If Bonelle was Will's daughter, then she had encouraged Mimi's relationship with the abusive Glen for no reason. If Mimi had left Glen, Bonelle would still have existed, and so would Isabelle.

Or would she? It was Glen's neglect that had pushed Mimi into Will's arms. Without Glen would Mimi have grown out of her teenage infatuation? Married someone else?

She ran a shaking palm over her face. Did Bonelle know? Was that the reason she hated Mimi and the Hall? This had to be the secret Mimi had written about. But why was Mimi still putting up with Jane and Glen?

Isabelle frowned as she read Mimi's message.

Are you sure you wrote the message?

Of course she was. But why hadn't Mimi seen it? Then Isabelle remembered that Mimi had never replied to her very first message, the one she'd written in London. This message had been written when she was in France.

It was as if the Hall itself had set out to bring Mimi and her together. But why? To encourage Isabelle to stay? To save the Hall form Bonelle and her developers?

A shiver ran through her.

'Don't be ridiculous; it's just a house.' Isabelle said aloud, as though it would make the words real.

She picked up her pen and wrote a hopeful message.

Well done for finding out. Now there's nothing to stop you from leaving Glen. I know you're thinking of Bonelle, but she's still quite young. I'm sure she'll get used to it. Children are a lot more resilient than we think. You have to set things into motion before Jane and Glen manage to turn her against you.

And my mum ends up hating you and probably me, she thought. Instead she wrote:

My mum brought buyers to the house when I wasn't there, and I caught her red-handed.

As she turned the page, she saw a letter glued on to it and read it.

Elisabeth Linley

21 August 1965

My dearest Mimi,

I'm afraid I've failed you. Please forgive me for writing, but I can't bear to be this close to you and not to see you. I know you've made your choice, and I understand, but I can't stop loving you. Knowing I might never take you in my arms again physically hurts. I wish I could turn back time, but would it have made any difference? If I had found a way of staying close to you?

Will you meet me one last time? I'll leave in a couple of days, and every day I'll be in our place waiting for you, in the hope that I will be able to hold you one last time.

I love you with all my heart. See you at the Moonlight Cove.

Yours always,
W

Chapter Forty

'This is for you, Miss.' Annie pressed an envelope into my hand.

I checked and couldn't see any address. 'Who gave it to you?'

'I'll have to go, Miss,' Annie said and fixed me with her gaze. Her jaw was clenched, and her chin raised. I knew that look of disapproval well.

I took the letter to Mama's rose garden, sat on the bench, and opened it. At the sight of the handwriting, I thought my heart would give out. Tears blurred my vision. I pressed my fist against my mouth to stop a howl that had made its way up from the depth of me. I inhaled, taking in the scent of the roses, until I calmed enough to read the letter that was trembling in my hands.

I read and reread it to make sure it was real. It had been eight years since the birth of our daughter. Eight years during which Glen and I had somehow managed to coexist. Eight years since that hole was burnt in my soul on the day Will left. And every day of the last eight years, I had prayed to set eyes on him just one more time, to feel his arms around me and the touch of his lips on mine. And now that the moment was here, I couldn't believe it.

'I'm off for a walk,' I said to Annie.

'Yes, Miss Mimi. I'll look after Miss Bonelle.'

'Thank you, Annie.'

Although I still could see that look of disapproval embossed on her face like a mask, I knew that my secret was safe with her. She'd proven to be a rock since I had become mistress of the Hall.

I stole another glance at myself in the hallway mirror and sneaked down the stairs onto the beach. Once I reached the Moonlight Cove, I looked around me once and slipped into the opening of the cave.

Will stood there.

I was rooted to the spot. All I could do was stare at him, wondering if he was real or an apparition.

One step at a time, he closed the gap between us, his eyes never leaving mine. His hands were warm as he cupped my face, and his breath stroked my skin as he bent and kissed me as though blowing life into me. His arms closed around me, pressing me against him so hard that I almost couldn't breathe, and yet I didn't want him to let go. His heart pulsated against mine and his scent enveloped me like a blanket.

'My beautiful Mimi, how much I missed you, my love,' he whispered. He took a step back and looked down into my eyes. My heartbeat quickened under his gaze. 'Mimi, I want you to come with me. I can't live without you.'

'Will—'

His finger on my lips silenced me. 'Please listen to me, love. I'm estate manager at Carnaich Lodge in Aviemore. We could stay there until we sort things out. Please say yes, my darling.'

The look in his eyes scorched my heart like hot iron, and the pain rushed through me. Every fibre in me wanted to give into temptation and say yes, to make a dream come true. God only knows how many times I'd fantasised about us living somewhere, far away from everyone and bringing up our daughter. But I knew that it was just a dream.

'Will, you know how much I love you, but how can I abandon the Hall? And Bonelle. I can't tear her from the only father she's ever known. She adores Glen.'

I swallowed down the knot of agony in my throat. Will squeezed me more tightly.

'There must be a way, Mimi. Please give us a chance, just … promise me you'll think about it. I'll wait for you here tonight after dark.'

'All right,' I said.

My head was spinning. I felt as though the cave was closing in on me. Oh, the cruelty of it all. I'd made a huge mistake and married the wrong man. I so wished I'd never set eyes on Glen. And amongst all this mess was my daughter. A shudder ran through my body. I put my hands on his chest as though to steady myself.

'Will… there's something I need to tell you.' I swallowed hard. 'Bonelle is—'

'Mummy, Mummy, where are you?'

I heard my daughter's voice, and my whole body immobilised. Sweat dripped down my back. Will moved into the shadows of the cave, and as I was about to reply, I heard another voice.

'Miss Bonelle, come along, I told you not to go in there on your own,' said Annie.

'But Annie, I heard Mummy; she's in there,' my daughter protested.

'Enough, or you'll be in trouble when I'll tell your mum.'

I felt sick to my stomach at the thought of what would have happened if Bonelle had discovered us. Bonelle shared everything with Glen. I would have played right into his hands. He would take Bonelle away from me in a heartbeat. A shiver ran down my spine, and I shook my head to dislodge the thoughts. Will took me in his arms again and held me. But the fear of being discovered had gripped hold of me.

I freed myself from Will's embrace. 'I must go. It's too risky.'

'Mimi, wait.'

Will kissed me one last time, and I hurried away, for fear that I'd never leave him otherwise. After a short while, I slowed my stride but didn't look back. The terror that had gripped me intensified, churning my insides with every step as I neared home.

'Where were you, Mummy?' Bonelle asked as we sat on the terrace enjoying a glass of lemonade.

'I went for a walk, my darling. Did you have a good time with Annie?'

'Yes, Mummy, we went to—Pa!' she screeched and ran into her father's arms.

'Hello, my princess,' Glen greeted her and picked her up.

'Pa, can we do some of our puzzle? Please?'

'All right, all right, come on then. But not for long. You know Pa needs to be away in a little while.'

Glen carried Bonelle inside without a glance at me. I felt a pang of jealousy at the closeness between father and daughter. Except he wasn't her father. Not by blood. *I'll be glad when he leaves for Edinburgh this evening*, I thought and followed them inside.

I saw Annie in the hallway. She fixed me with her gaze, and I knew she too had overheard me in the cave. I didn't blame her for disapproving of me. Annie's world was ordered with boundaries. Everything had its place, and there was no room for deviation.

'Is there anything I can do for you?' she asked.

I shook my head. 'Thank you, Annie.'

I hurried up the stairs, straight into my room. Once inside I locked the door behind me. Then I sat on the bed contemplating my fate. I was at yet another crossroads. A chill ran through me. Could I leave all this behind? What would become of the estate? Was life giving me a second chance? But this time it wasn't just about me. I had to think of Bonelle. Would she hate me for tearing her from her father? Of course she would.

I despaired at the hopelessness of it all. But a voice kept nagging at me. What if things settled down after a while?

But what would people say?

I needed to clear my thoughts. I reached for my diary, hoping there was a message from Isabelle that could inspire me. And indeed the answer was right in front of me as I read:

> **Now there's nothing to stop you from leaving Glen before Jane and Glen to turn her against you.**

> *Thank you, Isabelle, you have no idea just how much I needed to hear this. I just hope my courage won't fail me at the last hour. I haven't yet thought about what happens to the Hall when I go, but I must find a way out. The only thing I'm still not sure of is whether Bonelle would ever forgive me.*

> *I'm sorry your mother's so unkind to you. I understand you don't get on, but I'm sure she struggles with it deep down. I can't help thinking how awful I'd feel if Bonelle ended up resenting me like that.*

214

What if I didn't go with Will? Would that mean I would never see him again?

Chapter Forty-One

'Dr Rousseau—may I call you Isabelle?' asked Mr Morgan the next day.

'Of course, I'd much prefer that,' she said and sat back in her chair.

'Then you must call me James.'

Isabelle nodded, intrigued to hear what James had to say.

'Now that that's settled, I must warn you that there is a great deal to discuss. I'll try to keep the information as succinct as I can. I have prepared a copy of all the relevant documents. It's all in here.'

Isabelle's eyes widened as he handed her an envelope as thick as a medical encyclopedia.

'Thank you.'

James fixed her with his gaze. 'Please forgive me if I sound impertinent, but are you absolutely certain that you are completely committed to Lanesbrough Hall and the estate, and that you intend to carry forward your grandmother's legacy in full?'

Isabelle felt as though she was at her graduation again, taking the Hippocratic oath.

'Yes, I am, James. Particularly since my mother's stunt with the property developers.'

'Yes, that was rather underhanded of her. But we'll deal with that as and when there's a formal lawsuit.'

On hearing the last word, Isabelle's grip tightened on the envelope.

'You see, Mrs Lanesbrough left instructions for me that I could use at my discretion—of course within the legal bounds—to allow you to benefit from your inheritance sooner.'

Isabelle opened her mouth in astonishment and James held up his hand.

'Let me finish,' he said, mistaking her surprise as an attempt to disrupt his flow. 'As you're aware, the estate—the Hall, the cottages, the stables, other outbuildings, and the acreage—require upgrading. The farmland needs new fencing, and I'm sure even the grounds within the Hall could do with some TLC.'

Isabelle exhaled a long breath as the scale of her responsibilities was revealed.

'In addition, all the inventory at the Hall needs to be reviewed, updated, and re-evaluated for insurance and tax purposes before it can pass on to you. Is everything clear so far?'

Isabelle nodded.

'So, I have a plan.'

Isabelle was relieved; she wouldn't have a clue where to even begin.

He pushed a stack of papers in front of her. 'I've made a list.'

Isabelle scanned the lines and numbers on the first sheet, flicked through the rest, then looked back at James.

He chuckled. 'Please don't look so horrified. My intention was to make matters simpler for you. I shan't take you through the list, there is a copy of this in your pack.'

Isabelle sighed with relief.

'The most urgent matter is the inventory. Now, usually I would have to provide someone to be present in-loco and oversee the process. But if you were prepared to take on the task yourself, I could remunerate you for your time.'

Isabelle's interest piqued.

'I must warn you that it's only a small sum, but as you currently bear no financial responsibilities for the Hall, it might just be enough to help you out with your finances. It would be a daily rate of £100 pounds.'

Isabelle's jaw dropped. She'd earned that as a locum per hour.

'I can see from your reaction that you consider it rather an inadequate recompense for your time, but in my defence, it was your grandmother's suggestion.'

'You're right, but beggars can't be choosers,' she said considering her current job situation.

'However, if you were happy to project-manage the refurbishment you would be employed by the trust on a monthly salary of £3500 for the entire duration of the project. Of course, all the refurbishment expenses are paid by the trust, and you'd be given free rein with any interior designs, as long as you remain within the allocated budget.'

Isabelle's head was spinning like she'd done a twenty-four-hour shift at the hospital. She couldn't believe the lengths Mimi had gone through to plan everything. But she was in no position to make any decisions right now.

'Do you have any questions?'

Isabelle cleared her throat. 'Not at this time, thank you.'

It wasn't true; she had questions as long as her arm, but she doubted her brain was capable of processing even one more morsel of information.

'Then I suggest that you take your time reading through everything. I'd be grateful if you could let me know your decision by Tuesday.'

Isabelle counted the days. That left her four days to get through the bundle. James stood, which she took as a cue that the meeting was over.

Back at the Hall, Isabelle followed the smell of baking into the kitchen, where Mrs Murray had lined up scones on a rack to cool.

'Very good timing, Miss Isabelle. Sit yourself down; you look like you could do with a couple of these,' Mrs Murray said as she went about setting the table.

Isabelle realised she was hungry and cut through a scone, slathering it with butter and strawberry jam. Her eye caught the date on the jar, and she noticed it was one of the batches she had made with Mimi last summer. Another thing she would never experience again.

'Miss Isabelle,' said Mrs Murray, bringing her back to the moment. 'I just want to say I'm so glad you're here. I know how much it would mean to your grandmother.'

Isabelle reached out and gave Mrs Murray's hand a squeeze. 'And I want you to know how grateful I am for everything you've done and are still doing for me. I don't know how I would have managed without you.'

'I know dear,' Mrs Murray patted Isabelle's hands. 'And I'm sorry I can't help you with the things you want to know. But as I said, the Hall knows all, and I'm sure it will give up its secrets to you when the time's right.'

Would it? Isabelle asked herself as she sat in her room a while later with Mimi's diary. She took a breath and opened it up. Would Mimi have replied to her?

You have no idea just how much I needed to hear this...

'Bingo!' Isabelle said and punched the air.

The only thing is whether Bonelle would ever forgive me.

She just hoped this time Mimi saw it through. But as she read the last parther heart sank.

I'm sorry your mother's so unkind to you, and I understand you don't get on. What if Bonelle ended up resenting me like that?

Was this what was going to destroy Mimi's relationship with Bonelle? Did Bonelle hate Mimi for taking her away from her father? Or was it because in time Glen and Jane had turned her against Mimi? The only thing Isabel knew for certain was that Mimi had to leave that horror of a man. She began to write.

Mimi, I understand you're worried. But you're doing the right thing. Remember, Glen is abusive and manipulative. I know Bonelle is close to him, but do you really want her to grow up around a man like that? A man who has no respect for women. Will is there. He is her father. He's never stopped loving you, and I'm sure he'll support you through it all. You won't be alone anymore. Please just leave Glen and take Bonelle with you.

Chapter Forty-Two

Mimi, August 1965

At the sound of an engine, I knew Glen was gone. I went downstairs to spend some time with my daughter and to prepare her for what lay ahead. I found her in the living room, sitting on the window seat looking out onto the sea.

'Hello, darling, are you all right?' I sat down beside her, stroking her hair.

She shook her head but didn't look at me.

'What's wrong, sweetheart?'

'I miss Pa. Why can't I go with him? I'll have to wait four sleeps before he comes back.'

'I know, my love. But we can do some nice things to make the time go faster, what do you say?'

'Maybe. Pa said we're going to live in a house in Edinburgh. You could come too, Mummy,' suggested my daughter with a child's innocence, looking at me for the first time.

My chest tightened. Was Bonelle making this up? Or was Glen planning to take my daughter away without telling me? Of course he was.

'I'm sure that's not what your Pa meant, sweetheart.'

'Yes, he did. He said now I'm a big girl, I could live in Edinburgh and get to see Grandma Jane all the time.'

My heart froze. I took a moment to compose myself and couldn't help thinking that this was a sign telling me it was time for things to change. The thought strengthened my resolve. Maybe everything would work out after all.

'Come on, sweetheart, it's time for bed,' I said.

I put Bonelle to bed. As I lay there next to her, I asked myself over and over if I was doing the right thing taking her away from her father. Then I reminded myself of what Bonelle had said earlier. Glen was going to take her away, and I would never get her back. As soon as she fell asleep, I packed her bag with some of her clothes and deposited it in my room.

At ten the Hall was at last asleep. I picked up my bag, took one final look at my room, and headed for my daughter's bedroom.

'Bonelle, darling, wake up,' I said, kissing her brow and stroking her arm until she opened her eyes.

'Come on, darling, get dressed. We're going on an adventure.'

'But where are we going? It's still dark.'

'That's why it's an adventure, my love. Now, let's get you ready.' I helped her out of bed.

She yawned. 'Is that man coming too?'

Her question made my heart explode. Had she heard Will?

'What man?'

'The one you were talking to,' she said, rubbing her eyes.

For one moment I couldn't think. It was as though my brain had ceased.

'I want my red coat.'

Her voice jolted me into action. I couldn't backtrack now. I put Bonelle's coat on and led her by the hand. We had just reached the top of the staircase when the front door opened, and Glen walked in.

'And where are you going?' he demanded, staring up at me.

Horror seized me as I realised he knew, but how? Annie would have never betrayed me.

'Surprise, Mummy!' giggled Bonelle.

Then as clearly as I could see Glen crossing the hallway towards me, I knew that my daughter had given me away. She screeched with joy and ran down the stairs, hugging her father's legs.

'I knew you'd come!'

I tried to speak but my tongue was as paralysed as the rest of me, only my thoughts whirled like a storm.

'Princess, why don't you go to your room and Pa will come and see you in a minute?' said Glen.

The earlier sharpness had gone. His voice was sweet and soft like molasses speaking to Bonelle. I watched her walk back up the stairs with her bag clutched in her hand.

'Are you okay, Mummy?' she asked as she passed me. 'Did you like your surprise?'

Tears smarted my eyes. I so wanted to reassure her. But I only nodded, still unable to speak, and returned my gaze to Glen. Once she was in her room, Glen asked again, the timbre of his voice was full of menace.

'Where are you going, Mhairi?'

I watched him climb the steps one at a time. One hand slid up the banister inch by inch and the other swayed by his side. He looked like a fox baring his teeth as he cornered a chicken. I knew there was nothing I could say to talk myself out of this. It was already too late; my paralysis had given me away.

'Let me pass, Glen,' I said, when he was a couple of steps below me, and tried to cover up the tremor in my voice.

His laughter bellowed around me with such force that I almost lost my footing.

'Let you pass? Why? Are you in a hurry? Worried lover boy will leave without you?' He taunted me.

I looked at him standing there with the smirk on his face mocking me, and in that moment my contempt for him gave me the strength I needed.

'Glen, don't pretend you care. We both know you never really loved me.'

'And whose fault is that? You seem to have conveniently forgotten that it was your sordid affair that tore us apart in the first place. And surprise, surprise, you're at it again.'

The heat of anger rushed through my body. 'If you'd been a fraction of the man that he is, I wouldn't have needed to look elsewhere,' I shouted and had the satisfaction of seeing the smirk leave his face.

I was about to push my way past him when he reached for my hand. I jerked back and he grabbed one of the bag's handles instead. We struggled in a tug-of-war, then he clutched the body of the bag with both hands and pulled so hard that he lost his footing.

I watched as though I was hovering on the ceiling, looking down as Glen and the bag tumbled down the stairs. Clothes scattered on the steps like confetti. I don't know how long I stood there, immobilised by horror and shock. As the ringing in my ears began to subside, I was sure that I heard Isabelle's voice telling me to do something.

My hand circled the banister out of its own volition, and my legs carried me down the stairs. I kneeled beside Glen, pressed two fingers against his neck and tried to find a pulse. But my hands were trembling so badly, I couldn't be sure of anything. I willed myself towards the telephone, rang the doctor, and still with the receiver in my hand, slid down the wall, staring at Glen. He lay there like a grotesque puppet.

'Pa! Pa!' cried Bonelle, running down the stairs.

Her scream jolted me out of my stupor. I reached her just as she kneeled beside her father's body, hanging on to his shoulders and shaking him.

'Wake up, Pa, please,' she begged him, tears soaking her face.

'Bonelle, come away, sweetheart,' I said, holding her by the arms.

'No! I want my Pa! Let me go!' she screamed, trying to push me away.

I grabbed her by the waist and manged to drag her away a few steps.

'Let me go; it's all your fault. He only fell because you didn't give him that stupid bag,' she shouted, kicking out with her legs, and wriggling in my arms, trying to free herself.

Nausea choked me as I realised that she'd seen everything. I swallowed down the disgust I felt at myself and turned my attention to my daughter.

'Bonelle, sweetheart, it was an accident.'

I tried to soothe her, but my words were lost in her cries. They pierced the space. I have no idea where I found the strength to hold my daughter for as long as I did, until she was at last spent and flopped in my arms like a ragdoll. One of the maids, woken by all the commotion, approached me.

'Please take the child and settle her,' I said. 'Then get someone to go for Mrs Murray, tell her there's been an accident.'

Later that night as I wrote in my diary. I knew that my life had changed forever.

> *I tried Isabelle and I failed. How could I have been so unlucky? I wished I'd listen to you and left all those years ago. I know Bonelle is still young, but she is old enough to understand everything. She knows it's all been my fault. She blames me for her father's accident, and she hates me. My worst fear came true; it's all lost. What am I to do now?*

Chapter Forty-Three

That evening Isabelle sat in Mimi's study, enjoying a glass of wine and going through her finances. The London flat was booked out until September. That would pay the mortgage and bills. And now that she wasn't going back, she'd rent it out on a permanent basis, which meant the money James was offering her would keep her going until she could claim her inheritance in the New Year.

She considered how she'd feel about renovating the Hall instead of seeing patients. She had become a doctor to help others. It didn't take Freud to tell her that her career decision had something to do with Chloe's death. But thinking about finding a job in the medical profession again made her tense up.

Maybe she should just take a year out, sort out the Hall, and then think about going back. Yes, the idea of a sabbatical appealed to her.

She turned to the paperwork James had given her and reading through it, she realised that whilst there was a need for an overhaul, James had been right: the process itself was straightforward.

Isabelle opened the filing cabinet and took out Mimi's ledgers. The estate had its own dairy and meat production, including game. Some of the fields produced wheat, barley, and hay, but she still didn't have an idea of the scale in terms of manpower or expenses. But perhaps there was a way of running the estate as a business again.

Isabelle felt a twinge of excitement. A distant memory came to mind. Hadn't Mimi said something about only keeping animals? She couldn't remember when or why Mimi had stopped that side of business. But there was one person who might be able to help her.

Another few days went by before Isabelle had a chance to visit Hamish. She pushed open the wooden gate. The marigolds that Hamish had planted were in bloom, brightening the garden. The rosebush by the side of the door was now covering the wall like a red tapestry. She pressed the doorbell and waited.

'Isabelle!' called Hamish as he walked along the side of the house towards her, arms open. 'You're a sight for sore eyes, lassie.'

She followed him around the house to the garden.

'I thought you left us,' he said once they were seated.

Isabelle shook her head. 'Just a holiday. I'll be living at the Hall permanently.'

'That's good news.'

'Actually, that's why I'm here, I thought perhaps you could help me with a few things, seeing as your family managed the estate for so long.'

Hamish nodded, and Isabelle saw that look in his eyes again, as though he'd already slipped into the past. She listened as Hamish explained the workings of the Hall over half a century ago.

'Much would be still the same. Except it'll be difficult to get the manpower and of course now everything is more technology than farming, so it'd cost a fortune to set it all up.'

Isabelle asked Hamish if Mimi had been right about animal farming.

'Ah, Mimi always was a clever one. Yes, I think that could work. I hope I live long enough to see the Hall come alive again.' He looked down at his lap. 'I just wish with all my heart Mimi was still with us. You'd be making her very happy,' he said, wiping his eyes.

Isabelle was touched that although he was a stranger, the Hall meant so much to him.

'Mimi was a smashing lady, but a naughty lass,' he laughed, his eyes coming alive again.

Isabelle wondered why Mimi had never mentioned him in her diaries. 'So you were ... close?'

Hamish nodded. 'We all grew up together. After Mistress Catherine died—that's your great-grandmother—and what with Alasdair being away at school and the old master grieving his wife, the little lass seemed lost, so I took her under my wing a little. You know, just making sure she was all right. At weekends we'd go to the Moonlight Cove.'

The Moonlight Cove. The words reverberated around Isabelle's mind, but Hamish didn't seem to notice her reaction.

'Me and Alasdair used to go rabbiting at night,' he was saying. 'Pheasant and partridge shooting in the holidays. Those were the days.' Hamish took a deep breath. 'As we got older, I'd ride with him around the estate and check things were all right. Of course, by then he was my master, and I was working alongside my father, but we were still close until...'

Had he fallen out with Alasdair or Glen? Was this why Mimi hadn't ever mentioned him in her diaries?

Hamish was looking down at his hands. At last Isabelle broke the silence.

'I remember Mimi taking me to the Moonlight Cove,' she said. 'I went there the last time I was here. Do a lot of people know about it?'

'I don't know how many know of it, but not many would go there.'

Isabelle raised her brow.

'It was, and probably still is, within the boundaries of Lanesbrough Estate. and in those days things were different. Decent folks didn't trespass on an estate's grounds without permission.'

Isabelle nodded.

'Back in the day, and I'm talking centuries ago, smugglers used to bring everything from booze to weapons in under the cover of darkness. It was even said that there was a tunnel going from the back of the cave all the way to the Hall.'

'Really?'

'Yes! Alasdair and I certainly looked for it often enough as wee lads, hoping for treasure.' He laughed at the memory.

Isabelle watched the sun draw shadows over the garden, then she stood up and put her hand on his shoulder.

'I'll find my own way out,' she said and felt his hand on hers. 'Hamish, would you help me when the time comes?'

He looked up at her, and Isabelle saw tears brimming his eyes.

'It'd be my pleasure. I'd love to see the Hall again.'

Back at the Hall, Isabelle began to read the diary and realised she'd been too late again. She sat there with her hands covering her face, trying to take in the enormity of the trauma Bonelle had witnessed. She couldn't even begin to imagine what it must have been like for her. For the first time she understood why her mum hated Mimi and the Hall.

She also understood why Mimi had always made allowances for Bonelle's behaviour. And what of Glen? Was he dead? Is that why neither Mimi nor her mum ever spoke of him? She had to ask.

> **Mimi, that must have been horrific for you and Bonelle. Is Glen alive? I know you think it's all lost. Of course you and Bonelle are shocked and traumatised. But don't blame yourself. It won't help anyone, least of all Bonelle. You'll just have to be strong and ride this out. Don't give up, Mimi. Bonelle needs you! Don't let her push you away. Just promise you'll look after yourself and take care of Bonelle. I'm here for you. I send you all my love.**

Chapter Forty-Four

Mimi, April 1966

I walked up the stairs and the click of my heels on the floors echoed with each step. I took a seat outside the room and waited for Glen's consultant, Dr Monroe, to call me in. I was dreading his verdict. Glen had lost the use of his legs, but his consultant had thought there could be a chance of him walking again.

At the sound of the door, I opened my eyes and saw Dr Monroe ushering a woman out of his room. Her shoulders were stooped and when her eyes met mine, they told me what kind of news she must have received.

'Mrs Smeatson, please do come in.'

I straightened my back and tried to ignore the thumping in my chest. I entered the room that was furnished with a modesty that belied his status. A desk sat in one corner and a cabinet with index cards on the drawers stood against the wall. I sat and wrapped my coat around me to ward off the chill despite the balmy weather.

Dr Monroe looked like father Christmas, and my dealings with him over the months had taught me that I could trust his judgment, which he shared with a candidness I welcomed. He came straight to the point.

'I'm afraid, I don't bear good news, Mrs Smeatson. Despite the intense physical therapy your husband has received over the last ten months, he shows no sign of improvement.'

I stared at him.

'There's no sensation or mobility in his lower limbs. Whilst patients recover at different rates, sadly in case of your husband, we have seen no progress that would make us feel more hopeful about his prognosis.'

Dear God, I thought. I put my hand to my mouth as though trying to stop the words escaping my lips.

'As it stands he no longer benefits from being here, and I have arranged for his discharge. He will be sent home with a wheelchair, but it's a rather basic issue, so you may wish to look into purchasing a more comfortable one....'

I don't know how much longer Dr Monroe spoke because my brain shut down. Though I had contemplated that fate many nights, hearing Glen being condemned to a chair for life was too much to take in. I asked myself, like all those times before, if it was my fault. I sat as judge and jury in the court of my mind and the verdict of guilty was pronounced every time.

It was this guilt that had stopped me from leaving my crippled husband behind in pursuit of my own happiness with Will and of taking his only hope, Bonelle, away from him.

'How was school, darling?' I asked Bonelle one night over dinner, which seemed to be the only time we were all together. She spent more time with her father and his nurse assistant, Fiona, than with me.

'The same. Why do you keep asking?' Bonelle complained in a tone that did not please me, but I let it go, like all the other times since her father's accident. Still, I couldn't bear her coldness and dismissiveness that continued to lance my heart.

'Because I want to know about your day, darling,' I said, trying to ignore the pain.

'It's fine. Miss McGill said I'm very clever, and I told her I was just like my Pa.' She looked at her father. 'Isn't it true, Pa?'

'Yes, princess, you're my clever girl,' Glen said, sweeping his hand over Bonelle's hair, his eyes brimming with love.

'See, Mummy, there's nothing for you to worry about.'

I had to persist. I cleared my throat and tried to lighten my voice.

'What would you say if you stayed here this weekend and we went on a day out?'

Bonelle rolled her eyes. 'Mummy, you know we go to Edinburgh every weekend. I can't leave Pa to go on his own. Besides, Grandma Jane is taking me to the theatre.'

My cheeks were burning, and I had to look away. As I turned my head, I glimpsed Glen. The smugness on his face almost turned my stomach. Annie's voice brought me out of my reverie.

'Come, Miss Bonelle. Time for your bath.'

Bonelle slipped off her chair, bent down, and kissed his cheek. 'Night-night, Pa.'

'Sweet dreams, princess.'

'Night, Mummy.' She waved at me.

'Bonelle, come and give Mummy a kiss.' I called to her.

She rolled her eyes again and approached me. I was about to pull my chair out so I could give her a hug when she pecked me on the cheek and ran out. I sighed and looked up at Glen, who was smirking at me.

'I can see you're enjoying yourself, Glen. But this can't go on. We need to talk.'

'I'm not talking in here, with the servants having their ears on the door.'

'Fine, we'll go to your study.'

I stood and walked behind Glen as he wheeled himself. I wasn't sure I'd ever get used to that sight. I almost bumped into him as he halted to open his study. Fiona was sitting by the fireplace knitting.

'Fiona, would you mind waiting in the living room. I won't be long,' I said.

She gathered her knitting and left the room. I wondered what the woman must think of this relationship between husband and wife.

Glen wheeled himself behind his desk. He picked up his magnifying glass and bent over his papers.

The heat of anger rose through my body. 'We said we'd talk.'

'Then talk, Mhairi. What is it you want?' he asked but refused to look up at me.

What was it I wanted? Apart from my daughter, nothing bound us together but guilt and a sense of obligation on my part.

'For Bonelle's sake we should make more effort.' After a few minutes of silence I added, 'We should make more effort to be friendlier with each other. After all, we're still living under the same roof.'

But he carried on as if I wasn't there. My frustration rose.

'It's your choice, Glen. We've made the decisions we have, and we can't change the past, but we can have a better future.'

With that I walked out, wishing for the umpteenth time I had left him for Will the day I had found out I was pregnant. Back in my room, I opened my diary. I needed to talk to Isabelle before insanity took hold of me. I don't know what she must have thought of me; if she'd judged me, she'd never said so. I felt relief at the sight of her message.

> **That must have been horrific for you and Bonelle. Be strong and ride this out. Focus on Bonelle; don't let her push you away.**

> *It's been a dark time, Isabelle. Glen is alive but crippled for life. I don't know which is worse. I've been trying with Bonelle, but she just keeps pushing me away, determined to punish me. The pain of her rejection is unbearable. I wish she was as desperate to spend time with me as she is with Jane. Sometimes, I feel like she's slipping from my grasp like sand running through the fingers. I don't know what else to do. Please write to me.*

Chapter Forty-Five

Isabelle was lying on a blanket amongst Mimi's roses at the back of the Hall. She had her laptop open in front of her and was looking at online copies of *Country Homes & Interiors* and checking out prices on everything from curtains to kitchen cabinets. She was kicking her legs in the air and wriggling to the tune of 'Killer Queen.'

There was a tap on her shoulder. 'Hey, what are you up to?'

Isabelle let out a shriek, rolled onto her back and nearly sent her laptop flying.

'Angus! Are you trying to give me a heart attack?'

'Not again! You didn't used to be such a wuss,' he teased.

Isabelle noticed his complexion had improved, and he didn't look as drawn as last time they'd met. But he still didn't look his usual self.

'As you can see, I'm spending a relaxing day doing nothing before it all kicks off. I must admit it's quite fun to decorate an entire mansion on someone else's budget.'

After the struggles of the last months, the restoration of the Hall excited her. Angus crouched in front of her.

'I hear mischief brewing, little Belle.'

Isabelle laughed. She was amused that Angus still could read her like a book.

'It's a long story.'

'In that case, do you fancy a little outing, and you can tell me all about it?'

'Where are you taking me?'

'Hen Poo.'

'Are you kidding me?'

'Nope,' Angus said with a straight face.

She slapped his arm. 'Stop messing about, Angus.'

'Want to bet?'

'Fine.'

Some of her conviction was wearing off, but there was no way she was going to back down. It was a game they'd played many times when they were children, and Isabelle had to admit that she'd rarely won.

'You're on, Angus Fairbairn. The loser buys lunch.'

'Hang on,' Isabelle said half an hour later as they were leaving the car park. She took her phone out of her pocket as it started to vibrate. James's name was on the screen. Isabelle frowned at Angus and took the call.

'Isabelle, I hope you don't mind me calling you at the weekend, but I thought you'd like to know,' James said.

Isabelle's heart sank. 'Of course I don't mind.'

'I just saw an email from your mother's solicitors. They filed a lawsuit, I'm afraid.'

Isabelle felt a chill run through her. She looked up and Angus frowned at her.

'Isabelle are you there?' James's voice brought her attention back to the call.

'Yes,' she whispered.

'I'm sorry, Isabelle. I know it's not a surprise, but it still must be a shock. If it's any consolation, nothing major's going to happen any time soon. There'll be a preliminary hearing in a couple of weeks, but it'll be a good few months before a final hearing can happen.'

Isabelle clenched her jaw. How could her mum do this to her? And then she remembered what young Bonelle was going through and shook her head. Angus laid his hand on her arm and brought her back to the here and now. She looked at him.

Thank God he's here, she thought.

234

'I'd best let you go,' James said. 'Sorry for being the bearer of bad news. Try not to worry. I'll be in touch.'

After he ended the call Isabelle screeched in frustration. 'What kind of mother does this?'

'I know; I'm sorry, Belle. I heard everything. Come here.'

Angus put his arm over her shoulder. Isabelle nestled her head in the crook of his arm as they walked. Being pressed against his body made her tummy tingle, but Isabelle told herself to get a grip. Angus was just being a friend.

He tightened his grip. 'You know I'm here for you.'

'Thank you, I know.' She looked up and smiled at him.

Angus grinned back. 'Now, if I remember, we had a bet.'

Isabelle knew he was trying to cheer her up. To hell with Bonelle. She was not going to let her spoil her time with Angus.

Her eyes roamed over turrets and battlements of the castle in front of her. She raised her eyebrow at him.

'Ah, I doubt this is called Hen Poo.'

'No, you're right. That's Duns Castle. I'm surprised you don't know it.'

'I don't think I ever came here with Mimi. Or if I did, I can't remember.'

Angus led her away from the castle. A few minutes later, he swept his arm over the lake in front of them and said, 'Prepare to lose.'

'This is actually called Hen Poo?'

'Yup. And guess what?' Angus rubbed his stomach. 'I feel suddenly starving.'

'This is so underwhelming that I seem to have lost my appetite.'

'Oh really? Well, then in that case I have no choice.'

And before Isabelle knew it, Angus draped her over his shoulder, making her squeal with delight.

That evening Isabelle sat on the terrace musing over the days' events, and a warm feeling embraced her as she realised how much fun it was to be with Angus. But she had to stop fantasising about him.

Instead, her mind clouded with thoughts of the lawsuit. She had to do something. The only thing she could think of was to try and bring Mimi and Bonelle closer. Perhaps if she could do that Bonelle would lose her hatred of the house. She tucked her legs under her and opened Mimi's diary. But all hope left her as she learned what happened after Glen's accident.

It's all so sad, Mimi. I can't imagine what it must be like for you as a mother to be rejected by your own child. But please, you have to be patient with Bonelle and keep trying. Even though she rejects you, she's just a little girl who needs her mummy. Remember, every time she sees Glen in that chair, it reminds her of the accident. She is terrified of losing him or something happening to him; that's why she won't leave his side. Have you thought of getting her to see someone, like a counsellor? It might help. I hope things get better soon. Please hang in there, Mimi. I'm here for you.

She hoped there was time for their relationship to be salvaged.

Chapter Forty-Six

Mimi, August 1967

Though Glen had remained silent throughout our conversation, I started to notice changes. He and Bonelle now asked me to join them on their walks or to play boardgames or cards with them after dinner. As the weather warmed, we'd have picnics on the lawn or would go for a drive along the coast.

The turning point came on my birthday. I was sitting in Mama's rose garden, writing in my diary. Isabelle was right. I couldn't afford to lose my daughter. I just had to keep trying.

Thank you, Isabelle. Your encouragement gives me strength. I'm hoping she'll return to me if I keep trying. Wish me luck.

'Mummy, look what I've got for you,' Bonelle said, keeping her hands behind her back.

'What is it, sweetheart?' I asked and closed my diary. The smile on her face filled me with joy.

'Close your eyes and hold out your hands.'

I closed my eyes, though I wished I could have kept them open just so I could bathe in the sunshine of my daughter's smile and the sparkle in her eyes.

'Open now,' she said, after she'd placed something into the palms of my hand.

I opened my eyes to a posy of flowers that she must have collected from around the garden. My heart soared in my chest.

'They're beautiful, my darling. Thank you.'

She hugged me. 'Happy birthday, Mummy.'

I closed my daughter in my arms and for the first time since the horror of that night, she yielded into my embrace. It took all my strength to hold back the tears.

As the days passed it was like I had been given a new lease on life. Alas the honeymoon didn't last long.

It was the first day of September and Mrs Quinn's day off. Bonelle and I were in the kitchen baking a cake. I handed her an egg and showed her how to hold it.

'Just tap it on the edge of the bowl, grab it on both sides, and gently pry it open.'

'But Mummy, look, I squashed it.' She grimaced her displeasure.

'It doesn't matter, sweetheart. That's why I gave you a different bowl. I'll sort that out and you have another go.'

Fiona walked in. 'Miss Mimi, Mr Smeatson wishes to have a word.'

'Tell Pa we're baking a cake,' answered my daughter for me.

'Thank you, Fiona. I'll come as soon as we're finished here.'

Half an hour later, after I put Annie in charge of Bonelle, I knocked on the door and entered Glen's study.

'Fiona, would you mind helping Mrs Murray keep an eye on Bonelle and the cake,' I asked.

Fiona nodded once and left the room, closing the door behind her.

Glen swivelled around in his wheelchair. 'Sit down, Mhairi, we need to talk.'

I took a seat on the chesterfield and wrung my hands in my lap, wondering why I had been summoned.

'I agreed to go back to my post at the university,' Glen announced.

'I'm very happy for you,' I said. And I meant it.

He nodded in acknowledgment. 'However, as it will not be easy for me to come back to the Hall every week, I have decided to take Bonelle with me. We will live with Ma. She can continue at the same school as before. And Ma will be at hand to help when I'm busy—'

'No!' I leaped to my feet. 'You can't do this, Glen. I won't let you take my daughter away from me. Not after everything she's been through.'

'And whose fault has that been, Mhairi?' he snapped.

'No. I won't let you do this. I only just got my daughter back.' I walked over to his chair, looking down at him. 'You and that wretched mother of yours planned this all along. Didn't you think I knew?'

I smiled as I saw the thunderous clouds shadow his face.

'Yes, Bonelle told me that night. And you know what, that's what made my mind up for me.' I hissed at him and started to walk out.

'Perhaps because you're not fit to be a mother. And Mhairi, you may want to hear this before you go.'

I turned and froze at the sight of the smirk that split his face like a scar.

'I know your secret, Mhairi.'

All blood drained from me. It couldn't be. 'What do you mean?' I whispered.

His grin widened. 'I know about Bonelle, who her father is. I've known it since you told me you were with child.'

I opened my mouth, but nothing came out. I grabbed the back of the chair to steady myself.

'We'd been married for some time, and you hadn't taken. Didn't you find that odd? Ma told me she'd had some difficulties conceiving me, so I wanted to make sure I was … problem free before I discussed the issue with you. I received the test results only a few days before I came back to the Hall.'

I tried to breathe, but it was as if my lungs had closed up.

'You can imagine my surprise when you told me you were with child.'

The sound of his laughter tore through the haze in my mind and crystalised my thoughts. All that time I had wasted. All the heartache and yearning that could have been avoided. I could have been with Will. We could have been a family. I wanted to scream. But I stopped as another thought formed.

'In that case, Bonelle stays at the Hall. You have no claim on her.' I said, savouring my triumph.

'No, my dear. Bonelle is coming with me.' He pointed at me. 'And if you so much as *think* you can stop me, I will file for divorce on the grounds of adultery. Not only will you lose the custody of Bonelle, but I'll make sure to ruin you financially.' He steepled his fingers in front of his chest.

I gagged as nausea heaved in my stomach. I closed my eyes, breathed in and out, and chanted in my mind *He can't do it. He can't do it. He can't do it.* And with each breath, I realised that I couldn't take the risk. He *would* do it. And I'd lose Bonelle. At least this way I could see my daughter occasionally. I had played with fire and burnt everything to cinders.

I turned on my heel and left.

'Mummy, Mummy, come and have a look at the cake,' Bonelle cried as she saw me in the hallway. She ran and grabbed my hand.

'Okay, my love, show me.'

I swallowed my rage and pain and followed her into the kitchen.

Over the next few days, I spent as much time with Bonelle as I could. But the shadow of her departure was swallowing me a piece at a time with every day that passed.

'Have you got everything, my love?' I kneeled in front of her and stroked her face, tears stinging my eyes.

'Stop asking, Mummy,' she said.

'All right, love. I'll come and visit you next weekend and we do something nice? Right?'

'Okay, Mummy.'

'Bonelle,' Glen called from the car.

'Bye, Mummy,' she pecked my cheek, wriggled out of my embrace, and ran for the car.

I watched the vehicle pull away and let the tears of sorrow fall.

As the months passed. I saw less and less of my daughter. It was two weeks before Christmas, and I rang to remind her I was coming.

'Can I speak to Bonelle, please?' I asked the maid.

'Mummy.' I heard Bonelle a few moments later.

'Hello, darling. Remember, I'm coming tomorrow. I've got a surprise for you.' I was going to take her to see *Mary Poppins*.

'Oh …'

'What's wrong?'

'I forgot. Grandma Jane is taking me and my friend Cynthia to watch *Mary Poppins*.'

Was this a coincidence or had Jane and Glen engineered it to stop me from seeing Bonelle? It didn't matter. I wasn't going to upset my daughter either way.

'That's all right, my love. I'll come next week, and we'll go Christmas shopping.'

'I don't want to go, Mummy.'

'But darling, it'll be lovely to see all the lights and the carol singers. And then we come back to the Hall. We may even see—'

'Mummy, please. I said I don't want to go.'

'But why?'

'Grandma Jane is taking me to Jenners, and then we're going ice-skating with my friends,' Bonelle explained.

Panic replaced my frustration. 'But next week is Christmas.'

'Yes, Mummy, and I want to spend it with Pa and Grandma Jane in Edinburgh. Pa said I could. You can ask him. I need to go; Grandma is calling.'

'I love—'

But the line went dead.

On Christmas Day I sat in my room on my own, with my diary and Isabelle as my only companion.

> *I thought I had succeeded, but I'd underestimated Glen as an opponent and his hatred for me. And as for Bonelle, it's painful to see how little she cares for me. But I know I've been selfish because she seems happier now than when she lived at the Hall. I hope you had better luck than I did, and you and your mother have managed to put aside your differences.*

What kind of existence was this? Was I to spend the rest of my life alone? No. Now that Glen knew the truth and with Bonelle living in Edinburgh, what was stopping me from being with Will? He could come back to the Hall, and we'd be together again. It was the late sixties after all. The world had changed. I'd sacrificed my happiness for the community, and what had I received in return?

There were only few people of the old generation left, and their children preferred life in the cities than working the land. Besides, I had nothing more to lose.

I grabbed a paper and began to write.

My darling Will,

You must have wondered what became of me that day in August all those years ago when I didn't turn up. My biggest torment has been that you thought I didn't love you enough. Alas, it was not meant to be, for Glen found out, and in his attempt to thwart me, was met with a tragic accident that left him an invalid.

Do you see how I could not have abandoned him?

But none of it matters any more. Will you come back to me? There's so much I need to tell you. Please my darling.

With all my love,

Mimi

Chapter Forty-Seven

Thank you, Isabelle. Your encouragement gave me strength.
I'm hoping she'll return to me if I keep trying. Wish me luck.

Isabelle sighed with relief as she read Mimi's message. Maybe she hadn't been too late after all and had managed to salvage the relationship between Mimi and Bonelle. But her relief was soon replaced as she read of the events that followed. Glen was a right piece of work.

Then she reached the end of the diary and saw Mimi's last message.

> *It pains me to see how little she cares for me…she seems happier than she lived at the Hall. I hope you had a better luck than I had, and you and your mother have managed to put aside your differences.*

If you just knew, thought Isabelle. Bonelle sure was Glen's daughter, and what a despicable man he was. Yes, Mimi had made poor choices; still, it all seemed so unfair.

> **Mimi, I know it must be hard for you, but you have to follow Bonelle to Edinburgh. You can't just let her go like that. She's still young, you can still rebuild your relationship but not if you're miles away. Surely the estate manager could run the estate and you could go back to the Hall once a week? Please don't let the Hall stand between you and Bonelle.**

Isabelle exhaled and slumped back in the chair. But wasn't

she doing the same thing, letting the Hall stand between her and Bonelle? She couldn't just rely on Mimi; she had to find a way to patch things up with her mum. She couldn't let history repeat itself.

The chime of the doorbell disrupted her reverie.

'I'll get it,' Isabelle shouted as she reached the hallway.

'Hi,' she said as she opened the door. 'You must be Mr Wright. I'm Isabelle, please come in.'

He didn't look like a book expert, at least not the way she imagined one to look like. He reminded her of the fitness coaches when she used to do the classes in the park, except his demeanour resembled that of a professor.

Isabelle led Mr Wright to the library. She didn't miss his appreciation as he looked around the room.

'This is quite a collection you've got here. I was given a copy of the last inventory that was compiled in October 1956,' Mr Wright said.

'Yes, that was after my great-uncle died.'

'Do you know if there's a particular indexing system?'

Isabelle looked at him. 'I'm sorry, but I've never thought about it,' she admitted.

'Not to worry; it shouldn't be difficult to establish. Most estate libraries such as yours were referenced alphabetically or by genre. Of course, there are always deviations, such as referencing by colour or completely at random, which thankfully, I've not happened upon that often.'

Though Isabelle loved books, she was glad it was Mr Wright who was tasked with the job, not her. 'Can I get you a drink?' she offered.

'A strong coffee and a glass of water would be very welcome, thank you.'

Isabelle had just settled Mr Wright when Mr Jamieson arrived to evaluate the furniture, followed an hour later by Mr Miller, the art expert.

By Friday afternoon Jamieson and Miller had left, and Isabelle carried yet another tray of refreshments to Mr Wright. He'd warned her that he'd be needing another week if not two to complete his work.

'Ah, Isabelle, I've discovered this.'

She reached for the envelope addressed in Mimi's writing. It was sealed. She turned it around and gasped when she read the address:

Mr Hamish Williams, Estate Manager
Carnaich Lodge

There was only one estate manager in Mimi's diaries, only one she had written to: Will.

Was it possible that the reason Isabelle had never seen any mention of Mimi's childhood friend Hamish in her diaries was that Hamish was actually Will? How many of her own friends did she call by affectionate names? How many of those by their surnames?

Had the Hall finally let her in and given up its secret, as Mrs Murray had predicted it would? She said a silent *thank you* to the Hall, and the sunlight seemed to brighten around her in response. She could swear the Hall was smiling at her.

At last she had information she could act on.

'Thank you for finding this,' she said to Mr Wright.

'My pleasure.'

Isabelle carried her bounty out of the room. She thought she was going to burst with excitement as she ran through the Hall, calling and searching for Mrs Murray. She found her on the landing on the third floor, coming out of a bedroom.

'What in God's name is going on, Miss? I thought someone was being throttled,' said Mrs Murray, looking at her with a frown.

Breathless, all Isabelle could do was grin. She grabbed Mrs Murray's hand, dragged her back into the room and sat her on the bed.

'Mrs Murray, I know Mimi's secret. I know who Will is.'

'Thank the Lord,' said Mrs Murray. She clutched Isabelle's hand and looked into her eyes. 'The Hall has accepted its new mistress.'

Isabelle's phone rang. She smiled when she saw Angus's name on her screen and excused herself to answer.

'Hey, are you free for lunch?' he asked.

The flutter in her chest went up a notch. 'Meet you in an hour?'

Isabelle looked up to see Mrs Murray smiling at her with a raised brow.

Angus waved at Isabelle from a table when she entered the Fox & Hare. She made her way over and kissed him on the cheek before sitting down.

'You look happy to see me,' Angus said.

Isabelle grinned. 'You must have a six sense. There's so much I need to tell you.'

'Very mysterious. Let me get our order in first, and then I'm all yours.'

'A burger for me, please.'

'Coming up.'

Isabelle tried to remember how much she'd already told Angus. She'd definitely told him about the affair.

'So, shoot,' Angus said as he sat back down a few minutes later.

'You know how I told you about Mimi's diaries and that she had an affair with Will?'

'Yes, our own naughty Mimi.'

'Well, I found out that Will was my mum's real dad.'

'Holy cow.' Angus leaned forward in his chair.

Isabelle put up her hand. 'And I'm pretty sure that Will is really Hamish.'

'No way! You're kidding me?' Angus swiped his hair with his hand.

The waitress put two burgers on the table. Angus smiled his thanks then asked Isabelle, 'How did you find out?'

'The book evaluator found a letter in one of the books in the library.'

'Now what are you going to do?'

'I need to talk to Hamish. And I have to find a way to get Mum back to the Hall. This isn't the kind of thing you tell someone over the phone.'

'Have you heard anything from her at all?'

'No, but you know she really had a tough upbringing. I can see why she hates the Hall so much, and I guess in a way, Mimi.'

Angus pushed away his plate. 'It's all so strange. I just can't get my head around the idea that this is the same Mimi we knew.'

'I know. But I guess we all change.'

Chapter Forty-Eight

Mimi, September 1973

'Lanesbrough Hall.'

'Mum, it's me,' said Bonelle.

'At last! I've been ringing you for days. I wasn't sure Jane told you.'

I was used to my daughter avoiding my calls, but on this occasion I'd wished she'd called sooner.

'Why shouldn't she? I've been busy.'

'Yes, of course,' I said, not wishing to cause an argument. 'No matter. I thought I would take you out for your birthday tomorrow. We could go for lunch?'

I couldn't believe my daughter was going to be sixteen. Where had the years gone?

'Right, yes, well, tomorrow's not good.'

'But it's your birthday and I want to see you, darling,' I said, trying to ignore my hurt and irritation at her reluctance.

'We could meet the day after.'

'But why?'

I could hear the whining in my own voice like a child that couldn't accept a no. I heard Bonelle sigh and waited. I moved my neck from side to side to release the tension that was building up. She spelled it out to me at last.

'Because Pa and Grandma Jane planned a party for tomorrow.'

I hadn't been invited to my own daughter's sixteenth birthday party. It was as though someone had turned up the dial on my hurt and anger.

'And nobody thought of inviting me?'

Bonelle sighed again but remained silent. I had expected it from Jane and Glen but the fact that Bonelle hadn't said anything… I had enough of walking on eggshells around Bonelle for fear of alienating her even more.

'I'll tell you what, why don't I come to the party and the two of us go for lunch the day after. I can stay the night in Edinburgh.'

The silence stretched. I could hear Bonelle's breathing but no words were forthcoming.

'Bonelle?'

'Sorry, Mum, I don't think it's a good idea. The party is at the house. I'm not sure how Pa and Grandma … you know.'

Of course I knew. But I'd had enough of my daughter never considering my feelings.

'And what about me, Bonelle? How do you think it makes me feel that I can't be at my own daughter's special birthday? Don't you want me there?'

As soon as the words left my mouth, I regretted them.

'Don't *I* want you there? Mum, you were the one who *didn't want to be there*. Have you ever asked yourself what it must have been like for me? To know my mother cared more about a bloody house than she cared for me?'

The torrent of her anger almost knocked me off my feet. 'I never wanted to let you go. I was always there calling and wanting to see you, Bonelle. It was you who kept shutting me out.'

I was shaking all over. This was not how I'd envisioned the conversation going. Pain balled itself in my chest.

'I was a *child*, Mum. I was angry with you. Maybe you should have tried harder. Let's face it, nothing's ever mattered to you more than your precious Hall.'

Her words were lost in the sound of crying that tore at my very being. Isabelle's words rang in my ears through the haze of time. *Don't give up Mimi. Bonelle needs you!* The truth that I had failed my daughter was more than I could bear.

What was even more devastating was the realisation that I had let my duty to the Hall ruin my life. I'd sacrificed everything at the altar of this demanding God, including my flesh and blood.

I listened to her cry and then she hung up on me without another word.

Isabelle had been right, as always. I should have followed Bonelle. Not only did I lose my child, but I hadn't heard anything from Isabelle in years. Not since my diaries had burned when a fire had broken out in what used to be Glen's study.

His wretched magnifying glass had been like a torch in the sunlight. Thank goodness Annie had noticed before worse damage had been done. I had thought she too had enough of me, but what if it had been the fire?

I must write to her and explain.

> *Dearest Isabelle, I only just realised that you may not have been able to write because of a fire that burned some of my diaries. You were so right, and I wish I had listened to you all those years ago and followed Bonelle to Edinburgh. She hates me and I have only myself to blame. I'm not sure I can ever right our relationship. I'm grief-stricken. Please write to me.*

After I finished I felt encouraged that perhaps I might hear back from Isabelle at last. It was time I took control of my life. I couldn't change the past, but I had to give the future my best go. I put the diary aside and dialled another number, for my lawyer.

'Mr Morgan, please. It's Mimi Lanesbrough.'

'Mrs Lanesbrough, what can I do for you?'

'Would you be free to come over this afternoon?'

'Let me check … Not this afternoon but I could come in the next couple of hours.'

'Perfect, thank you.'

Relieved, I replaced the receiver.

I was pouring over papers when there was a knock on the door.

'Come in.'

I stood as Mr Morgan entered the room. 'Please, take a seat,' I said as I shook his hand. 'Annie, can you bring some tea and sandwiches, please.'

'This must be urgent,' Mr Morgan said and steepled his hands in front of him.

'Actually, it's been something I should have dealt with some time ago. I appreciate you coming at once.'

He nodded, waiting for me to speak.

I took a breath. 'I want to divorce my husband.'

As the words left my mouth so did a heaviness I'd lived with for so long that I'd forgotten it was there. Mr Morgan raised an eyebrow and studied me with for a few moments.

'Very well,' he said at last. 'On what grounds?'

'Desertion. He's lived in Edinburgh for the last eight years.'

He nodded. 'I'll see to that.'

'Thank you. I also want to update my will as a matter of urgency and remove my husband's name. My daughter is sixteen. I know she'd be too young to manage her inheritance if anything happened to me, but is there some sort of trust I could set up?'

'Of course, it's common practice. If you wish, we could put the entire estate including the Hall into a trust fund.'

'Thank you.'

'However, we may have to do this first before filing for the divorce or the removal of your husband as a beneficiary from your will. This should limit his ability to claim against the estate. But I will have to look into it,' he said, making some notes.

'I understand.'

'My firm could act as trustees unless you have someone else in mind?'

That question underscored my loneliness in a way that I could no longer ignore—I had no one else. So as soon as Mr Morgan left, I sat with a pen in my hand hovering over a piece of paper. Will hadn't replied to my first letter all those years ago. But I had to try one more time.

My darling Will,

It seems a lifetime has passed since I wrote to you last time. Did you get my letter? Or perhaps you chose not to reply? I couldn't bear the thought that you may have stopped loving me. I've asked for a divorce and soon I'll be finally free and after all those years of just existing, I owe it to myself to grasp for happiness. Do you think it wrong that I'm reaching out again? I hope not. But if you do, then please forgive me.

With all my love,
Mimi

I sealed the letter and went on the search for Annie.

'Could you please send this letter off for me,' I said.

She looked at the addressee and stiffened. The downward curve of her mouth left no doubt that she disapproved. We stood there in a silence that was weighed down with words that neither of us wished to speak.

'Thank you, Annie, that's all,' I said at last, unable to hide my dismay at her impertinence.

As I walked away she called, 'Miss Mimi.'

What now? I thought as I turned and fixed her with my eyes.

'He married last month,' she said and handed me back the letter.

Those four words shattered my heart into a thousand pieces.

Chapter Forty-Nine

Isabelle was at the kitchen table with Mimi's diary and the unopened letter in front of her. She was glad she'd told Angus about her discoveries and wondered what the letter to Will said. She opened it and read.

> *It seems a lifetime has passed since I wrote to you last time. Did you get my letter? Or perhaps you chose not to reply?*

Isabelle sat there thinking. So, Mimi had already written once to Will. Or she should say Hamish. Why hadn't he replied? She had to find out. She took Mimi's diary, hoping she had listened to her and followed Bonelle to Edinburgh.

'What the hell happened? Why is Bonelle sixteen?'

Isabelle read as fast as she could and shook her head. A small fire was all it'd taken to destroy her chance to change the future. So far she'd not managed to alter one single thing about the past. Isabelle exhaled slowly as she reached the end and realised that to Bonelle the Hall must have been like a sibling that took away Mimi's love and attention. Like Chloe's illness and then her death had taken Bonelle from her. She wrote:

> **I'm so upset you didn't see my last message; I wish you had. At least now Glen will be out of your life once and for all. It's just such a shame that Will has already married. I know you must be devastated. It is so unfair. Life can be so.**
>
> **Perhaps though, it is time to let him go and move on. I know it'll take time, but you have to start thinking of yourself and maybe slowly building a bridge with**

Bonelle. I know it's been a while, but you have a degree. Maybe you could look into starting your career. I love you, and I'm here for you.

As Isabelle closed the diary, she couldn't help worrying. How many more setbacks could Mimi take? Apart from the staff at the Hall, she'd lost everyone she ever loved. It was time for Isabelle to take things into her own hands. She picked up her phone and clicked on her mother's name.

Her pulse beat to the ringing tone.

'I hope you're ringing to tell me you changed your mind,' said Bonelle.

No, I'm not but, I've got to get you to the Hall, thought Isabelle but said, 'Something like that.'

'I see.'

'But it's a bit complicated,' Isabelle rushed on. 'I thought maybe you could come over and we'll sort it out?'

Isabelle chewed her lip as she waited for an answer.

'Fine. But this better be the end of it.'

Isabelle silently thanked the universe as she hung up. She had to get things moving.

The next morning, Isabelle parked the Volvo in front of Silcraig farmhouse. It was time to for the truth to come out in the place where everything had started. Besides, the last time they'd spoken, Hamish had said that he'd like to see the Hall again.

Hamish was already walking towards her. His appearance seemed to mirror the significance of the occasion for him she thought as she gave him a hug and caught the scent of cologne.

'You're ready?' Isabelle asked after they'd settled in the car.

'As ready as I'll ever be.'

His features were taut, and his usual smile missing. They spent the short trip in silence, and Hamish wiped his brow with his handkerchief every few minutes. Isabelle drove up the drive and parked in front of the Hall.

'Here we are.' She looked over at Hamish who seemed frozen in place.

'Can you give me a few minutes?' he whispered without looking at her.

'I'll wait outside for you.'

Isabelle left the car and wondered what it must be like for him to return to the Hall with all its memories, considering her own apprehension was making its way up to her chest. After a few minutes she heard the crunch of gravel as Hamish disembarked from the car.

'It's been sixty-one years since I last was here,' Hamish said with a tremor in his voice.

Nearly twice as long as I've lived, thought Isabelle. She couldn't begin to comprehend what it must feel like.

'Would you like me to leave you alone for a bit? I could set up everything on the terrace. It's only a picnic lunch so take as much time as you need.'

Isabelle brushed his arm and went indoors. She'd just sat down when Hamish joined her.

'The rose garden,' he said, bending his head at intervals to breath in the scent. 'Can I?' he asked.

Isabelle nodded and watched as he picked a single lilac rose, holding it to his face as he walked back to the table.

'This was Mimi's favourite place. When she wanted to be alone, you'd find her sitting there.' He pointed to the bench. 'Right next to the lilac rose, with her knees drawn up to her chest, lost in her own world. Aye, so many memories ...'

'I can imagine.' Isabelle took a sip of her wine. 'And soon the Hall will look more like its old self.'

'That's grand that the Hall will return to its former glory. Mimi would be very proud of you.' He patted her hand. 'Do you mind if I take a stroll around?'

'Of course not.'

An hour later Isabelle saw Hamish coming up the lawn and went to get their coffee and Mrs Murray's cake.

'You're spoiling me,' he said and sat down.

Isabelle placed the tray on the table and poured coffee into their cups. She noticed a calmness about him. Her feeling of unease grew at the thought she was about to unsettle him by bringing up the past. Her shoulders tensed and her mouth felt dry. She took a sip of her coffee and rolled back her shoulders.

'Hamish, can I ask you something?'

'Anything, lass.'

'Do you know someone called Will, who was close to Mimi?'

Isabelle watched all colour drain from Hamish's face. The look of astonishment in his eyes was an affirmative. He rubbed the flat of his hands over his face, took a breath that juddered in his chest. and nodded.

Isabelle's head went into overdrive. Guilt at being the cause of his distress competed with her excitement at the prospect of hearing the story from Mimi's lover—her own grandfather. Eventually, she found her speech.

'Would you like me to get you a drink?' she offered.

Hamish nodded again as though he no longer could speak. She returned with two bottles and glasses.

'Whisky or brandy?' she asked.

'A dram of the Balvenie for me if you don't mind.'

Isabelle handed Hamish his whisky and poured herself two fingers of Hennessy XO.

Hamish raised his glass to Isabelle. '*Slàinte mhaith.*'

She smiled at his use of the Scottish toast for good health. She took a sip and almost choked on her drink at Hamish's next words.

'Will was my nickname. Alasdair started it when we were young. He used to call me by my surname, Williams. It shortened to Will at some point and somehow it stuck.'

So Hamish *was* Will. Somehow, hearing it spoken aloud made it real in a way to Isabelle that reading about it hadn't. A rush of adrenaline made her body buzz.

'Excuse me a minute,' she said and got up from the table.

As soon as Isabelle was inside, she ran to her bedroom and sat on the edge of the bed, closed her eyes, and focused on her breathing. She then took the box out of her wardrobe and carried it outside, where Hamish was still sitting, lost in his own world.

Isabelle set the box in front of him and sat down before her legs failed her. 'I believe these are yours.'

The expression on Hamish' face spoke volumes. As tears gathered in his eyes, he reached for the letters with trembling hands, and he held on to them. He played with the ribbon. He wasn't looking at her; his eyes were fixed on an indeterminate point in the distance. Isabelle held her breath.

'She was—is—the love of my life, but destiny had different plans for us.' His voice shook with sorrow and regret. 'I remember the first time I realised I'd always love her. We were in the stables after her ride, and she told me she was going to St. Andrews to study. I'll never forget the feeling. It was as though someone had taken a scythe and slashed my heart.'

Tears fell down his face. Isabelle reached and stroked his hand as though she could rub away his pain.

'The loss I felt was so all consuming. In hindsight I think I must've had a premonition because the next time she visited the Hall, I heard over the grapevine that she was walking out with a young fellow.'

Isabelle saw the lines on his face deepen and watched him take a breath as though to dislodge the entrenched pain of loss. She had so many questions, but she didn't want to disrupt his reverie.

As though reading her mind, he explained, 'You see, in them days things were different. I would never have stood a chance, what with me being one of the staff and she from a family of landowners.

'For a few years, I only saw glimpses of her here and there, but then things changed when Alasdair died. The Hall went to Mimi. She stayed here, and Glen went back to St Andrews to wrap up their lives there.'

Hamish stopped as though to gather strength for the next part of his story. Isabelle was spellbound. When reading the diaries, she had tried to fix the image of Mimi and her lover many times but somehow it had always seemed like a story.

'In our grief we found comfort in each other for a short while. When Glen came back from St Andrews, he caught us together, and I had to leave for her sake.'

He closed his eyes. Isabelle could see the strain on his face.

'I came back one more time and begged her to come away with me, and she said she'd think about it. We were supposed to meet that night in the Moonlight Cove. I waited until dawn, but she never came.'

Isabelle's heart ached for him.

'Years later, I was told her husband was an invalid. There had been an accident or some such thing and by the time the news reached me that he had passed, God rest his soul, I'd married my lovely wife, Elsbeth. I loved her, but not the way I loved Mimi. I just couldn't.'

Isabelle was stunned by the depth of Hamish's love for Mimi after all these years, and for a moment her thoughts wandered to Angus. Would he ever love her the way Hamish had loved Mimi? Nonsense. He probably still saw her as little Belle, his childhood friend. Hamish's words brought her back to present.

'It was only after my Elsbeth was gone that I could come back here. I wanted to see Mimi again, but I was already too late. Mimi too was gone. Sometimes I wish I'd gone before her; it's been like losing her all over again.'

Hamish stopped. Isabelle waited for him to say more but nothing came. He slumped in the chair, and Isabelle thought he looked every year of his age. She was about to tell him of the letter Mimi never sent to him. That she too always loved him. That he had a daughter, and he was her grandfather, when she saw all colour drain from his face. He was gasping for air.

Her training kicked in. She jumped off her chair and helped him to sit upright. She just hoped he was not suffering a heart attack.

'Hamish, I need you to look at me.' But his eyes were still fixed skyward. 'Hamish, look at me.' She placed her hands on the sides of his face and brought his face down.

'I'm...'

'I want you to breathe with me, nice and slowly. In ...' Isabelle inhaled 'and out,' she exhaled.

To her relief, Hamish started to copy her. Eventually his breathing evened out and he stood.

'I'm okay, now. I'll be off, lass, and thank you.'

Isabelle thought he still looked unsteady but understood he needed to get away; the exhaustion was written in every line on his face. And if she was honest, she too needed the break. The rest had to wait for another day. She didn't think he could cope with more revelations today.

'Come on, I'll drop you off. And you have to promise me you'll see your doctor.'

Chapter Fifty

Mimi, September 1978

Dear Diary,

How long has it been? Since that day five years ago when I learned of my failure on my daughter's sixteenth birthday and that Will had married, I've been shrouded in the blackness of depression and condemned to the Hall as my prison. Even knowing I had Isabelle didn't help, for she must have been tired of hearing the disaster that's been my life. I wish I'd been brave enough to end it once and for all. But alas I've always been and remain a coward.

Today is another special milestone in my daughter's life. It's Bonelle's twenty-first birthday, and soon there'll be her graduation. I've received a formal invite in the post, not sent by my daughter but by Glen, the man who didn't sire her but through some cruel twist of fate has become the father she worships. Yet as her mother who carried and gave life to her, I've been cast aside and treated as a stranger for so long that I now truly feel like one.

I shook my head to rid the morose thoughts that had become part of me. There was no point, and as always I had only myself to blame.

I read Isabelle's message again, urging me to build bridges with Bonelle and move on from Will. As so many times before, my mind skipped the passage of time, taking me back to that night thirteen years ago, and I asked myself yet again if I would have gone away with Will had I known what pitiless plans the future had in store for me? But Isabelle was right, I needed to think of myself.

My darling Isabelle, I could not have wished for a kinder and more loyal friend than you. I don't know how I didn't drown in my own misery and self-pity all these years. But you're right, as always. It's time I took charge of my life. Though perhaps it's too late for Bonelle and me, I like the idea of finding a way to put my degree to use. But enough of me. How have you been? Did you resolve your differences with your mother? And what about your sweetheart? Is he still engaged to that other woman?

An hour later the car pulled in front of the hotel. I walked the few steps into the foyer, and with every step my pulse quickened. I stopped at the banquet Hall and my eyes roamed the room in search of Bonelle. My heart stopped as I spotted Glen in his wheelchair by the window, Jane's hand resting on his shoulder. I followed his line of vision, and my eyes fell on my daughter, now a woman surrounded by friends.

At least she's happy, I thought, which was really all that mattered. She noticed me only when I was in front of her.

'Mum,' she said and let me hug her for a moment that was not enough to still a fraction of my yearning for her.

'Hello, my love, happy birthday. How have you—'

I didn't finish my sentence as Bonelle screeched with delight at the sight of more friends. But I didn't mind. I'd have time to speak to her later. As I turned around, I met Glen's stare. My back stiffened, and I swallowed hard to supress the myriad feelings that threatened to break the surface. Nausea rose in my throat as he wheeled himself towards me.

'Hello, Mhairi.'

I nodded. I knew I couldn't control myself if I spoke. Yet the words forced themselves out of me.

'Why haven't you signed the divorce papers?'

'Oh, Mhairi.' He laughed and shook his head before he fixed his blazing eyes on me with such disdain that my breath caught. 'Surely, even you can't be that naive? But I forget, you are. Do you think that after you condemned me to a wheelchair and ruined my life I'd give you carte blanche to be with your lover boy?'

I had to summon every ounce of strength not to strike his face, and I all but ran out of the room before I lost control. I was about to head for the washroom when we were ushered to dinner. It seemed as though my ordeal was not over yet.

As we sat down to dinner, the weight of hurt crushed my chest when I realised I was seated at the opposite end of the table to my daughter, who was flanked by her father and Jane. And I had no choice but to play my part despite the humiliation. I was not going to spoil my daughter's birthday.

The next few days I spent in an even bleaker darkness than a mausoleum. I had at last emerged at Annie's insistence for breakfast when she came in.

'Miss Mimi, there's an urgent call for you. It's Miss Bonelle.'

I dropped my napkin and ran into the hallway, feeling heat cursing through my body with anticipation.

'Bonelle—'

My daughter's howl invaded my being.

'Bonelle, my love, what's happened?' I raised my voice, trying to make myself heard, but my question was met with more wailing. 'Bonelle, darling,' I tried again but to no avail.

A feeling of dread descended on me, penetrating every fibre of my body as I waited for her cries, hiccups, and silence to subside, before I got my answer.

'It's Pa.'

My heart stopped. 'What about Pa?'

'He's ... he died,' she said in a voice so void of any life that the hairs on my neck stood up.

'What—'

The line went dead. I don't know how long I stood there with the receiver in my hand and Bonelle's words ringing in my ears before Annie appeared by my side and led me to the living room.

'Can I get you a coffee, Miss?'

'A brandy please, Annie. And tell Malcom to collect me as soon as he can.'

'Miss Mimi, you're shivering.'

Annie handed me the glass and helped me take a sip. She then wrapped a throw over my shoulders and began to rub my back as I sat there, staring into space, before the warmth of the brandy and Annie's hand seeped through me.

Alas my relief was short-lived. My stomach tightened as the car pulled up at the house in Regent Terrace. The image of the first time I had visited flashed before my eyes. I'd been so full of joy and excitement walking up these steps with Glen by my side.

The maid opened the door and led me into the drawing room where I found my daughter asleep on the sofa and Jane sitting next to her in another kind of oblivion. I swallowed the bile in my throat.

'I'm truly sorry for your loss,' I said, knowing my words could not touch her grief.

Jane looked at me with eyes void of any life. Weariness overtook me. I took the chair next to Bonelle and began stroking her hair that draped over the arm of the sofa like golden gossamer. The unfairness that she too had lost her father so young broke my heart. I felt defeated by my own helplessness. It seemed like an eternity that we all sat there like a frozen tableau.

'Jane, what happened?' I asked when I gathered the courage to face her grief.

'He had a heart attack last night,' she whispered then stood and left the room, leaving me to wonder why my daughter hadn't reached out to me sooner.

The cold hand of resentment at Glen for alienating Bonelle from me clutched at my heart. I shook my head. What was the point? But the bitterness I felt at the loss of all those years refused to leave me just because Glen was dead. After a couple of hours, Bonelle's head stirred under my hand.

I looked down and she opened her eyes, blinking at me, as though she didn't know who I was.

'Hello, my love,' I said as she propped herself up on one elbow. 'Let me get you some tea.'

'No, thanks, Mum. I'm fine.'

'Bonelle, darling, why don't you and Jane come back with me to the Hall and let me take care of you?'

'Thank you, Mum, we're fine here.'

'Then why don't I stay here for a few days? What do you say?' I encouraged her, trying to hide my hurt that she refused to let me comfort her.

'It's fine, Mum, really,' she said and looked away.

I didn't know why after all these years I kept hoping that perhaps one day I would get my daughter back.

Chapter Fifty-One

On Monday Isabelle awoke to the sound of metal crashing and men shouting. What on earth was going on? She looked out of the window and saw that men in hi-vis vests and safety helmets were setting up a scaffolding. Worried that she'd overslept, she checked the time. It wasn't yet eight.

When she walked into the kitchen a bit later Mrs Murray shook her head. 'There won't be any peace in the house with all that noise.' But her eyes told Isabelle that she was secretly pleased.

'Mrs Murray, there's something I'd like to discuss with you,' said Isabelle. The idea had come to her last night, after she'd read more of Mimi's diaries.

Mrs Murray put the coffee on the table, shoved a plate of toast in front of Isabelle, and sat down, looking at her.

'How do you feel about living at the Hall?' Isabelle asked.

The fold between her eyebrows deepened. 'But I already have the cottage, Miss.'

'Yes, and of course you can keep it if that's what you'd prefer. But I feel you're a big part of the Hall and should live under its roof.'

Mrs Murray widened her eyes. 'You don't mean that, Miss?'

'Of course, you could have the guest suite. We could convert one of the adjacent rooms into a kitchen, and that way you'd have your own apartment. What do you say?'

Mrs Murray looked down at her lap. Isabelle hoped she hadn't somehow offended her. She was about to say something when Mrs Murray looked up at her.

'Thank you, Miss Isabelle, that'll suit me very well,' she whispered and looked down at her lap again.

A lump rose in Isabelle's throat. She walked over to Mrs Murray and kissed her on the cheek.

'No, it's me who needs to thank you.'

Though she had appreciated Mrs Murray's help since her grandmother's death, it was through Mimi's diaries that she had understood what Mrs Murray had done for her family, a debt that Isabelle could never repay.

The previous few weeks, Isabelle had been rushing everywhere, sorting out builders who seemed to work at the speed of lightening. The painters and decorators had also arrived a couple of weeks earlier. There were around fifty men poking and prodding the Hall, but the Hall seemed to take it with grace.

Isabelle was in the study, preparing an update for James when there was a knock and the door opened before she had time to respond. Mrs Murray rushed inside and closed the door behind her, catching her breath.

'You'd best hurry-up, Miss. Your mother just arrived and she's not a happy lady.'

Isabelle cursed. Bonelle must know now that Isabelle had duped her.

'Thank you, Mrs Murray. Where is she?'

'I managed to settle her in the kitchen with a cup of coffee,' she said like a proud mother who had dealt with an unruly child.

'Thank you, I'll be a second.'

'I'll leave you to it, Miss,' Mrs Murray said and left the room.

As Isabelle diverted her attention back to her update a thought crossed her mind. Why hadn't she asked Mrs Murray whether her mother had an inkling of what had happened all those years ago? What if Glen had told Bonelle about her parentage to spite Mimi? She wouldn't be surprised if he had. Maybe she could find the answer in Mimi's diary.

Isabelle ran to her room and picked it up. She was shocked at how much Mimi had suffered. But what broke her heart was that she'd thought of taking her own life.

How much more would Mimi and Bonelle have to go through? she wondered as she read about Glen's death.

Her poor Mum. She tried to think what it would have been like if she'd lost her father a decade ago? She shook her head. It was too horrid to contemplate.

After reading Mimi's message, Isabelle was relieved to see there was still hope. She picked up her pen.

> **I'm so glad you're over the worst. I would have been devastated if anything had happened to you. You're such a strong woman, Mimi. It's unbelievable how much you've been through. I'm so happy to hear you're thinking of doing something with your degree. Nothing has changed between Mum and me. It's all so hopeless. Angus and his fiancée broke up, but I really think he just likes me as a friend. Please be there for Bonelle.**

Isabelle closed the diary, shoved it into the drawer, and went downstairs.

'Hi, Mum,' she said as she entered the kitchen.

Bonelle was dressed all in white, but Isabelle doubted her outfit would stay like that with all the dust and dirt.

'Isabelle, what's the meaning of all this?'

Despite her mother's tone, Isabelle wondered if it'd been a good idea to bring Bonelle here under false pretences.

'The Hall is being refurbished Mum, that's all.'

'I can see that Isabelle, but why?'

'Because although Mimi looked after the Hall, a lot of things were neglected. The last time the Hall was fully refurbished was when great-uncle Alasdair took over. That was over sixty-years ago,' she explained, parroting the information James had told her.

'Why am I only finding out about this now? Didn't you say we were going to finish this business?'

'Yes, we will.'

'We'd better, Isabelle. I haven't jetted over here to waste my time on your antics.'

Isabelle let her have the last word, considering the task she still had ahead of her. 'I'm sure you must be tired, the guest room on the second floor is ready. Why don't you have a rest, and we can talk over dinner?'

Isabelle didn't see her mum the rest of the afternoon. It was six thirty and the builders had just left. Since her discovery that Glen wasn't Bonelle's father, she'd spent hours wondering if she should tell her mother. Why should she be the bearer of bad news? In the end she'd decided it was the right thing to do. However, now that the moment was here, anxiety was creeping up Isabelle's body, lodging itself in her chest. She sat on the terrace with a glass of chardonnay and two of Mimi's diaries. She watched the waves, imagining they were washing away the tension.

'I've been looking for you everywhere,' said Bonelle.

'Sorry, I thought you were still asleep. Would you like a glass of wine?

'Yes, the same, please.'

Isabelle poured her mother a glass and topped her own. She would need it. She could sense a current of tension in the atmosphere, or maybe it was just her. Anger at Mimi for dumping this on her flared up inside her. But there was no point in delaying the inevitable. She took a sip of her wine, braced herself, and spoke.

'Mum…' Isabelle cleared her throat, tried to ignore her mother's look of irritation, and pushed on. 'I found Mimi's diaries. There're quite a few of them, but you need to read this part.'

Isabelle handed over one of Mimi's diaries and pointed to the section she had marked, noticing the tremble in her hand as she did so.

'Just leave it here, I'll have a look later,' Bonelle said and looked away.

'Please Mum, just look at it.'

'I said I do it later,' snapped Bonelle. 'Besides, we were going to talk about the Hall.'

Isabelle ignored her mother's remonstration and carried on. There was no way she wanted to delay this.

'Please, Mum,' she said again with more assertiveness than she felt.

'Oh, for goodness' sake, Isabelle, stop being so melodramatic. What could possibly be so important that it has to be done right this minute?'

'You'll see.'

That got Bonelle's attention. Isabelle's heart sank as she also realised that her mum didn't know the truth. She held her breath as Bonelle picked up the diary and opened the page. The colour drained from her mum's face and her eyes widened as she read Mimi's words:

Bonelle was type A. My blood type was O and Glen's B.... There was no chance that Bonelle's could be A, unless one of her parents had the blood types of AB or A. Bonelle was Will's daughter.

Isabelle knew the words by heart. She tried to imagine what it would be like to realise that everything she'd known to be true for her entire life was a lie.

Bonelle's shriek made Isabelle jump.

'If it proves anything, it's that she had a sordid affair, the news of which is nothing new to me. But this,' she hit the page with her hand, 'this is preposterous. A wild fantasy of a delusional woman.'

Bonelle swept the diary off the table, making the glasses clink from the force.

Despite having prepared herself for the worst, Isabelle still couldn't help feeling shocked at her mother's reaction. She fixed her eyes on her glass of wine and watched her thumb and index turning the stem over and over as she tried to order her thoughts. So she'd been right. Her mother had known all along about the affair. But she hadn't a clue that Hamish was her father. Maybe it'd make it easier if she knew more about Hamish? She had to try.

She looked up at her mum. Bonelle's face was so red it looked as if the skin had peeled off her face, and Isabelle could see the flesh underneath. The veins on her temples were pulsating and her eyes were fixed on the ground.

'Mum,' she whispered. 'It's not a fantasy. I've met Hamish. He's a nice man. You should meet—'

'Enough of this nonsense, Isabelle. I had the best father I could have ever wished for. I have no interest in that impostor.'

Despite her rage, Isabelle could see Bonelle's eyes were tearing. Her own chest tightened with anger at Mimi. She needed to do something. Isabelle pushed the other diary towards her mum. The one where Glen admitted Bonelle wasn't his daughter.

'Mum, please—'

'No! I've had enough of you, Mimi, and this miserable place,' shouted Bonelle.

She stood and the sound the chair made as it crashed against the stone masked her mother's footsteps as she strode indoors.

Isabelle sat with her head in her hands. There was nothing more she could do. For once her mother had all her empathy. She too would have reacted that way if someone told her that her father wasn't her real father. Maybe she shouldn't have said anything after all. Her shoulders slumped with the weight of the responsibility.

The sound of gravel crunching and a car horn disrupted her thoughts. Isabelle reached the front door just as Bonelle was dragging her suitcase to the taxi.

'Mum, where are you going? You said you'd stay the night.'

'I changed my mind.'

She closed the taxi door in Isabelle's face, who in that moment hated both herself and Mimi. She watched the taxi go then walked back into the Hall. She saw Mrs Murray standing in the middle of the hallway with her hands folded in front of her.

Isabelle held her gaze. 'You knew, didn't you?'

'Yes. That's what killed her.'

Isabelle's heart raced. 'What do you mean?'

'You'd best come and sit—'

'No, please just tell me what happened,' Isabelle said.

'It was the afternoon of the day she passed. She asked me to make some tea and join her by the fire. She had something to tell me, she said. Anyhow, we had almost finished the tea when she told me Hamish—or Will as he was known back then—was Miss Bonelle's father.' She looked down.

Isabelle couldn't understand why Mimi hadn't told anyone sooner.

'Unbelievable, after all those years.'

'I know,' Mrs Murray nodded. 'She'd barely finished when her eyes went funny. She put her hand to her head and passed out.'

Chapter Fifty-Two

Mimi, August 1982

The French sun was blazing down on us as we waited to be ushered into the church. I was standing with the groom's parents, who didn't speak a word of English, and a few others.

'Good God, this heat,' I heard a gentleman say, wiping at his brow with a handkerchief.

At last, someone I can talk to, I thought and seized the opportunity.

'It is rather relentless,' I said.

'Yes, you'd think after all these years of living here, I'd get used to it.' He pushed his hat back in place. 'By the way, I'm Pierre, Pierre Brown.' He offered his hand.

'I'm Mimi Lanesbrough. Are you a native, Pierre?' I asked, though judging by his surname and his accent, he must have an English heritage.

'My mother was French, and my father was English. I lived in both countries but moved here permanently about six years ago. What about you?'

'Oh, Scottish through and through,' I said and laughed.

'Well, you don't sound it, if I may say so. You must be one of the bride's guests then?'

'Yes, the bride is my daughter. And you?'

'I've known Jean-Francois's family forever. We were—still are—neighbours. They're a great couple. Both rather ambitious young people.'

That was news to me, as Bonelle never shared anything with me. And it hurt that a stranger knew more about my daughter than I did.

'Ah, I think it's time,' said Pierre as the groom arrived. 'I'd best leave you to it.'

At all my daughter's milestones, I'd been left on my own. Not today.

'No. Please, Pierre, would you mind sitting with me?' I asked.

'It would be my pleasure, Mimi. See you in a moment.' He tipped his hat and went ahead.

I straightened my back, looked at Jean-Francois, and began my march to the altar, all the while keeping my eyes glued to the figure of Christ with his crown of thorns that seemed to reflect the thorns in my own heart.

I lowered myself next to Pierre in the front pew and squeezed his hand in thanks. It didn't take long before silence fell upon us, and music played that to my surprise was not the 'Wedding March.' I assumed it must be the French equivalent.

I turned around and watched Bonelle stride into the church on the arm of the groom's father. Despite myself, my heart ached that the father she'd known and adored wasn't leading her up the aisle, knowing she must be thinking of him, and that she had a father who could have been here for her, had I been brave enough to put them in touch.

Still, I could see the joy in her eyes as she stood next to Jean-Francois. In the couple of days that I'd got to know him, he'd won me over.

As I watched the ceremony, my mind wandered through the maze of the past, and as each image obscured the next, I prayed for Bonelle's happiness.

The sound of cheers brought me back to the present.

Pierre touched my hand. 'Shall we?'

I nodded and followed him outside. After the photographs were taken, I walked up to the newlyweds.

'What a lovely ceremony that was.' I kissed Jean-Francois and hugged Bonelle.

'Thanks, Mum,' she said and for the first time in so long, she yielded into my arms.

Perhaps this is a new dawn for us after all, I thought and soaked up the feeling.

Back at the villa, we sat at a table on the terrace right by the beach. The setup reminded me of the Hall.

'What is it you do, Pierre?' I asked before taking a bite of my fish.

'I paint. But I used to be in the city. What about you?'

'I live at Lanesbrough Hall and run my family's estate. It used to be quite a versatile farming business, but five years ago I set up a breeding program.'

'And you've been doing all this on your own? Bonelle mentioned her father had passed.'

'Yes, he did.' I didn't want to share the details of the catastrophe that had been my marriage with this man. 'I have some help, but I guess the responsibility is mine.'

Yes, I thought, *a responsibility that I'd never been prepared for and one that I let ruin my life.*

'That's very impressive indeed. I have a love of country estates. Imogen, my wife, and I used to stay at one whenever we could.'

'Your wife's passed away?'

'Yes, that's when I moved to France. Too many memories.' He shook his head. 'But I seem to have brought my loneliness with me. You can't escape the ghosts of the past.'

'I couldn't agree more.'

I sipped at my glass as we watched couples taking the floor.

'Shall we?'

Pierre took my hand and led me to the dance floor. Our bodies merged as we swayed to the music. It felt good after all those years I'd spent in the depths of depression without a human touch.

I closed my eyes, determined to savour every moment, until I heard Pierre whisper in my ear.

'Let's go for a walk and watch the sunset.'

As we ambled along the sea, I thought of how much I'd been enjoying the day. It was as though a box had been unlocked inside me and life was streaming again in my veins.

Pierre turned to face me. He held my gaze in a way no man had done since Will had left. He took my face in his hands and his lips touched mine. For once I gave into the moment without inhibition. And I realised how much I'd missed being desired.

'I'll call you this evening. Yes?' Pierre said the next day as we stood at the airport.

'I'd like that, and you must come and visit.'

'Of course. You won't get rid of me that quickly, Mimi Lanesbrough.' He bent and kissed me.

I waved one last time, feeling as if I'd been given a new lease of life. I couldn't wait to tell Isabelle. She was still the only friend who knew everything about me. I just hoped that after all this time, she'd still be there.

I settled in my seat, opened my diary, and as I saw her message, my eyes teared at her kindness.

I too am glad I escaped that place I was in. It felt like my soul had died and I had been left only with the shell of a body. You'll be pleased to know I followed your advice and set up a breeding program on the estate. But at long last, there's light.

And with every word I wrote, I relived the joy of my daughter's wedding day. At last, a new chapter had begun.

Chapter Fifty-Three

It was the beginning of September, and the Hall was transformed. Isabelle and Mrs Murray had watched as the builders dismantled the scaffolding and packed up their tools. The loaded trucks disappeared down the driveway for the last time and peace returned.

'Come on, Mrs Murray; let's have a look around.'

Isabelle grabbed Mrs Murray's hand and they walked into each room, admiring their creation. They arrived at Mrs Murray's apartment. The day before, Isabelle had made several journeys in the old Volvo to move Mrs Murray's belongings from Burn Cottage. Now the rocking chair was by the window, and the photographs took a place of pride on the mantlepiece. A throw was draped over the bed and a chest was sitting at the foot of it.

'Do you like it?' Isabelle asked.

'It's very comfortable; I already feel at home.' Mrs Murray put her hand on Isabelle's shoulder. 'I can't thank you enough.'

Isabelle thought of her mum again and wished she could see the Hall. She'd been worried about her. Since her last departure Bonelle had ignored all her messages and calls, until yesterday when she had sent a one-liner saying *I'm fine*.

Isabelle rolled her eyes; there was no way her mum could be fine. How could she? Part of her wished she'd never discovered the diaries and letters. But there was nothing she could do. She'd never imagined that her relationship with her mother could get this close to breaking point.

Had she done the right thing by telling her about Hamish? Isabelle had asked herself this question so many times, and though part of her regretted it, the other part of her knew Bonelle had a right to know. She just hoped that in time she would forgive her.

After they finished the tour, Isabelle left Mrs Murray to prepare for her guest. To her delight, it was a warm and sunny day; it seemed the summer was persisting. Isabelle had just placed a basket of bread on the table when she heard Angus's footsteps.

'What a treat; thanks Belle.' He gave her a hug and kissed her on the cheek, which made Isabelle's stomach flip.

'Come on, I'll give you the grand tour,' she said and pulled him indoors.

She walked him through every room, showing off the Hall.

'Wow, this looks amazing. The Hall's really come alive. You could have a career in interior design if you ever tired of being a doctor.'

'I can't take all the credit I'm afraid. It was a joint effort with Mrs Murray,' she said, pleased that Angus liked it. 'How's work coming on? You said in your messages there'd been some kind of disaster?' she asked as they made their way back outside.

'Yeah, it was pretty intense, but all is fine now.'

'I'm glad it's over. It's been a while since I had one of those weeks at work.' Isabelle poured them some wine.

'Yes, but everything with the Hall and your mum hasn't been exactly a walk in the park.'

Isabelle sipped her wine. 'No, it hasn't, and the worst is yet to come.'

Toward the end of lunch, Angus asked, 'Have you heard anything about the court date yet?'

'Yes. Apparently, it's going to be in a couple of months.'

He ate the last of his baguette, then stood to help clear the table. 'It must be tough for you. I just don't get it.'

'That makes two of us.'

He grinned. 'And all because our Mimi was such an adventurous, naughty girl.'

'Angus Fairbairn watch your language,' she joked and with a flick of her wrist swiped him with the tea towel.

Angus grabbed the other end. 'That's not very ladylike, Miss Belle,' he said and pulled on the tea towel.

Isabelle lost the tug-of-war and started running before Angus could flick the cloth at her, squealing as she saw he was gaining on her. Angus grabbed her around the waist and turned her around to face him.

'Got you, little minx,' he said, holding her.

Before she knew, his lips moved over her face, kissing her brow, her eyes, her cheeks, and the tip of her nose. The thrill of each touch reached every corner of her body, immersing her in pleasure. When he finally kissed her lips, she thought she had been set on fire.

'I'm sorry to interrupt you.'

Isabelle and Angus pulled apart at once at the sound of a voice—Alex's voice.

Isabelle's stomach whooshed like a rollercoaster. She turned and looked at Alex, who just stood there, staring. Her face was a picture of bleak calm. Isabelle nestled into Angus's arm like it was a shield that could protect her. She wasn't sure she could have remained standing without his support. She fixed her eyes on her sandals, no longer able to hold Alex's gaze, which seemed to scream at her *How could you?*

'Alex, what in God's name are you doing here?' Angus raised his voice. A tremble invaded Isabelle's body where it touched his.

'I've come to talk to you in person, after you ignored my messages and calls. And blocked me. You weren't at the cottage. I rang your mum and she said you'd be here.'

'I'm sorry you made the long journey, but there's nothing to discuss, Alex.'

'Please Angus, can we just talk, in private?' Alex asked, not looking at Isabelle.

Isabelle was surprised Alex had taken what she'd seen in stride, given her own insides were roiling with embarrassment, resentment, and a pinch of guilt for good measure. Isabelle doubted she could contain her discomfort for much longer and was about to remove herself, but Angus tightened his grip around her.

'You can say whatever you want in front of Belle,' he said.

Isabelle felt a frisson of warmth, which was soon replaced by a tightness in her chest.

'Very well,' said Alex. 'Can we at least sit down? I've had a long journey and little sleep. Could I have a coffee please, Isabelle?'

Isabelle felt a flash of heat and shot Alex a look that said, *How dare you turn up out of the blue and uninvited at my home and be demanding.* But the expression in Alex's eyes softened the tightness in her jaw—but only just.

Angus let her go, and Isabelle hastened her steps. If Alex thought she could get rid of her, she was mistaken. It was clear as day that Alex had an agenda, and it did not include Isabelle. As soon as she was inside, Isabelle ran to the kitchen, whizzing around like she was possessed. She piled everything on a tray and walked out as fast as she could.

She could hear Angus speaking outside and halted to listen, wondering what he'd say in her absence.

'Alex, I know it's awful, because I went through it. The first month was an absolute nightmare. There were times when I thought I'd never get out of it.'

Isabelle felt a tinge of guilt for eavesdropping on them, but she couldn't help herself.

'I'm sorry, I know I was wrong. I made a mistake, Angus. I should never have left.'

Isabelle's heart sank. What if Alex managed to persuade Angus to get back together with her? Maybe she should make an appearance after all.

'You hated it here. You turned into someone I barely recognised,' he said.

Isabelle approached with the tray. She hadn't seen Angus this agitated in a long time.

'I know—' Alex said.

'Look, I'm sorry you feel that way. But there is no us anymore. I've moved on with my life, and I'm glad I have.'

'Yes, I can see that,' Alex shot Isabelle a look as she put the tray on the table. She stood. 'You know what, you're welcome to each other,' she said and walked away.

Angus sighed and held out his hand to Isabelle. She went around the table and sat on his lap, leaning into his chest.

'I'm glad it's finally over.' He kissed her.

And so am I, thought Isabelle. At last, everything was falling into place.

Later that night, Isabelle read about her parents' marriage. Her heart warmed at Mimi's message, and she found her own words reflected back at her. But she'd been heartbroken that Mimi had suffered another bout of depression for so long. There had to be an end to all of this.

> **Mimi, I'm so happy for you. Please just enjoy it all. And this time, don't let the Hall stand between you and happiness! By the way, I just thought I let you know, Angus kissed me today. And his ex-fiancée turned up out of the blue but thank God he sent her packing. I still can't believe it.**

And she buzzed with excitement for the future.

Chapter Fifty-Four

Mimi, May 1987

It was late afternoon, and I was luxuriating in Pierre's arms. Since the day of Bonelle's wedding, Pierre and I had kept in touch. He was my friend and my lover. The only regret I had was that neither of us was prepared to give up our homes, but anything was better than those years of loneliness.

'I missed you,' he whispered in my ear.

'And I missed you.' I nuzzled into his neck, breathing in his warmth.

'You must be very excited,' he said as he stroked my hair.

'Of course. I can't wait. Jean-Francois is at the hospital. He said he'll call the house as soon as there's a change.'

Pierre's his eyes danced at me. 'Until then, I have you all to myself.'

I laughed and kissed him. 'Have you got anything special—'

The phone disrupted the moment.

'That must be him.' I quickly picked up the receiver.

'Mimi, you'd best come over. It's all happening very quickly,' said Jean-Francois, giving me the details.

We rushed to the maternity ward.

'We're here for Bonelle Rousseau,' Pierre said, my French still not up to the job.

'*Un moment, s'il vous plaît,*' said the nurse and consulted a board.

'Mimi, Pierre.'

I turned around to see Jean-Francois rushing towards us. The look on his face made my heart sing.

'All done. I've got two beautiful daughters,' he beamed at us.

I hugged him. 'Congratulations.'

'Come on, they should be back in the room.'

'I'll let you have a few moments, then I'll join you.' Pierre squeezed my hand.

What a thoughtful man he was.

I walked into the room. My heart swelled with joy at the sight of my daughter with my granddaughters in her arms. Three generations of women.

Bonelle looked up at me. 'Meet Isabelle and Chloe.'

My heart missed a beat. 'Isabelle?'

'Yes, after my grandmother. Don't you like it, Mimi?' asked Jean-Francois.

'No, no, it's beautiful. It's just … I know someone with that name.'

What a coincidence that my granddaughter should have the same name as my friend, I thought.

I bent down and kissed them. 'They're exquisite,' I said as I stroked them and watched my daughter feeding them.

'There.' Bonelle pointed to Isabelle after they stopped feeding.

I cannot describe the feeling that overtook me as I sat there holding her. It was as though all the years of loss, heartache, and sacrifice had been wiped away by magic, and for the first time there was nothing but joy in my heart as I gazed down at Isabelle.

'Oh my God, Jean-Francois, call the doctor.'

My head snapped up at the panic in Bonelle's voice, and my body shivered with fear at the sight of Chloe, who lay in her arms turning bluer by the second. My grip around Isabelle tightened as though whatever had befallen Chloe might take hold of her.

In the commotion that followed I watched through a haze as the doctor and nurses whisked Chloe away. I hadn't even held her yet. I thought, *Please, dear God, let her be all right.*

Jean-Francois was holding Bonelle, and her wailing was piercing my soul. Isabelle's cry pulled my attention back to her.

Though my heart was bleeding for Bonelle, I had to take care of Isabelle.

I stood up and said, 'I'm taking her out.'

Jean-Francois nodded at me, tears running down his face.

Pierre put his arm around me. 'Mimi, what's happening? I didn't want to disturb. Is the little'un all right?'

'I hope so.'

I carried on rocking Isabelle until she calmed, then we sat there in agony of waiting. I didn't dare taking my eyes off Isabelle for fear she'd suffer the same fate.

'I'll get us a coffee and baguettes,' said Pierre.

'Thank you for being here.'

He kissed the top of my head and was about to go when Jean-Francois came towards us. He looked as though all life had left him. I held my breath and waited for him to speak.

'Chloe's stable. The doctors say she has some problems. They'll do more tests tomorrow. They're keeping her in the intensive care, there's nothing we can do tonight.'

'How's Bonelle?'

'They had to give her something. She was hysterical. The nurse said the girls need to be bottle fed.'

He wiped his hands up and down his face. I put my hand on his arm.

'Look, Jean-Francois, you need a rest. Why don't you go home? I can stay here with Bonelle and Isabelle.'

He shook his head.

'You need to keep your strength up for tomorrow. Let me help,' I urged.

'She's right, Jean-Francois,' Pierre said. 'Come on, I'll drive you home.'

Pierre led Jean-Francois away as I made my way to Bonelle's room, where I camped with Isabelle for the night and all the next day as Bonelle sat by Chloe's bedside.

On the second day Jean-Francois found me in the hospital garden with Isabelle asleep in my arms. My back straightened as I saw the dread in his eyes. I stood but seemed unable to take any steps towards him.

'The nurse said they've finished operating on Chloe. The doctor will be seeing us soon.'

He put his hands on his face and his body shook as he stood there and sobbed. Holding back my own tears, I put my arm around him and held him as close as I could without squashing Isabelle.

'I'm sure she'll be fine,' I said but my words were drowned by Isabelle's cry, as though she too was giving voice to her worries.

'Come here, ma petite.'

Jean-Francois took Isabelle in his arms, and we went back to the ward where the doctor was already awaiting us.

'The operation was successful, but I'm afraid there are no guarantees with congenital heart disease. I'm sorry. We'll monitor her for the next few days, and if she remains stable, you can take her home.'

We had been back at home for two weeks. But I was still worried about Bonelle, wondering how she'd be able to take care of the girls on her own after the trauma.

'I rang the Hall and told Fraser I was extending my stay,' I said to Jean-Francois when Bonelle and the girls were asleep.

'Thank you, Mimi. I was worried about what would happen when I go back to work.'

'I know.' I patted his hand.

'It's just …' he looked away.

'What is it Jean-Francois? Tell me.'

'It's Bonelle. She seems so focused on Chloe.'

'Of course, that's understandable.'

'Yes, yes. It's just, you know, when the girls cry or need feeding or nappy changing, it's always Chloe first. The other day, you were out with Pierre, and I was making a call. I had to stop because I could hear crying and when I went up, Isabelle was lying in her cot and Bonelle was feeding Chloe. My poor little baby was so upset, looking all red and sweaty with distress. When I asked Bonelle, she said Chloe came first.'

I didn't want to worry him more by saying I had made similar observations. 'Have you thought of getting a nanny to help Bonelle?'

'To be honest, I wasn't sure how she'd take it.'

'I'm sure she'll be fine. Why don't you start looking, and I'll stay until you've found someone.'

'Thank you, Mimi.' He leaned across the table and kissed my cheek.

That night I wrote to Isabelle.

Though it has been a challenging time, you should know that one of my granddaughters is called Isabelle. I couldn't have chosen a better name myself. I hope she'll be as wise and kind as you, my dearest friend.

Chapter Fifty-Five

Isabelle knocked on Hamish's door.

'Coming, coming.'

At the sound of his voice, Isabelle's heart dropped into her stomach. She didn't think she could get through this.

The door opened after a few minutes, revealing Hamish. 'Ah, Isabelle, what a lovely surprise, lassie. I haven't seen you in a while. Come on in,' he said and hugged her.

'Yes, it's been busy.'

Isabelle followed Hamish into the kitchen, where she was greeted with the smell of freshly baked bread. A pot of tea, a dish of butter, and what looked like homemade jam were sitting on the table. Hamish collected two cups and put them on the table.

'Sit down, the tea's just brewed, and the bread's still warm. Tuck in.'

The sheen of sweat on his brow belied Hamish's chirpiness. Was it because he was unsure how she felt about his affair with Mimi? Isabelle's mind was whirring. She had to stop to take a breath. It felt as though her lungs were stitched together.

'You're all right, lass? You've gone all quiet.'

Isabelle saw concern in his eyes and got flustered. She wished she could fob him off, have a bit of chit-chat, and leave. But it couldn't be any worse than when she talked to her mum. And she needed to tell him. She felt it was the right thing to do. Mimi had wanted to. Isabelle knew she needed to get on with it before she ended up confusing the man.

'Hamish, you know Mimi's daughter—my mother—Bonelle?'

'I knew of her, but I've never seen her. Is she all right?'

'She's your daughter, Hamish,' Isabelle blurted out.

Hamish's eyes widened, and his face paled. The piece of bread in his hand dropped on his plate. He just sat there. Isabelle waited for what seemed like an eternity. But then, as though he had absorbed the meaning of the words, he covered his face with his hands. His frame trembled with the force of his emotions.

Isabelle was trying to suppress the lump in her throat. As with her mum, she couldn't begin to imagine the significance of this moment for him. After some time, Hamish raised his head, and his face was contorted with pain. Isabelle's heart went out to him. She took his hands in hers, and they just sat there as though neither could find the words that would do this pivotal moment justice.

'Why didn't Mimi tell me?' he asked in a whisper.

'She was going to. You know that night you were waiting for her?'

'Yes.'

'She was coming to see you. She was going to go away with you. She wrote to you twice. Once when Bonelle was sixteen—'

'I never got a letter.' Hamish rubbed his hands over his face.

'And later, when my grandfather—' Isabelle stopped, realising Hamish was her grandfather. 'I mean, when her husband, Glen, died, she wrote to you.'

Hamish sat upright. 'But how is it possible? I don't understand.'

'I don't know why you didn't get the first letter, but she never sent the second. She found out you'd just got married.'

Isabelle took the letter out of her handbag and handed it to Hamish. She watched him read it. It was a long time before he looked up at her.

'You know, I often wondered if there'd been anything I could have done differently.'

'I'm sorry,' Isabelle said. It's all just so sad.'

Hamish nodded. 'It's a lot to take in.'

Isabelle stood, understanding he needed to be alone. Hamish got to his feet and enveloped her in his arms. Then he stood back, holding her by her shoulders, looking into her face. Isabelle's heart warmed to see the light had returned to his eyes.

'Thank you for what you've done for me.' He kissed her brow. 'Who knew that at the tender age of eighty-seven, I'd be finally a grandaidh!'

'And I'm Scott's niece.' She inwardly grimaced at the idea of Charlie's boyfriend being her uncle.

'In a manner of speaking.'

'What do you mean?'

'Elsbeth could never carry a bairn. After the third loss, we stopped trying. In the end we adopted Scott.'

'Ah, that's why he's so much younger than Mum.'

Hamish nodded. 'Now, tell me, does your mother know?'

'Yes.'

'And from your expression, I guess she wasn't happy.'

'She didn't even want to know who you were. I'm sorry.'

'Don't apologise,' said Hamish. 'I'm sure it's come as a terrible shock to her. Now, wait a second; I've got something for you.'

He gave her shoulder a squeeze and left the room. Moments later, he returned and handed Isabelle a box.

'Take this; you can give it back to me later.'

She hugged him and left. And now there was one place she needed to go; one she had avoided for long enough.

With flowers on the graves and birds twittering in the background, the cemetery looked like a park. Isabelle wound her way to Mimi's grave and was met with a rose growing by the head of her grave. She suspected it must have been either Mrs Murray's or Hamish's work.

She sat, crossed her legs, and considered everything that happened since Mimi's death. It had been quite the journey. Did she wish she hadn't taken on the challenge? No. Though she was still sifting through her feelings, it pleased her that she had moved to the Hall and discovered the past.

She opened the tin Hamish had given her, and the ghost of a perfume escaped like a genie from a bottle. Her chest tightened when she recognised the scent as Mimi's Chanel No. 5. The papers were held together with a twine. She took them out of the box and opened the first letter. Love and passion leapt from the pages. She reached the last line of the last letter and could no longer see the words, the tears that were blurring her vision started to flow at the thought of all the heartache and pain Mimi and Hamish had been through.

Next, she opened Mimi's diary and read Mimi's account of her own and Chloe's birth, and the trauma her parents had gone through. No wonder Bonelle had been so protective of Chloe. But did it excuse her mother from neglecting Isabelle herself? At least now, she could tell Mimi some things.

> **Mimi, I'm Isabelle, your granddaughter. I still don't know how all this is possible, how I've been able to talk to you. You see, I hoped I could change the future so both yours and my relationship with Bonelle would be better, but it didn't work. You were the one who left me the Hall and asked me to find out its secrets. I'll admit, at first I was really upset and angry at you for dumping it all on me. But you'll be pleased to know that Hamish, your Will, now knows the truth. He never stopped loving you, Mimi.**
>
> **But as you can imagine, Bonelle didn't take the news well at all. I hope in time it all sorts itself out. I'm so glad you and Pierre are still together. I love you, Mimi, and miss you so much.**

Isabelle was about to close the diary when another thought struck her. She froze. Chloe would die soon. She couldn't bear the thought of reading it in Mimi's diary. It would break her heart all over again.

But perhaps she didn't have to.

She had failed to warn Mimi about Alasdair's death. She had mistakenly told her to remain with Glen, meaning that her relationship with Bonelle had crumbled. Apart from being moral support, she'd had no impact on Mimi's life at all, so she had no idea if she could change the past. None.

This time she had to try; she had to save Chloe.

She picked up the pen and twisted it between her fingers. She had saved lives before when she had worked in the hospital. She had saved lives as a GP. Never had she saved a life with a pen. It was such a small thing. So ordinary. So every day. She swallowed, put the nib to the paper, and wrote:

Mimi, there's one more thing. It's very important. You have to go to France. No matter what happens, stay with Chloe on the second of July 1993. Please, please promise me you'll do that. I'll explain everything when we talk next.

Chapter Fifty-Six

Mimi, July 1993

I was in the garden with my diary open on my lap, staring into the distance as I tried to comprehend that my friend Isabelle was my own granddaughter. How was this possible? How could she have reached out to me from the future?

I would never know, but I knew that at times, the only thing that had kept me going was the thought of Isabelle being there.

I picked up the diary again and tears smarted my eyes as I read that she had managed to tell Will the truth.

> *My sweet angel, I can't thank you enough for everything you've done for me. I too wish I was there and that I could see Will one last time. I'm so glad that he finally knows the truth, that I never stopped loving him. And my heart warms to know that his love for me never died. I love you with all my heart, darling girl and just so you know. I'm in France as you told me.*

The knowledge that Will had never stopped loving me meant the world and led to a few nostalgic tears of what might have been. For a moment I was tempted to try and find him, but to what end? What we'd had seemed like another lifetime, and Will was living his own life. As was I. Since Alasdair's death, I was finally happy. Pierre's love had been calm like deep waters compared to the storm that marked my passion with Will, and I knew that at this stage in my life, I preferred the steadiness and serenity of Pierre's companionship.

Another thought left me unsettled: If Isabelle was my granddaughter, then it meant that the terrible mother she had spoken of was none other than my Bonelle. I'd seen her disinterest in Isabelle from the start, but to know that this never changed— how could Bonelle do this? I picked up the pen.

I too worry about Bonelle, my darling girl. But let's hope she'll come around. I'm afraid I have only myself to blame, as I already told you. But I'm sorry that you seem to be paying the price.

I'd just closed my diary when the tranquillity was pierced by Bonelle's voice.

'Mum, I'm going to have a nap. The girls will be watching their cartoon.'

'All right, darling. I'll keep an eye on them.'

And remembering my promise to Isabelle, I followed Bonelle into the living room where the girls were.

'What are you watching?' I asked as I took a seat on the sofa.

'*The Jungle Book*,' Chloe said over her shoulder. 'It's *boooring*.' She elongated the last word.

'Why is that then?'

She rolled her eyes at me. 'Because there's no princess.'

She was such a madam.

'I don't want to watch this. I'm going outside,' Chloe said and stood.

Isabelle's shoulders tensed and she reached for her sister's arm. 'Chloe, stay here. You know we're not allowed.'

'It's all right, darling. You watch your cartoon. I'll go out with Chloe.'

Isabelle looked at me and smiled. 'Thank you, Mimi.'

I could see the relief on her face and wondered what would have happened had I not been here. Then I remembered something that Isabelle had written in my very first diary, which had remained with me in my darkest moments; the thing that had always made me feel that Isabelle understood my grief.

She never liked me as much as my twin who died when we were really young.

Was I here to save Chloe's life? I held a trembling hand out to my young granddaughter. 'Come on, then.'

But she just ignored me and ran ahead. By the time I made it outside, she was sitting by the pool, dangling her feet in the water. I picked up my book where I'd left it on the recliner but couldn't read it. What was going to happen to Chloe and when? I had to watch her like a hawk.

I don't know how much time had passed when I heard her shout, 'Ouch, ouch.'

'What's the matter, my love?'

I stood and saw Chloe clutch at her foot and before I knew, she slipped from the poolside and fell in with a splash. My heart stopped as I saw Chloe inhale a lungful of water and start gasping for air.

I jumped into the pool and paddled desperately towards her. As soon as she was within reach, I swept her into my arms. Her eyes bulged and her chest contracted as she coughed.

'Isabelle! Isabelle!' I shouted.

I carried Chloe from the pool, tapping her back with the flat of my hand. We had just sat down when Isabelle came rushing towards us.

'Mimi, what's wrong?' Isabelle came to halt by my side. 'Chloe!'

'Get your Maman, quick,' I said.

My eyes never left Chloe, who was now retching. I propped her forward and rubbed her back to soothe her.

'It's all going to be fine, my love.'

Moments later, Bonelle came racing from the house, her face rosy from sleep, her eyes frantic. She kneeled beside us and took Chloe in her arms.

'Chloe, darling, what happened? Are you all right'

Chloe nodded. But it was some minutes later before she could speak.

'I fell in the pool and swallowed some water, and then I couldn't breathe.'

'I told you not to go out,' said Isabelle.

I looked up and saw the worry on her face. 'Come here, angel,' I said and pulled her down onto my lap. 'You did very well.'

I kissed her head, and she nuzzled into my wet clothes. Bonelle stared at me. She was as pale as Chloe.

'Thank you, Mum. I don't know what would have happened if you hadn't got to her on time.'

'I'm glad I was here.'

Bonelle gathered Chloe up. 'Let's get you to the doctors, darling. Just to make sure everything is all right.'

I took Isabelle's hand. 'Let's go in then, my love. I need to get changed.'

A little while later, I found Isabelle in front of the TV and settled myself on the sofa with my diary. I looked up at the young Isabelle and still couldn't get my head around it all. Was this the same little girl that would reach out to me in the future to save her sister?

> *My sweet Isabelle, I did as you told me. You saved Chloe from drowning. You did it, my angel. I love you with all my heart.*

I buried my six-year-old grandchild a month later. Not because of her accident; she had been given the all-clear from that. She had died in her sleep three weeks later, her heart had just given in.

A loud scream tore me out of my rumination, I rushed to the sofa where Isabelle was kicking and tossing in her sleep.

'Isabelle, sweetheart, wake up. It was just a bad dream.'

I swept away the hair that was stuck to her face and stroked her head. When she at last opened her eyes, they were full of terror. I lifted her up and took her in my arms.

'It's all right, Mimi is here, my love,' I whispered into her ear and kissed her head.

She pressed her body into my chest, her arms wrapped around my neck, as though her life depended on it.

'It was horrible, Mimi,' she said and burst into tears.

I tightened my grip, my heart breaking for her. I wished I could absorb all her grief and pain. I'd offered to bring her back to the Hall with me when Bonelle had a breakdown after Chloe's death.

'I miss Chloe, Mimi, so much.' Her breath hitched.

'I know, my darling, we all miss her. But I'm sure she is happy playing with the angels,' I said with a confidence I didn't feel.

My father had told me about my mother being with the angels when she died, and I had found that comforting as a child. At last, Isabelle calmed enough to unpeel herself from me.

'Can I visit her sometime and play with the angels?'

She had the ability to ask the most heart-wrenching questions. My eyes misted with tears, and I had to blink a few times to stop them from falling.

'One day, my darling, one day, you will.' *But I hope to God that it wouldn't be anytime soon.*

Isabelle nodded and seemed satisfied with the answer.

'I'll tell you what, let's give you a quick wash, get you changed, and we'll go say hello to the little lambs. What do you say?' I said, injecting as much brightness as I could into my voice.

'Is Angus coming with us?'

'No, sweetie, he's with his mummy, but we can go and get him tomorrow,' I offered.

Angus had been a Godsend. And if I'd been reading Isabelle's messages correctly, he would one day be more than just a friend to my granddaughter.

Isabelle nodded in agreement, and once she was washed and dressed, we headed for the barn.

'Oh, look at them, Mimi,' Isabelle said, her eyes wide with disbelief. 'Can I hold one please?'

'Just sit on that bale, and I'll bring you one.'

I retrieved one of the new-borns for her and watched a spark of joy lighten her eyes as she took the little lamb onto her lap.

That night and every single night after that for the next two months, Jean-Francois called to talk to Isabelle and me.

'Isabelle, sweetheart, it's your Papa on the phone,'

'Papa!' Isabelle paused and listened. Her hands held the receiver. 'Yes, I was a good girl. Wasn't I, Mimi?'

I nodded my head. Isabelle, like her mother, was a daddy's girl.

'And I held a baby lamb and saw the big cows.'

It was a joy to see her excited.

'Yes, I will, Papa. I love you.'

She held up the receiver towards me.

'Thank you, darling. Why don't you go to the kitchen and get your hot cocoa and biscuits from Mrs Murray?'

'How's Bonelle?' I asked as soon as I was sure Isabelle was out of the earshot.

'Terrible, Mimi. Just terrible. She is in that bed all day. She doesn't talk, doesn't move. She refuses to get washed, dressed, or eat. I don't know what to do.'

'I'm so sorry, Jean-Francois. What does the doctor say?'

'He's given her medication, but she won't take it. He said if she carries on like this, he'll have to put her in a psychiatric hospital. And I have to go back to work. It's all very difficult.'

He sounded close to tears. He too had lost a child, and yet he wasn't allowed the luxury of grieving.

'Of course, you need to get back to work. Jean-Francois, could you organise an assistant nurse for Bonelle please? I will cover the expense. That way you can go back to the office and hopefully by the time the summer's over, there'll be some progress. You just look after yourself and give my love to Bonelle.'

'Thank you, Mimi, I'm much obliged. And you're sure it's okay for Isabelle to stay a little longer?'

'Isabelle's no problem; it's a joy to have her.'

My poor, poor Bonelle. I couldn't even begin to imagine how she must be suffering, losing her child. No wonder she'd disappeared into herself. I just hoped that at some point soon, she'd remember that she had another daughter who still needed her.

I put the phone down and went to the kitchen to collect Isabelle.

'Goodnight, Mrs Murray,' Isabelle said, waving a little hand at Annie.

'Mimi, can I sleep in your bed?' she asked as we were walking up the stairs.

'You have your own lovely bedroom, sweetie.'

I didn't want the child to become used to having someone with her at night. With Chloe gone, she'd have to sleep on her own. The sadness of it all was just devastating.

'But what if the bad dreams come?' she asked, and her voice shook with anxiety as we walked up to her room.

'I'll tell you what, why don't we read a story and I promise I'll stay until you've fallen asleep. Then I'll leave the pretty light with the stars on for you and the light in the corridor so if you did wake up you can come and find me next door? What do you say?'

She nodded.

'Can you read *Peter Rabbit?*' Isabelle asked as we settled in her bed.

'Of course, I can.'

And with her body nuzzled into mine, I read to her until she fell asleep before I made my way to my room. It was time I wrote to Isabelle. I opened the diary and took the pen with a heavy heart.

My darling Isabelle, I'm so sorry. I did my best, but it seems life had other plans.

When the day arrived that Isabelle had to go home to Bonelle, she didn't want to go.

'But Papa, I want to say with Mimi and Angus,' she said, her eyes brimming with tears.

'I know, chérie. But your maman and your school friends miss you. You can come back and see Mimi in summer, and we can call her every day.'

'And this is for you,' I said, handing her a parcel wrapped in tissue paper.

'What is it, Mimi?'

'Why don't you open it and see for yourself?'

She unwrapped her present, and her eyes brightened with delight at the sight of the toy rabbit.

'It's Peter Rabbit! He can tell me the stories when you're not there. Thank you, Mimi,' she said and threw herself in my arms.

I held on, not wanting to let her go, knowing I'd miss her. But she'd given me an idea. As soon as they left, I picked up the house phone.

'Mr Morgan, I wish to change my will.'

Chapter Fifty-Seven

Two months later

Isabelle jumped up with joy as she read Mimi's message.

'I did it, I did it, I did it! Chloe will live,' she shouted into the room and relief washed over her.

She had saved her sister. But shouldn't she feel different? Isabelle stood still, wondering what it would feel like to have her life changed around her. Would she just blink and know she'd had her twin by her side all her life?

She probed at her memories of Chloe and gasped. Chloe hadn't died from drowning that day. But Isabelle didn't have a grown twin sister. No. Chloe's heart condition had killed her when they were only six. Everything she had done had been for nothing. Chloe had never been meant to have a life.

With trembling fingers, she turned the page, already knowing what she was going to read. It was like losing Chloe all over again. Isabelle put her head in her hands and sobbed.

After a time, she quietened. Something *had* changed, something inside her. The guilt that had crippled her like a disease all her life was gone. The loss of it made her feel weightless. Chloe's death hadn't been her fault. Her sister had died, yes, and that was what had spurred Isabelle to go to medical school, but her death had been the result of a heart condition, not a heartless twin sister. Perhaps now she could put the past where it belonged and embrace her future.

She picked up the pen.

Mimi, I can't thank you enough for saving Chloe from drowning. I love you so much, and I wish you were still with me. I'll never forget everything you've done for me. You'll never know how much you meant, how much you mean to me. I'll always miss you.

Snow crunched under her feet as Isabelle stepped outside. The gravestones were buried under a white cloak. She wound her way around, orienting herself by the names and dates, afraid to walk over someone's resting place. As she drew closer, she recognised the figure at Mimi's grave.

'Hello, Hamish,' she said and laid a hand on his arm.

'Isabelle, how are you?' He hugged her.

Isabelle laid her Christmas posy on the grave, and they both stood there in silence, each lost to their own thoughts. She still couldn't comprehend that Mimi was lying beneath the earth and snow. It was not worth thinking about. She chose to focus on Mimi being somewhere 'up there,' playing with Chloe and the angels. She heard footsteps behind her and looked around to see her mother. Isabelle hugged her.

'Mum, I'm so happy you could make it.'

'Me too. The delays were awful. I'm sorry I couldn't tell you when I'd be arriving.'

'What matters is you made it.'

'Hello, Hamish,' Bonelle said.

Hamish nodded and smiled. 'I'd best be off then.'

'Isabelle told me you'll be joining us tomorrow.'

Hamish looked at Isabelle and then at Bonelle. 'Only if it's not a pro—'

'We'll see you then.' Bonelle smiled at him.

Isabelle could have kissed her mum as she saw Hamish's eyes well up before he turned and walked away.

'Thank you, Mum.'

'I've been thinking a great deal since I left here. It took a long while to process everything, to readjust the lens on more than fifty years—my entire life. But in the end …'

'I understand.' Isabelle laid her arm around Bonelle's shoulders.

'I decided it was time to make my peace with it all and for that to happen I need to learn to forgive. But, above all, I realised I needed to *be* forgiven.' Bonelle looked down at Mimi's grave.

Isabelle gave her a sideway glance and noticed the traces of tears. Her mother was keeping her gaze on the headstone. Isabelle wasn't sure if Bonelle was speaking to her or Mimi —or perhaps both.

'I know I've been a poor mother to you all your life. Since Chloe's death I felt so guilty, and that made the grief and loss so much harder to bear. I know Chloe's death wasn't my fault, but as a mother, you always blame yourself.'

Isabelle's heart was pounding in her chest. But she didn't dare to so much as breathe in case her mother stopped talking.

'I kept telling myself I still had you, that you needed me. But my rage and my grief … I thought it had destroyed any love I had left. In my darkest moments, all I wanted was to join Chloe.'

Isabelle was listening to every word, but it felt as though she was dreaming. She'd always guessed, but now through Mimi's diaries, she understood her mother. At last the barriers between them were coming down.

'I know the way I've treated you is unforgiveable, Isabelle. I just didn't have the strength to set aside my grief and comfort you in yours.' Bonelle's voice trembled.

Isabelle tightened her grip on her mother's shoulder. Both to comfort Bonelle and to calm the tremor that had taken hold of her own body. She'd waited so long—so, so long—to hear these words. Yet now the only thing she felt was sadness for herself, for her mother, and for her sister, who'd never had a chance at life. And of course, Mimi.

'Your father was the only one who had enough courage and love to get through. He stepped in where I faltered.'

Isabelle nodded. Yes, she didn't know what would have become of her without Jean-Francois, and of course Mimi.

'I know I failed you miserably, and there's no excuse. By the time I had halfway come to my senses, I realised I'd been hiding from you for so long that I'd become a stranger to you. You'd found a replacement for me in Mimi.'

'I can't begin to imagine what it must feel like losing a child. But I know it was bad enough losing a sister.'

'Believe me, I was truly grateful to Mimi for saving Chloe's life that day. But a part of me still resented her for destroying my father's life and putting the Hall before me. And it got worse as I watched her taking away the affection of my only child.' Bonelle shook her head. 'I know it was irrational, but I couldn't help the feeling.'

Isabelle wished Mimi was there and could hear Bonelle speak. But she would tell her in the diary later.

'I feel nothing but remorse for wasting my life and alienating those who loved me and whom I should have loved.'

Isabelle didn't know what to say. She needed time to get her head around everything.

'But that's changed. I've decided not to contest the will.'

'Really, Mum?'

'Yes.'

Isabelle kissed her mother's cheek.

Bonelle squeezed her hand. 'And I'll be moving back to Scotland once I've managed to get my affairs in order. I'll live in Edinburgh. That way I'll be close but won't be breathing down your neck.'

Bonelle looked at her for the first time. There was sadness in her eyes, but at last the coldness was gone.

'I know I can't turn back time, but I want to make the best of the time I've got left. I know I can't ask you to forgive me, but I hope you'll give me a chance to be a better mother to you. A chance I never gave my mother.' Bonelle laid a hand on Isabelle's arm. 'And I just want you to know how proud I am of you, just for being you.'

Isabelle looked at her mother, taking in the plea in her eyes. She opened her mouth, but Bonelle held up her hand and silenced her.

'There's one more thing.'

Isabelle cocked her head, trying to figure out what was coming next. She wasn't sure she had the capacity for any more emotions or revelations.

Bonelle reached into the pocket of her coat. 'Turn around.'

Isabelle did so and felt her mother's hands brushing against her neck as she clasped a necklace around her neck.

Isabelle lifted the necklace up and saw it was the locket that her uncle Alasdair gave to Mimi on her eighteenth birthday. And with it, Isabelle realised, she'd always carry a part of Mimi with her.

Isabelle turned around and saw Bonelle smiling at her, eyes glossy with tears.

'I know I'm fourteen years too late, but I know Mimi would have wanted you to have it.'

'Thank you, Mum.'

Bonelle folded her into an embrace. And for the first time since Chloe's death, Isabelle felt safe in her mother's arms.

The church bells chimed the hour.

'Shall we head back?' Isabelle asked as Bonelle loosened her grip on her.

'You go ahead. I'd like to stay a little longer.'

Back at the Hall, Isabelle followed the smell of coffee into the kitchen and found Angus sitting at the table.

'Hey, you're back. I missed you,' he said.

He held up his face towards her; Isabelle bent and kissed him. Angus took her arm and lowered her onto his lap.

'I hope you didn't mind me telling Bonelle where you were.'

'No. I'm glad you did. It was quite something.' Isabelle shook her head at the turn of events. 'We talked. I mean properly, you know?'

Angus nodded.

'It was extraordinary. Bonelle apologised for everything: not being a good mother and how she had let me down.'

'Wow, that's a first,' said Angus.

'Right? Honestly, it was like all these years, she'd been frozen and only now had come alive.'

'That's wonderful, my darling. I know how much it means you.' He tightened his arm around her waist. 'It's hard to believe how much everything has changed since that day in hospital.'

'It feels like another lifetime. Looking back, I'm so glad I followed Mimi's wish and didn't give into my doubts.'

'So am I. You were very brave.' Angus kissed her brow.

Isabelle looked up at him and smiled. 'Do you know, that's exactly what Mimi said in her letter. But I never thought of it that way. I just had to do it.'

Angus nodded and stroked her hair. He lifted the chain that was caught in his hand.

'What's this?'

'Oh, Bonelle gave me that.' Isabelle pulled away and showed Angus the locket.

'A family heirloom, hey?'

'As a matter of fact it is. It was Mimi's. It gets passed on from mother to daughter on her eighteenth birthday.'

Angus raised a brow at her. 'Let's hope we won't end up having just boys then.'

Isabelle cocked her head and searched his eyes. Was he messing with her?

'Are you serious?'

'I mean it, Belle. I want us to settle down and start a family.'

Isabelle could swear her heart stopped beating for a moment. Was this actually happening or was she dreaming?

Angus cleared his voice. 'I hadn't imagined it this way, but will you marry me, Belle?'

Isabelle cupped her hand over her mouth. 'Oh my God.'

He laughed. 'I wouldn't go that far. Angus will do.'

Isabelle slapped his arm. 'You're incorrigible, Angus Fairbairn.'

'I know, but that's no reason for making me wait.'

Isabelle held his gaze, her eyes tearing with the intensity of her emotions.

'I'd love to!'

She couldn't wait to tell Mimi.

Acknowledgements

Thank you to my readers; I hope you enjoyed *Lanesbrough Hall*.

I would also like to say a BIG thank you to everyone who helped me on my journey to create Lanesbrough Hall. My editors, Becky and Bryony at Cornerstones, whose critical eye and valuable advice shaped my writing. Kathleen at Creative Classics Publications US who took a chance on me and together with her team added the final touches and brought *Lanesbrough Hall* to you readers. My book designer, Cherie at Chapman & Wilder, who dressed Lanesbrough Hall with her gorgeous cover design.

Last but not least, I want to thank my family and friends. My husband, Simon, for his tireless support over the last three years, for putting up with me when my writing monopolised our evenings and weekends, and for making it possible for me to take three months off and finish my book. My son, Connor, who gave his time generously and would chew through the plot with me and read the various drafts. My friend Greg who encouraged me to pursue my dream every step of the way. My dogs Jax, for sitting at my feet and keeping me company during the long hours, and Axl, for dragging me away from my desk to play frisbee with him for some respite.

Elisabeth Linley was a clinical psychologist and a Reiki Master in another life. An avid reader, she always aspired to write a book. In 2019 alongside her day job, she finally picked up that pen and gave voice to Isabelle and Mimi. *Lanesbrough Hall* is Elisabeth's debut novel, which she hopes will bring you as much joy reading it as it gave her creating it. A lover of animals and nature, she lives in the English countryside with her husband and their two dogs.

Lightning Source UK Ltd.
Milton Keynes UK
UKHW041226080922
408498UK00004B/162/J